D0912383

RESCUING ISABELLE

Guardian Hostage Rescue Specialists BRAVO Team, Book 2

ELLIE MASTERS

JEM Publishing

Copyright © 2022 Ellie Masters
Rescuing Isabelle
All rights reserved.

All rights reserved. This copy is intended for the original purchaser of this ebook ONLY. No part of this ebook may be reproduced, scanned, transmitted, or distributed in any printed, mechanical, or electronic form without prior written permission from Ellie Masters or JEM Publishing except in the case of brief quotations embodied in critical articles or reviews. This book is licensed for your personal enjoyment only. Please do not participate in or encourage piracy of copyrighted materials in violation of the author's rights. This book may not be re-sold or given away to other people. If you would like to share this book with another person, please purchase an additional copy for each person you share it with. If you are reading this book and did not purchase it, or it was not purchased for your use only, then you should return it to the seller and purchase your own copy. Thank you for respecting the author's work.

Image/art disclaimer: Licensed material is being used for illustrative purposes only. Any person depicted in the licensed material is a model.

Editor: Erin Toland

Proofreader: Roxane Leblanc

Published in the United States of America

JEM Publishing

This is a work of fiction. While reference might be made to actual historical events or existing locations, the names, characters, businesses, places, and incidents are either the product of the author's imagination or are used fictitiously, and any resemblance to actual persons, living or dead, business establishments, events, or locales is entirely coincidental.

ISBN: 978-1-952625-42-8

Dedication

This book is dedicated to my one and only—my amazing and wonderful husband.

Without your care and support, my writing would not have made it this far.

You pushed me when I needed to be pushed.

You supported me when I felt discouraged.

You believed in me when I didn't believe in myself.

If it weren't for you, this book never would have come to life.

Also by Ellie Masters

The LIGHTER SIDE

Ellie Masters is the lighter side of the Jet & Ellie Masters writing duo! You will find Contemporary Romance, Military Romance, Romantic Suspense, Billionaire Romance, and Rock Star Romance in Ellie's Works.

YOU CAN FIND ELLIE'S BOOKS HERE: ELLIEMASTERS.COM/BOOKS

Military Romance

Guardian Hostage Rescue Specialists

Rescuing Melissa

*(*Get a FREE copy of Rescuing Melissa when you join Ellie's Newsletter*)*

Alpha Team

Rescuing Zoe

Rescuing Moira

Rescuing Eve

Rescuing Lily

Rescuing Jinx

Rescuing Maria

Bravo Team

Rescuing Angie

Rescuing Isabelle

Rescuing Carmen

Military Romance

Guardian Personal Protection Specialists

Sybil's Protector

Lyra's Protector

The One I Want Series

(Small Town, Military Heroes)

By Jet & Ellie Masters

EACH BOOK IN THIS SERIES CAN BE READ AS A STANDALONE AND IS ABOUT A DIFFERENT COUPLE WITH AN HEA.

Saving Ariel

Saving Brie

Saving Cate

Saving Dani

Saving Jen

Saving Abby

Rockstar Romance

The Angel Fire Rock Romance Series

EACH BOOK IN THIS SERIES CAN BE READ AS A STANDALONE AND IS ABOUT A DIFFERENT COUPLE WITH AN HEA. IT IS RECOMMENDED THEY ARE READ IN ORDER.

Ashes to New (prequel)

Heart's Insanity (book 1)

Heart's Desire (book 2)

Heart's Collide (book 3)

Hearts Divided (book 4)

Hearts Entwined (book5)

Forest's FALL (book 6)

Hearts The Last Beat (book7)

Contemporary Romance

Firestorm

(Kristy Bromberg's Everyday Heroes World)

Billionaire Romance

Billionaire Boys Club

Hawke

Richard

Brody

Contemporary Romance

Cocky Captain

(Vi Keeland & Penelope Ward's Cocky Hero World)

Romantic Suspense

EACH BOOK IS A STANDALONE NOVEL.

The Starling

~AND~

Science Fiction

Ellie Masters writing as L.A. Warren

Vendel Rising: a Science Fiction Serialized Novel

To My Readers

This book is a work of fiction. It does not exist in the real world and should not be construed as reality. As in most romantic fiction, I've taken liberties. I've compressed the romance into a sliver of time. I've allowed these characters to develop strong bonds of trust over a matter of days.

This does not happen in real life where you, my amazing readers, live. Take more time in your romance and learn who you're giving a piece of your heart to. I urge you to move with caution. Always protect yourself.

ONE

Izzy

SOMEDAYS, I WANT TO PINCH MYSELF, BECAUSE THIS KIND OF LIFE never happens to a girl like me.

Now, if my four, overprotective, overbearing, and overly paternalistic brothers would back off and let me enjoy myself, this could be the perfect life. They will *not* get off my case and demand I *go home.* Where it's *safe.* In their defense, there was the whole abduction-in-the-jungles-of-Nicaragua bit and the subsequent running-for-my-life thing.

But I'm good. Totally fine. I don't need them hovering over me to be safe.

Safe feels a whole hell of a lot like oppressively smothering. I love my brothers, but they can be way over the top when it comes to their baby sister.

However, I've successfully put them off.

At least for a bit.

That trip home needs to happen, but I'm going to stonewall them for a little bit more.

I'm not ready to step away, especially when it comes to days like today.

And my view?

It's one in a million.

"Whatcha thinking, Izzy?" My best friend in the whole wide world, my abduction-and-running-for-my-life-buddy, Angie, gives me the eye.

She knows exactly what I'm thinking.

Hell, every female within sight of the spectacle in front of us is thinking the same damn thing.

That's due to the six mighty-fine Guardians flexing their muscles in a virile display of jaw-dropping, fantasy-inducing, testosterone-infused masculinity, and my dirty mind is overflowing with all kinds of wicked fantasies.

"I'm not thinking anything you're not." I cross my arms and give her a look. "Your mouth is open, and you're drooling." I call her out for calling me out.

Angie likes to think, since she's got a ring on her finger, that she's above ogling the drool-worthy display, but she's totally guilty of checking out not just her beau, Brady, but all the men of Bravo team.

Just.

Like.

Me.

Her heart may belong to Brady Malone, but she watches them all.

"Oh yes, you are." She reaches over and pinches me. "And if I'm drooling, you're foaming at the mouth. You so want a piece of Booker Holloway." She pinches me.

"Hey, stop that." I yank away and rub at my skin. "That hurt."

"Not until you admit you've got the hots for Bravo Two." Her light-hazel eyes twinkle with amusement. Yeah, she's having fun with me.

"I won't."

But the thing is—she's totally right. I've got a major lady boner for Booker Holloway, especially after what the women of Alpha team told me about how he made ends meet before he became a Guardian.

Before he became a US Navy SEAL.

It's deliciously naughty.

My man is an ex-exotic dancer—was an exotic dancer. Evidently, he doesn't do that anymore.

Bummer.

Although, he supposedly taught the men of Alpha team how to bump and grind on their women.

In Vegas, no less.

But that's a different story.

"You don't have to say it because it's scrawled all over your face." Angie makes a circle in front of my face, then preens in victory because she knows she's right.

Booker used to star in an all-male revue on the strip in Vegas. He's got the moves and the body for it. I don't doubt it for a second. Not that I didn't do my due diligence and confirm for myself.

I've got the pictures and the proof; after a little detective work and an assist from Mitzy, the technical lead for Guardian HRS. I call her a wizard because that woman is amazing. She makes me feel like an underachiever.

Which I'm totally not.

Straight A's in high school were followed by straight A's in undergrad, and those continued in Pharmacy school, where I graduated —with honors.

I'm a valedictorian three times over. I thought that was pretty badass until I met Mitzy. I've come to realize, I'm merely ordinary, at least when I try to measure myself up against the talent hired on at Guardian HRS.

"I hate you." I tighten my arms and hunch inward.

I hate that Angie's right, but there's no denying the truth. The scariest thing is, I think he may like me too.

"Want me to ask Brady if Booker's into you?"

"No!" That makes me cringe.

Isn't it funny how no matter how old we get, we never leave the schoolyard? Here I am, pining over a boy, thinking he might like me, but too chickenshit to get off my ass and find out.

"Hey, lunch break is almost over." Angie starts packing up the remnants of her meal. "We have to get back to orientation."

Our new employer definitely offered us a sweet deal. Two actually. One for each of us. They hired me on as a pharmacist. I'll be working at Guardian HQ's onsite hospital during my initial onboarding, but then I'll shift to the pharmacy at the Facility where Guardian HRS is looking to expand.

Angie got the same offer—to work for Guardian HRS that is. She's not a pharmacist but rather an ophthalmologist. She'll remain at the onsite hospital, joining their current Ophtho team.

"What if we fake tummy aches? Tell them we need fresh air to recover?" My gaze turns back to the men scaling the sixty-foot wall in front of us.

Bravo team is a little over two-thirds of the way to their objective. They're joined on the wall by two robots. Four-footed things, they scale the wall like it's nothing, putting the Guardians to shame. Every day at Guardian HRS some new futuristic tech makes me shake my head.

"I think that'll go over like a ton of bricks. Come on. You can watch them tomorrow too."

Bravo team is in between assignments, which means they fill their days working various scenarios and honing their skills. As for Bravo team, my bestie is currently engaged to Brady, the man who single-handedly rescued us from the Coralos cartel after they abducted our entire medical team.

He's the lead for Bravo team. They call him Bravo One.

Booker's Bravo Two. Then there's the rest of the team: Rafe, Hayes, Alec, and Zeb.

The whole team looks like they're carved out of granite—all hard lines and rough edges—perfect specimens of the male form.

"*Le sigh.*" I lean back and press the back of my hand over my forehead in a dramatic gesture. "They're all stinking hot."

"But you have the hots for one." Angie giggles. "And from the looks he gives you, the feeling has to be reciprocated. I could ask Brady to look into it."

"No! Don't you dare. And I'm not into Booker. He's an overprotective, over-bearing ass." My lips twist, turning my smile into a frown. "That man is flawed, with a capital F, as in over-bearing, over-protective, and over-everything. He's just like my brothers, and you see how I react to their demands."

"I do, and you love that about Booker." She continues to tidy up our picnic spot. "It's what draws you to him."

"Does not."

"You can't lie to me." She turns her attention back to the rock wall the men scale as a part of one of their training exercises. "The air sizzles when the two of you get close."

"Don't know what you're talking about, and as far as sizzle, look who's talking. You and Brady are like lightning with the way you make the air crackle."

I lean back and tilt my head, getting a really fabulous look at the way Booker's ass fills out his pants. He traverses an overhead reverse incline with a full ruck on his back. One of the robotic dogs waits patiently for its turn to traverse the same overhang. Working with the robots, Bravo team is testing their operational readiness.

The man reaches out with powerful arms. His deft fingers feel around for a blind grip. Once he's set, his body swings out into open space. I can't help but gasp, worried he might fall the fifty feet between him and the ground.

But he doesn't.

Booker uses the momentum of his body to his advantage. He hooks a boot on a rock overhead, then hand over hand, pulls himself up the rock face. That gives me plenty of time to admire the way he fills out those black tactical pants of his. The man has a mighty-fine ass, and from what little I've seen of the front package, there are delights to be had there as well.

Once he's past that obstacle, it's time for the robot to follow. It scrambles across the inverted overhang like it's nothing, reminding me of a spider or a crab. Unlike either of those, the robots only have four legs, plus one arm-like appendage, that does double duty as a head and arm.

As for Booker, my mind is totally in the gutter. As for the gutter, Angie leads me into a trap.

"I bet you'd kill for Booker to get bossy with you."

"Shut up." I smack her in the arm, but the heat in my cheeks tells the truth.

Can't help it. I love a man who knows what he wants. When he goes after it with single-minded determination, I turn into a swoony puddle of goo.

It's true. I like a man who knows how to take charge, but only in the bedroom, and only when I'm in the mood. Meaning, that overprotective shit better not flow into any other part of my life.

The problem with Booker is he's not the kind of man who knows how to turn off his natural protectiveness. His take-charge attitude is a 24/7 kind of thing as well.

And I don't respond well to that—except in the bedroom.

With my cheeks aflame, I gather my trash and pack up the rest of my lunch.

"I really hate you."

"You love me far too much to hate me."

"I do." I tilt my head back, wanting one last view of the spectacle that is Bravo team.

They're near the top of the sixty-foot artificial rock wall. Not aware of the specific objective of this training exercise, I don't know if they did well or failed. Knowing the way Brady leads his team, and how Booker backs him up, I bet they busted expectations.

Angie and I stand, then police our picnic spot, making sure we leave nothing behind. As we do, my phone rings. I pull out my cellphone and glance at the screen.

"Ugh! Will they ever stop?"

"Your brothers?" Angie's eyes flash with mirth. "Which one?"

"Elder Dingleberry." That's what I call my oldest brother.

He's a decade older than me and likes to think that gives him parental privilege over my life and my life choices.

He was the loudest when it came to expressing concern when I first joined Doctors Without Borders.

I loved that job.

Absolutely *loved* it.

My first nine-month contract found me in the Caribbean, where I worked with my team to stamp out parasitic infection, provide life-saving immunizations, and dole out anti-malarials and antibiotics like they were going out of style.

Talk about a dream job.

My life's been blessed. I've never wanted for anything. To give something back to those less fortunate than myself is the golden goose of selfless acts.

My second contract brought me to Nicaragua, and while the first two months were amazing, the abduction thing was less than stellar.

Elder Dingleberry feels that proves his point about how dangerous my work with Doctors Without Borders was. He wants me close to home where he, and the other Dingleberries, can watch over me.

I'm one of those people who believe every cloud has a silver lining. As horrific and terrifying as that might have been, it brought Angie and me together. Before that event, we were cordial colleagues. We worked side-by-side but never connected. Now, we're practically inseparable.

We'll still be together when we're old and gray. It's one of those *life-ships*. That's what my mother calls a lifetime friendship. Angie's definitely my life-ship.

Even when she's being a pain in the ass, like right now—teasing me about Booker.

The hissing of rope running through carabiners snaps my head up in time to see the six Guardians rappelling down that sixty-foot rock face. I don't know how they do it, but they all kick off the wall at the same time, swing out, then gently arc back inward. Their feet touch the wall one time, then they kick off and drop to the ground.

It's like watching water ballet. They're so in sync with each other, it's like they're a living, breathing machine working in unison.

Since I'm currently holding my breath, I'm going to call it breathtaking, because I'm certainly amazed, impressed, overwhelmed, and a little bit tingly down there. More so when Booker looks in my direction and gives one of his devastating winks.

Dear lord, just shoot me now. Because now he knows I've been watching him.

Angie clutches the ring tied around her necklace. Like me, she's breathless and overtaken by these strange emotions.

The ring on that necklace belongs to her late husband. On her finger, however, the diamond engagement ring Brady gave her glitters in the light.

I envy my best friend. She found, not just one, but two soul mates to love. Whereas I've never dated. Never experienced young love—thank you Dingleberries.

No man stands a chance against my brothers.

My phone rings—again.

"Aren't you going to answer?" Angie looks down at my phone.

I swipe away the incoming call with a growl forming in the back of my throat.

"No."

"They'll just keep calling."

Angie's not wrong about that. After our Nicaraguan jungle adventure, we both moved to California. We share a small, two-bedroom townhouse while we figure out our lives.

In this case, *figure out* means however long Angie's going to make Brady wait to tie the knot for real.

He's always at our place, and where Brady goes, Booker follows. Those two are tight.

All that's to say, Angie hears my phone go off day and night. My brothers are persistent bastards.

"You know …" she gives me a sideways glance, "if you don't talk to them, one of them, if not all four, are going to come out here and drag you home."

"They'd like to think they could." I shove the phone deep into my back pocket.

"All I'm saying is what they've told me."

I forget my brothers text Angie as well. It's a two-pronged attack. Annoy me, and my bestie, hoping one of us will cave.

"You're not answering those texts, are you?" I narrow my eyes with suspicion.

"I wouldn't do that to you." She gives me a look, almost

offended, but smooths it out with a smile. "But I will tell you the texts are getting more and more insistent."

"I'll go home when I go home, and not a minute sooner."

"Hey, I'm on your side. Just telling you what they're saying to me."

I stop and pivot. Grasping her hands, I give them a little squeeze. "And that's what I love about you."

"What?"

"That you put up with my family drama. I regret ever giving them your number. You're a saint for putting up with them."

"It's not that hard to ignore a text."

She gives me a look like I'm overreacting and am overly grateful, but Angie doesn't know my brothers. They're not ones to stop at a text.

"Well, how about we get through the rest of the afternoon. I'll text them when we get home."

"Um, Izzy …" She gives me a look. "You didn't forget, did you?"

"Forget about what?"

"Brady and …"

"Oh shit." I cover my mouth. "I did."

It's Friday night, which means Brady and Booker are coming over for dinner. Since Angie can't cook worth a damn, I volunteered to whip up one of my amazing dishes.

"But that's perfect." My step lightens. "I can talk while I'm cooking. It's a natural kicking them off the phone stopping point."

"Okay, but please, no drama with Booker tonight. Will you promise to behave?"

"I always behave." With a shake of my head, I skip a step or two ahead of her. "He's the one who's always putting his foot in his mouth."

"Great …" Angie rolls her eyes. She almost looks disappointed, but she loves me. "You're not going to behave."

"I will if he does."

"Just shoot me now."

There it is. Angie's eyes do a double flip and triple twist with that eye roll.

"What do you care? The moment the food's done, you and Brady are going to get all lovey-dovey, leaving Booker and me to …"

"You could get cozy with him."

"Not happening."

"I'm telling you. The two of you would make a nice couple."

"I don't want *nice.*" Nope. That's not what I want at all.

And I'm not wrong about Booker. He's over the top, moving from tolerable to unbearable Alpha asshole in a split second.

Unfortunately, he's exactly the kind of man I'm attracted to.

TWO

Booker

"You ready yet?" Brady calls out from inside his gear locker.

Each Guardian team has their own space within the building we claim as our own. Four teams with four bullpens and a gear locker for each man. This all surrounds a briefing room where we plan and debrief all our missions, both active and training.

"Almost." I turn off the shower and shake the water from my hair.

All the sweat, grit, and grime from our training exercise is gone, leaving me smelling my best for another night with the most infuriating woman in the world.

I should've gone out with the guys.

Rafe, Zeb, Alec, and Hayes showered, changed into civies, and left Brady and me behind. They're hitting the bars, while I hang with Brady, his fiancée, Angie, and Isabelle LaCroix—aka the most infuriating woman in the world.

I hang with Brady because he's going to see Angie. Nine times out of ten, Isabelle is with Angie, and since I *want* Isabelle, I'm there too.

"I should've gone with them." The wet tile draws my eyes. My toes wriggle in the water while my chin lifts.

But I can't see my reflection in the mirrors.

Steam fills the room, forming a dense fog. Moisture coats the mirrors, not that I need them. I'm well aware of how I look.

Which is why my frustration with Isabelle grows with each passing day.

She's not getting the hint.

Or she's messing with me.

I'll have to resort to hitting her over the head to knock some sense into the woman if she doesn't get it soon. Not that I ever would—hit a woman—but I've never had to work this hard to get a woman into my bed.

My balls are getting bluer by the day.

"I seem to remember telling you to go with them." Brady rattles the wire fence of his personal locker, stowing his weapons and gear until tomorrow. "Maybe then you'd get laid and stop being a bitch."

"Asshole." My teeth clench with irritation, but Brady's right.

As for getting laid, I'm in a major dry spell, and it's all because of Isabelle.

Since the moment I laid eyes on her, I haven't wanted any other woman. It's been just me, my hand, and an endless wealth of dirty fantasies about the raven-headed vixen with cornflower-blue eyes.

"I didn't want to leave you alone with Angie and Isabelle." I act like I'm doing him a favor, which is total bullshit.

"You don't think I can't handle the two of them alone?" Brady snickers. The scarring on his face turns that grin into a bit of a sneer. "Are you forgetting the day and a half I spent alone with them in Nicaragua?"

I'm well aware of the day and a half he spent with Isabelle.

"*That* doesn't count." There's a possessive rumble in the back of my throat I tamp down before Brady calls me out about it.

"And why is that?"

"That was work and this is …"

"Play?" There's that tone again. "Maybe Iz isn't into you?"

"She is."

Or will be.

I just need to lay on the charm and convince her that she's mine.

"You should go out with the guys. I'm sure they haven't gotten far. Call a car and have it drop your ass off at whatever bar they're terrorizing for the night."

"Not interested in drinking."

"Right, I forgot. Your body is your temple." There's that low chuckle again. "And I'm not talking about drinking. You need to get laid."

"Just because I watch what I put in my body, doesn't mean …"

"Relax, dude. Geez. You're grouchy as fuck."

"Am not."

"Are too, and speaking of … Make a move on Izzy already. I'm tired of watching the two of you prowl around each other."

"If you haven't noticed, she's not into me."

"Only because you're a dick to her."

"Am not."

"Are too."

"You're full of unwanted insight tonight."

"That woman's got you twisted around her pinky finger and you're too blind to notice. You're playing right into her hand."

"I'm not twisted around her finger." My ego takes extreme offense to that comment, but I say nothing to Brady about it.

The thing is—I keep stepping wrong with Isabelle. Don't know why that is, but she's not interested, or impressed.

So why are you still chasing her?

I'm not chasing her.

That little voice inside my head can go fuck itself. I don't chase women. They fall at my feet. And that's not arrogance speaking.

It's simple fact—backed up by a lifetime of experience.

Women have been falling at my feet from the day my voice deepened and muscle packed on my scrawny frame.

When I turned eighteen, and could legally work in Vegas … Well, let's just say, I've *never* had to work for it.

As for the gig on the Strip, someone needed to feed my four little sisters and keep a roof over their heads. That sure as shit wasn't my deadbeat dad, or my mom who scraped by on minimum wage and crappy tips at the diner she worked at all night. That woman worked her ass off for her kids.

But it wasn't enough.

It was never enough.

"I'm not arguing with you." Brady secures his gear locker and tugs on the lock, making sure it's fully engaged. "You and Iz need to figure shit out or stop breathing the same air. You don't have to come over for dinner."

I want to go to dinner.

It's the only time I can be alone with Isabelle.

Such a pretty name, I prefer it over the jarring Izzy she prefers, or Brady's annoying nickname—Iz.

She hates it when I call her Isabelle.

Absolutely hates it.

Which is probably why I use her full name. There's just something about getting her fired up that drives me crazy and heats my blood.

Maybe tonight, I'll get to …

Naw, that girl is driving me fucking crazy and I'm not going to go all Alpha-male on her. I have a feeling that's the surest path to a permanent *dis*-invitation to dinners at her place.

"I'm coming for dinner."

"I know. You can't *not* show up." Brady shakes his head. "I don't know why you don't just take her to bed already."

"She's not that kind of girl. Have you noticed how that kind of shit totally turns her off?"

"Oh, I've noticed. I've also noticed how that totally throws you off your game. Either step up to the plate or move on."

"I'll step up, once I know she's not going to chew me up and spit me out." I rub at the back of my neck. "Women are supposed to be easy."

"What man has ever said women are easy?"

"Me." I give him a look. "I've never had a problem getting a woman in my bed before. Not like this."

"That's because you don't want Izzy in your bed."

"Sure as shit I do." I give him another look, like he's a crazy man.

"Not saying you don't want that with Iz, but for the first time in your life, you want her standing beside you too." Brady crosses his arms over his chest and gives me the look. "That's why you're off your game. The girl stumped you."

"I don't know what you're talking about."

"You know I'm right." He shrugs. "Which is why you're struggling."

He knows what's going on in my head better than I do, and he's right about all of it.

I'm tired of fucking for the sake of fucking.

It bores me.

Not that I'd refuse.

But seeing how Brady and Angie look at each other, the way they watch out for each other, makes me want something like that too.

Hate to say it, but I'm ready to settle down.

I've sown enough wild oats to feed an army. It's time to plant roots and look to the future. At thirty-one, I'm ready for the next step.

"Hurry up and get dressed." Brady shakes his head, laughing at me under his breath. He leans against the wall and crosses his arms over his chest while I tug on street clothes.

"Dinner's at their place tonight?"

"Yeah."

"Why? We have the better view."

"Dunno. Angie said Izzy wanted to cook and the kitchen at my place isn't up to snuff."

Isabelle's a great cook. Fabulous comes to mind. If she's cooking, that's one boat I'm not rocking.

"Dinner at the girls' place it is then."

"If you'd ever get dressed." He gives me a look that says shut up and hurry up.

I get it. He's eager to get home to Angie.

As for me, I've got the entire evening open. Kitchen issues aside,

"You can't help it, can you?"

"Help, what?"

"You insult me when you don't know what to say."

"I do not."

"You do, but let me simplify things. I want you. I *crave* you." I let my voice get husky and rumble in the back of my throat. "I want to devour you. I'm not afraid to put it out there. Why are you afraid to do the same?"

Her lids draw back. Whether that's in fear, surprise, anger, indignation, or something else, is way beyond my limited mental capacities. Right now, I'm splitting mental faculties between two heads; and one is getting larger by the second.

"That's a bit presumptuous." From the flaring of her nostrils to the way her pupils dilate and blow out her gorgeous, blue eyes, I struck a nerve.

What nerve that might be, remains to be decided.

"What's presumptuous?"

"You know."

"Actually, I don't." I cock my head. "I could take a stab at it, considering I read people fairly well, but I'm going to give you a chance to come clean."

"Come clean?"

"That is what I said."

"You are so …"

"Full of it. Yes, you already said that." I crack a grin because I suddenly realize how much I enjoy this back and forth. I usually don't get this much time alone with Isabelle. Generally, I have to share her with Angie and Brady.

"You're incorrigible." She blows out a breath.

"Why? Because I'm not afraid to put you to question."

"Put me to question? What the hell does that mean? You're interrogating me now?"

"No, I'm asking a very simple question."

"And what is that?"

"Are you attracted to me?"

"That's a silly question." She goes into defensive mode, folding her arms across her chest.

"Why?"

"Because that's not the answer you want."

"How do you know it's not what I want? It's a very direct question. Are you attracted to me?"

"You're too polished. Too swoony."

"Swoony?"

"Yes. You're not only attractive, but you're every woman's wet dream. You ooze sex appeal. And I bet you used that during your exotic dancer days to double your tips."

"Damn straight I did. I was there to make money. Which means, I did whatever it took to double, triple, and quadruple my tips. I sold those women a fantasy and delivered it with a silver platter. At the end of the night, that's what allowed me to put food on the table when I got home."

"Well, that's exactly what I don't want."

"What's that?"

"I don't want to be sold a fantasy. It's an empty promise. Or worse, something that's not real. I'm not interested in the fantasy. I can dream about you all night long, but that doesn't mean I'm stupid enough to do anything about it."

"Well, at least we settled something."

"What's that?"

"That you not only fantasize about me, but I'm in your dreams as well."

"That's not what …"

"It's okay. I fantasize about you too." I wink at her and love the way her cheeks turn bright red.

"You're impossible."

"Perhaps." I glance around, wondering where Angie and Brady got off to. Knowing them, they're probably getting in a quickie while Isabelle and I try not to kill each other. "Now, about the bet."

"What bet?"

"Our bet." I tuck in my shirt, making sure I look good for her.

"There's no bet." She's suspicious, and for good reason. Isabelle gives me stink eyes and turns her attention back to the stove.

I've almost got her. If I play my cards right, *my* bet will turn into the kiss I want.

"I want in on the bet." Brady barges in on us. His brows tug tight as he assesses the situation.

Fucking way to cock block, man.

I hide my irritation behind a scowl.

"I don't even know what he was talking about, but there's no bet." Isabelle points to the cupboards. "Now, why don't the two of you make yourselves useful and set the table?"

Brady gives me a *What-the-fuck* look, but I ignore him and grab some plates. As I set the table, he whispers in my ear.

"What the fuck did you do?"

"Nothing."

"Nothing, my ass. What happened to not starting a war?"

"I started nothing."

"From the looks she's throwing, Iz wants you dead."

"That's not what she wants." I keep my voice to a whisper because Isabelle's eyes are definitely drilling a hole through my back.

"And you think you know what she wants?"

"Damn straight, I do."

"What?"

"She wants me." I lower my voice to a whisper. "And for the record, that was terrible timing." With that, I crook a grin and spin around to meet Isabelle stare for stare.

Yeah, this is just the beginning between the two of us.

FOUR

Izzy

"WHAT THE HELL WERE THE TWO OF YOU DOING?" ANGIE ENTERS ON the heels of Brady, and like him, she reads the room in less than a millisecond.

Not that it's hard to figure out something's off between me and Booker. The air crackles with the residual energy of our exchange.

She pulls me aside, whispering so the guys don't hear us. "Were you arguing again?"

I yank her down the hall. Passing by her bedroom, the question of what she was doing with Brady is a moot point. They can't keep their hands off each other.

"At least someone's having fun." My smile tips into a frown.

I hate admitting it, but I'm jealous of Angie's relationship with Brady.

"I thought we could leave the two of you alone for a second without starting World War III." Angie blushes and bites her lower lip.

"It's not like that, but yeah. We were doing what we always do." I shrug.

No reason to hide it. Our verbal exchanges rarely progress to shouting matches, but they come close.

Often, I question why I even bother, if we're so obviously incompatible, but then I look at him, and that flutter in my belly returns.

It's there now. A light fluttering sensation with a tingle—down there. Man, I'd love to jump his bones. Give me one night to get him out of my system. One night not to fall desperately in love with a man I barely know.

Yeah, that's what I need.

One magnificent night.

There's just something about Booker that draws me. I'm like a deranged firefly happily flitting toward the bug zapper and certain doom.

I know I shouldn't.

I know he's dangerous.

But I can't stay away.

"Argue?" Angie's left brow lifts, calling me out.

"Yeah." I hunch my shoulders, ashamed with myself for not being able to act civil around Booker. "A little." I pinch my thumb and forefinger together.

My gut tells me he's not such a bad guy. I mean, the man's a Guardian. He dedicates his life to saving others. If that's not the epitome of a *Knight in Shining Armor*, then I don't know what is.

"I'd say there was a bit more than a *little* arguing going on." Angie glances down the hall, checking on the guys. "Are we going to have a problem at dinner? I'm tired of dinners where Brady and I pretend the air's not sparking between you two."

"I'll be civil. As for Booker? I make no promises."

"Then let's see to our guests and devour the amazing meal you made for Booker."

"I didn't make it for him."

"Girl, you've talked about that dish since we met, and you've never made it for me. What changed?"

"Changed?"

"I assume you made it for him."

"I didn't. I just felt like cooking it tonight."

I totally made it for Booker and hate that I lie to my best friend.

The silly thing is that I don't know why I care, or why I went to the effort of cooking for him.

Maybe, I did it because there's a part of me that's missing home. Mom makes this dish.

The Dingleberries might have a point. Maybe it's time to take a few days off?

Maybe I need a good dose of home?

Or maybe, I'm foolishly trying to impress a man that I can barely stand to be in the same room with?

"Of course, you did." Angie sees right through my bullshit. "Just cooking it for yourself." She takes my hand. "Now, let's get in there before the food gets cold."

I'd love to have what she has; a man who's strong, but willing to let his woman in behind his shields. Hell, I'd just settle for a fuck buddy, which is funny considering Booker's practically begging to be exactly that.

If I want him to stay the night, he will in a heartbeat. The sex would be fabulous. I can tell that by looking at him. A man who looks like him, knows how to please a woman. My fear is what happens after I let my guard down.

Because I will.

I'll fall hook, line, and sinker because I'm weak like that. But he's a player, and I'm not interested in playing games.

Not when it comes to my heart.

Not when I know I'll lose.

Not when I've already fallen hard.

But how can it be love when I don't know the guy?

It's a feeling in my gut, a warmth in my chest. It's the way the world seems to make sense when he's around.

Yeah, I'm sunk.

"You ladies going to join us?" Brady's deep voice calls out. "Or are you going to keep whispering behind our backs?"

"We're not talking behind your back." Angie grabs my hand and drags me back to the living room.

"Sure sounds like it." Brady winks at his fiancée, then turns his gaze on me. "I hear this is a special recipe. If it tastes half as good as it smells, we need to hurry up and get to the good part."

"It is a special recipe." I can't help but beam with pride. "Passed down through the generations because it's so wonderful."

While Brady and Angie take a seat, Booker comes to the kitchen.

"Can I help bring anything out?" The tone of his voice is different from before.

There's no sign of the harshness from our earlier verbal exchange. Since he sounds sincere and wants to help, I figure I can do the same.

Be civil, that is.

"Yes, thanks. The bread's in the oven keeping warm. Oven mitts are right there. You can take that straight to the table and put it on the hot pad."

"I can do that." He leans in toward the stovetop. "That really does smell incredible."

His breath whispers against my neck, lifting the fine hairs on my skin and sending a tingle of electricity down my spine.

My breaths accelerate, and I don't dare move.

He takes in another deep sniff.

"Yeah, that smells amazing."

Booker's not talking about my mother's secret recipe.

"Thanks. It tastes even better."

"Well then, I can't wait to try it, and hear the story behind it."

With no further prompting, he slips on the oven mitts and takes the hot rolls I made to the table. While he does that, I ladle out four bowls of my mother's infamous Junkyard Stew.

Booker returns and carries two of the bowls to the table, setting them down in front of Brady and Angie. He waits for me as I carry the remaining two to the table. He takes the bowls out of my hands, almost acting like a real gentleman.

"Is there anything else?" He glances toward the kitchen, then places the steaming bowls on the table.

My family's special concoction of spices floods my senses. Yeah, this is a killer dish—even if it's just stew.

"Nope. This is it." When I go to sit, Booker surprises me by holding out my chair and helping me scoot in. "Dig in."

I wait for the three of them to try out my mother's stew, a bit nervous about their reactions.

Stew isn't generally considered a gourmet dish—thus my nerves—but my mother's brew takes heartwarming to a sublime treat of the senses.

Booker's eyes widen with his first taste.

"When you mentioned stew, I did not imagine this. What's in it?"

"Izzy is amazing in the kitchen." Angie looks at me with a smile and gives me a thumbs-up. "I've never had soup ..."

"Stew." I correct her.

"I've never had a stew that melts in your mouth before. And the flavors. It's rich, complex, and—simply amazing."

"This is beyond good, Iz." When Brady takes a sip, his eyes close with appreciation. "It's amazing."

"You're supposed to take the bread and dip it in the stew." I show them what I mean.

It's true, the stew is magical, but combined with my homemade bread, it goes a step beyond.

Dinner conversation ceases as my friends devour the meal. Booker, along with Brady, fill their bowls up three times, and they demolish the bread.

Angie opens a bottle of wine, something I always forget, and we sit back chatting about everything and nothing.

"We watched your training on the wall with the robots." Angie takes a sip of wine. "What was that about?"

Booker gives me a look that makes my belly do this little loop-de-loop kind of thing. Something about the way he does it makes me wonder what's going on inside his head. Especially after our conversation about fantasies.

I doubt he realizes how close he came to nailing my deepest secret on the head.

"The tech team wanted us to put the robots through their paces in a vertical space. Damn things put us to shame. They scaled the wall like fucking spiders." Booker sets his wine glass on the table and grabs the last piece of bread. He uses that to sop up the last of his stew.

"I'm continually impressed with what Guardian HRS can do." I can't stop staring at Booker.

Clean-shaven, square jaw, prominent brow, he looks like a superhero. Many would say, in real life, he is a superhero.

All the Guardians are.

Fierce protectors, they risk everything to save those who can't save themselves.

Brady saved me.

If not for the Guardians, I'd still be in that jungle, or dead. There was always that possibility.

Brady jumps in, describing the various tests they put the robots through. I follow less than half of the conversation as he and Booker discuss things about sticky feet and self-aware robots that can scale sheer rock walls.

The conversation comes to a lull. The wine hits me, putting me in a relaxed state. This is what I miss. It's what I want in my life.

A sense of belonging to something greater than myself.

Growing up with four older brothers, we often sat around the dinner table long past when the food was gone. We'd talk about everything and anything. My parents provided what guidance they could, while trying not to pry too deeply into their children's lives.

I miss that.

After two contracts with Doctors Without Borders, it's been far too long since I've been home. As obnoxious as the Dingleberries have been, I feel that urge to go home.

This is my hard-headedness getting in the way. If my brothers weren't so obnoxious and demanding, I probably would've visited sooner.

It needs to be my idea, and I finally think I'm ready. It's been a few weeks since the Guardians rescued me and Angie from the jungles of Nicaragua. That's enough time to take the edges off the whole experience. Meaning, I'm good to talk about it and answer the million questions the Dingleberries will throw at me.

"How about you?" Booker's deep voice snaps me out of my thoughts.

"I'm sorry. What were you asking?"

"I was asking about Guardian HRS orientation. How's it going for the two of you?"

"Kind of slow, to be honest." Angie wipes her mouth with a napkin. "I'm ready to dive in and get back to seeing patients, but there's a lot of in-processing. Way more than I thought."

"Well, if anything, the Guardians are a thorough bunch." Brady leans back and taps his belly. "Iz, when Angie told me you were making stew, I had my doubts, but that was the best meal I've had in ages."

"Thanks." I push away from the table to begin clearing the plates, but Booker shakes his head.

"She who cooks does not do dishes." He reaches for my bowl. "Let me."

"You seriously don't have to do that." I scoot back and grab Angie's and Brady's dishes. "I'm a bit weird about that."

"What do you mean?" He joins me on my way to the kitchen.

"I find doing dishes soothing."

"You *are* weird about that."

Behind us, Brady asks Angie about our day. I give their conversation half an ear as she relays the boring bits.

"You kept the bracelet?" Brady's voice expresses surprise. "It's kind of ugly."

"Yeah, but you gave it to me." Angie sounds wistful. "I'm attached to it now."

"It's not much more than a bit of knotted string."

"With a tracker in it. If you hadn't given it to me, who knows where I would be now."

I know about the bracelet and her attachment to it. When Brady rescued the two of us in Nicaragua, he gave Angie the bracelet.

He's not wrong about it being not much more than a bit of knotted string, but it's the tracker embedded within it that saved Angie's life.

While the Guardians literally swooped in to save me—first,

worst, and last helicopter ride of my life—Angie was taken. Brady had to leave her behind.

It eats at him. I see it in the pain of his expression. The guilt over saving me while losing her to the Coralos cartel.

But it's because of the tracker that the Guardians were able to find Angie and the other members of our team who were also abducted.

"What did you pick?" Booker's deep voice makes me jump and lifts the fine hairs at my nape.

"Excuse me?"

"The tracker? Angie was saying how the technical team introduced you to the trackers. I was wondering what you picked."

He refers to the startling array of trackers embedded in pretty much any, and every, type of jewelry known to mankind.

It's something Guardian HRS does for its employees. That, along with a coded emergency message, are all a part of their many, and varied, security protocols.

"I didn't."

"What do you mean you didn't?" Booker's brows practically climb off the top of his head.

"I opted out."

"Why the hell would you do that?"

While his brows levitate off his forehead, mine bunch together, nearly touching.

"Because it's invasive." Why am I defending my actions? I look him square in the eye.

"You need one. First thing tomorrow morn …"

"Whoa." I hold up a hand. "You're not the boss of me."

"It's not invasive. It's meant to provide a sense of security and protection." He grabs my upper arms and gives a light squeeze. "And I'm not trying to boss you around. Consider me a concerned citizen."

"Concerned, or not, I'm not in the jungles of Nicaragua. I don't need it, and I'm not a fan of Guardian HRS always knowing where I am and what I'm doing. I don't want it."

Not that Guardian HRS spies on their employees. Mitzy was

very clear about the embedded trackers being a passive system during the briefing.

That means they're not actively sending data. Supposedly, they're activated only in an emergency. There's not some tech guy in a closet keeping tabs on Guardian HRS employees.

Booker's expression darkens. He's on the verge of losing control, but he manages to rein it in with one long, deep breath.

All the while, my skin heats beneath his hands. Booker and I *never* touch. We're more than standoffish around the other, but the moment his hands touch me, it's like getting struck by lightning.

My entire body wakes up and comes alive beneath his touch. It's all I can do not to squirm.

"You never know when you're going to need it." His glare makes my insides twist, almost as if I've done something wrong. "And there's no way to know whether what happened in Nicaragua will follow you."

"Follow me?" My caustic laugh is building into something derisive and not at all friendly.

I'm not a fan of my actions being questioned by anyone; Dingleberry or Guardian.

"There are unresolved issues." He presses his point.

"Like what?"

"What Jerald said before he died, for one thing." He gives me a look like this should all be obvious.

Truthfully, I'm eager to put the whole wretched experience behind me.

Jerald was one of our mechanics and general helpers. When our medical team was taken, he was kidnapped with us. The only females, Angie and I, were immediately separated from the men. The first night we narrowly escaped rape when Brady showed up on the other side of a river that flowed next to the encampment.

What followed after that was a day and a half of the most terrifying moments of my life.

I'm afraid of water; we went for a swim.

I'm afraid of heights; we descended a steep path around a waterfall.

That's where I injured my ankle, which ultimately led to Angie being left behind. Since I couldn't walk, Brady carried me out of the jungle. Angie ran behind us.

The rest of Bravo team swooped in on a helicopter and scooped me out of the jungle, but Angie was retaken by the cartel. That bracelet Brady gave her is the only reason the Guardians were able to track her down. In the end, they rescued not only her, but the rest of our team.

All because of the tracking device in that bracelet.

Everyone *except* Jerald.

We thought he was being held separately, since he wasn't medical, but it turns out he was working with the cartel.

He later tracked down and attacked Angie, saying something crazy about diamonds. As far as I know, no one knows what he was talking about.

Booker continues to loom over me. Sculpted chest huffing and puffing as he tries to rein in his anger. Damn, but the man smells amazing; spice and musk and, holy hellfire, I could sniff him all day long.

Wrong move. I place my hand over his chest—*holy moly wow cow, that's some muscular definition*—and push him away.

He releases my arms, but only to fold them over his broad chest and scowl down at me.

"Until that's sorted, you need a tracker."

"What part of *I don't want one* do you not understand?"

"What part of *it's for your safety* do you not get?"

"Look, I grew up with four overprotective brothers. I don't need to add an overbearing Guardian to the Dingleberry squad."

"The, what?"

"The Dingleberry squad. It's what I call my brothers when they get overbearing, overprotective, and overly obnoxious."

"Caring about you doesn't make me overbearing. If you could get out of your own way, you'd understand what it means."

"Talking down to me like I'm some child who doesn't know what's good for me is a sure-fire way to piss me the fuck off." I lift on tiptoe, needing to equalize some of our height difference. It does nothing because he towers over me, but it makes me feel a little better.

"I'm not talking down to you."

"This conversation is over." I turn on my heels and stomp down to my bedroom, leaving Booker to clean up after dinner.

What I need is distance from Booker.

Space to work him out of my system.

Orientation for Guardian HRS is in progress, which makes texting my new boss, Skye Summers, more than awkward.

After a little back and forth, I tell her why I need a few days to go home, playing up the trauma angle from my recent abduction. She has zero problem with me taking a couple of weeks off.

I wanted a couple of days.

Don't think I can survive a couple of weeks with the Dingleberries.

While still fuming over my conversation with Booker, I book a midnight flight out of California to Laredo, Texas. Then I pack a bag, including the most important thing: a rabbit's foot that's seen better days.

Given to me by Jerald on the first day of our mission for *good luck*, I kept it with me all through the harrowing escape through the jungle.

Suspicious by nature, I believe the mangled rabbit's foot saved my life. Considering I faced practically all my fears during that escape, the rabbit's foot goes with me everywhere.

It's threadbare—or is that furbare?—and looks like it's been put through the ringer, but I place it around my neck and write a note to Angie.

I could leave in the morning, but if I stay the night, I might lose my nerve. Packed up and ready to go, I call for a car to take me to the airport.

Midnight check-in at the counter goes smoothly. Security is a breeze. All that's left is boarding and getting over my fear of flying.

That fear isn't enough to keep me from air travel, but I'm definitely what they call a nervous traveler.

I kiss the mangled rabbit's foot just prior to takeoff and again just prior to landing. It's not as scary as a helicopter, but I'm still afraid of flying. The rabbit's foot may be a bit of foolish nonsense, but it got me out of the jungles of Nicaragua intact, and it'll get me through this flight.

I text the Elder Dingleberry an hour before the plane touches down. I want my visit to be a surprise and tell him to let no one know.

When I make it through baggage claim, tears fill my eyes.

All the Dingleberries are there. They move as a group toward me, then fold themselves around me in one massive group hug. I didn't realize how much I missed them, and the tears catch me by complete surprise.

"Hey, sis." Gareth, the eldest, soothes me with his deep Texan twang. "How was the flight?"

Gareth knows about my many, and varied, fears. There's a twinkle in his eye, teasing me, but affection resides there as well.

"Hey." I lift on tiptoe to kiss his cheek. "Guess I survived another brush with death."

"Brush with death?" His bright blue eyes twinkle. "You do know the air travel industry is one of the safest on the planet?"

"Doesn't matter." I firm my lip and stand my ground.

The twins, Jude and Parker, grab my bags, each giving me a peck on the cheek. Then Colton, youngest of the Dingleberries, loops his arm through mine.

"We have missed you, little sis."

He rubs his knuckles over the top of my head, making me screech and laugh. Colton keeps a hold of my arm as Gareth marches our group out to the parking deck.

Damn, this feels good. Why did I wait so long to come home?

FIVE

Booker

"SHE LEFT?" MY EYES PINCH, AND MY MOUTH GAPES, DISBELIEVING Brady's news. "What do you mean she left?"

"That's all I know. Angie said, when she woke up, Iz left a note that she was going home."

"Going home to stay? Or going home to visit?"

Did my bullheadedness, and our constant bickering, finally drive Isabelle away? I certainly hope not.

I grill Brady for information while combing my fingers through my hair.

"Was it because of me?"

"Honestly, I don't know, but I doubt it was because of you." He gives me a strange look. "What, exactly, is going on between the two of you?"

"Don't know what you're talking about."

"Sure as shit you do. You just asked if she left because of you." He sweeps out his arm, emphasizing his point. "I can't tell if the two of you dislike each other, or if you're in some twisted mating ritual."

"Mating ritual?" I scoff at his comment. "That's an image I won't get out of my head anytime soon."

"From my point of view, it's like watching a lion and lioness circling each other. We're all wondering who's going to pounce first."

"Another odd image." I give him another look. "And Isabelle isn't a lioness."

She's far more precious than that. She's soft and delicate, more like a cuddly kitten than a ferocious lioness.

Brady needs to get his metaphors under control.

"Isabelle?" He arches a brow. "Got your own name for her, I see."

"You call her Iz." My tone comes off way more defensive than I'm willing to admit.

"I do?"

"Yeah."

"Guess I do, but that's only because she's like a little sister to me. We bonded through the whole jungle thing. That kind of thing tends to stick."

I wish that had been me instead of Brady.

Honestly, I'm jealous and pissed off. I played my part in rescuing Isabelle, getting her into the helicopter, but Brady did the heavy lifting.

He spent a day and a half with her and Angie, hunkering in a cave overnight, swimming them downriver, navigating a waterfall, protecting them from a sniper, and running to the evacuation spot where the rest of Bravo team came into play.

All I did was walk Isabelle over to the helicopter. Definitely *not* hero material. Brady is her hero, and I hate every bit of it.

It should've been me.

Not that I can speak a word of that out loud. It would destroy my friendship with Brady and make me look like a total tool.

Isn't that the word Isabelle used?

Brady's right about one thing. All Isabelle and I do is argue. If she were any other woman on the face of the planet, I would've turned my back on her and moved on already. I don't need that kind of shit in my life.

But I find turning away from Isabelle physically impossible. For some unknown reason, I'm drawn to her, and that scares me to death.

"Do we know where her home is?" I kick myself for never asking. There's so much about her that I don't know.

"Why? Are you going after her?" Brady gives me a look like I'm a crazy lunatic.

"Don't be an ass." I rub at the back of my neck and pace the length of the conference room.

Since Brady and I live right next to each other, we generally drive to Guardian HQ together. Today, we're a few minutes early for a pop-up briefing called by CJ, head of the Guardian branch of Guardian HRS.

"You've got it bad." Brady's enjoying this. His shoulders bounce with his laughter.

"Don't start that shit with me." I spin around and point at him, but it's all for show.

I know it.

Brady knows it.

Shit, everyone knows it.

"Why?" He shrugs. "Nothing to be ashamed about." He gives me another look. "Felt the same way about Angie. Meaning, I've been in your shoes."

"Isabelle isn't like Angie. Angie knows how to take care of herself. She's a survival specialist. Isabelle isn't."

"Don't I know it." Brady gives a little chuckle. "But we're not in the jungle. I'm sure Izzy knows how to handle herself on US soil."

We talk a lot, and Brady told me all about how Angie is different from other women.

She's a rugged, outdoorsy kind of gal. They're a match made in heaven. Isabelle isn't like that. She's not rugged, and definitely not outdoorsy.

I worry what might happen if the Coralos cartel decides on a bit of retribution after our rescue of her team. That part of the rescue —the part not involving Isabelle—I was a part of.

As was Brady and the rest of Bravo team.

Brady took down the leader of the cartel when we rescued Angie. Put a bullet right through his head. The rest of Bravo freed the other hostages, all men, and pretty banged up after the torture they endured.

If anything, what remains of the cartel, whoever rose to the top, will be coming after Guardian HRS and not the two women we saved.

"Well fuck." I pace the length of the conference room as frustration builds inside of me. "Did you know she declined the tracker?"

"Angie mentioned it." The nonchalant shrug he gives pisses me the fuck off.

"And?" I can't believe he's not worried.

"And, what?"

"She needs to be chipped."

All the Guardians are chipped.

One to find and one to hide.

I carry two embedded chips within my body. We all do.

It's a safety measure. For those who work in support roles for Guardian HRS, they're given the option of taking advantage of the varied tracking devices created for emergency situations. We're in the business of saving lives, which means we tend to make a lot of enemies.

After Forest Summers, visionary and creator of Guardian HRS, was taken as a prisoner by his lifelong nemesis, John Snowden, the tracker program was implemented.

"Izzy can make her own decisions. Not everyone opts for that." Brady's right about that.

Like any mandate, there are always those few who object. With a Guardian, there is no opting out. It's a part of the job requirement and nonnegotiable. All other Guardian HRS team members have a choice.

"Why are you stressing about it? Iz just went home. She'll be fine."

"Fine?" I pull at my chin. "You know that shit in Nicaragua isn't settled."

"Angie told me Iz has four older brothers. I'm sure she's fine." Brady's dismissive tone makes me grind my teeth together.

Am I the only one concerned about Isabelle out there all alone?

She may have four older brothers, but that doesn't mean they know shit about protecting her.

Civilians never know what to look for, what to be concerned about, or what to do if the shit hits the fan.

"I hope you're right."

Brady forgets rule number one.

Never assume.

As far as Nicaragua goes, it turns out that's the focus of our meeting. CJ called the meeting with Bravo team, but all the higher-ups show up.

Mitzy's there from the technical team. Sam, who's in charge of all of Guardian HRS sits in. Then there are the two heavy hitters, Forest and Skye Summers.

They're a brother and sister power duo; the visionaries who created the Guardians in the first place, as well as The Facility where their rescues find respite from their ordeal and learn what they need to move past their trauma.

Technically, Forest and Skye aren't blood related. They grew up together in foster care and endured unspeakable trauma at the hands of their foster father.

But that's a story for another time.

I keep my trap shut during the preliminary part of the briefing. It's really a rundown of the mission and what intel we obtained.

Which isn't much.

"Does anyone know what Jerald was talking about?" Brady focuses in on Mitzy.

As lead of our technical team, the rainbow-haired pixie knows pretty much everything about anything.

"As far as the diamonds go?" Mitzy gives a little flick of her hair. It doesn't move. She's got it glammed up with some kind of glitter gel. Her psychedelic hair sticks out in all directions.

Somehow, it looks right on her.

"Come on," I blow out a breath. "Are you telling us, with all your Mitzy Magic, you've found nothing about diamonds?"

"No, meathead. I have not. And just because some dead guy

spouts off at the mouth about diamonds doesn't mean I can magically find out what he was talking about." She gives me the eye. "And it's not like there's any evidence to go looking either. Everything from that mission was taken by the cartel. Angie and Isabelle escaped that first camp with nothing but the clothes on their backs."

Something about what Mitzy says tickles a memory. Try as I might, I can't bring it up.

"Aren't there other things to look for?" Brady props his elbows on the table and cups his face.

"Like what?" Mitzy's irritation ups the tension in the room.

"I don't know. What do people do with diamonds these days?" Brady's trying, but he's on a fishing expedition.

I'm with Mitzy on this.

We have nothing.

"Mitz—it's a good question." The deep rumbly bass of Forest Summers makes the air vibrate with latent power.

I remember the first time I met him. I'm a few inches over six feet, yet he towered over me. White-blond hair, eyes like ice, he's a formidable man. Reminds me of a Viking king. Although, he looks a little less than I remember. Paler. But that's surely my memory being off.

"We should consider every angle." Forest Summers pressures Mitzy.

One of the many things Mitzy is good at is acting like the rest of us are idiots. The one person she can't get away with that is Forest Summers. The man operates in a whole other sphere of existence than us mere mortals.

A high-functioning Asperger individual—I think the PC thing is to say *On the Spectrum*, whatever that means—Forest is gifted with a truly unique intelligence.

"How about we step away from the Nicaraguan mission and look at this from a different angle?" The soft voice of Doc Summers brings quiet to the room. "Diamonds are one of the best ways to transfer capital from one place to another."

"True." Forest nods. "Diamonds are an excellent way to launder money."

"So is art." Mitzy pipes in. "Did you know the illegal sale of art, and art forgeries, is nearly a trillion-dollar industry?"

"True," Doc Summers says, "but art is difficult to move and subject to degradation by the elements. Not so for diamonds. We're thinking about this the wrong way."

"How so?" Sam, who's been quiet so far, joins the conversation.

"Angie and the rest of her team said they were being questioned about the movement of guns. Of course, none of them knew anything about any weapons. Angie told me several times how they unloaded their gear as a team. It would be pretty difficult to hide weapons and ammunition."

"Weapons, yes," CJ agrees. "Ammunition, or other explosives, could easily be camouflaged." He looks to Hayes. "Isn't that right?"

I'm the team's medic, trained and licensed as an EMT, and I have a fascination with munitions, but Hayes is our explosives expert.

"There are many ways explosives could be packaged to look like medical supplies." Hayes speaks with a rumbly voice, carrying the barest trace of a southern accent, but he looks like a mountain man with a barrel chest and shaggy beard. "As a gel, it can be packaged in bottles, generally glass, to be mixed with accelerant at a later time. Anything plastic could be fuses to be used in bomb making." His eyes pinch and he leans back, thinking hard.

"How would they keep the medical team from accidentally using any of those things?" Doc Summers speaks up.

"That's the thing." I chime in. This, at least, is something I listened to. I clear my throat and continue. "After listening to Isabelle explain how she kept her pharmaceutical supplies, there's no way she wouldn't accidentally use those vials, if there were any explosives there in the first place. All I'm saying is that it's possible, but highly unlikely."

As team medic, I have a deeper understanding of what might be found in a medical pack. I don't have the info Hayes has because I never sat in on the debriefings of Angie and Isabelle.

I was too busy being a *tool*, as Isabelle would say. Damn, but I certainly fucked shit up with her.

"Back to diamonds." I tap the table with my fingertips. Everyone looks at me. "How much are we talking about?" When I don't get an immediate response, I rephrase my question. "I mean, diamonds are nearly indestructible and relatively easy to transport. Any idea how big something like that might be?"

Mitzy flips open her tablet. The light from the screen casts a blue glow on her face. The room goes silent for a minute, until Mitzy lays her tablet on the table. "Well, the easy answer is there is no easy answer."

"That's all you've got?" My frustration grows, but that's only because the hairs at the back of my neck stand up like lightning rods. The feeling we're missing something grows and grows.

"Well, we all know the basics." Mitzy shifts to lecture mode. "Cut, color, clarity, and carat all combine to determine the individual price of a diamond. One carat is about 0.2 grams. Of course, most diamonds mined are either too small or too inferior to produce a gemstone quality product."

"What kind of numbers are we talking?" CJ asks.

"Let's just say this, to produce a single, one-carat diamond, it can take mining upwards of a million rough diamonds. A one-carat diamond, depending on cut, color, and clarity, can cost anywhere between two to nearly thirty-thousand dollars."

"Wow." I pull at my chin. "If you have a hundred of those …" My voice trails off as I try to imagine what that might look like.

"It depends on what diamonds you have, but let's say you had fifty diamonds, at the bottom of the range, we're talking …"

"A hundred thousand dollars," Forest answers. "Enough to fill a thimble, I'd say."

A thimble?

"Sounds about right." Mitzy agrees with him. "If you had the same fifty diamonds at the top of the scale, you're talking an easy million and a half." She glances at me. "Thimble-full is about right."

"So, Jerald tracks Angie down to the resort in Costa Rica, blathering on and on about diamonds, then tries to kill her?" I drum my fingers on the table.

"What was it he said exactly?" Doc Summers looks around the table.

Only Brady was there. After we finally rescued Angie, she and Isabelle spent a few days at a resort in Costa Rica. It was the mandatory vacation Brady took after Doc Summers released him from Medical Hold after a year's long recovery following the explosion in Cancun and his extensive burns.

He let Isabelle and Angie use the hotel room, then joined them later. Isabelle flew out, coming to Guardian HQ rather than flying home to her family, while Angie and Brady made good use of the private suite.

"He wasn't making any sense." Brady glances around the table. He's mentioned this before, during several debriefs following that mission. "He wanted to know where Angie's backpack was, and his as well. He rifled through hers before she caught him doing it. After that, he went berserk, screaming about the diamonds."

"It wasn't just the diamonds." Mitzy lifts a finger. "He asked her about a rabbit's foot."

"He did." Brady's eyes get as large as saucers.

"How much did we say a thimble full of one-carat diamonds was worth?" I look around the table. "How about what can fit inside a rabbit's foot?"

"Shit." Brady leaps to his feet and I'm right there behind him. "Get Angie on the phone and tell her to meet us at her place."

"Why?" Doc Summers' question is nearly drowned out by the commotion of our entire team scooting back and standing up.

I look to Brady and he returns a nod.

"Because," I say, "I think we know where the diamonds are."

"Let's roll." Brady clasps my arm.

"Wait a second." Mitzy's high-pitched voice cuts through the chaos. "Don't we have Jerald's backpack? Brady, did you bring it back with you?"

"No. The local officials confiscated nearly everything except our personal belongings. I'm pretty sure we didn't, but I don't think it matters."

"Why?"

"Because he wasn't looking through his pack when Angie caught him. He was looking through hers."

"Oh shit." It feels like the bottom of the world dropped out from beneath me. "Didn't he say something about Isabelle?"

"I don't know." Brady shrugs. "I wasn't there, but Angie would know. I just shot the guy."

SIX

Izzy

"Didn't you catch any sleep on the plane?" Colton twists around from the passenger seat of Gareth's truck.

I sit in the middle of the back seat, like I have since I was born, sandwiched nicely between Jude and Parker.

"Sleep? On a plane? Are you crazy?" I playfully tap the back of his seat. "I'm not going to die with my eyes closed."

"I love that you haven't changed a bit." Jude jabs me gently in the ribs.

"You act as if I've been gone forever."

"Feels like forever," Parker grumbles beside me.

Jude and Parker are twins, alike in nearly every way, except for their eyes and a half-inch difference in height.

All the Dingleberries look the same. Broad of shoulder, in the six-foot club, handsome with the same cornflower-blue eyes and raven-black wavy hair we all share.

"Well, our little sis is home now." Gareth, Elderberry of the Dingleberries, makes it a pronouncement.

"I'm only home for a couple of days."

Despite Skye's willingness to let me take a couple of weeks off, I'm eager to get back—to my new home.

Funny, that's the first time I've thought of any place other than the small town of Leighton, Texas, as home, but it feels right. I'm building a life with Guardian HRS that combines my pharmacy degree with my need to serve the less fortunate.

I can't do that here.

"Does Mom know that?"

"Um, hello?" I glare at Gareth through the rearview mirror. "Me coming home is supposed to be a surprise." I make a gesture encompassing the cab of the truck. "You didn't keep my secret with the Dingleberries, but you damn well better have with Mom. I wanted to surprise her."

He's always been the spokesperson of the group, but then again, he's the eldest.

I take a moment to look at my brothers through different eyes. Not as the boys who not only helped to raise me, but as the men they've become.

"Calm down. They only know about it because Jude saw your text on my phone before I did. He told Parker and Colton." Gareth's eyes twinkle as he smiles back at me. He shifts his attention back to the road.

My brothers were a lot to handle growing up as the only girl. They sheltered and protected me, something I didn't appreciate nearly enough as a child, but that protective instinct became overbearing once I started college.

I was trying to learn who I was going to be as a woman, while they all still treated me like a child. They scared off every boy who showed a lick of interest.

Thus, my woeful lack of a dating history.

"Yeah, sis." Jude pokes me in the ribs again. "I can't believe you didn't want to let us in on your little secret."

"I wanted it to be a surprise." I fold my arms across my chest and tuck my chin, feeling grumpy. "Y'all don't keep surprises."

"You don't give us enough credit." Parker gives me a look. "We didn't tell her."

"Did you tell Dad?"

"No." Parker looks up toward the roof and shakes his head. "He would definitely tell Mom."

My brothers are strong men. Solid men. Capable men. They've figured out all the adulting stuff. Next to them, I feel as if I'm barely getting my feet wet with the whole being a grown-up.

Although, compared to them, I'm the only one who's spent any significant time out of the country. They've all been to Europe and enjoyed the pleasures of cruising through the Caribbean, but I'm the only one who's gone native.

"So, she doesn't know?" I glance around the cab of the truck, looking for confirmation.

"She doesn't," Gareth answers for the group.

He's also the instigator of the group.

He arranged for their cruise to the Caribbean, which *happened* to coincide with my first nine-month contract with Doctors Without Borders. It was his way of checking up on me.

Knowing what they would think about my living conditions, I met them at the dock and kept them busy the entire day with an aggressive itinerary that hit all the tourists' hotspots.

If they saw the conditions I was living in, they would've kidnapped me and taken me home.

That was my first contract with Doctors Without Borders, and I was still figuring out how the relief agency operated. It was hard work, harder than I imagined, but it was immensely fulfilling.

"We're really glad you're home." Colten's eyes soften as he twists in his seat to look at me. Closest to me in age, he understands some of my plight. Youngest of the brothers, he struggled to find his identity out from under their shadow.

"How's business going?" I ask.

Colten set up a business a few years ago flipping houses. It began as summer work with a contractor in high school and has evolved into a multi-million-dollar endeavor.

"Business is booming." He grins, full of pride over his hard work. "We're expanding."

"That's amazing." I lean forward and place my hand on his shoulder, squeezing with affection. "I'm so happy to hear that."

"What are you going to do, now that you're back in the States?" Colton's question sounds innocent on the surface, but I feel the Dingleberry Squad coming down on me. "There's always work with me. Like I said, we're expanding, and I could use a good office manager."

I practically choke.

"I'm not letting you strap me to a desk." I give him the eye. "Besides … Hello! I'm a pharmacist. Why would I want to work as an office manager?"

"After what happened to you …" Gareth gives me one of his stern Elder Dingleberry looks. "I would think staying close to home sounds a whole lot better than risking your life God knows where. You're not working for that outfit again." He lays down his words as if they're law.

As if I'll follow happily along.

"That *outfit* is an internationally renowned relief organization. What happened in Nicaragua …"

"What happened in Nicaragua nearly cost you your life, and they're obviously not prepared to handle stuff like that." His brows bunch together, pissed and angry.

"What happened in Nicaragua was outside of their control, and we were rescued."

When I was a new pharmacy graduate, I worked for six months at the local pharmacy before deciding it wasn't for me. Which sucked, considering how much time and effort I put into getting my pharmacist license.

Needing to get out from under the shadow of my brothers, I went to our mother first, asking for her blessing. She gave it eagerly, knowing how much I needed to establish myself as a woman without my brothers breathing down my neck.

I found my calling.

Excited by the relief work, I immediately signed on for a second contract. That brought me to Nicaragua.

I did much the same thing in the Caribbean as I did in Nicaragua. Our job was to provide life-saving immunizations, antibiotics, anti-parasitics, anti-malarials, along with dental, optometry, ophthalmology, and mental health professionals.

It was the first time I exercised my pharmaceutical skills without backup, and I had freedom to think outside of the box. It was also the first time my life was ever in serious danger.

But we were rescued.

The men of Bravo team saved us and introduced me to Guardian HRS; a place that meets all my needs.

I actually don't know who arranged for our rescue. My assumption was Doctors Without Borders contracted with Guardian HRS to extract us, but that doesn't go with what I know about Angie and Brady.

Those two had a connection three years before, when Angie buried her husband. Evidently, Luke, who was a trauma surgeon on the Air Force's Special Surgical Operations Team, came across Brady's team of SEALs during one of his missions.

Brady found us because he recognized Angie on the local news.

"What's wrong? No witty comeback?" Gareth isn't pleased with my answer, but he's kind of being a dick, pushing the way he is. "At least, you're finally home where you'll be safe."

"You're wrong about Doctors Without Borders, and I'd sign up for another mission with them in a heartbeat if I didn't already have a job."

My hand flies up to cover my mouth. I'm not ready to break this news to my family.

"You, what?" Colton twists around in his seat again, pinning me with a look.

My belly flutters with the combined shocked and judgmental stares of my older brothers.

Well, shit.

"What do you mean you already have a job?" Gareth's gaze through the rearview mirror turns dark and stormy. "Where? And with whom? Better not be with those guardians." He doesn't place the right emphasis on the Guardians.

"Why not?" I firm my chin and straighten my shoulders, getting ready for the fight that's coming.

"People like that tend to attract trouble."

"You're wrong about that," I fire back at Gareth. "They're heroes and rescuers who make the world a better place."

"Sis, outfits like that have huge targets on their backs. I'll give you the rescue part, considering they rescued you, but I'm telling you, the people they rescued you from are the kind of people who hold grudges and act on them."

"You're wrong."

"How do you know?"

"Because I know."

I actually don't know and hate that he poses a completely valid question. I hate that it never occurred to me.

The Guardians rescue trafficked women and children from the worst kind of people on the planet. They must make a lot of enemies.

Is that why they offer those damned trackers? Have they had issues of retribution in the past?

Not wanting to have to defend Guardian HRS, I shut down on my brothers, refusing to answer any more of Gareth's questions.

Jude, Parker, and Colton say nothing as Gareth scolds me and my life choices.

"You've gotta stop this nonsense." When he uses that judgmental tone with me, I can't help but curl in on myself.

I hate how he makes me feel like I've done something wrong when I've done nothing wrong. Despite what happened, my decisions were sound.

Nicaragua, and what happened there, was a once in a lifetime event. Something so far out there that the chances of it happening again are practically zero.

I want to say all of that to him, defending my actions, but I have to respond to that last comment first.

"What the hell does that mean?" I rub the palms of my hands on my jeans. "It's not nonsense."

My cheeks heat as my anger flares.

Gareth's words hurt because deep down, what he thinks of me

matters. I seek his approval now, as I have my entire life, and it hurts that this is all I get.

"Look, Mom let you go to the Caribbean. We didn't step in, although we had our concerns."

We, meaning the Dingleberries.

My brothers act as if they're equals to our mother in telling me how to lead my life. When I was a kid, that was true. I didn't know any better. They were all so much older, and wiser, than me.

But I'm older now. I see their protectiveness through a different lens. I wouldn't change a thing about my childhood. With four older brothers to protect me, my childhood was exceptional.

If a boy tried to bully me. They took care of it. If a girl tried to hurt me, they took care of it. If I struggled in my studies, they helped me with tutoring. They came to all my piano and ballet recitals. They smothered me with nothing but good intentions and the deepest love.

But I'm not a little girl anymore. I don't need them to protect me from the world.

"Mom didn't *let me*. I told her ..." I try to stand up for myself.

"You got lucky with that mission." Gareth interrupts me, pressing his point. "But Nicaragua? Could you have picked a hotter hotspot of civil unrest and military action?"

"It's not like that. We were never in any danger."

"Never in danger!?" Gareth's voice rises.

He shouts at me in a rare display of losing his cool. It's a bit terrifying, to be honest. He's generally the calm one, the cool one, the voice of reason. He's none of that now. There's real fear threading through his voice.

I press my knuckles to my breastbone, realizing how deeply my brothers care about me. How much they love me.

"I wasn't." Despite any of that, I defend myself, but only because Gareth leaves me no other choice.

I'm not a little kid anymore, and they need to understand my life's my own. My choices are mine. As are the consequences.

"Hello, you were *abducted* by a cartel." His voice trembles in anger and fills with frustration. "That's the very definition of *danger.*"

"I know what happened, but that doesn't mean the work is unsafe. It was …" I grit my teeth, trying to find the right words. "What happened was an unusual event."

"Unusual?" He glares at me and I don't miss the way his grip tightens on the steering wheel. "Why are you defending them, when you know I'm right?"

"Because Doctors Without Borders does incredible work throughout the world. They do that *despite* civil unrest and military action. For the most part, they're insulated from the violence precisely because of their humanitarian aid. I'd go back in a second and sign up for another contract if I wasn't working for the Guardians."

"The Guardians?" The muscles of Gareth's jaw bunch as he grits his teeth. "That's who you're working for? That's your new job?"

"Yes." I curl in on myself, feeling like I've done something incredibly wrong.

Jude, Parker, and Colton remain eerily silent. Normally that means they side with Gareth and are simply letting him deal with the problem. What I wouldn't give for one of them to be on my side for once.

"You're not working for them." Gareth makes a proclamation.

"You can't …"

"Look, we almost lost you. We're not going through that again, and you're not putting Mom through that kind of terror ever again. She was beside herself with worry."

"You don't get to decide …"

"We're not discussing this further. Your old job is still there. Later today, we'll head over there and get your job back."

"I'm not working in Leighton." Our hometown is suffocating. "I already have a job." One I can't wait to begin.

"We'll see about that." When Gareth digs in, I already know I've lost the battle, but I'm not willing to lose the war.

"Yes. We'll see." I cross my arms over my chest and say nothing for the rest of the ride home.

My brothers join me in silence, having nothing to add to my exchange with Gareth.

I'm not interested in furthering this fight, but it's not over. It's not over by a long shot.

SEVEN

Booker

All of Bravo team descends on Angie's modest townhome, with Mitzy, CJ, Sam, Forest, and Doc Summers in tow.

Angie holds the door as everyone marches inside. Brady and I take up the rear.

"When you said as soon as possible, I thought something was up." Angie's lids pull back, surprised and alarmed. She gives Brady a quick peck on the cheek. "What the hell is going on?"

"I'll tell you inside." Brady moves in, pulling Angie along behind him.

I take the door and close it behind me, double-checking to make sure it's latched. Not that anyone is watching, or would barge in, but it's an old habit I refuse to break.

"Please, make yourselves comfortable." Angie makes a sweeping gesture, indicating the small living room and modest dining area.

Our crowd takes up every available seat. Rafe, Hayes, Alec, and Zeb sit at the dining table, while Mitzy, Forest, and Doc Summers sit on the couch. CJ and Sam pull out the two stools by the bar.

Angie takes the last remaining chair, leaving Brady and me on our feet. "So, what's this about?" She looks between Sam and CJ, then sweeps her gaze to gather in Mitzy and Forest. "Seems like something pretty important if you're all here." Angie pauses a moment, then shifts her attention to Forest. "Are you feeling okay?"

"Just a bit under the weather. I'm sorry we barged into your place." Forest clears his throat and leans back. He kicks off the conversation. "We have good reason to think …" His voice trails off as a fit of coughing overcomes him.

After Angie's comment, I look at Forest thinking he doesn't look much different. A little pale, perhaps, but nothing big.

"Do you still have the rabbit's foot Jerald gave you?" My words come out hard and fast, almost accusatory in their tone, although that's not how I intend them.

I'm simply worried for Isabelle and need to do something.

With Isabelle gone, my senses are hyper-alert. Knowing she's out there in the world, unprotected, with a potential threat against her life, I'm amped on adrenaline with no outlet for the excess energy.

"I think so. Why?" Angie responds softly, curious but confused.

"Because we think Jerald hid diamonds inside of it." Brady backs me up.

"Excuse me?" Angie looks around the room, surprised. "Diamonds? Why?"

"It's the perfect currency when dealing in the illegal sale of weapons and arms." Forest gets his cough under control and his deep rumbly voice brings to mind booming thunder and boulders grinding together. "The Coralos cartel questioned your team about weapons, but what if that's not what you were carrying?"

"I don't understand." Angie looks around the room. If anything, she's more confused.

"During your debrief, you mentioned they asked about guns." Sam shifts on his stool. "Your colleagues said the same thing. All their interrogations centered around smuggling weapons to the *Laguta* cartel; their rival."

"What does that have to do with diamonds?" Angie's smart and doesn't miss a beat.

"As we all know," Mitzy likes to recap, and when she does, she often goes into what I like to call lecture mode. "Nicaragua is a hotbed of civil unrest with two marauding cartels in the midst of a border dispute. The *Coralos* cartel hold much of the southern part of the country, while the *Laguta* cartel holds the north."

She looks around the room, receiving nods from all. We know this well.

"The mission you were on operated smack dab in the middle of hotly disputed territory. For some reason, the *Coralos* cartel thought your group was smuggling weapons to the *Laguta* cartel, but we think it wasn't weapons at all."

"You think it was diamonds?" Angie glances at Brady. A soft smile fills her face when she looks at him.

"Exactly. From what Jerald said before his untimely death ..." Mitzy gives Brady the eye.

She's not happy Guardian HRS missed out on the opportunity to question Jerald.

In Brady's defense, Jerald held a knife to Angie's neck and would've killed her if Brady hadn't taken the shot. As it is, a healing wound slashes across Angie's face, marring her natural beauty.

"About the diamonds." Angie shifts in her seat. "I remember how crazed he sounded. So, you think he was smuggling diamonds and not guns?"

"Yes." Sam nods. "We think the *Coralos* cartel got it wrong. Although we're still trying to piece everything together. There are still a lot of holes in what we know."

"A lot of holes," Mitzy chimes in. "Can you take us back to when he gave them to you and why?"

"Gave me, what?" Angie's eyes pinch. "I never saw any weapons."

"Sorry." Mitzy holds out her hand. "Let me back up just a bit. When Jerald was in the honeymoon suite with you, he went through your backpack."

"He did." Angie nods. "But he asked where the diamonds were. He didn't say anything about a rabbit's foot."

"We have reason to believe he hid the diamonds in the rabbit's feet that he gave to you and Isabelle." I jump in to explain because we're doing a piss poor job of it.

I also want to hurry this along. If Isabelle's in danger, I need to be by her side.

"He did."

"Can you get it?" Sam cuts in.

There's an urgency in his voice I share. Sam's an old pro at this kind of shit, and if he's alarmed, I know my gut's steering me right.

"Um, sure." Angie rises from her seat and glides across the room. "Just a second." As she disappears down the hall, Brady follows.

I move in right behind them and hover just outside of her room.

Angie goes to her closet, where she rummages around for a bit.

"You think he put diamonds in the rabbit's foot?" She lifts out a box, holding it for Brady to set aside.

"Are you sure you have it?" With the way she's unloading her closet, I'm concerned it's lost.

"Oh yes. I put it with my passport in the safe when we moved in. Just got to shift some stuff around to get to it. Izzy and I went on a shopping spree after we moved in and things are a little messy in here." She holds out another box, looks like a bunch of shoeboxes stuffed in a larger box. "Hang on. Just a minute."

There's silence for a second, then an electronic beep. Angie backs out of the closet holding a white rabbit's foot in her hand.

"Here you go." She hands it to Brady.

He gives it a quick once over, then looks at me and tosses it. I snatch it out of the air and look at it too.

There's nothing unusual about it.

Covered in white fur, it's soft on the outside, but tough and leathery underneath the downy white fur. Little toenails stick out of the toes.

"Don't know why people get these when it's not so lucky for the rabbit." I give it another look, seeing nothing out of the ordinary.

"You're not a believer, I take it?" Angie smiles at me.

"Not in the slightest. I don't believe a rabbit's foot brings good luck. I'm more of the kind of guy who believes we make our own luck."

"Well, some people do." She glances toward Isabelle's room,

trying to tell me something, but I'm too dense to decipher what she says.

Then it hits me.

"She's a believer?" I step back from the door and turn toward Isabelle's room.

"She sure is. Carried her rabbit's foot with her from sunup to sundown, and probably slept with it too. She said it would bring her good luck. She had it with us when we escaped too. Carried that poor thing all through the jungle, and knowing how she thinks, I have a feeling it's with her right now."

"You're shitting me?"

"I'm serious, and she is too. You might want to keep that in mind when you see her. Honestly, I think that rabbit's foot gave her the courage she needed to overcome her fears. Sometimes, a rabbit's foot can be more than a simple lucky charm." Angie gives a soft smile.

In that look, I know she's rooting for me and Isabelle. It feels good to have someone on my side because Isabelle sure as shit isn't convinced we belong together.

As for having the rabbit's foot with her right now, I don't like that at all.

Not one damn bit.

"Why would she take it with her? She's not in the jungle." I just don't get it. I've never understood superstition.

"Booker …" Angie places her hands on her hips. "She's terrified of flying. I bet she took it for good luck to make sure the plane didn't crash."

"Shit, I really hope you're wrong." I run my fingers through my hair, hating how they shake.

I don't believe in luck, but I do believe in hunches. Mine have never steered me wrong, and that feeling in my gut tells me things are very wrong.

"Is it worth looking?" The urge to search Isabelle's room comes with a lot of conflicted feelings. The last thing I want is to destroy her trust; a search would do that and far more.

"It won't take a second." Angie turns toward Isabelle's room.

"How can you be so sure?" I follow behind her, rubbing the back of my neck. It's been tingling since we arrived, and that's never a good thing.

"Because she keeps it on her nightstand." Angie's eyes flicker with amusement. She's having fun with me.

"Why would she keep something like that, especially after what happened with Jerald? I'd think she'd toss it out after he tried to kill you."

"Like I said, she believes it brings good luck, and it did …" Angie gives me another look. This time, it's harder, delving deep, and turning serious. "For her at least. It doesn't matter who gave it to her. What matters is that she conquered her fears, swam in a river, climbed down a waterfall, and flew in a helicopter—with the doors open, I might add. All of that far outweighs *who* gave it to her. What matters is what it did." She places her hand on my arm. "Remember that when you see her."

Angie seems to know every thought in my head. She's certainly reading my mind. The moment we're done here, I'm hopping on a plane to Isabelle's hometown.

"Where did she go?" I scratch my head, feeling all kinds of bad that I don't know such a simple thing about the woman I'm obsessing over.

"She went home." Angie's brows pinch.

"I know she went home, but where is home?"

"You don't know where she lives?"

"There's a lot I don't know." That's a deficiency I intend to rectify as soon as possible.

"She lives in Leighton, Texas, a small border town in Texas, and she has four older brothers who are just as overbearing and overprotective as you are. For the record, she's not a fan."

"Why are you telling me that?"

"Because I like you, Booker, and I don't want you to mess things up with Izzy. She's pretty awesome, and I think the two of you belong together. But if you go after her, guns blazing, she's not going to like it."

"You're basically telling me not to breathe. I'm a protector at heart. It's who I am and literally what I do."

"That's exactly what you can't be around Izzy. It rubs her the wrong way. She's worked her entire life to get out from under her brothers' overprotective shadow. Don't give her a reason to transfer any of those emotions to you. At least, not if you plan on staying in her life."

Angie steps inside Isabelle's room while Brady and I hover in the hall. Not a moment later, Angie's back.

"Well, it's not there." She holds out her hand. "Can I see mine?"

I hand it over.

She holds it up, examining it like Brady and I did.

"And you really think there's a fortune of diamonds in here?"

"According to Mitzy, anywhere from a few hundred grand to a million and a half."

"Holy shit." She tosses the rabbit back at me like it's a hot potato. "I really hope you're wrong."

"Why?" I shrug and shake the rabbit's foot, hearing nothing.

"If I've been carrying around a fortune in diamonds …" She presses her hands against her cheeks. "Maybe that's what the leader of the cartel wanted? He wanted the rabbit's feet, not to …"

Brady and I exchange a look. I arch my brows, asking Brady if he wants me to take that comment, or ignore it.

Brady places his palm to the small of Angie's back. "Luv, we don't think they knew about the diamonds."

"You don't?" Her eyes widen, realizing her fears were spot on.

"If they knew, they wouldn't have tortured the others asking about guns. It wouldn't make sense."

"Oh, but if they didn't know about the diamonds, and we weren't smuggling guns, what the hell was going on?"

"That's what we intend to find out." Brady turns toward the living room. "Let's talk to the others."

As they move out, I can't help but peek inside Isabelle's room. It's neat and tidy with everything in its place. Next to her bed is a nightstand. There's a small lamp and a phone charging station. What isn't there is a rabbit's foot.

My gut clenches and the hairs on the back of my neck tingle. Isabelle needs protection until we sort this out. She and Angie both need protection.

I don't care if my overprotectiveness rubs Isabelle the wrong way. I'll do anything to keep her safe, even if it means destroying any chance of a future we might have.

I head back to join the rest of the group. Mitzy's head snaps up and her gaze latches onto the rabbit's foot in my hand.

"Here." I toss it to her and Mitzy surprises me by catching it out of the air.

"Great." Mitzy stands and waves at Zeb. "Up you go."

Zeb moves out of the way, giving his seat at the table to Mitzy. He joins me against the wall, leaning back with his arms crossed.

"Wanna bet how long this takes?" His sly grin brings an answering smile to my face.

"I give it five minutes."

"I say less than sixty seconds."

We shake and I lose.

Mitzy finds the secret compartment and spills dozens of loose diamonds all over the table.

"Well, shit." I hand over a dollar bill and grit my teeth.

All we're doing now is wasting time. I need to get to Isabelle.

EIGHT

Izzy

The silence in the truck is oppressive. Gareth doesn't like that I have a mind of my own and am exercising it contrary to his desires.

My life is mine, and I'll determine the path it takes. What I won't do is remain in the small border town of Leighton, Texas, for the rest of my life, working for my brothers.

My dreams are bigger than that.

My aspirations aim higher.

My need to make my mark on the world drives me away from my hometown.

As for coming home, Mom is completely taken aback. She hugs me, then scolds my brothers for keeping my homecoming secret. After all of that, she decides we'll have a feast to celebrate.

I stand with her in the kitchen. Flour coats my hands, dusts my forearms, and there's even some on the tip of my nose.

Beside me, Mom prepares her signature dish, beef wellington, a complex dish, but that's Mom. She excels at everything she touches.

"I still can't believe it." Mom mixes the spices for the meat while I work on the dough that will wrap around the tenderloin.

"That I'm home?"

I love the warm feeling blooming in my chest. Even though I didn't want to come home, I'm happy when surrounded by my family. That includes the Dingleberries, despite their faults.

Perhaps happier than I realized.

I didn't think I missed my family this much, but maybe I'm just really good at compensating?

"That your brothers kept it from me." Mom shakes her head and fixes a hard stare on my brothers.

She's a beautiful woman. Mid-fifties, she's lost none of her regal looks. Her bright-blue eyes shine with vigor and her midnight-black hair is only now showing signs of gray at the roots.

"To be honest," I lower my voice and whisper, "I didn't think Gareth could keep it secret."

"But all four of them?" She looks toward the living room where my brothers lounge on the couch and argue about what show to watch.

They've been at it for over half an hour and still haven't landed on anything they can all agree on.

"Well, I hope it's a good surprise." I bite my lower lip, knowing my homecoming is the best kind of surprise but needing motherly reassurance.

"Oh, honey." She turns toward me and the soft smile on her face warms my heart. "Anytime I get to see you is a blessing. Especially now that you're out on your own."

"Am I?"

"Excuse me?"

"Out on my own?" I give a lift of my chin in the direction of Gareth. "If it's up to them, I won't be allowed to leave. Gareth already has me working for Colton as his office manager."

"Ignore them." Her laughter is like bubbles, softly bursting in the air. "You are on your own path."

"Tell that to the Dingleberries."

She snickers beside me.

I don't remember how old I was when I first started calling my brothers the Dingleberries. I was very young and knew nothing about swearing, but I certainly created my first expletive.

In our house, swearing is expressly forbidden, so we get creative. Instead of calling my brothers overbearing-assholes-who-can-fuck-the-hell-off, I dubbed them the Dingleberries.

It encompasses all the above, although I don't think they've figured that part out.

For years, my brothers tried to get me to stop calling them Dingleberries.

Come to think of it, maybe they know exactly what I mean when I say it.

Mom, however, always gives one of her serene smiles. She gently tells me to stop, but the twinkle in her eyes speaks the truth. I take it as tacit approval to continue.

Needless to say, I never stopped.

It's always been my belief Mom felt I needed something to deal with my brothers. The name stuck and no one tries to get me to stop now.

I'm glad it brings a smile to my mother's face.

"Since you brought it up, what *are* your plans?" She turns toward me and stops what she's doing. "Now that—well, that whole ordeal is over?"

We've talked on the phone about what happened in Nicaragua. Mom is wise enough not to rehash that trauma. Although, she worries.

As for what we talked about, I didn't lie about being abducted, but I didn't delve into any of the gritty details. All I told her was it happened. We were never in any real danger. And that we made it out safe and sound.

Okay, maybe I stretched the truth. I may have told one, or two, white lies, but there's no reason to make her worry about something that happened in the past.

"Are you saying you're not a part of the Dingleberries' plot to keep me in Leighton, Texas?"

Our small town lies along the border between Mexico and Texas. The LaCroix family owns several thousand acres, which we run cattle on and drill for oil. The ranch has been in the family for generations. My brothers manage it with my father, who is out in the field with a new drilling contractor.

"Honey, when you came to me, and were so excited about working with Doctors Without Borders, I knew this town was too small for you." She glances toward my brothers. "Your brothers have always been tied to this place. Gareth's wanted to take over the ranch since before he learned to ride. They've all put down roots, but you, my dearest daughter, never did." The serenity in her smile warms my heart.

"Does that make you sad?" I work the dough, kneading it almost past the point where it's done. "That I won't be here?"

"To see my children succeed in life is a mother's greatest blessing. At first, I was sad, but you've always wanted to know what was beyond the horizon. You're a wanderer at heart. A great explorer. I've known since you were a little child that you would one day leave me."

"I'm sorry."

"Don't be." She cups my cheek. "Look at what you've already accomplished. How many lives are better because of you?"

I don't know how to answer that question. It's far more than I can count. My work has impacted hundreds of lives, if not thousands, and I want to continue helping others.

"Be careful, or my head will swell."

"I've never feared your ego would get the better of you. You have a soft determination that drives you. It's a strength many would overlook, or see as weakness, but it's there, pushing you onward. I'm just wondering where that might be. Since you haven't mentioned it, I take it you aren't signing another contract with Doctors Without Borders?"

"I'm not." I curl my lower lip between my teeth, not sure if I should tell her my plans. Although, it's best coming from me rather than one of my brothers. "I got a job."

"You did?"

"I did." I look down, knowing this next part will be hard on her. "It's in California."

"California?" She pauses a moment, taking it in. "I suppose that's closer than living in another country. Tell me all about it."

Over the next twenty minutes, while we prep dinner, I tell her all about the Guardians and their mission to make the world a better place. She listens, silent for the most part, interrupting only to have me explain something she doesn't understand.

"And you're happy there?"

Her question makes me take a long, hard look at the choice I made. The thing is, while I'm happy to be home, I can't wait to get back to Guardian HQ and begin my new job.

"I am." My face beams with joy.

"How long will you be here?"

Skye Summers said I could take two weeks to visit my family. I decided on a few days. Now, I'm thinking I want to stay longer.

"I have two weeks before I need to get back. I left in the middle of orientation, but that can wait. I don't have to start working in the pharmacy on any particular day."

With Mom by my side, I can handle the Dingleberries.

"That sounds wonderful." She wraps her arm around my shoulder and gives me a hug. "We should probably go through your room."

"Why?"

"To decide what you want to take with you to your new home."

"You're wonderful." I give her a kiss on the cheek. "And I love you."

"I love you too. Now, how about we get back to getting dinner on the table? If those four aren't fed on time, they turn into monsters."

We laugh because it's true. My brothers notoriously run on their bellies.

"When do you think any of them will settle down with a woman?" My brothers need some of their wildness tamed.

"Now that's the million-dollar question. I'm not getting any younger, and a mother deserves grandbabies after raising a bunch of hellions."

"They're not that bad."

"You know they are."

"Any prospects?"

Now that I think about it, I've heard nothing about whether any of my brothers are dating.

"Your brothers have scared off most of the local candidates. Any woman stepping into that mess needs to be strong enough to wrangle all four of them."

My brothers are tight. They're best friends and fiercely protective of one another. I can see how intimidating that could be for a woman trying to break into this family.

I suppose I shouldn't be so dismissive of their protectiveness toward me.

I never had a confidant growing up and always wished for a sister, but that wasn't mine to have.

In many ways, I'm jealous of the bond between my brothers. As a girl, I was excluded from most activities. If it wasn't that, my age widened the gap even more.

Not that they didn't include me in some things. My brothers took me everywhere they could, but there are some *things* teenage boys can't do with a sister tagging along, especially one who's still in grade school.

I'm the little sister to four older brothers. It's both a blessing and a curse. I both love and hate them, even when they're bossy.

And it's not as if I *hate* them.

I don't.

I love them too much for that, but sometimes, they make it difficult to like them.

"What about you?" My mother nudges me with her elbow. "Any prospects in your life I should know about?"

"No." My answer comes too fast; either that or there's something in how I say it that spikes her curiosity.

"Who is he?" Her smile beams so bright, it makes her eyes shine. "Anyone special?"

"I said no."

"Honey, there's saying no, and then there's saying *No*."

"But I really mean no."

"If you say so." She turns back to her work.

"I'm not lying. I'm not seeing anyone."

"That's okay, honey. You'll tell me when you're ready."

"But …" My phone rings.

With my hands covered in flour, I look for a towel to wipe them clean, but the number isn't one I recognize. I let it ring and go to voice mail.

"Aren't you going to answer?" Mom gives me a look.

"If it's important, they'll call back." No sooner do the words tumble out of my mouth than the phone rings again.

I stare at the phone, letting it ring, as a funny feeling comes over me. I can't say why, but something tells me I don't want to pick up.

The call goes to voicemail once again, and I breathe out a sigh of relief. However, the moment I turn back to the dough, my phone rings for a third time.

"Hey, sis …" Gareth calls out over his shoulder. "You gonna answer that?"

"Sounds important." Mom wipes her hands on her apron.

I don't have one—an apron, that is—because I decided I didn't need one since I was *just going to help*. Now, I'm elbows deep in flour and sticky dough.

Mom hands me a towel, then picks up my phone while I fumble getting my hands clean.

She angles it toward my face, to unlock the screen, then puts it to her ear.

"Hello?"

"*Who is this?*" Booker's harsh tone blares through the speaker.

"Who is this?" My mother is a stickler when it comes to manners. Booker's digging himself a hole he knows nothing about.

"This isn't Isabelle. Now, who the fuck is this?"

I cringe as my mother pulls the phone away from her ear. She turns it toward me. "Honey, whoever is on the other side of this call needs his mouth washed out with soap." Her grip tightens and I brace for what comes next.

"Young man, swearing is for vagrants and thieves. Some would say it's a sign of low intelligence, but I say it's simply rude and disrespectful. I don't tolerate it in my house."

"Ma'am, not knowing who you are, but guessing you're Isabelle's mum, I will say only this: the size of your swear word vocabulary is directly linked to your overall vocabulary. Since my repertoire of swear words is vast, my overall vocabulary surpasses most. And if that's not enough, my IQ is in the top one percent. So, I neither have low intelligence, nor am I in your house and subject to your rules. If I were, I would not swear, but what you will do immediately is hand the damn phone to Isabelle."

I cover my mouth to hide, not my surprise, but the laughter bubbling up from within me. Booker's voice comes through loud and clear.

Even the Dingleberries stop arguing over what to watch on TV. The silence in our house is so overwhelming one can hear a pin drop.

Mom looks at me. Stares at the phone. Then looks at me again.

She hands it to me, steady as a rock with an expression on her face I can't quite make out.

She should be offended, but she's not.

She should be irate, but she's not.

Instead, her expression is one of intense reflection.

"Honey, I am very curious to meet your beau, but let him know not only is swearing not allowed, but I don't tolerate speaking back to your elders in my house, or in my presence."

I reach for the phone, but unlike her, my hand shakes.

Her calm delivery makes those words a mandate. In this household, that's the law.

Colton looks at me, eyes wide, and mouths *What the fuck?*

I ignore him and snatch the phone out of my mother's hand. Her lips twist into a knowing smile and there's a glimmer in her eye.

"What the fudge, Booker? Nice way to make a scene."

"Isabelle, where the hell are you?"

"Stop calling me Isabelle. And I'm at home. Why?"

"I'm on a plane."

"You're, what?"

"You heard me. I'm on a plane …"

"Yes, you said that. I want to know why you're on a plane and why I should care."

"We don't have time for this. Do you have the rabbit's foot?"

"Excuse me?"

"The rabbit's foot. Do you have it with you?"

My face scrunches with confusion at the very odd conversation.

My brothers crawl over the back of the couch and close the distance. They lean on the counter and listen in.

I really wish I turned down the volume on my phone, but there's nothing I can do about that now.

"Who the hell is that?" Gareth jumps when Mom snaps him with her towel.

Flour pops in the air, creating a white puff that slowly settles down on the marble countertop.

"Sorry." Gareth hangs his head for a millisecond, then turns his attention back to me. "Who is it? And what is he talking about?"

I make a shooshing gesture and grip the phone.

"FYI, my entire family can hear your booming voice through the phone."

"Good. They need to hear this. Put me on speaker."

"Fine." There's really no need. Booker's loud enough as it is, but I switch him to speaker and turn the volume down. "You're on speaker."

"Who's with you?"

"My mother, who you've already met and offended, along with the Dingleberries."

"The what?" Booker barks out his words.

"Sorry. My four brothers. It's me, Mom, and my brothers."

"Do you have any weapons in the house?"

"Why the he …" I glance at my mother, knowing her proficiency with snapping that towel and rephrase my question. "Why would you ask that?"

"Because you're in danger."

The way he says it makes the world tilt and wobble around me.

Booker is many things, but he's not one to make a mountain out of a molehill, meaning he feels there's a real threat against me.

"What do you mean our sister's in danger?" Gareth snags the phone out of my hand and ups the volume to full blast.

"Who is this?"

"Gareth, Izzy's oldest brother."

"Good. Are there weapons in the house?"

"There are, mind telling us what the fu—what's going on?" Gareth checks himself with a wary glance to our mother.

Mom has her towel in hand and twists it in her grip. She says nothing, but there's nothing for her to say. It's all scrawled on her face and the way the blood drains out of it.

I place my hand on her wrist, stilling the fine tremors, and take the phone back from Gareth.

"Booker, I know you mean well, but you just dropped a major bombshell and everyone here is freaking the eff-out. What's going on?"

"Jerald stashed diamonds in the rabbit's feet he gave you and Angie. We confirmed that with Angie's rabbit's foot and believe we'll find the same in the one you carry." Booker pauses to take a breath, then continues. *"You need to put it in a safe place. The team and I are on our way. We'll be there in less than two hours. In the meantime, you need to stay someplace safe."*

"Why?" The trembling in my hand increases. "Why would they suddenly come after me?"

"Because we believe they're looking for you and Angie both. No one knew where either of you were because you came into the US on a Guardian HRS flight. There's no record of you traveling, but the moment you bought a ticket home, you put yourself on the radar."

"Don't you think it's a bit of a stretch that anyone would notice?"

"Luv, you'd be surprised the kinds of resources these operations have at their fingertips."

"Why not just stay here until you arrive? I've got my brothers and we have guns."

It's very Texan of us. I grew up around guns; not only am I comfortable with them, and around them, I'm exceptionally proficient with my rifle.

We all are.

"Booker, we have plenty of firepower and enough ammunition to fight off a small army. Staying put is the best option."

"It's the worst possible option. The one place they know to go is to your parents' house. And Mrs. LaCroix, my apologies for the swearing, but your daughter's life is important to me."

"I'm glad to hear that, Booker. She's important to me as well, and I agree with my daughter. It's safest if we stay put. The chances of anyone tracking her down that quickly is downright small."

"I'll have to politely, but firmly, disagree. You're all in danger." There's a slight pause on his end of the phone. *"Isabelle, you didn't tell me if you have the rabbit's foot with you."*

"I have it." I pull it out from beneath my shirt.

The minute the rabbit's foot is in the open, Colton snatches it out of my hand. He shakes the mangled rabbit's foot next to his ear, then turns it over and over in his hand.

"I don't see anything that looks like a secret compartment."

"Trust me. It's there."

Booker isn't one to get excited about much of anything.

Is it possible he cares about me?

Or … am I reading too much into things?

"We'll stay here and wait for your arrival. After that, we can decide what to do next." I snatch back the rabbit's foot from my brother and turn it around in my hand.

"Next is that I take you back to Guardian HQ and never let you out of my sight until we've eliminated the threat."

"I don't get why the *Coralos* cartel cares about me. Don't you think you're blowing this out of proportion?"

"Mitzy's digging as we speak, and it's not the *Coralos* cartel we're worried about."

"It's not?"

My brothers try to follow our conversation but give me strange looks. I failed to tell them much about my abduction and subsequent rescue.

I admit I played most of it down, and since it never made the news here in the US, they don't have anything to go by except what I told them.

I've learned to keep the details light if I want any peace from my brothers and their overprotective instincts.

"No. It's not." Booker's tone turns from serious to deadly. *"Mitzy just informed us that known Laguta contacts just touched down in Laredo."*

"Okay …" That shakiness in my hands spreads to the rest of my body. "What does that mean?"

"It means they're at least an hour ahead of me." His voice deepens, turns huskier—sexier. *"Isabelle, they're coming. They're coming for you, and I'm not going to be there to save you. You need to get out of there. For God's sake, for once, please don't fight me on this."*

My brothers exchange looks, speaking in a language that belongs solely to them. No words are exchanged, but an entire conversation takes place.

"Booker," Gareth speaks for my brothers, "what do you suggest we do?"

NINE

Izzy

Dinner is a bust.

Gareth and Booker chat for less than a minute before the phone call ends.

Next, there's a flurry of activity as we head to the basement and the gun safe. All my brothers carry. When we each got our driver's licenses, the next stop was to get a concealed carry permit.

Life on a working ranch, raising and protecting cattle, comes with a lot of risk. Between the random coyote, wild boar, and ever-present rattlesnakes who threaten the herd, going out without being armed is foolish.

I have my concealed carry permit, but since I don't work on the ranch, I rarely carry.

In less than twenty minutes, all six of us pile into the cab of Gareth's truck and back out on the highway. We're loaded down with rifles, shotguns, pistols, and enough ammunition for a small army.

Jude called our dad, updating him on what's happening. Dad's on the ranch, with the drilling team, looking at one of the new drill sites. That's where we're headed.

It's the most secure place I know.

In my usual position, squished between Jude and Parker, I stare at the back of my mother's head, where she sits on the bench seat between Gareth and Colton.

Booker isn't happy about Gareth's decision to meet up with our father. He wants us nowhere near anything LaCroix related. However, Booker fails to realize exactly how vast our family ranch is.

If there are cartel members looking for me, by the time they search the house, we'll be long gone, and there's no way they'll find us on the ranch.

Almost no way.

But if they do, we've got numbers on our side. With the Dingleberries, me, Mom, my father, and his men, who are all expert shots with a pistol, rifle, and shotgun, we are a formidable force.

Not Guardian-formidable, but Texas-Ready-for-Anything.

Normally, when we're all together like this, boisterous conversation fills the air. Right now, there's nothing but pensive silence. It lasts far longer than I expect and breaks exactly how I fear.

"What the heck happened in Nicaragua, Izzy?" Gareth glances at me through the rearview mirror.

"I told you." My voice is small, like how I wish I was right about now.

I've avoided the *interrogation* up to now, hoping my ordeal would blow over and disappear as far as my family's concerned.

Now, however, the questions won't stop.

"You told us shit." He quickly glances at our mother. "Sorry, Mom."

"It's okay." Her soft voice remains strong and calm, unlike the anger boiling over in Gareth's tone. "Izzy will tell us now."

"Mom …" I slide my hands between my knees and curl inward.

I've been dreading this moment ever since the *Coralos* cartel shoved us into the back of their trucks. The rabbit's foot saved me then, and I can't help but believe it will save me now.

We all took a look at the mangled thing. It didn't survive its jungle adventure through water and mud very well, but I'm not giving it up.

None of us were able to find a secret compartment containing a fortune in diamonds.

Part of me still believes this is overblown.

Except Guardian HRS sent the entire Bravo team to collect me. They wouldn't do that if the threat wasn't real.

My stomach twists and turns. Real fear bubbles up inside of me, as well as guilt over putting my family in danger.

The Dingleberries are in full protective mode. Almost as if they've been practicing their entire life for exactly *this* moment; to protect their little sister.

Mom sits quietly, letting Gareth lead, but she's really the one in charge. It's that quiet strength she mentioned earlier. I get mine from her.

"Head to drill ten." She glances at her phone, then places it in her lap. "Your father is there with his men. I told him what's happening." She glances in the rearview mirror, catching my eye. "Isabelle, that gives you plenty of time to fill us in on what really happened in Nicaragua."

A woman of many expressions, the stare she levels at me now is one that can't be ignored. Her demand will be met.

I inhale and brace for the worst.

"What do you want to know?"

"Don't go down that road. This isn't a game of twenty questions. Tell us what happened in Nicaragua." Firm, and broking no nonsense, my mother lays down the law.

"Well, I'm not really sure what to say. We were setting up at the next village on our itinerary. There was some distant shooting in the hills."

"Active gunfire and you were setting up camp?" Gareth huffs out a frustrated breath. "I knew something like this would happen."

"No, you didn't. They wouldn't still be in business if the work wasn't safe."

"I'd think the very definition of safe would be not getting kidnapped."

"It was an *a-nom-a-ly*." I stress each syllable, knowing I won't be heard.

How am I going to get Gareth off my back? It feels like a lost cause.

"Gareth, let her finish." There goes Mom again, controlling the peace and the situation.

"The area we were working in is in an area disputed by two rival cartels. It wasn't uncommon to hear gunfire in the distance. We set up our clinic—it's not a camp—like we always did. Camp makes it sound like we're a bunch of kids spending the night in the woods. The work I was involved in …"

"Isabelle, stick to the story." Mom steps in, squashing an old argument before it builds into something larger.

"Well, the gunfire got closer, and the *Coralos* cartel drove into where we set up for the day. They thought we were running guns for the *Laguta* cartel and took the medical staff hostage."

Along with Jerald.

Never understood why they took him and not the other mechanics and drivers we had with us.

"Why the medical staff?" Jude's soft voice belies his strength. He's the biggest of my brothers, the strongest, and got into too many fights when he was younger. Almost killed a man in a bar brawl and never fully recovered.

"We thought it was for ransom. They didn't take our interpreters, just us. Again, that's not uncommon. Kidnapping rich Americans is a thriving business in that part of the world."

The more I speak, the less solid my footing feels, defending my previous choices.

"They took a video and broadcast it on local news. I assumed to send to family members for ransom or to Doctors Without Borders."

"We never received any communication."

"I think that's because of Brady."

"Who?"

"Brady. He's Bravo One, leader of Guardian HRS's Bravo team. He just happened to be vacationing in Costa Rica, and he recognized Angie in the video."

"And he got the Guardians involved?"

"I'm not sure he ever officially got them involved. Like I said, he knew Angie and came to rescue her. I just happened to be extra on the side."

"What does that mean?" Colton's inflection rises with confusion.

"He knew Angie's husband back when he was in the Navy, and because of that, he came to rescue her. I was baggage because the cartel separated Angie and me from the others."

"Why would they do that?" My mother's question is a good one but not something I want to answer.

There's no need to tell her what the cartel leader planned for us *women*.

A shiver races down my spine with the memory of the leader's words.

He told the guards to take Angie and me down to the river to clean up. We knew what would happen next. Ushered to the bank of the river by four men with guns trained on us, that was certainly the blackest moment of my life.

The unrelenting terror made me sway on my feet. It didn't feel real, like I was living someone else's nightmare, but it was all happening to me.

"Mom, you know what they were going to do." Parker leans forward and places his hand on my mother's shoulder.

My brothers understood immediately. It takes Mom another half-second to catch up.

Her choked sob turns my stomach. I never wanted her to know how bad things almost got.

"But you don't have to worry about that." I rush my words, trying to make it sound better than it was. "Nothing bad happened. Brady rescued us. He took out our guards, then had us join him in the river."

"The river?" Parker gives me a look. "You? In water?"

My fear of water, as well as many other things, is well known.

It comes from when I was five and got swept into a drainage ditch during a flash flood. Gareth saved me. Jumped in, risking his own life to save mine.

Maybe that's where his overprotectiveness stems from?

Funny. I never thought about it that way.

"Yes. We floated down a river, hid in a cave overnight, more swimming in the river—well, floating actually. Brady helped me. Then we scaled down a steep waterfall …"

"Whoa, wait." Colton spins round in his seat to look at me. "You scaling down anything is unbelievable."

"Well, I did it. Then Brady …" I pause, thinking I'll leave out this part of the story. "Anyway, Brady half carried me to this field where his team landed in a helicopter …"

"You flew in a helicopter?" Jude knocks my shoulder with his. "Our scaredy-cat sis scaled down a waterfall *and* flew in a helicopter?"

"I did, and that's basically what happened in a nutshell."

"You certainly overcame a lot of your fears …" Gareth gives me a long hard look. It's assessing in its intensity, almost as if he's seeing me in a new light.

"Our sis is growing up." Colton gives me a final look as he twists back around to face front.

"Running for your life will do that." All I can do is shrug.

I did conquer several fears during that escape. I'm proud of that. Proud that I didn't let fear overwhelm me.

Dad always said fear can paralyze the mind, and we must face our fears. He made my brothers face theirs but never pushed me to face mine.

Was that because I'm a girl? His *baby girl*? Or something else?

All I know is I'm surrounded by people who love, cherish, and protect me.

For some ungodly reason, I find it stifling. Mom's right about being driven to live, see, and do more than what I can in Leighton.

Perhaps it's because of that love that I feel such a great need to give back to those less fortunate than myself?

My phone rings and all conversation with my family comes to a screeching halt. I gave them the Cliffs Notes version of my ordeal in Nicaragua, but it feels like it's enough to answer their need for more.

"Hello?" Don't know why I say that when Caller ID says it's Booker.

"Where are you?" His tone is more controlled, and deathly calm.

"We're driving down the road and we're about ten minutes out from the ranch."

"Good." The way his voice wraps around that word makes my heart thump. *"We're a few minutes out. Mitzy's got Smaug in the air."*

Parker gives me a look, but I shoosh him.

"Isn't that a bit overkill?"

"Considering six cartel members just pulled up the drive of your house, I'd say no, it's not overkill."

"My house?"

"Yes. I told you this was serious."

"Booker ..." Real fear fills me, making my hands shake.

"It's okay. I'm on my way."

There's possession and protection twining in and around his words.

For the first time since we met, I don't find it annoying, irritating, or infuriating. Instead, I take in a deep breath. I may be surrounded by my brothers, but Booker will be the one to keep me safe.

I know it. I feel it. It settles deep inside of me, taking root and grabbing hold.

"Where are you going on your ranch?"

"Drilling station ten."

"Do you have coordinates?"

"Coordinates?"

"Yes, GPS ..." There's a slight pause, then Booker's back on the line. *"Never mind. Mitzy found it. We'll see you there."*

"Okay."

How? How will he 'see us there?' Is there anything the Guardians can't do?

"And, Isabelle ..."

"Yes?"

"Mitzy's tracking your phone. Whatever you do, don't lose it. It's the only way for me to find you."

Our argument over the tracking devices comes to mind. My

cheeks heat with embarrassment for not only refusing one but claiming I didn't need it.

Famous last words, right?

I'm never going to live that down.

Gareth adds to our speed, and to my surprise, Mom says nothing about him going ten over the speed limit. Everyone's a bit keyed up, but I still kind of feel like it's a bit over the top.

As far as this world goes, I'm a nobody. Yet, I've got cartel members hunting me down, Guardians swooping in to save the day, and my family circling protectively around me.

It feels like a dream, yet it's all too real.

We pull up to the grand gates at the entrance to the family ranch. They automatically sense the transponder in the truck and slowly draw open.

From this point on, the highway disappears, taking its paved roads with it.

The dry, dusty heat of southern Texas bakes the ground. Gravel crunches beneath the tires as we pull onto family land. With the hard-packed dirt, there's no need for Gareth to slow down. He does drop his speed a little, but we head off toward the hills in front of us.

The land here is hard and unforgiving. Despite that, we're blessed with relatively temperate lands. Meaning, grasses grow on our land rather than the sturdy scrub brushes seen in other parts of Texas. Several small streams flow into our land, nourishing the ground to supply water and nutrients to the grasses.

It's a good place to raise cattle but far from hospitable. Deceptive in its beauty, if someone gets caught out here without water, it's not uncommon for them to die from thirst in a couple of days.

Despite the presence of water, heat exhaustion takes its toll on the most physically fit person.

We know this from those who attempt to cross the border in the heat of summer and the bodies left behind. It's sad but an undeniable truth about life on the ranch.

It's also another reason everyone around here is armed while working the ranch. In addition to the occasional coyote who harries the herd, people driven by desperation create threats all their own.

We don't turn in those we find. We feed them, give them water, treat any life-threatening injuries, then gently escort them off our land with warnings not to return. What happens after that isn't our concern.

That's the uneasy stance our father took on the political quagmire that is the Texas-Mexico border issue.

Fortunately, it doesn't happen often. Nevertheless, the moment we cross onto our land, Jude and Parker pull out their pistols and check the load. Colton does the same not a few minutes later.

The silence in the cab is thick enough to cut with a knife.

No one speaks.

Meanwhile, I squirm in my seat, feeling foolish for not accepting the tracker from Guardian HRS, terrified that my family's at risk, and angry this is happening again.

I've had my fair share of bad shit happening to me.

"What's that up ahead?" Colton breaks the silence and points about a half mile down the road.

We all look where he points.

To two vehicles blocking the road.

Trucks that don't belong on LaCroix land.

"Fucking shit." Gareth yanks the wheel hard to the left.

We careen off the dirt road, bumping over the uneven ground.

Gareth steps on the gas, flooring it.

Dirt, grit, and rocks spit out from beneath our tires, as does a plume of dust.

TEN

Booker

Isabelle's in danger, and I'm not by her side.

I nearly break my phone with the vice grip I have on it. Frustration flows through my veins, building to a fury boiling up within me.

We land in Laredo, Texas, and immediately unload our gear from the jet onto a helicopter diverted for our specific needs.

It comes as no shock that I know the pilot.

"Hey there." I stick out my hand. "It's Booker. Nice to see you again."

"Booker?" Ariel Black tugs at her chin. When I open my mouth to remind her where we met, she holds up a finger. "Give me a second." Her eyes close for a fraction of a second, then pop open. "I flew you to a container ship headed down the Mississippi about a year ago."

"That's the one."

I'm surprised she remembers.

That was a mission where I filled in as support for Alpha team.

Bravo was nonoperational on account of injuries sustained during an explosion at a shipyard—aka, a rescue gone wrong.

Brady took the brunt of the blast when he yanked Rafe out of the blast radius. Brady's burns were extensive—the scarring covers most of the left half of his body and some of his face. Rafe lost his foot and lower leg, not that you'd know it with the prosthetic he wears. The others suffered injuries as well, but Brady and Rafe fared the worst.

Brady's recovery took the better part of a year. Rafe's was nearly as long.

That mission put my EMT skills to the test. I barely got Brady and the others, who were also wounded, out of there alive.

"I remember." Ariel smiles sweetly at me. "Alpha team was on a mission to rescue a woman placed on a containership for delivery. Ah, what was her name?"

"Moira."

"That's right."

Moira is a beautiful siren who was captured and intended for delivery to a waste of human flesh.

"You and …" She snaps her fingers, reaching for the memory.

"Griff." I don't wait for her memory to fill in the gaps.

We're working on borrowed time.

"That's right. We were in a support role that turned into a rescue. Ha! I still remember him rappelling down to scoop her off the ship. How is she doing? Are she and Griff …"

"She's doing well, and they are very much together—with some thanks to you."

"Nope. No." She shakes her head. "I definitely didn't do that. I was just the pilot—a glorified bus driver. Although, I do remember some difficulty with the radio …" Her serene smile lifts my spirits.

She's a war-decorated pilot several times over, who now runs medevac flights out to oil rigs in the Gulf of Mexico and happens to fill in *as needed* when Guardian HRS calls.

She disobeyed orders during that mission, claiming radio difficulties, but that was only because we were told to back off. Ariel Black isn't the kind of woman who backs off. She goes in guns blazing, and that night, she helped save a life.

"You boys about ready?" she calls out to my team.

"Locked and loaded." Brady trots over and sticks out his hand. "I have heard good things about you."

"Oh, I hope not!" Her laughter is rich and full, unfettered and free. "That means my reputation is slipping."

"Hardly." Brady gives a nod of respect.

She's a knockout, but it's clear she's worked most of her career with men. Ariel Black doesn't bat an eye at our gear, our guns, or our formidable size.

"Well, let's get you boys in the helicopter and headed out. No time to waste." She points to the helicopter bay and circles her arm, ushering us in.

We're old pros at this and are in our seats and strapped in before she can walk around and climb into the pilot's seat. Her helmet goes on, with its integrated headset, and she spins up the rotors.

We grab the headsets hanging overhead and dial to channel two when she flashes two fingers, telling us what frequency she'll be on.

Soon, we're in the air, flying out of Laredo and headed toward the small border town of Leighton, Texas. After we clear the city, there's nothing but an open highway below us, rugged land spreading out as far as the eye can see, and what remains of the Rio Grande.

"It's greener than I thought." I glance down, surprised by the verdant fields below.

"We're near the delta. That's the Rio Grande below us, draws a line right along the border," Rafe chimes in with useful geography facts. It's a thing of his. The man is an encyclopedia of random facts. "Did you know it's the fifth longest river in North America? Twentieth longest in the world."

"No, but I do know it forms the border between Texas and Mexico." I'm not a wealth of random facts, but I know that much.

"Well, it originates in the Rockies and flows through steppes and deserts on its way to the Gulf of Mexico. As for it being greener than you thought, while most of Texas is dry and arid, the Rio Grande is nearing its end here. As it meanders across a coastal plain, it creates a fertile delta. We're just at the beginning of that. Which is why there's grass and some of it's green."

"If you say so, Mr. Know-It-All." Over the years, I've learned not to question Rafe. I seldom bet with the man when it's over anything book-worthy. He invariably wins.

"What did you say Izzy's family farms?" Like me, Hayes hangs half in, half out, of the helicopter.

We're all adrenaline junkies, but Hayes takes it to another level. In addition to being our explosives expert, he's an avid fan of extreme sports. You name it, he's done it.

"Ranch. Not farm."

Since Isabelle's trip home, and all that followed, I've done a deep dive into her background, and that of her family. "Her family owns several thousand acres. They run cattle but also drill for oil and natural gas."

"Ah, now that's interesting." Rafe opens his mouth to begin a compendium of the leading drilling and mining industries in Texas, but I'm one step ahead of him, courtesy of Mitzy's skills.

In addition to natural gas and oil, there's an abundance of silver, lead, gold, uranium ore, and gypsum buried beneath the soil.

From what I read about LaCroix Industries, they're focused mostly on cattle and oil drilling.

Which means, her family is rich.

Not that I ever would've guessed from the Isabelle I know, but it explains much about her gentle nature as well as her temper.

Odd how she suppresses any accent. I never noticed a Texan twang in her speech.

"Overwatch to Bravo-One." Command and Control breaks into our conversation, speaking through our personal gear rather than Ariel's headsets.

"Bravo-One. Copy." Brady replies for the team.

"We've got activity on the ranch."

My gut does a thousand-foot drop to the ground.

Those words are never good. Brady's gaze cuts to mine, where he tells me without using words to keep my shit locked up nice and tight.

It's not unusual when working with a group of guys over the years, to develop a nonverbal language all our own. I'm not talking a word here and there.

There's a big difference between a look that says *Stop being an Ass* to one that conveys everything Brady just did when he looked at me.

Whatever Overlord has to tell us, it isn't good. I claw at the leather seat, digging my nails in, and steel myself for the worst.

"Go on." Brady's voice is calm. Cool. Level.

It lacks the fire burning in my gut. The all-out rage that follows bad news.

I know it's coming, and I brace.

"Activity on the ranch. Two vehicles. A dozen men. Subject's vehicle is off-road. Others in pursuit."

Brady holds my gaze, telling me to settle the fuck down when every cell in my body demands I jump out of the helicopter and rescue my girl. He knows my feelings for Isabelle are more than they seem.

Hell, everyone knows.

Everyone but Isabelle.

"Bravo One, active gunfire. I repeat. Active gunfire." CJ reports what Mitzy's high-flying drone, *Smaug*, sees.

It's a play-by-play, live-action report on what's happening on the ground.

"Ariel, we've got action." Brady switches to the internal comms in the helicopter.

"Copy. Instructions?" Her voice is smooth as silk, but that's what I've heard about the battle-hardened pilot. She's cool under pressure.

Wish I could say the same.

"Overlord, relay coordinates to Ariel. We'll take them out from the air."

"Will do. Tread easy. Let's not start a war." CJ's modulated voice tells us to proceed cautiously, but there's no proceeding cautiously when my woman's involved.

I give Brady a look. He shushes me with his hand. In that look, he reads me and answers right back.

Bravo team is going to war.

ELEVEN

Izzy

"Gotta step on the gas, Gareth." Parker leans out the window, checking the progress of the two trucks in pursuit.

Gareth's truck bounces wildly on the uneven ground, but it's rugged and built to last.

With articulating axels, we launch over bumps, sail through the air, and land with slightly less than bone-jarring force.

"All of our rifles are in the back." Colton fires out curse after curse, despite our mother's presence.

"I can …"

"*No!*"

The resounding shout from all of my brothers at the same time has me covering my ears.

This isn't the first time I offer to crawl through the narrow pass-through in the rear window.

It's also not the first resounding *No!* I receive from the Dingleberries.

We slowly gain ground, but it's two against one.

Two trucks against one.

Twice as many men against the six of us.

Our rifles and shotguns, are locked securely in the compartments over the wheels. If we stop to let one of my brothers jump out of the truck and into the truck bed, we'll lose the lead we barely maintain.

"But we need …"

Another harsh bump lifts me out of my seat. Thank goodness for seatbelts or that would've been my head slamming into the headliner.

Still, I think I'm right.

The first *pop* of gunfire rings out.

Gareth swerves, but the shot falls short of our truck.

"Enough of this." I slam the sliding window open and unbuckle before Jude and Parker can stop me.

"Izzy—stop!" Parker calls out, but I ignore him.

While Gareth drives, I twist in my seat and plan my attack.

I'm small, but the window isn't much bigger. Deciding to just go with it, I dive through the window like I'm diving into a pool.

And promptly get stuck at my hips.

The truck launches into the air, crunching down with force. My hips take the brunt of that bump, leaving me gasping in pain.

Jude pulls on one leg, trying to drag me back inside the cab, while Parker tries to push me through the small window.

Another *pop* of gunfire dusts the ground a few feet behind our truck.

We careen over a berm and drop into a gulley. Gareth swerves right, keeping us from colliding into the steep bank on the other side.

That little bit of momentum is just what my body needs to slide the rest of the way through the window.

Keeping low, I crouch in the back of the truck.

Gunfire sounds all around me. Either I'm exceptionally lucky, or they're horrible shots. My hand drifts to the rabbit's foot securely tied around my neck.

The first vehicle in pursuit flies over the berm behind us and crunches into the opposite bank.

Its partner follows suit, narrowly avoiding a collision. They back up, spitting rocks out from under their tires, and lurch back into motion.

A shot rings out, making me duck. But they're too far and too unstable for a precision shot.

I open the locker over the left wheel and pull out heavy canvas bags filled with ammunition. These I pass through the gap in the window.

My brothers carry their sidearms on them, but their rifles and shotguns are in the locker.

Heavier, clunkier, more difficult to manage, I thread those through the gap in the rear window one at a time.

With the left wheel locker emptied, I turn my attention to the one on the right. Not as full as the other one, there's more ammunition at the bottom. Resting on top is my competition rifle.

Another shot from the pursuing vehicle rings out.

They know they're too far and on too unstable of a platform to aim with any degree of accuracy. The same can be said of me, but I've got something they don't.

Expert training.

I open the heavy canvas bag with my ammunition inside and pull out a few rounds. Then I scoot back to brace against the cab.

Locked and loaded, I bend a knee and use that to steady my aim.

Gareth flies down the gulley. Steep banks on either side keep us contained, but I know this land.

Gareth does too.

With the truck bouncing, I take aim, but hold my shot. Even I can't hit the side of a barn with the way the truck bounces over the uneven terrain.

But that will soon end.

This system of gullies empties out onto a dry riverbed.

Hard-packed sand fills the center of that riverbed, which means everything will smooth out in just a little bit.

"Izzy, what are you doing? Get back inside. It's not safe out there," Jude calls out, waving for me to climb back inside the truck.

It's not safe out here, but only marginally safer inside the truck.

Bullets penetrate glass just fine, a fact all my brothers know.

I ignore him and center my breathing, going back to the tips and tricks ingrained by my father when he first taught me to shoot.

Bringing everything down to a center focus, I hold my rifle with a steady grip. The moment the ground beneath us smooths out, I put my eye to the scope and place my finger on the trigger guard.

Beneath us, heat-baked sand smooths our ride. I take in a slow breath, aim for the front right tire of the lead truck chasing us, and slowly squeeze the trigger.

The tire blows out.

The truck swerves hard to the right. Dust kicks up in a thick plume as the truck comes to a halt.

"She hit the tire!" Parker shouts and gives a hoot, urging me on. "Go! Go!"

The vehicle behind the one I hit swerves to avoid hitting it.

I once again place my eye to the scope. Set my sight on the left front tire and take in a slow, centering breath.

I squeeze the trigger, but our truck bounces over a grouping of rocks.

My shot goes wide.

Shit!

We climb out of the riverbed, leaving the smooth sand behind. Determined to get rid of the last truck, I take aim again.

But the ride's too chaotic.

I can't get a clear shot.

Frustrated, I prop my rifle beside me while watching the other truck slowly gain on us.

Gareth pushes his truck, demanding its best. The back tires dig in to the loose rock and scree of the bank. We stall for a moment, then the tires dig in.

Up and over, the truck climbs the bank and sails right on over it.

I catch air over the rise, and land with a grimace and a groan.

Reloading, I take aim on the vehicle following us.

We trade shots, but nothing hits. With a curse, I put my weapon down.

This is pointless.

Twisting around, I glance ahead. Gareth heads toward the drill site, where our father waits with more men.

Another *pop* of gunfire rings out. It hits the tailgate with a *ping* that sends my heart into a full-scale riot. My gut clenches, and a sickening wave of fear washes over me.

Wiping the sweat from my brow, I steel my nerves and take aim again.

I try for the tire.

My shot's lined up.

A deep breath in to steady my aim, then I gently pull back on the trigger.

A flurry of gunfire rings out. On its heels is a loud explosion as our left rear tire blows out.

"Shit!" My finger continues its squeeze on the trigger but goes wide as Gareth tries to control the truck.

We veer wildly to the right, running on the rim of the tire, but that won't last for long.

We're essentially dead in the water.

Or will be.

I take aim …

My finger squeezes.

The concussive blast of my rifle makes my ears ring, but I hit the lead tire of the truck.

Like the one before, the truck jerks left as the front tire blows out.

Leaning back, I breathe out a sigh of relief.

But they score another hit.

Our remaining rear tire goes out.

We're toast.

I bounce in the bed as the truck cants left then right, rocking so violently I'm afraid we might flip.

Solid under pressure, Gareth maintains control.

Nevertheless, we come to a screeching halt … Out in the open.

Vulnerable.

Shots fire.

The men in pursuit pile out of their vehicle. They're not giving up.

"Out! Out! Out!" Gareth orders everyone out of the truck.

The doors pop open and my brothers peel out.

Mom comes out last. She stands next to me, rifle in hand, armed and determined to protect her young.

Parker reaches up to help me out of the back of the truck. I hand over my rifle as well as my ammunition.

"Come on, sis." Gareth gestures for me to get out. He holds up his arms, and I go to him.

Placing my hands on his shoulders, I hop out of the back of the truck. He catches my hips, lowering me to the ground.

"Get to the hood," Gareth yells at me to get in front of the truck.

Colton and Mom load their weapons and set up their shots.

Gareth and I race around to the relative safety provided by the truck.

Parker hands me my rifle as he crouches in the dirt behind the front fender. My heart bangs away inside my chest, but I otherwise feel surprisingly calm.

As if time stands still …

I take in a breath, exchange a look with my mother, then brace for what comes next.

I'm a competitive shooter, ranked nationally while in college, but this will be the first time I take aim on a human.

Tires are inanimate objects.

I didn't hurt anyone, but these men are relentless.

"Get down." Gareth pulls me and Mom down to the ground while Parker, Jude, and Colton trade shots with the men trying to close the distance.

Colton hits one.

That's all it takes to slow the advance of the others.

They crouch behind small boulders, trading gunfire with my brothers until there's a lull, or they get cocky and run to the next boulder that provides cover.

I glance over the hood, looking through the windows, and grit my teeth.

The men from the first truck I disabled sprint to join their fellows.

The six men shooting at us will soon double to twelve.

"What do we do?" Adrenaline rushes through me, making my hands shake.

"They're advancing on us." Jude steps back to reload.

I realize how he and Parker trade shots, maintaining a steady barrage to slow the men.

Once Jude reloads, Parker steps back to do the same. Twins, those two share a unique bond.

Colton tries to join, but there's no way for him to do so without coming out from behind the cover of the truck.

I glance behind us, noting the terrain. It's a series of gullies that wind through the land.

"Gareth, what about …" I point toward the gullies. "At least we'll have better protection."

The truck does a good job of protecting us, as long as the men are a certain distance away, but our lower legs remain at risk.

If any of them decide to start shooting under the truck, we're done.

"It'll work." He taps Colton on the shoulder. "Take Izzy and Mom. Stay low. We'll keep them pinned down."

Mom places her hand on Gareth's shoulder. It's almost as if she wants to say something, but she gives a little shake of her head and turns toward me instead. "You ready, honey?"

Colton and Gareth exchange expressions.

No need to be a mind reader to know what they say between themselves.

Colton slings his rifle over his shoulder, then grabs a bag of ammo in each hand. He turns to me.

"Run fast. Stay low. They shouldn't see us from where they're at."

"Okay." I sling my rifle over my shoulder and grab my ammo pack.

Mom does the same. As good as I am, she's a better shot than me.

"I'm sorry, Mom. I never meant for …"

"Hush, honey. We'll have time for words later."

"Okay." For some reason, my eyes well up with tears. I turn toward my brothers—toward Gareth. "And once we get there, you'll join us, right?"

I need Gareth to tell me that's the plan.

There's no way I can leave them behind.

The look in his eye speaks volumes.

He and my brothers will do whatever it takes to keep me safe.

I get that. I recognize the sacrifice, but I refute it.

There has to be another way.

But we're too exposed, unlike the men shooting at us who hide behind rocks.

This is the only way.

"On three." Colton checks with me, then Mom.

We both nod.

"One … Two … Three!" Colton takes off, hunching low.

It's not a sprint.

It's more of a slow hustle as we stay hidden below the truck.

Hopefully, Gareth's right and they won't know we've gone. Although, it'll be obvious soon enough.

It's about thirty yards to where the gully branches off.

Shots ring out behind us as we sprint to relative safety.

Colton jumps over the bank and drops a few feet. He holds out a hand for Mom, helping her down. I scoot down on my butt, letting my feet slide over the loose scree and rock in a semi-crouch.

The moment I'm down, I spin around, check my weapon, and take aim. Mom mirrors my pose.

"What are we going to do, if …" The words get lodged behind the lump in my throat.

The only way to get these men to stop is to do more than simply wound them.

I've never taken a human life, and I only hunted the one time.

Tears filled my eyes as my father congratulated me on my first kill, but I never got over killing that deer.

I went from shooting a defenseless animal to competitive riflery and never looked back.

Now, because of me, my brothers, mother, and maybe even myself might have to take a life.

Mom will have to kill. There's a fire in her eyes. She's not happy with her kids in danger, but she's prepared to do what she must.

"Mom, I've got this." Colton fishes into his pocket.

He pulls out his phone and hands it to Mom.

"Call Dad. Tell him what's happening. See if he can send men …" There's no further need for him to finish.

Mom takes the phone, dials, and puts it to her ear. She scoots down and makes the call.

Meanwhile, Colton and I exchange looks, then take aim.

Our view isn't the best.

With the truck thirty yards away, the men behind it another fifty yards further, our shots are complicated to say the least.

We have to lie down covering fire, without endangering Gareth, Jude, or Parker. It sounds easier than it is.

But we provide cover for my brothers.

Colton signals that we're ready.

Jude and Parker don't turn their backs, too busy laying down suppressive fire, but Gareth waits for our signal.

The moment he taps Jude and Parker on the shoulder, Colton and I spread out to cover their retreat.

The three of them sprint for cover, not worrying about whether the men will see them or not because Colton and I lay a wasteland of suppressive fire to cover our brothers.

Bullets fly, but they go wide. My brothers slide into the gulley without a scratch.

"Your father's on the way. His men are out with the truck but are coming back. He's heading out on Brutus." Mom's speech is devoid of emotion. She says only what we need to know.

Despite that, her hands are steady. Her grip on her gun is firm.

Goddamn, but I have a kickass family protecting me.

Dad is on his way.

Brutus is one of our many ATVs. Each has a name. Brutus is a Razor ATV, which means it's a beast over rugged terrain, and it seats four.

"He can't ride that here." My brows tug tight. "It has no protection."

Dad will be a sitting duck.

Gareth spins around. He scans up and down the gulley, then his attention snags far to the left.

"What if we …" He pauses, trying to think.

I look down the direction he faces, where the gulley branches and deepens.

"Izzy, do you know where we are?"

"I do." Pointing to the south, I know exactly where we are.

When I was five, a flash flood caught me unaware. I was out with my brothers, exploring like we always did, when a thunderstorm blew through without warning.

The sudden deluge didn't have time to soak into the parched ground, and the runoff spilled right into the gullies—where I played.

The flash flood dragged me nearly half a mile toward a culvert that funnels under the road. Gareth barely got to me before the fast-running water sucked me under.

Thus, my fear of water that remains to this day.

"Do you remember how to get to the road?"

"I do."

"Okay." He comes to a decision. "You, Colton, and Mom get to that culvert. We'll tell Dad to grab you there."

"And what about you?"

"We'll make do."

Make do?

What the hell does that mean?

There's only one way this ends.

Either my brothers kill a dozen men, or those men kill my brothers.

Once those men overrun our position, they won't spare my brother's lives when they see I'm not there.

With my heart lodged in my throat, I find myself speechless and paralyzed. It takes Colton grabbing me to get me going.

We duck down for the first few hundred feet, but then the gulley deepens enough for us to stand. Once that happens, we break into a run.

It's a good mile, maybe a bit more.

Behind us, it sounds like a warzone as my brothers buy us the time we need to get away.

Mom calls Dad, telling him where we're headed.

I grab the rabbit's foot around my neck, praying for a bit of good luck, but then I suddenly release it.

That foul thing's brought me nothing but trouble.

I'll be glad to get rid of it.

TWELVE

Booker

"Shots fired." Mitzy's voice comes in too loud.

Too clear.

Fuck!

My teeth grind as I sit in the helicopter. We're still ten minutes out, and now those assholes are shooting at my girl.

I'm going to kill the fuckers.

"Copy that. Details." Beside me, Brady thinks like a commander, demanding more information before dropping his men into a hot zone.

"Two trucks in pursuit. Unclear where Izzy's headed. Not in the direction of the drill site."

"Copy that." Brady looks at me.

Dropping into a hot zone is the least preferable action, but Isabelle and her family are in clear and imminent danger.

"We can take them out from the sky," I offer a suggestion.

It wouldn't be the first time we laid down suppressive fire from the air. Unlike a combat helicopter, however, this one is meant for saving lives, not taking them. There are no guns built into the helicopter, but we have our own.

"Agreed." Brady's sharp nod says he's on board. "Ariel, take us in for a low pass. We'll take out as many as we can."

"Kill order?" I only ask because I aim to kill as many men as I can.

"Negative," Brady says.

Fuck me.

Talk about raining on my parade.

"We need them alive, Bravo Two. Don't get creative."

"I won't."

I'm not a fan of wounding versus killing, but I'll follow orders.

"One truck is out. Front tire shot. One in pursuit, six men inside." CJ's voice is smooth as silk and as calm as a summer breeze. It takes a lot to get CJ excited. *"Focus on the lead truck."*

"Good copy." Brady closes the communication loop, letting all know he heard and understands.

"Looks like they're headed for a series of gullies," CJ's voice crackles over the phone. *"I hope they have a reason for that."*

Me too.

For the most part, the land is flat for miles. Rolling hills march off in the distance, but that's about it.

Here, the last bit of the Rio Grande spreads out into a watershed as it nears the Gulf of Mexico, splitting and dividing again and again.

In the dry season, that leaves a network of steep gullies cutting through the land.

After a significant rainstorm, those gullies can turn into deadly flows of water on account of run off from the parched ground.

They impede vehicles, making it treacherous, if not impossible, to navigate over and through them.

"More shots fired. The men in the second truck are on foot. Advancing."

Shit.

These guys do not give up.

"Back tire is out." CJ's play-by-play churns the bile in my stomach.

There's no need to say which truck. The only one that would have its rear tire blown would be the one Isabelle's in. I hold my tongue and check my weapon.

Rafe and Hayes do the same. Zeb and Alec already have their guns trained on the landscape below.

We fly toward the vehicles, which means we can't see them from where we sit in the back.

"ETA?" Brady calls out to Ariel.

"Five minutes."

"Copy." He glances at me and gives a nod.

I'm not supposed to kill anyone, but I probably will. I know it, and he knows it. In my defense, we don't need twelve prisoners to interrogate.

A handful will do.

"They lost the other rear tire. Vehicle slowing."

If it's slowing, the one in pursuit is closing in.

"Last vehicle out. Repeat, last vehicle out. Front tire blown. Looks like it's a ground fight." CJ's deadpan tone carries no emotion. *"The LaCroix's are taking position at the hood, returning suppressive fire. Damn they're good."* CJ continues his up-to-the-minute broadcast.

My brows tug together.

"Booker, your woman's family is pretty damn smart." CJ moves from telegraphic speech to something more descriptive. *"There's a gulley about thirty yards in front of them. They're splitting forces. Two women and a man retreating to the gulley."*

Two women. Isabelle and her mother.

"The ones that stayed with the truck are laying down suppressive fire, protecting the retreat, and now …" His voice trails off.

I find myself leaning forward, as if that will help me hear any better. It's reflexive, as if CJ sits in front of me rather than speaks directly into my ear via the headset I wear.

"All six are now in the gully. It's good cover. Excellent choice." CJ rarely lays down praise that easily.

CJ would expect something like that from his Guardians, but these civilians are impressing him with their tactics.

As for their choice, it's excellent only if they can hold their position.

It's the only cover around, but if they're overrun, they're done.

"How far?" I can't help but check in with Ariel. Brady should be the one to do it, but we're too close for me to step back now.

"Two minutes. I need direction, boys. What's the call?" Ariel speaks exactly like CJ.

Here we are, flying into a hot zone where we're all at risk, and she's cool as a cat. Fuckin' nerves of steel in that one, but I remember her temperament from when I flew with her before.

"We make one pass, incapacitate as many as we can from the air, then we land." Brady lays out his plan succinctly.

"Land?" Ariel calls back. "Not if they're still shooting. Sorry, but that's …"

"We'll fast rope it." I offer an alternate suggestion.

Fast roping out of a helicopter is a little different than rappelling but comes with similar risks. Fast roping is—well, much faster than rappelling.

It's only an option when unencumbered by our heavy rucks, and unlike rappelling, we don't use a harness. Instead, we use hands, knees, or feet to slow us down, getting us on the ground much faster.

And I need to be on the ground.

I need to be with Isabelle.

"Agreed. One pass to take out as many as we can, then drop us on the far side of the gulley, out of range of their fire. We'll join them on the ground." Brady calls out our next steps.

It's a solid plan.

"We've got movement on the ground," CJ calls out.

"Go on." There's a sudden stillness in the helicopter as Brady waits for CJ to elaborate. *"Our group on the ground has split. Three run along the ditch. Three are staying."*

Shit.

I look to Brady, knowing the call he's going to make and hating every bit of it. The thing is, we can't leave the three who stayed behind to face the remaining men alone.

They're not trained warriors but civilians in need of aid. Knowing one of the three running away must be Isabelle, my gut clenches with what needs to happen and what I want instead.

Brady looks at me, and we communicate all of that within the span of a breath. There's no need for words. I give a sharp nod, letting him know I've got my shit locked down tight.

"Stick to the plan." Brady sets us in motion, but the warning is for me.

Flying in low, skimming over the ground, Ariel sets us up like a pro. Four of us lean out the left side. We take out six of the men moving up from behind, wounding them with shots to their legs. No running, walking, or crawling for them.

They're effectively incapacitated.

Which leaves the front six perilously close to overrunning the three brothers Isabelle left behind.

The men advance steadily, despite suppressive fire laid down. They make it to the back of the truck Isabelle's family used to escape, placing them less than thirty yards from her brothers.

Ariel races through the air, swinging us out wide and out of range of the gunfire, before sweeping around behind the brothers. On her mark, we grab the thick ropes and slide down. In less than a minute, all six of us are on the ground.

Our presence does not go unnoticed. The relief in the faces of Isabelle's brothers is a palpable thing.

Bravo team does what we do best.

We advance.

Guns raised.

A lethal force coming to enact justice.

But our orders are to wound and incapacitate.

Not to kill.

My trigger finger is itchy.

Sweeping my weapon left to right, I move away from center of mass kill shots and go for the legs. If I get lucky, maybe I'll hit a femoral artery.

A guy can hope.

By the time we reach the gulley, the remaining men are down. That doesn't mean they're not a threat. While they nurse leg wounds, their weapons remain within reach.

Bravo team drops into the gulley. Rafe, Hayes, Alec, and Zeb take position, monitoring the wounded while Brady and I get the brothers out of the line of fire.

"You're Izzy's brothers?" Brady asks the obvious, but it's one way to say hello.

"Yes." The eldest looks between us. He's got the same black, wavy hair as his sister, along with the arresting-blue color in her eyes.

"Name's Brady. This is Booker."

"Don't know where you came from, but sure glad you're here. I'm Gareth." He twists around and points. "My brothers, Jude and Parker."

"Nice to meet you." Brady shakes with the men, getting the introductions done.

I follow suit.

Alec and Zeb lift from their positions and disappear over the rise. Their job is to separate those men from their weapons. After that, they'll provide first aid.

As the saying goes, you can't interrogate a dead man, and I want answers.

"Isabelle?" I look down the ditch, following the path she took.

"She's safe. Colton and our mother are with her. Our father is coming, going to meet them on the road and take them to the drill site."

"Have they …"

"Boys, I have a situation." Ariel's voice cuts through our comms, patched in through Mitzy's controls. *"There's a fire on one of the rigs. I have to go."*

"We've got it from here." Brady waves his hand over his head. "Thanks for the assist."

"Sorry, boys. I'd love to stay, but …"

I get it. Lives are on the line, and three things that never go together well are drill, rig, and fire.

While Ariel leaves us to save lives, we clean up the mess down here on the ground.

The helicopter angles away, nose dipping down as she piles on speed and flies toward the Gulf.

Once she's gone, I turn my attention back to Gareth.

"How far is this drill site?" I need my girl in my arms.

"Five miles."

Brady and I exchange a look. I know exactly what he's thinking.

"How were you planning on getting there?" One look at the steep sides of the gulley makes me question Gareth's mad dash off-road.

"Less than a quarter mile that way, these walls disappear where the riverbed widens. I thought to make it there and cross over."

He points in the opposite direction of where Isabelle and the rest of her family went.

"I assume you've got a jack in that thing?" Brady climbs the steep edge.

While we talk to Gareth, the rest of our team disarms the men we took out, then they tie tourniquets around their legs.

"I do." Gareth arches a brow in question.

"Good, because while we can run the five miles, I'd rather not. How about we change out your tires with those from the other truck and get on our way?"

"I don't have just one. I've got two, and they're both Hi-Lifts."

"Even better." I tap Gareth on the back. "How about you take the rear wheels off your truck, while your brothers and I find you a fresh pair."

Gareth's smile reminds me too much of Isabelle, but the faster we get his truck back in the game, the sooner I can hold Isabelle in my arms.

Jude and Parker join me in a jog to the nearest truck. I jack the back of the truck up with the Hi-Lift while Jude takes one wheel and Parker takes the other. In less than a few minutes, we've got two fresh tires for Gareth's truck.

Maybe there is such a thing as good luck.

Rafe and the others finish their first aid efforts as we roll the tires back to the truck. By the time we get there, Brady and Gareth have the two bad tires off the rear axle.

We work quickly. The whole process takes very little time.

There's a brief debate about the men. In the end, we take three of them, hoisting them into the back of the truck.

Me, Zeb, and Alec keep watch over the men as the rest of our team and the three brothers load up in the cab of the truck.

We head over to the drill site.

"We've got action at the drill site," CJ cuts in on the comm.

"What do you mean, action?" There goes my gut again, clenching in anticipation of bad news.

"The father picked up three people at the road. Returned to the drill site, and now there's a helicopter lifting off."

I look to Gareth who hears the message.

"We have a helicopter at the drill site. Almost impossible to manage this much land without one. Our father takes it to the drill sites when he visits them. He's probably coming to check on us."

Probably.

But I won't believe that until I see it with my own eyes.

"You might want to step on that gas." I turn my attention to our support team. "Mitzy, where is that helicopter headed?"

"Um …" The hesitation in her voice makes my blood boil. *"You're not going to like the answer to that."*

Fuck!

THIRTEEN

Izzy

HALFWAY TO THE CULVERT, THE *CHOP, CHOP, CHOP* OF AN INCOMING helicopter turns my head. I stumble and nearly trip, surprised by the new arrival. Although, I shouldn't be.

I find my footing and slow my run. Booker said he was coming, and there's no doubt in my mind he's on that helicopter.

Not quite noon, the heat of the day has yet to settle over the land, but it's going to be a scorcher. With no clouds overhead, and the still air holding in the heat, the sun will bake the ground and all the creatures who inhabit it.

Right now, I'm one of those creatures.

It's been a few minutes since we left Gareth and the others. At first, we hunched down, hiding our flight, but the moment we were safe from the gunfire, Colton had us pick up the pace.

Perspiration beads my brow and drips into my eyes. I use the back of my sleeve to brush the salty sweat from my eyes and control my breathing as much as I can.

Colton hangs behind me and Mom, urging us to run faster.

My heart beats a mile a minute.

It's not the run. We're all in good shape. Mom runs several times a week, as do I.

Then there's Colton, a cross country superstar in high school and college.

Our bodies adapt to the exertion easily, but that's not what makes my heart run away from me.

It's fear.

We have to run, but it feels all kinds of wrong leaving Gareth and the twins behind.

"Who's that?" Unlike me, Mom pulls to a stop and shades her eyes, trying to make out the helicopter. "That's not one of ours."

We have a small fleet of helicopters on the ranch, three to be precise. They rotate in and out of service, with one always in maintenance.

Dad and the Dingleberries are all certified pilots. I'm the only one who isn't, but then, I'm the only one afraid of heights.

Colton and I come to a standstill while Mom peers at the helicopter.

"It's circling around …" Colton stands beside her. "But it's not coming for us. Izzy, could those be your friends?"

"Booker said they were on their way." A quick glance at my watch confirms the timeline matches up. "They should've landed in Laredo by now." I shrug. "The Guardians never cease to amaze me, but since that helicopter isn't coming toward us, I'd say they see what's happening on the ground. They're helping Gareth and the twins."

"Good. They need it." Colton places his hand on our mother's arm. "You good to run? It shouldn't be much farther."

"I am." Like me, Mom is a bit winded.

I hate to admit I'm glad for the breather, but we can't rest for long.

Colton shows no sign of exertion, but he's a runner; always has been. While I racked up medal after medal in competitive riflery, he was a track and field all-star athlete.

He continues to stare off into the distance, watching the helicopter. Despite his words, he's torn like me. He's here to get Mom and me to safety but wishes he was with our brothers.

We're not quite a mile away from where we left Gareth, Jude, and Parker. While I normally run a mile in under eight minutes, doing that cross-country slows me down.

"Look how it's moving now—circling around behind them." Mom continues to shade her eyes.

"They probably took out what men they could from the air and are circling around to join them on the ground."

"How do you know that?" Colton gives me a strange look.

"Because I've seen them practice something similar during training."

"You watch them train? I thought you were manning their pharmacy."

"I am." I trip over my words a bit. "Or, I will be once in-processing is done."

"And that gives you time to *watch* them?" Colton winks at me.

I've never been able to lie to him. He always knows.

"For the record, I take my lunch break with Angie. She and Bravo One are a thing."

"Bravo One?"

"Sorry. Brady is Bravo One."

"And what is Booker?" He's not buying my shit.

"Bravo Two."

"And you're sweet on him."

"Don't start with me. Angie likes to watch Bravo Team train during lunch breaks, and since I'm her friend, I join her."

"Because you're her friend?" He gives me a look.

"Yes. It's pretty much what we do at lunch, every day." I prop my hands on my hips. "Think what you will, but that's the truth."

"That is only half the truth, little sis. You've got your eye on this Booker."

It annoys me when Colton sees through me, but he's never violated my confidence. Closest to me in age, he kept my secrets and covered for my exploits. Out of all the Dingleberries, he's the one I like the most.

He never tried to *parent* me or act like an uncle rather than a brother. Gareth is the worst about that.

But Colton's right about one thing. I can't get enough of watching the way Booker moves.

"You should see them train."

"I should, should I?" The corners of his lips tilt into a mischievous grin."

"There was this one day they practiced various exit techniques from a helicopter."

Colton's grin grows wider. I want to punch him in the gut but restrain myself.

"It was just like on TV, only way more awesome."

"If you say so, sis."

"I do say so. They did this thing where they landed and had to get themselves and their gear out of the helicopter in under a minute. Then they rappelled out with all their gear."

I remember how my mouth gaped and my heart leapt to my throat when they leapt off the skids with bulky packs weighing them down.

My stomach practically hurled in sympathy for them.

"But that was nothing compared to fast roping it down."

"Huh?" His brows tug tight together. "What's that?"

"It's different from rappelling." I go on to explain what I learned after asking that very same question. "If you ask me, jumping out of a helicopter trusting nothing but your grip on a rope is insane. I mean, I get jumping out of a plane. You've got a parachute. And I get rappelling too. At least there you're tied in with a harness, but they literally leap out of the helicopter using nothing but their hands and legs to slow them down enough not to crash into the ground like a pancake."

"Sounds like something I'd like to try. Maybe we could get Dad ..."

"You speak one word of that to your father and you won't sit for a week." Mom, who's been silent this whole time, gives Colton her mom-look.

That thing is like staring Medusa in the face. We all turn to stone, and there's a bit of ass puckering too.

I love the look on Colton's face and figure he deserves that after teasing me about Booker. But I like him and save him from our mother's glare.

Knowing the Dingleberries, next time they're all off together, they'll be taking the helicopter up to do exactly that.

Mom knows it too.

"The coolest thing I watched was an extraction where they're on the ground. A helicopter flies overhead dangling a rope. They clip in to the rope and hang from it as the helicopter literally lifts them off the ground." I pantomime the whole thing, even the jerk when they lift off. "They just dangle beneath the helicopter as it flies off."

Talk about ass puckering. That's something I'm definitely putting on my never-ever-in-a-million-year's list.

Nope.

Never going to happen.

Not in this lifetime.

"And I love all the lingo. Like infil and exfil. Makes everything sound cool."

"I bet." Colton's smile is back.

"What do those mean?" Mom puts away her Medusa face to ask the question.

"Infil is how they begin a mission, infiltrating into an active engagement. Exfil is the opposite. It's how they're extracted following a mission. Every bit of it fascinates me."

None nearly as much as one Guardian in particular.

Booker definitely gets my heart racing, but then he invariably ruins it by acting like a little shit.

Men are their own worst enemies. And he's not little. Not by a long shot.

Damn, my heart races just thinking about him.

"Is that so?" Mom gives me a look. "I'd say there's a little bit more than that going on."

"What do you mean by that?"

"Nothing." Mom keeps her thoughts to herself but flashes a secretive smile.

"Don't *nothing* me. What does that mean?"

"Only that your friends are going to a lot of trouble to help you.

Or maybe, it's one determined man in particular." She gives me a look. "Like one with a particularly colorful vocabulary? I think you're sweet on him."

"I am not." I stamp my foot and curl my fingers into tiny fists. Nothing gets by Mom.

She's still playing that conversation with Booker over in her head and jumping to all kinds of conclusions I'm not ready to face.

"It's not like that. This is what Guardians do. They help where they're needed, and we don't need them. Gareth, Jude, and Parker need them."

"I'm sure they do, hun. I'm sure they do ..." Her voice trails off as she watches six men slide down ropes to the ground. "Hey, looks like they're rappelling, or fast roping ..." Her voice trails off as we watch from a distance.

I'd give a million bucks to know what she's thinking.

From where we stand, Bravo team looks tiny. Like little ants sliding down a tiny string.

I wish I was there instead of here.

I'd feel better with Bravo team around me, especially Booker.

"Come on." Colton snaps my attention away from Booker to the gulley we stand in. "We're less than a quarter mile from the culvert."

And our father will be there.

Any hint of his family in peril and the man moves mountains.

The three of us lope into a jog. Our pace is slower than before, but only because we breathe easier knowing our brothers are getting the help they sorely need.

Also, and there is no reason to voice this out loud, but if that helicopter is filled with anyone but the Guardians, it wouldn't waste time on my brothers.

The pilot would fly directly toward us.

Toward me—and the diamonds they think I have.

The three of us stick out like a sore thumb against the scree and brush, not to mention the protective shelter of the gulley's bank doesn't help us if someone's searching from the air.

Colton urges us on.

A few minutes later, we stop at a culvert I know far too well.

Even now, years later, and with not a drop of water in sight, the fear of getting swept away sends tendrils of fear slithering down my spine.

I choke with the memory, and my entire body trembles. A whole-body shudder wracks me from head to toe.

Thankfully, neither Mom nor Colton notice.

While they climb up the bank, I approach the grate covering the culvert as it goes under the road.

My stomach knots at the danger I inadvertently put my family in, and all because of a mangled rabbit's foot.

I really believed it was my good luck charm.

It saved me from getting raped when Angie and I were captured by the Coralos cartel.

It helped me overcome my extreme aversion—aka phobia—to water.

I braved the heights of a waterfall, steeling myself to peer over the tumbling water to admire a rainbow in the mist few have ever seen.

It helped me climb into a helicopter and keep myself together as I struggled with my fear of heights.

The thing's supposed to be lucky, but it's more like a bad luck charm.

And all for what?

I shake the rabbit's foot, trying to hear the rattling of what's supposed to be millions of diamonds inside.

There's nothing.

And I want nothing to do with it. As long as this thing's in my possession, my family's at risk.

But what can I do with it?

It's not like I can toss it.

Hello, millions of dollars in diamonds?

But keep it with me?

Once again, I wish Booker was with me instead of helping my brothers.

As much as Booker and I fight and argue, something simmers between us. It's a banked heat getting ready to explode.

I feel it in the way my pulse races when he's near. In the way I gasp and tremble when he *almost* touches me. I feel him everywhere when we're in the same room.

What that is, or might be, I'm afraid to label. It's likely all in my head, but I really hope it's not.

I'm more than a little sweet on the guy. I'm head over heels falling for him.

Mom seems to think Booker likes me, but she's never heard the way he speaks to me.

Or the way I talk back.

Yeah, we're definitely not relationship material. And while I'm thinking about all of this, that lightness in my belly returns. That fluttery, tingling sensation that tells me I'm in trouble.

I more than like Booker, but he's not coming for me. He's here because there are millions of dollars at stake. He came for the rabbit's foot.

And that's exactly what I'm going to give him. Hand over the rabbit's foot and be done with the whole thing. While I'm at it, I may need to rethink my decision to stay with the Guardians.

I don't think I can live in a place—work in a place—where I might have run-ins with a Guardian I both hate and secretly love.

It feels like I've regressed to junior high and I don't like it. Not when I'm finally establishing independence from my overly protective brothers.

But Mom gets it.

She understands my need to break out from beneath the LaCroix name and make my own mark on the world. I'm tired of being the little sister and only daughter of a ranching dynasty. People think money solves all problems, but they don't understand it creates more than it solves.

"Come on, Izzy!" Colton shouts down at me. "I see Dad." He waves for me to hurry up.

"On my way." I glance at the grate over the culvert and abandon my plan to tie the rabbit's foot to the grate.

It was the briefest of thoughts; tie off the rabbit's foot and tell the Guardians where to find it.

Without the damn rabbit's foot, my family will be safe, and that's all that really matters.

But there's no way I can be that irresponsible. What if the tie comes undone? Or if a coyote finds it too tantalizing to pass by? What if there's another thunderstorm and a flash flood that sweeps it out to the Gulf of Mexico?

I abandon any thoughts about leaving the rabbit's foot behind and tuck it back inside my bra.

FOURTEEN

Izzy

By the time I climb out of the ditch, Dad is nearly upon us.

He slows down before stopping, allowing the dust plume the Razor kicked up to dissipate rather than cover us in dust. He drives Brutus—my dad loves to name his vehicles.

An off-road monster, Brutus is a four-person ATV and a beast with articulating axels, rugged wheels, a monster motor, and tremendous torque that can power through anything.

While the light breeze blows the dust to the side, the three of us crawl inside and buckle up.

Mom leans over to Dad, and the two of them kiss. It's brief, there and gone before I realize it, but what a tender kiss it is.

I want *that* in my life; a connection between two people binding them together forever. The kind of love encompassed by a gentle press of the lips.

I want a love that transcends time, and I want to be a part of affection that lasts a lifetime.

High school sweethearts, my parents married the day after they graduated college. Dad went to work for his father on the ranch while Mom used her degree in accounting and finance to manage LaCroix Industries.

Right after their kiss, Dad reaches over and covers Mom's hand. It's another of their tender and sweet touches; a love language only they share.

That's definitely what I want.

Unlike me and Booker, who are constantly at odds, in the twenty-five years since I was born, I've never seen my parents argue.

Never.

Not once.

"Colton." Dad says hello, and so much more, in a minimum number of words. It's more of an acknowledgment than a greeting. "Good to see you."

Dad's not a talker.

"Thanks for getting us." Colton readjusts his seat. Brutus doesn't give a man his height much legroom in the back, but he squeezes in.

"I saw a helicopter in the distance …" Dad won't ask. To him, it's a waste of words because the question's implied. He's worried about his sons.

"Friends of Izzy. Her employers sent a team to protect her. They're called Guardians."

"Good to know." Without another word, Dad steps on the gas and yanks on the wheel. We execute a tight turn and race back the way he came.

"I was out with the crew when you called, I took the helicopter. Unfortunately, they're several minutes behind me."

He would've flown the helicopter to us, but it's a Scout Aero with only three seats abreast. Not enough room for the four of us, unlike Brutus.

"With the Guardians, we should have all the help we need." Colton places the butt of his weapon on the tip of his boot and gives me a look. "Right, Izzy?"

It doesn't escape my notice, Dad's yet to say anything to me, and I don't know what to make of that.

Not that he's upset with me. He's angry his family's in danger, but he doesn't blame me. My father would never do such a thing.

Not acknowledging me, however, only tells me how deep his fear runs. He's famous for bottling up his emotions, and he's doing that now.

I wish I shared that quality. My mouth gets me into more situations than I'm willing to admit, and my emotions often spill over into what I say.

We take the road to the drill site in relative silence. Rock and gravel crunch beneath the tires. Overhead, a hawk calls out. A pair of buzzards fly in a spiral, high in the sky, sniffing out something dead.

Since we move at a good clip, there's plenty of wind to take the edge off the building heat.

I sit in the back of Brutus with Colton, staring out at the land I grew up on. I miss this place. I miss my family, but it no longer feels like home.

Isn't that weird?

As for where home might be, I'm at a loss. It might be with the Guardians in California, if I stay with them. Or it might be back with Doctors Without Borders, traveling the world and bringing health care to those without.

Despite what happened in Nicaragua, I don't blame any of that on the relief agency. They do good work in the world, and I like being a part of something bigger than myself.

Maybe that's why Leighton, Texas, no longer feels like home.

There's no place for me here.

My brothers will work the land, manage the cattle, and monitor the drilling. That doesn't leave anything for me.

"Looks like my team made it back. Although, I'm glad we don't need them." The tone of his voice is one of profound relief.

So much for keeping his emotions bottled up.

Mom grips her cellphone, clutching it in her lap. The moment we're out of the Razor, she puts it to her ear.

Colton climbs out and stretches, lifting his arms high overhead then touching his toes. His hands go to the small of his back as he twists side to side.

The moment I climb out of Brutus, Dad grabs me and pulls me tight to his chest.

He says nothing.

Not. A. Word.

But he folds me into a massive bear of a hug and holds me for what seems like forever.

I wrap my arms around his waist and hug him right back, tighter and fiercer than he holds me.

He kisses the crown of my head, an expression of the deepest love, then hugs me tight again.

Mom's got Gareth on the phone, and snippets of their conversation reach our ears.

"We're good, Mom. No one's hurt."

Gareth's comment brings a smile to Mom's face, and if I'm not mistaken, she wipes a tear from the corner of her eye.

"The Guardians took care of the men. We changed out both rear tires and will be there in a few minutes."

"Can't wait to see you." Mom blows out a deep breath.

She turns to the rest of us and has the brightest smile on her face. Her next words are directed to us, or rather, my father. "Our boys are safe."

And daughter.

I almost want to add that. It's not uncommon for the only daughter of the LaCroix family to be left out, but I'm not willing to tempt fate.

No one would be in danger if not for me.

"Come on. Let's get everyone inside. I'll let the men know they can get back to work."

Drilling Station Ten is a misnomer. There's no actual drilling at the station.

Scattered around the three-thousand-acre ranch are upwards of three hundred plus oil pumps. Each drilling station manages twenty to thirty drills scattered around the ranch. Cyclone fencing encircles each drill, keeping cattle, coyotes, and humans away from the actual drills.

That fencing is electrified, further discouraging any attempts of unauthorized humans trying to get in, and it does a pretty good job of keeping the cattle away too. It doesn't take long for them to learn to give the fencing a wide berth.

Coyotes learn that too.

Rabbits, mice, and other small mammals are another matter. They aren't as smart as the cattle. It's not uncommon for them to get ensnared in the fencing and electrocuted.

Or maybe they are?

Smart, that is.

I remember finding more than one rabbit warren and mice colony safely ensconced inside the wire. Since the wire keeps out their predators, it's probably a safe place to build a home. But it comes with peril.

Every time they leave the safety of the fence, they risk electrocution going out and coming back in. Hard price to pay for a bit of safety.

Life is tough in the wild.

"It's nice to have you home, Izzy." Dad takes my rifle from me, putting it on the back rack on Brutus, then he drapes his arm over my shoulder and guides me across the gravel parking lot.

Mom and Colton follow a few steps behind us.

"It's good to be home."

"You sure about that?" He gives me a look; one I've never seen before.

"Of course, I'm sure. Why would you say something like that?"

"Because, my dearest, and favorite daughter, you're a wanderer at heart."

"I'm your only daughter." I tap him playfully on his chest.

It's a running joke in the family that I'm his favorite daughter. Took me until I was ten to figure out that didn't mean his favorite child.

My parents never play favorites with their children. We're all equally loved, but it was embarrassing when I finally figured out the joke.

Dad drops his arm from around my shoulder to open the door of the steel building that is Drilling Station Ten.

Inside are bunks for five men, a kitchen, rec room, and of course, the heart of the drilling operations; a massive bank of computers controlling everything.

The door swings out.

I cross the threshold and pull up short with a gasp.

Five men, who I know well, are on their knees.

Charlie Tompkins, Sam Hodges, Tom McBride, Bruce Ackles, and Fred Asher kneel with their hands tied behind their backs and guns trained on them.

Fury bunches their shoulders. Anger speeds their breaths, but they've been subdued and are no threat to the two gunmen.

Those men look up as I enter.

Fred Asher suddenly lunges forward, trying to knock down one of the men.

Instead, his temple meets the solid steel of the pistol, knocking him out cold. Bruce tries to do the same to the other man, but the second gunman is faster.

Bruce is clocked over the head with the butt of the weapon by the second man and slumps to the ground. Blood oozes from the cut while I stifle a scream.

After taking Fred out, the first man swings his pistol in my direction and aims it directly at my heart.

Dad halts behind me and grabs the back of my jeans. He's about to yank me out of there, but the gunman fires a shot right over our heads.

The air pulses with the concussive report, making my ears ring and my lungs seize.

Hands up, we shuffle inside, but Dad keeps the doorway blocked, ensuring Mom and Colton remain out of sight.

Dad takes a step inside and lets the door slam shut behind him —closing us in.

At least Colton and Mom remain outside where they're safe, and there's no way they missed the gunshot.

Colton's smart. He'll figure out something.

The gunman trains his weapon back on me. His menacing expression makes my blood run cold. The ferocity in his eyes is like staring death in the face. He's fierce with wavy, dark hair and soulless, black eyes.

In dirty trousers and a sweat-stained T-shirt, his foul stench permeates the air and reaches for me from across the room. Those malevolent eyes latch on to me and send chills shooting down my spine. My entire body shivers.

"You must be the *senorita* we've been sent to find." An evil grin twists his face into something truly terrifying.

The thick accent is familiar to my ear. No reason to guess. This man is from Nicaragua, and I know exactly what he wants.

Will this nightmare never end?

"Come, *senorita*. It is time to go." He gestures with the gun—as if I'll follow happily in line and surrender my freedom, and likely my life.

"I'm not going anywhere with you. Your men outside failed, and you're outnumbered."

His dark gaze twists back to the five men, two of whom are out cold while the rest remain on their knees.

"Is that what you think? That we're outnumbered?" He shoots Charlie Tompkins in the chest.

Charlie's body jerks, then slumps.

"No!" I take a step forward, hand reaching for a man I adopted as my uncle when I was three.

Charlie always greeted me with smiles when I was a little girl. He never minded when I joined my dad on the ranch, letting me ride on his shoulders more often than not.

I know all those men. They're close, like family, and it twists my guts seeing them hurt because of me.

Dad grabs my upper arm and pulls me back.

Tears stream down my face, thinking Charlie's dead, but his body jerks.

Thank God, he's still alive.

"My daughter's right. Your men are down, and we have more on the way. There's no way you're getting out of here, and there's no way you're taking my daughter."

The man's eyes narrow as fury bunches his brow. If we're not careful, he'll murder us all.

I yank the leather thong with the rabbit's foot out from under my shirt.

"Is this what you want? Take it. Take it back to your boss. Leave me and my family alone."

Charlie groans. Sam Hodges shifts to help his friend, but what can he do with his hands tied behind his back?

"Yes. We want that, too, but you are the one I was sent to find."

"What?" I take a step back, backing into the solid wall that is my father.

"You're not taking my daughter anywhere." My dad pushes me to the side and steps in front of me.

Protecting me.

The man aims his weapon at Sam's head. "Do you really want your friends to die?"

"Don't shoot them." I try to step out from behind my father's protection, but he pushes me behind him again.

"Then come here, *senorita*. I'm tired of waiting."

I do the bravest thing I've ever done. I shake off my father's protective grip and step forward.

"If you want me, let them go."

"Or, I could shoot them." His lips twist into a snarl.

"Do that, and you'll never have me." My heart lodges somewhere in my throat, making it difficult to think, let alone speak.

"Izzy …" My father's warning isn't lost on me.

"It's okay." I place a hand on his chest, turning so I can see him. "Booker will find me."

I don't know how.

I refused the very thing which would help in a situation like this, but he will find me.

The stranger's attention shifts to the second man. "Call the others."

The second man fishes into his pocket and pulls out a radio. It squawks for a moment, then the man speaks into it in Spanish too rapid to follow.

A garbled reply comes back in English.

"I'm going to fucking kill you."

My heart nearly stops because that's Booker's voice.

The gunmen glance at each other, only now realizing the truth.

Which makes me cocky.

"That's right. All your men are down, and you've got a team of special ops Guardians on their way."

His lids pull back at that comment.

That's right, asshole. Game. Set. Match.

"Who flies the helicopter outside?" He watches us closely.

Dad says nothing, but he must've twitched, because the gunman's gaze narrows in victory.

"You fly it?" He doesn't wait for my dad to answer. "You fly us. Or we kill your friends."

"I'm not flying you out of here, and you bet your ass I'm not letting you take my daughter."

Unlike me, my father's voice is stone cold and solid.

"Really?" The man moves too fast to follow, but the report from his gun makes my ears ring.

Sam crumples beside Charlie.

I scream, then wring my hands in front of me.

"We can't … You have to …" I tug on Dad's arm, frantic and fearful for our friends.

"I'm not …" He bites out the words, but I can't let his heroism lead to the deaths of men I basically grew up around.

I wouldn't be able to live with myself.

"He's going to kill them all." My gut churns, and my heart's off at the races, pounding inside my chest at breakneck speed.

"But, Izzy …"

"The Guardians will find me." I lower my voice to a whisper. "*Booker* … Will. Find. Me. You have to trust me."

"I love you, baby girl." He grabs my shoulder and pulls me close, folding me into his arms. "And I trust you." The words spill out of him, coated in defeat. "But you're ripping out my heart."

"There's no other choice." I look at Tom, Fred, Bruce, Charlie, and Sam. "We can't let him kill them."

"You're wasting time." The gunman shifts his gun to Tom McBride. This time, he presses the barrel of his weapon to Tom's forehead.

His friend shifts on his feet, eyes darting left then right. He's antsy and trigger happy. If we don't deescalate this soon, we'll lose more men, but if we stall long enough, the Guardians will be here.

Hopefully, Dad's thinking the same thing.

"We go now." The gunman waves his pistol, finger on the trigger rather than the trigger guard. If he flinches, the gun is likely to go off.

I wish the helicopter was out the way we came, but it's parked behind the building.

"Matias?" The second man's anxiety spikes.

"We have to go." I pull on my dad's arm, urging him not to waste more time.

His face is wiped of expression. Those emotions of his are buried deep inside. Dad gives a sharp nod.

"The helicopter is this way." He takes my hand and leads me past the dining area, through the rec room, and down the long hall lined with the sleep rooms to a door leading outside.

The two gunmen follow, leaving Tom and the others to do what they can for Sam and Charlie.

The moment I open the door, heat slams into me with physical force. I stagger and shade my eyes from the noonday sun.

What little breeze we had before abandoned us.

I kick up dust walking toward the helicopter, trying to do anything to delay.

Dad glances left, then right, looking, I hope, for Colton or Mom. He, too, moves slowly.

We drag our feet.

A shot rings out from behind us.

The second man goes down with a shot to his knee.

But that distracts me. I should've run. I should've done anything other than stand still and watch the man's leg give out.

Matias grabs me, placing his gun to my temple.

"One more shot and she dies." Matias glares at my father. "Get in the helicopter or watch while I put a bullet in her head. Her blood will be on your hands."

Fear courses through me. I gag and cough, unable to draw breath as Matias drags me toward the helicopter.

All of a sudden, our pace picks up. I'm herded toward the helicopter.

The second gunman limps behind us, dragging his injured leg.

Dad climbs inside the helicopter. The moment he does, the gunman forces me inside. He looks to my father.

"Do not be a hero. *¿Comprende?*"

Dad's jaw bunches as he grinds his teeth together.

"Matias?" The second man takes a look at the number of seats —there's only three—and completes the simple math in his head. His eyes widen, but he's not quick enough.

Matias shoots him between the eyes, killing him instantly. Then he turns his weapon back on me.

"No funny business, señor. Do not stall. You fly now."

"And where are we going? This thing has limited range."

"Across the border."

"I can't do that, there are rules …"

"I don't care about rules. Fly. If you don't, I will kill the *senorita*, and then I will kill you."

Blood rushes past my ears, pounding with fear. My entire body quakes.

My fingers shake.

My lips tremble.

A hollowness fills my chest, despite the beating of my heart.

It's the feeling of despair.

Dad completes the preflight checklist in record time and spins up the rotors.

How long until Booker arrives?

Where are the Guardians?

As I ask these questions, a dust plume rises not more than a few hundred yards away.

Hope rises within me, even though I know they're too far.

They won't make it in time.

I reach for Dad's leg, placing my hand on his thigh. I need that connection, or I'll go out of my mind with fear.

The one thing Matias does not do is take the stinking rabbit's foot from me. The despicable thing still hangs around my neck.

With a grimace, my father places his hand over mine. The gentle pressure helps to ease my fear, but this is a one-way trip.

I feel it in my bones.

Now, all I have to do is make sure my father gets out alive. Matias is a killer with no compunction about who he kills, friend or foe.

The body of the other gunman sprawls on the ground, emphasizing my fears. What an elegant solution to too many people and not enough seats. Matias killed his partner without blinking.

Cold, brutal, and efficient.

That man's dead, and we will be too if Dad doesn't take off.

With the Guardians racing toward us in Gareth's truck, Dad lifts us into the air.

They miss us by seconds. As I look down, Booker squats in the back of the truck, weapon trained on the helicopter. Two others from Bravo do exactly the same.

But they don't take the shot.

My gaze locks with Booker, connecting us across the distance.

In Booker's expression, I feel every emotion under the sun, but the one that's the strongest is rage. Beneath that lies another emotion, one I'm too scared to admit.

But I feel it too.

I feel it despite all our fights and all the words spoken in anger.

I feel it deep inside, where I will treasure it until I die.

I feel the desperation of a love never expressed.

Not able to bear the flood of emotions running through me, I squeeze my eyes shut and say goodbye to my mother, goodbye to my brothers, but most importantly, I say goodbye to Booker.

The Guardians are a fierce organization, capable of many things, but what they're not capable of is rescuing me.

Even so, Booker will come for me.

That's what I fear the most.

I fear he'll sacrifice his life to save mine, and I'm not worthy of that kind of love.

FIFTEEN

Booker

Gareth LaCroix, Isabelle's eldest brother, comes to a skidding halt at the building.

Two minutes too late.

My teeth grind in frustration while the helicopter carrying Isabelle lifts off.

While it dwindles in size.

While it heads south—away from me.

I exercise my extensive vocabulary of curse words.

Zeb and Alec give me a look. In that brief nonverbal exchange, they vow to do whatever it takes to help me get her back.

Brady radios back a status update, letting Guardian HQ know what happened. Not that they don't already.

Smaug is in the air, tracking the whole damn thing.

The moment we stop, I'm up and out of the truck. Our three *passengers* groan and leak blood all over the back of the truck.

Don't fucking care.

They deserve it.

A woman comes over to greet us with a rifle slung over her shoulder. She wears it like she's used to the heavy thing, and she's the spitting image of my Isabelle.

"You must be Booker?" She sticks out her hand while my brows tug together.

"How did you know?"

"Any man who looks at my daughter, the way you did when she was being taken, tells me everything I need to know."

"It's nice to meet you, ma'am."

"Likewise." She gestures toward the building. "We have wounded we need to take care of before we do anything else."

Like chase after Isabelle and the dead man who took her?

He signed his death warrant the moment he laid hands on my woman.

While every instinct within me demands I go after Isabelle, I'm not immune to the needs of the wounded. I'm both a warrior and a healer. The healing side of me balances out the warrior side. I figure when it's time to weigh the balance of my scales, I'll come out on the right side.

"I'm a medic. Let me help."

I follow her inside and immediately go to work on the wounded while Brady and the others figure out our next steps.

Two LaCroix employees are shot in the chest, but still alive. I do a quick primary and secondary survey while Isabelle's mom grabs a first aid kit.

"Have you called 911?" I call out to Mrs. LaCroix over my shoulder as I take a closer look at the wounded men.

Two of the men are merely knocked out with a blow to the head. Two others are shot. Those are the ones I tend to first. A fifth man appears uninjured.

"Tom, what happened?" One of Isabelle's brothers, the youngest and only one I've yet to meet, cuts the Zip ties around Tom's wrists.

"We were with your dad when he got the call. Jumped in the truck quick as we could while he flew the helicopter. When we got here, your dad was gone. Took the Razor to get the others. When we walked into the building, two men jumped us. Tied us up, and you see the rest." The man looks at me. "Who are you?"

"Name's Booker. Tell me what happened to them?" I point to the four wounded men.

"That crazy bastard clocked Fred and Bruce in the head. Then he shot Charlie and Sam in the chest."

Isabelle's mother returns with the first aid kit. I expect something small and unhelpful, but am surprised by the full medical pack she has slung over her shoulder. She tosses the pack on the ground and opens it like a pro.

"What do you need?" She looks at me with complete focus, and I get she's a no-nonsense kind of woman.

"Wraps and bandages. The bullet went right through …" I point to one of the men, not knowing who's who.

"That's Charlie Tompkins." Tom makes the introductions. "Sam Hodges is the other."

"Well, the bullet lodged in Sam's chest. He's not bleeding as much as your other friend, but we can't move him until a team gets here."

"Why's that?"

"The bullet could shift, and if it's near an artery …" No need to finish that sentence. It's self-explanatory. "Tom, come help me out."

Over the next ten minutes, I do what I can to stabilize the two men. Then my attention shifts to the others.

They rouse easily. My cursory exam reveals no evidence of skull fracture. As to what might lie beneath, that's way beyond my skills.

"I've got this." Mrs. LaCroix squats beside Charlie Tompkins. She gestures toward the door. "Your team is outside, if you want to rejoin them."

"I think I will. Thanks, ma'am."

"No problem, and, Booker?"

"Yes, ma'am?"

"Izzy promised me you would find her. I'm counting on you to fulfill that promise."

"I'll move heaven and earth to find her, ma'am. You can count on that."

"Thank you."

With one last check on the wounded, I move to rejoin my team.

Outside, I shake hands with Jude and Parker, making more formal introductions than before. The one from inside joins us and thrusts out his hand.

"I'm Colton. I take it you're Izzy's man?"

"Not sure she would agree with that statement, but I'm Booker." I scratch the back of my head. Why does Isabelle's family seem to think we're a thing?

Isabelle and I are far from a couple. We're a rolling verbal barrage at best.

Fire burns in my belly knowing she's more at risk now than a few moments ago. It feels as if I'm always a step behind. One of these days, that'll be one step too many.

Rafe and Zeb lean casually against Gareth's truck while Alec and Hayes guard our three passengers. I go over there, feeling an obligation to see to their wounds, even if I'd rather watch them bleed out.

Fuckers went after my girl and don't deserve to live.

"What's our status?" I close in on Brady.

He looks up and waves me over.

"Better than you'd think."

"Considering I think this is one massive clusterfuck, I'd say things couldn't get much worse."

Isabelle's brothers make no bones about joining our briefing. Bravo team makes room to include them as Brady debriefs us.

"I know it looks bad." The look Brady gives me says to keep my mouth shut and let him continue.

There's no problem with that. My rage isn't controlled, but I channel it in a positive direction.

From now until she's found, every breath I take, every step I make, it will be in pursuit of rescuing Isabelle.

"We've got great leads," Brady continues.

"How's that?" Gareth speaks up.

"Because Mitzy's working her magic."

"Who's that?" Colton scrunches his brow.

"She's our technical lead." I jump in, filling the gaps, then turn my attention back to Brady. "What is she cooking up?"

"Facial recognition." Brady gestures to the truck with our three prisoners on board.

"I don't understand," Gareth pops in again, too eager to do something.

I understand that urge. It washes through me with a vengeance. I also know that sometimes the best next step isn't to do something but rather to do nothing.

I call it getting our ducks in a row. That comes from good intelligence and thorough planning.

There's nothing we can do for Isabelle and her father right now. But we can regroup, strategize, and plan. With Mitzy on the job, that step's already in motion.

"I'll explain …" Brady takes back the conversation. "She's using facial recognition to figure out who these men are …"

"How does that help?" Frustration rims Gareth's eagerness.

I like the guy. I like the way he takes care of his own. That's something I respect.

And I know exactly what Mitzy's doing.

"She's using facial recognition to not only identify these assholes but to trace back their steps until she finds something we can act upon."

And one of those steps will be to identify the man who kidnapped her.

"Is there security on this building?" Brady addresses his question to Gareth.

"There is." He points to the corner of the building as well as to the telephone poles that supply power to the building.

"How is it accessed?" Brady asks.

"We have an app …" Gareth withdraws his phone and lifts it. He taps the screen and brings up the feed.

"We need you to give access to our tech team." Before Gareth can interrupt him again, Brady pushes on. "Hopefully, he gave us what we need."

"And we'll track him that way." I nod, seeing the brilliance of Mitzy's plan.

"How does that help us?" Jude, the taller of the twin brothers, speaks up.

"Easy." The massive grin on my face isn't going away anytime soon. "I know exactly what Mitzy's doing."

"Care to share?" Gareth leans back and crosses his arms over his broad chest.

"The man took Isabelle." I want to see if anyone else comes to the same conclusion. If so, then I'm on the right track.

"Exactly." Rafe nods.

"Holy shit. You're right," Zeb joins in.

"Do y'all mind telling the rest of us what the fuck you're thinking?" The agitation in Colton's voice rises.

The looks he exchanges with his brothers say they all share the same thought.

I hold out a hand.

"We thought they came to retrieve the rabbit's foot. Its twin, the one Angie was given, holds millions in diamonds. We assume the same goes for the rabbit's foot Isabelle has."

"I looked at that thing and didn't see any secret compartment holding diamonds." Colton's irritation wains. He's beginning to see what I see.

"If all he wanted was the diamonds …" Rafe says, "he would've taken it from Izzy and that would've been the end of it."

"But he took Isabelle," I jump in. "That means, she is his target, not the rabbit's foot."

"But that makes no sense." Gareth isn't convinced. "What would she know? She's a pharmacist. It doesn't add up."

"It says a shit-ton." Brady wrangles the conversation back to his lead. "It means something else is in play. We're missing something vital. Right now, our objective is to head back to where we left the others and send their faces to our technical team. Mitzy and the others will chew through what they can, backtracking their movements as only they can …"

"Until they converge," Gareth finally gets it. "That's fucking crazy, but I see how it could be done. If you have the right tech."

"We have the right tech *and* the best minds on the planet," Brady speaks with pride, and for good reason.

"Booker, take Rafe, Hayes, and Alec with you. Gareth, I'll need you to take them back. Zeb, you stay with me, guard the three we've got." He glances around. "We've got ambulances on the way and local authorities. I'll deal with them. If you can, bring the wounded back. It'll make things easier."

"And while we're gone?" I arch a brow.

"While you're gone, Zeb and I are going to have a nice long chat with our newest best friends." Anger surges in and out of Brady's voice.

I get his anger. After rescuing Angie and Isabelle from the *Coralos* cartel, he's furious Isabelle's back in peril.

He mentioned briefly how he feels about Isabelle. It's not the same as me, but he's protective of her, like a brother would be.

Rafe lifts his AR-15. "Hell, I'm ready. Let's go."

"We should take two trucks." Gareth glances at his brothers. "That way, if we run into any resistance …"

"Good call." Brady acknowledges Gareth's insight. "Booker, split your team between the two vehicles." He turns his attention to the twins. "Which of you want to go with them?"

All three brothers raise their hands, but Brady shakes his head.

"Colton, we don't know how long before the authorities arrive, but you're the only one who can tell them what happened here."

"Mom can. She was with me. To be honest, you won't be able to stop me from going." Retribution and revenge spark in his eyes.

"Fine. That'll do." Brady swings his gaze to the twins. "You two want to flip for it?"

Parker looks to Jude and shrugs. "Your call, bro."

"I'll go with. You can stay and help them interrogate the prisoners."

"Works for me." Parker shoves his hands into his pockets and stares at the dirt.

Damn, but Isabelle has an amazing family. From her brothers to her mother, I have nothing but respect for the way they come together in a crisis.

Not all families are like that.

"Then it's a plan. The seven of you load up, and Gareth …"

"Yes?" Gareth turns his stormy eyes on Brady.

"Booker's in charge. Leave the handling of the wounded to my team. Follow his orders. Don't fuck up and be a hero. We're trained for this and know what to look for. That's not saying you don't, it's just saying we're far more experienced with this kind of shit, and my men are protected with armor, whereas you and your brothers aren't."

"Can't say I like it, but message received. We'll help as we're told." Gareth grudgingly gives in.

My respect only grows.

This isn't the time to be measuring the size of our dicks. Gareth is man enough to understand and strong enough to set his ego to the side.

I'm going to like this man.

"Once we're done here," Brady continues, "we'll need to return to Guardian HQ and prep."

"And what about us?" Colton asks. "Are we just supposed to sit and wait?"

"If you want to see your sister again, that's exactly what you'll do. Not casting any shade on you. You and your brothers know how to handle yourselves, but we're experts in hostage rescue, and you don't want to go where we're going, or do what we'll have to do."

Brady's words sink in, not just for Colton, but for all the brothers.

Taking another man's life leaves a mark on your soul.

We're warriors, trained to do whatever it takes. We've stared into the mirror and come to terms with what that means for us.

Brady's sparing Isabelle's brothers from having to face that darkness. Fortunately, they're wise enough to grasp the message.

There's an overall lessening of tension among us all. We can't chase off after Isabelle, but there are actionable steps that get us one step closer.

We split up. My group loads up into Gareth's truck and the

truck belonging to their men. Brady and Zeb head over to the back of the truck and the three men inside.

I sit in the front with Gareth, while Colton slides into the rear with Alec. Jude, Rafe, and Hayes pile into the other vehicle.

"We left nine men behind. They're wounded, but not incapacitated. Drop us on the other side of that gulley. My men will go in and ensure it's safe. Once I let you know, you and your brother can drive around to that spot you said you were going to cross at. You meet us there, and we'll load up."

"Sounds like a plan." Gareth's grip on the steering wheel tightens. "Do you really think you'll bring our sister home?"

"I will, or die trying."

The corner of Gareth's mouth bounces with a smile.

"I like you, but as Izzy's eldest brother, I'm obliged to say that if you ever hurt her, we're all coming for you."

I tilt my head back and laugh. "I wouldn't have it any other way."

It's a short drive back to the gulley but takes a few minutes longer as we're not racing at breakneck speed like before.

During that drive, I chew on everything we've learned.

The diamonds are only a piece of the puzzle. The capture of Isabelle's medical team by the *Coralos* cartel is another piece, but we're missing the bigger picture. What that might be, I don't know. Right now, I don't give a damn.

All I care about is that Isabelle is of value to whoever took her. I hope she realizes her value. They'll fuck with her, but they won't kill her.

Not until they get whatever it is they want out of her.

Hang on, Isabelle. I'm coming for you.

SIXTEEN

Izzy

"I can't fly over the border." Dad holds the controls in a death grip.

"You will." Matias's deep voice sounds like a growl, and within it lies a life-or-death threat.

"There are …" My father's doing what he can to save me.

Only, it's too late for that.

"*Senor,* I don't care. Fly."

"Where?"

"Over the border, *gringo.*"

My father's frustration is a palpable thing. He grits his teeth and heads due south. I keep one hand in my lap and the other on my father's thigh.

The touch grounds me.

"They will stop us." Dad doesn't give up. "Local authorities will be there when we land."

"The authorities?" Matias's laughter reminds me of a barking dog—harsh and feral.

"They won't stop an American helicopter. They only care about illegals coming over the border, and we're not landing at the airport."

Dad doesn't respond, and I stay quiet as I can, meek as a mouse, but my mind spins with ideas.

Since I opted out of the tracker, how can I let Booker know where I'm being taken?

There's my phone. I have that. By now, Booker's alerted Guardian HQ. No doubt they're already tracking me.

But if I lose the phone?

This is the tricky part.

What then?

Since there's nothing for me to do other than sit quietly between my father and Matias, I work on possibilities. I figure it's best to think ahead rather than figure things out on the fly.

When Dad climbs, gaining altitude, our unwanted guest jabs me in the ribs with his gun.

"No, *señor.* We fly low, under the radar. I know what you're doing, but no sneaky business."

The grinding of my father's molars against each other sends a spine-tingling shiver down my back. The stench of my captor is so foul it coats my tongue and floods my nasal passages. I turn toward my father, not that it helps in the cramped cockpit.

The Scout Aero is designed to fit three, but it's a snug fit. My father is a large man and Matias, although several inches shorter than my father, is big-boned and overweight.

I keep my hand on my father's leg, needing the physical connection, but it ends far too soon.

Leighton, Texas, is one of scores of border towns strung all along the US-Mexico border. The only thing separating the two countries is the majestic Rio Grande.

Within ten minutes, we cross that boundary. As soon as we do, Matias scans the ground, looking for something only he knows.

Dad continues south, ignoring the squawking coming through his communications panel. Despite flying low, it's impossible to avoid the ground radar.

Border agents take note of our illegal entry into Mexico. I can only hope they intervene. People will be sent out to investigate. The only question is will it be in time?

"There." Matias points at the ground.

I look between my feet where the floor of the helicopter is made of see-through panels, a necessity for helicopter pilots when they land, and see nothing but dry ground, roads, and a smattering of tent stalls.

It looks like an open-air market.

A riot of colors dots the ground, each one representing a booth where locals trade with eager tourists searching for the best bargain.

"I can't land in the middle of that." Dad gives a shake of his head.

"You will." Matias's tone brooks no nonsense.

"If I do, we all die." He gestures below us. "See the wires? Those will make us crash."

"Then over there." Matias points to a dirt lot just opposite the market.

Unfortunately, there are no wires impeding our descent. I know because I check for them. Some small part of me prays there is no place for us to land and that we have to turn around and go back.

But that is not the case.

Dad angles down and descends. The rotors kick up dust, sending it outward in a whirlwind.

The moment the skids touch down, Matias unlatches the door and pushes it open. He grabs my arm, practically dragging me out of the helicopter as I try desperately to grab hold of my father.

If I could just get free, Dad can take off, and we'll be rid of Matias.

But that isn't what happens.

With the downdraft of the rotor whipping sand and dust into my eyes and mouth, I squeeze my eyes closed and let Matias take me where he will.

He forces me into a loping jog and jambs the barrel of his gun against my ribs.

We head toward the road and a long line of parked cars.

"Scream and I kill you. After I kill you, I will shoot your father, then I will go to your home and kill your family. You do not want to test me."

His words keep me from doing just that.

He yanks me from car to car until he finds one that's unlocked with the keys dangling from the ignition.

Opening up the driver and rear passenger doors, he forces me into the driver's seat. Keeping his weapon trained on me, he slides in behind me.

"Drive!"

I'm not used to actual keys, which makes me fumble for what to do with the key. My mind desperately tries to think of a way out of this, but there is no escape.

Across the way, my father sits in the helicopter, his face a mask of rage and desperation. He's probably trying to decide what he can and can't do.

It's hopeless. That's all I can say.

"Do not make me hurt you, *puta.*" His threat turns my blood to ice. "I've been told to deliver you alive, but not undamaged."

Undamaged?

Holy hell, do I want to go down the path of what that might mean?

No.

Most definitely not.

When we stop at a traffic light, sirens sound in the distance. Most likely, those are local officials sent to arrest my father for his unauthorized crossing.

The moment the light turns green, two police vehicles blow through the intersection. I ease on the gas, feeling desperation within me grow.

But that's when I see a tiny box beneath the traffic signal.

I don't know how much is similar between the United States and Mexico, but I bet some of their infrastructure is the same. That means traffic cams.

Traffic cams mean other cameras recording the comings and goings of civilians at gas stations, ATMs, parking lots, and almost anywhere.

If I can get my face out there, Guardian HQ will find me.

I blow out a deep breath. As long as I have my phone, they can track me. When I lose that, there is another way, but I need to be smart about it.

"Where am I going?"

"I will tell you." Matias leans back, but if I think he relaxes his guard, he doesn't.

That gun of his sits rock steady in his lap, and it's trained on me. Following his directions, we wind through the city, heading South. With no air conditioning, sweat beads my brow. When I roll the window down, Matias surges forward, pressing the gun to my neck.

"Roll it up."

"But it's hot."

"Roll it up." The gun presses harder against my neck.

His directions make little sense to me, except that they take me farther from my father and the border.

"Pull in here." Matias taps the side of the headrest, ordering me to stop.

We're at a complex of buildings, a shopping center for the locals.

"Pull into that spot."

I do exactly as I'm told.

He opens his door. As he climbs out, the gun stays trained on me.

For some reason, my heart ramps up, banging around like a kettle drum. Once Matias is out, he opens my door, grabs my arm, and hauls me out of the vehicle.

"Open that mouth of yours and it will be the last thing you do." His malevolent gaze sends tendrils of fear shooting through me.

"But …" The press of cold steel against the small of my back forces my mouth closed.

What are we doing here?

That's the question I want to ask, but it soon becomes obvious when he peers inside the windows of the parked cars.

We walk up and down two rows before he finds what he wants. It's yet another vehicle where the owner left the keys inside.

He forces me inside.

He forces me to drive.

We repeat that seven more times over the next day and a half.

I know what he's doing. He's trying to throw off anyone who might be following us.

Fortunately, I still have my cell phone. I cling to that with all my hope. Booker's words come back to me, over and over again. If I have my phone, he can find me.

Unfortunately, sometime between hour thirty-eight and forty of our drive south, the battery dies.

It's nearly enough to break me.

Just north of the Nicaraguan border, Matias forces me out of a beat-up station wagon and into the back of a van.

The back.

Something inside of me dies because he no longer needs me to drive. We're met by two men and they lock me inside a modified freezer with a small breathing hole drilled into the bottom.

With fear coiling within me, growing bigger as the minutes pass, we enter Nicaragua.

I'm back where it all began, and I'm terrified.

SEVENTEEN

Booker

"WHAT DO YOU MEAN, IT STOPPED?" I PACE IN AND AROUND THE rows of computer terminals, glancing at the screens, not really knowing what I'm looking at.

Which is fine. I don't need to know what's on the screen. I just need Mitzy's staff to hurry the fuck up and find Isabelle already.

My fingers clench and tighten into fists made impotent by lack of data, and my feet are wearing the carpet thin as I make a circuit of the room.

In the back, I pass CJ and Sam. They seem to have taken up residence and lounge on a pair of folding chairs propped up against the wall.

I grimace as I pass, letting them know exactly what I think about all the fucking waiting and spinning our wheels.

Out there, Isabelle's all alone, kidnapped by a lunatic who shot one of his own men rather than let him get captured like the others.

This waiting game, collecting intelligence, is nothing short of torture.

I need action.

I need to go after my woman.

I need Isabelle safe in my arms.

Halfway back to the front of the room, I reengage with Mitzy.

"It means …" She looks up from the terminal, which currently occupies her attention and gives me the eye.

She's about to shoot back something snarky.

I'm totally not in the mood for snark.

Have at me, Mitzy. Give me a reason …

Maybe she senses my mood because her eyes soften along with her tone.

"It means the battery's drained, but don't worry. We're still working it from the other end."

The moment she tells me what I already know, Isabelle's phone battery is dead, it's like getting kicked in the gut by a mule. Takes the wind right out of me, leaving me gasping.

But Mitzy offers hope.

Another way …

"Do you really think that'll work?" I scrub at my hair, running my fingers through the strands.

"I'm ninety percent positive."

From a woman who lives and breathes numbers, ninety percent leaves ten too many percents hanging in the balance.

When that comes to Isabelle, that's too much left to chance.

Mitzy leans back and gives me her undivided attention, which is unheard of—Mitzy rarely pulls herself away from the screen for anyone.

It means a lot. More than I'm willing to admit. One deep breath and some of the tension drains from my body.

I'll shamelessly cling to any bit of hope.

"And the other ten percent?"

It's a question I don't need to voice. Mitzy knows exactly what's on my mind.

"Will take longer." Her attention moves back to the screen and I get the hint.

The longer I keep her from her work, the longer it'll take her to find my Isabelle.

I return to my pacing and make another circuit of the room.

I should leave her team alone. There's about a dozen of them busy working on this one project. Probably more in rooms I don't see.

They're doing something monumental. I call it crazy. Mitzy acts like it's no big deal.

From the pictures we took of the men we fought in Leighton, Texas, her team is using crazy tech to track the movements of those men—in reverse.

The main monitor, nearly the size of a small movie screen, sits at the front of the room. Displayed on it is a map of North, South, and Central America. Overlying that are thirteen red *strings*.

They're not really strings. They're more like threads of a tapestry joining those men together.

Working backward, using footage from traffic cams and other surveillance cameras that upload their data into the cloud, Mitzy and her team are backtracking each man's movement as he made his way to Leighton.

All threads converge into a red mass right over Isabelle's home.

Initially, it's a thick interwoven rope that begins to unravel across the border.

My pacing brings me back to where CJ and Sam watch the data unfold. Like me, they're eager to get Isabelle back. She may be new to the Guardians, but she's one of our own.

There's a lot of interest in getting her back.

"Booker, we're making progress." CJ tips his chair back against the wall, letting it rest on two legs. His tone is meant to calm, but it frustrates me instead.

He may run the Guardian branch of Guardian HRS, but he does that in concert with the tech and intelligence teams Mitzy oversees. In many ways, the two main branches of Guardian HRS are complexly interwoven.

"I know." A glance at the main monitor says he's right.

What CJ doesn't mention is how my scowling presence affects those in the room.

I make them nervous.

"Do we know anything substantive? It's been almost two days."

"You see what we know." Sam clears his throat. "Most of the threads that die out are from low-ranking gang members. They were brought in as a show of force but aren't otherwise associated with the *Laguta* cartel. A handful are one step up the ladder. Their trails take them directly into Nicaragua, which says they started off as a group."

A group that bastard Matias leads.

People don't understand how advanced facial recognition is these days or how ubiquitous surveillance cameras are in the environment. It's far easier than I realized to track people's movements.

Mitzy's team takes that to the next level, developing associations.

Such as whether those men are known gang members. We figured all of that out within a couple of hours. It's the four remaining men who give Mitzy's team the fits.

The trails of three men simply disappear, no longer trackable as they vanished into Nicaragua's dense rainforest.

Matias's trail, however, makes a detour to the capital city.

Those are the threads Mitzy's team focus in on.

"I'm still unclear about one thing." I lean against the wall and fold my arms across my chest.

"What's that?" CJ slouches in his chair, but only an idiot would say the man's relaxed.

"Isabelle and Angie, along with the rest of their team, were picked up by the *Coralos* cartel because the cartel thought they were using Doctors Without Borders to move weapons. We thought that meant guns. Maybe munitions."

There was that one conversation about transporting explosives in gel form and primer fuses.

"Correct." Sam rocks forward and twists his neck to look at me. "What's the question?"

"There were no guns."

We all know this.

"And no munitions." CJ drags his hand down his chin.

"I didn't know that had been confirmed. We talked about the

possibility, tossing ideas around, but we didn't have proof." I kick off the wall, ready for another round of pacing, but Sam surprises me.

"We got the answer just this morning." Sam kicks a heel over his opposite knee and leans back in his chair. "Forest had his CIA contacts look into the medical gear left behind."

"Left?" My brows bunch. "I thought the *Coralos* cartel took all the gear?"

"We thought the same. They rifled through it, but they didn't take it. They left it on the side of the road. Of course, the villagers pilfered what they could. Gave our CIA friends a run for their money tracking it all down, but they managed. When they tested it for explosive residue, they found nothing."

"Then I don't get it. Why would they think Isabelle's team was moving weapons?"

"Probably misdirection by the *Laguta*." CJ's low Texan twang is barely discernible.

"How would that help?" I scrub my jaw and pull at my chin, trying to puzzle it all out.

"It's a test for one thing." Sam taps his leg.

He glances at CJ, who nods in agreement.

"Ah, I see." My fingers twitch. I hate standing around doing nothing. "You think they tossed out a juicy morsel to see what happened?"

"That's what we're thinking." Sam nods. "The CIA believes the *Laguta* cartel is sniffing out a traitor in its ranks. That misdirection was theirs."

"Were the diamonds another?" Instead of pacing around the room, I make a three-stride circuit in front of Sam and CJ.

"Possibly," Sam props his hands on his knees and gives me a look. "You mind pulling up a chair. Feels like I'm getting whiplash watching you pace."

A low growl works its way out of the back of my throat, but I grab a folded chair and shake it out.

Out of all the amazing tech gear Guardian HRS comes up with, what the fuck are three grown men doing sitting on plastic folding chairs?

Couldn't afford the metal rejects from the military?

"So, you're saying they're ferreting out a rat in their ranks?"

"That's one way to put it." CJ bounces his knee. "Feed one man information about transporting weapons. Feed another something about diamonds. See what your enemy goes after, and you've found your rat."

"Damn, that's one blood-thirsty business." I don't like the fucking chair. It's too small for my ass.

I push on my knees and get back to pacing. At least that makes me feel like I'm doing something.

"Agreed." Sam shakes his head the moment I pass back in front of him. "Back to the matter at hand." He gestures toward the main monitor. "Most of the men sent to retrieve Izzy are bottom of the barrel in terms of the power hierarchy. Nothing more than hired guns from street gangs the *Laguta* cartel contracts with to provide muscle on an as needed basis. Matias Gonzales, however, is one of their lieutenants."

"How sure are we about that?"

It makes sense. From what the men from the drilling site told us, Matias is definitely the man in charge.

"Hard to say." Mitzy joins us. She drags a folding chair with her and places it smack-dab in the middle of my path. She sits backwards and gives me a look.

When I don't respond, she puffs out a breath. Then she props her forearms on the back of the chair and places her chin over the back of her hands. With a flutter of her lashes, she grins, pleased as punch to interrupt my pacing.

"As for Matias being a lieutenant," she says, "we're going with intel provided by the CIA. It's good info, probably correct, but not vetted by my team, and not likely to be anytime soon."

"Why's that?" I spin the chair I previously sat on and straddle it the same way Mitzy straddles hers.

"Because our main priority is getting Izzy home." She rolls her eyes like that's the dumbest question she's heard all day.

"Fine." I don't let the snide comment eat at me, but I'm understandably fired up. "So, this Matias is not a minor player but rather a low-ranking leader of the *Laguta* cartel?"

"Correct." Her reply is crisp and to the point.

"Meaning they sent someone they could trust to retrieve Isabelle?"

Something about this feels off.

"Also correct." When Mitzy nods, her psychedelic hair shimmers in the light.

"Why would they do that?"

"Good question." Mitzy and CJ exchange looks. "As far as we know, Izzy is no more involved than Angie or any of the others."

"It can't be Isabelle they want." I shake my head. It makes no sense.

"I don't think it's Izzy." Mitzy leans back and stares at the ceiling.

"Then what?"

"I think it's us." She tilts her head and pins me with her gaze.

"Us?"

"Yeah. The mysterious Guardians who sent a man to rescue two women within hours of their capture. That video the *Coralos* cartel took was recorded immediately after their capture and distributed to the local news networks. They were looking for a response."

"From the *Laguta* cartel." I chime in, following Mitzy's logic.

"Exactly. They wanted to get the news out, letting the *Laguta* cartel know they captured their couriers."

CJ blows out a breath. "They were looking to start a war with their rivals. What they got instead was an organization they'd never heard of, rescuing two women right under their noses. Brady sent them on a merry chase when he rescued Angie and Izzy."

"We rescued the rest of their team." I can't help but jump in. "Not all of this tracks. There are still holes."

"Like Jerald." CJ lifts a finger, emphasizing the point.

"Exactly. They kept Jerald alive, hoping he'd lead them to the girls." I agree with CJ. "Because, why? Because Brady rescued them?"

"Maybe?" Sam tugs at his ear.

"No way to know for sure," Mitzy interjects, not convinced. "All of this is conjecture. Nothing but assumptions pulled out of thin air, and you know how I feel about assumptions." She crosses her arms and gives us all the eye.

Everyone knows what Mitzy thinks about assumptions. If it's not based in hard science or backed by solid fact, she doesn't like it.

And for good reason.

Assumptions are a good way to get killed in this business.

"But it's all we have." In this, I disagree with her philosophy. "Sometimes, you have to make assumptions. I know how men like this work. For argument's sake, let's say the *Laguta* cartel crafted a plan to ferret out a snitch. One was fed weapons. The other diamonds. Jerald was the courier for the real package, which we now know are diamonds, not weapons. He gave them to Izzy and Angie in the rabbit's feet and told them to keep it with them at all times."

"Right. It kept his hands clean." CJ rubs at his jaw. "Or it would've if Angie and Izzy weren't rescued by Brady."

"Right, but only Isabelle had her rabbit's foot on her. Angie's was in her personal backpack, which the *Coralos* cartel took when they kidnapped the team."

"Yes, but they didn't know they were looking for diamonds. They were told weapons were being smuggled instead." CJ tips his head back and closes his eyes. Like me, he's been up most of the past forty-some hours.

"I assume the diamonds would eventually be used to purchase the weapons?" I look to Sam who knows more about stuff like this.

"Most likely." Sam nods. "It's an easy way to move money."

"Just to clarify, we think Jerald was working with the *Laguta* cartel?"

"From the extent of his injuries, the *Coralos* worked him over pretty well. Hard to think he was working for them." CJ blinks forcibly and stifles a yawn.

"Mitzy, don't let this go to your head, but I agree we're making a shit-ton of assumptions."

"Don't worry, I don't need you to tell me I'm right." The way she wrinkles her nose, teasing back, makes her look even more like a mischievous pixie.

"Isabelle, though." I circle back around to what matters most to me.

To *who* matters most.

"We're working on the assumption they want her because they think what? What value does she have?"

"Well, they probably want to know who the Guardians are, for one thing." CJ doesn't look me in the eye when he says that. "Next on their list will be where the rest of their diamonds are. Izzy knows the answers to those questions."

"What about Angie? Has there been an attempt on her?" Brady will flip his shit if they come after Angie.

"Unlike Izzy, Angie is invisible to them. Untraceable. Now that Izzy's been taken, Angie's keeping a low profile and zero internet footprint. Besides Brady, who won't leave her side, we've assigned additional coverage just to be safe. But the moment Izzy flew home, she lit a beacon for anyone looking to find her. It doesn't take a tech genius to put together a search routine like that."

"I'll take your word for it." To me, it sounds pretty high tech.

"As for Izzy …" Mitzy turns back to the main screen and aims her remote at the monitor. A new picture pops up. "Clearly, Matias is good at his job. He swaps out vehicles like they're going out of style, and he didn't stop for the night."

New lines appear on the monitor; these in blue.

"Each one of these," she says, "are one of the cars he appropriated. The red line is the geo-locator on Izzy's phone. It goes out just north of the border."

And that's why this sucks as much as it does.

"What do we do now?" I can't help but slump, feeling defeated.

"Turn our attention to the other ten percent," Mitzy says. "We track Matias's routines. Extrapolate from there. Trace his digital footprint and see how he receives messages and missions. I know it looks bad, Booker, but we've still got a lot up our sleeves. I'm working on something that will make all of this unnecessary."

"What's that?"

"Using what we know of Izzy's phone; it's location, direction, and speed, we're tracking all of the phones that were in the vicinity of her phone. It's going to take some time for *Jacen* to crunch through the numbers, and deal with all that data, but if I can separate the unique signature of Matias's phone from the rest, I'm fairly confident I can use Matias's phone to find Izzy."

Jacen is Guardian HRS's resident supercomputer, and its name is a nod to HAL, the supercomputer in "2001: A Space Odyssey."

At the time when the movie was made, the screenwriters took the letters from IBM, the major player in computers of that era, and shifted one letter earlier in the alphabet. Forest Summers did the same with JCN. But since our resident supercomputer is a generation older than IBM, Forest shifted the letters the other direction.

Mitzy's words release the steel band constricting my chest.

There's hope.

I can finally breathe easier.

"You wouldn't shit me about this?" I turn the full force of my stare on Mitzy.

She bats it away with a blink of her pretty lashes. "No, Booker, I most definitely wouldn't, but it's still going to take time. Time you should spend getting ready for when I send out the call."

"Oh, I'm ready."

"No doubt you are, but you're tall and scary, and your presence intimidates my team. How about you back off for a bit? Let us do our thing while you pump up your muscles, or do whatever it is a Guardian does when he should be prepping a mission. Like sleep? Ever try that? You're no use strung out and exhausted."

"Ha. Not funny."

"I'm not kidding." She points to the door. "Don't let the door hit your ass on the way out."

"You're really kicking me out?"

"I'm really kicking you out." She stands and folds the chair. "You're doing no one any favors hovering. Focus on your area of expertise and let us focus on ours. We're all working to save your girl."

"Fine. I'll go."

As I exit the room, something still doesn't sit right with me.

The *Laguta* cartel took Isabelle.

They want her. Not the millions contained within the two rabbit's feet. And, let's face it, a couple of million in diamonds is chump change to an operation like that.

What are we missing?

EIGHTEEN

Izzy

My lids bounce from lack of sleep and general exhaustion.

The moment Matias forced me into the modified freezer, claustrophobia closed in, stealing my breath and accentuating my fears.

My brothers tease me about my multiple phobias, but I can't help it.

The air's too thick. It's too thin. It's not there at all.

I gulp, trying to breathe, feeling the darkness press in on me.

I twist inside my tiny prison and sip from what I assume is an air hole. If it's not, I'll soon be dead, suffocated in the back of a van somewhere in Central America.

What a way to go.

We stop several times. One particularly jarring lurch forces my eyes wide.

Total blackness greets me, and the stale air turns my stomach. Swallowing down bile, I breathe through my nose and repeat in my head *I will not throw up. I will not throw up.* Over and over, I let it repeat until the sickening feeling passes.

The only thing worse than being shoved inside a freezer is being locked inside of it with the stench of your own vomit for company. Fear licks at my frazzled nerves. It tingles at the back of my neck.

Prickles around my lips. Air hunger from hyperventilation makes me gasp. Not to be left out, my fingers tremble and my body shudders.

Hope fades as despair lurches like a relentless drunkard into the forefront of my thoughts. There will be no escape from this.

I kick at the walls of my prison, bang away with my fists, and scream at the top of my lungs, but nobody answers.

Nobody cares.

My mind drifts to my father, to being dragged away from his loving hands.

All through that harrowing first day and night, Matias pressed relentlessly toward the border. Secretly, I hoped to make my break for freedom along the way, but Matias was always one step ahead of me.

When exhaustion pulled at him, he made me pull over, trussed me up until I could barely move, and shoved a sock in my mouth as a gag.

While I suffered, he leaned his seat back and slept. I spent most of the next day tied up in the backseat, let out only for the occasional bathroom break.

He untied me, then marched me in to use the facilities with his gun pressed to my side and threats levied upon my family if I tried to scream or otherwise alert anyone to my predicament.

We drove for three agonizing days. My nightmare only increased when men met him with the van and this cursed box of death shoved in the back.

And now?

God only knows where I am now.

Muffled conversations reach my ears, too garbled to make out; not to mention in a language I barely understand.

My imagination takes over and goes wild, filling in the gaps with horrific things.

We arrive at a border crossing, or at least I assume, because of the voices.

Male voices demand Matias and his friends state their business and provide identification. It's all in garbled Spanish, but I make out enough to get the gist.

If I kick hard enough, will they hear me? Will they free me?

But kicking only makes breathing more difficult. Yelling makes my head swim from hypoxia. Locked inside this freezer, I'm slowly dying, one brain cell at a time.

The muffled sounds turn into garbled laughter, then the van moves on.

The guards don't hear me. They don't free me. Hell, they're probably in league with Matias.

I lie on my back, breathless with terror. Fear swims in my veins, growing and swelling into full-on terror.

The ground beneath the tires turns rough, jostling me inside my living coffin. The constant bouncing messes with my body, adding motion sickness to my growing list of complaints.

While I clutch at my belly, praying I don't puke in this damn box, my lungs struggle, and my heart pounds.

My pulse hammers in my ears, going berserk as I try to calm down. Fear is a mind-killer, and I need to think. I need to find a way out of this.

But there is no escape.

My thoughts spiral to dark places and take me with them until I float in a sea of nothingness.

Not sure what wakes me, I blink away the sleep in my eyes. The road beneath us smooths out.

No more jarring bumps scare me. It feels like well-kept pavement; a rarity on the roads we traveled to get here. Wherever *here* is.

We move fast. Or, at least, it feels fast. Then we slow, taking turn after turn, lurching forward, slamming hard to a stop.

That urge to retch returns.

Finally, we stop and the engine cuts out. The van lurches first to the left, then to the right as men exit the vehicle.

The doors to the back of the van open. The whole vehicle dips as someone steps inside.

My heart kicks in, sending a fresh surge of adrenaline coursing through me. My breathing ramps up and my entire body trembles. That tingling at the back of my neck returns.

Sudden, blinding light forces me to blink furiously. I fight the hands that pull me out of the freezer, but I'm too weak.

Matias is too strong.

"You can fight, but you can't change what happens next. Will you walk with dignity or will you fight like a she-cat?"

"I *want* to rip your balls off and feed them to your face."

"Such a shame. She-cat it is." He handles me roughly and forces me to my feet.

I do my best to give him my fiercest scowl, but he only laughs in my face.

"*Senorita*, you are like a kitten; cute, but tiny. Don't give me a reason to hurt you."

"You need a reason?"

"I was instructed to deliver you, but if you resist me, I can't be held responsible for what happens next."

The urge to spit in his eye overcomes me, but I bury that impulse as deep as I can. I'm not stupid. That isn't a threat.

And I'm so thirsty, there's no spit to spare.

After my eyes adjust to the bright light, I spin in a slow circle while he watches me.

I believed the freezer would be my coffin, but no such luck. I stand in front of a grand estate.

"This isn't the …" My brows tug together.

"Jungle? Is that where you thought I was taking you?"

"I …" Speechless, all I can do is gape.

Massive walls surround me. Not stucco, or brick; it looks like stone, maybe marble?

We're in some sort of motor courtyard. The van sits in the middle. A fleet of black limousines sits against a far wall. Six in total. Five garage doors line the far end of the courtyard.

Behind us, a heavy metal gate slowly swings closed. Beyond that is a road—maybe a long driveway? I question it because there are no cars and no buildings out there.

All around me, thick walls soar twenty or more feet in the air. Concrete forms beneath my feet hold the gravel that crunched beneath the van's tires.

And then, there are the planters. Massive man-sized pots dot the walls, spaced about twenty feet apart; they hold various tropical trees along with brilliant flower displays.

It's breathtaking.

And disturbing.

That fluttering in my belly returns and the twitching of my fingers is back. A sense of wrongness overcomes me and following close behind that, fear rears its ugly head.

"Follow me." Matias takes off, covering the distance to an elaborate gate at a fast clip.

He doesn't wait for me to join him, nor does he look behind him to see if I do. Open-mouthed, I suck in the humid air. Behind me, one of the men from the van clears his throat.

I jump and stumble after Matias. The moment I pass through the ornate gate, I manage three steps before pulling up short.

I've entered another world.

Incapacitated by emotion, all I can manage is to stare wide-eyed and unbelieving at the magnificent fountains and delicately manicured flower beds that decorate a stunning inner courtyard.

In the middle of the courtyard, a six-tiered fountain sprays water ten feet into the air. It falls like a gentle rain and splashes into the tiered basins. From there, it spills over each basin to cascade into a pond at the base.

The sound from the fountain is meant to soothe, but I find it terrifying.

Birds of Paradise sport colorful blooms, thrusting up from the center of lush leaves. Bougainvilleas, my favorite flower, sport a rainbow of colors from stark white to rose and all the way to the deepest purple. Lilies dot the ponds. Orchids and bromeliads hang from fanciful trees, drawing the eye up to the lush vegetation.

Off in the corner, a wrought-iron cage stands empty. Its door slightly ajar. Inside, is evidence of life. Droppings from a tropical bird, monkey, or other denizen of the jungle.

The walls drip wealth and I am in an altogether unexpected place.

"*Senorita* LaCroix?" Matias calls my name, pulling me from my thoughts.

I spin around, confused, terrified, and unclear what's happening. My hand covers my belly in a vain attempt to quell the shakiness I feel deep inside. I do it to keep my fingers from trembling and telegraphing my fear.

Although, why is beyond me.

"Who are you?" I take a step back, placing what distance I can between me and this strange man.

The two men from the van follow me in, blocking my escape. They shift their feet, widening their stance. Dark shades cover their eyes, making them appear more menacing—as if that's possible.

Beneath their suit jackets, attire wholly unsuited to the temperate heat, they wear shoulder holsters filled with impressive weaponry.

"Come." Matias sweeps out his arm, gesturing through an elaborately decorated archway.

All around me is marble and stone; soaring far over my head, this place knows how to make an impression. It feels heavy, weighted with history, but all the construction is new. There's nothing of the Spanish influence that touches most of Central America.

"Is this your home?" The tugging of my brows can't be helped. I try to turn my face into an expressionless mask, but it's not possible when I'm so incredibly overwhelmed.

"No, *senorita*. Not mine."

"Then whose?"

"You will soon meet the man who sent me to fetch you."

"I told you, whatever you think I have, or know, you're wrong."

"Your words are wasted on me, *senorita*, and your host doesn't appreciate when his guests keep him waiting."

Clearly, Matias will share nothing with me. My fate lies inside this monolithic building, which I'm only now realizing is the family home of an excessively wealthy man.

I don't know what to call the men behind me, but they are definitely there to ensure I do as Matias commands.

I suck in a shaky breath and take a step in the direction Matias wants me to go. He falls in beside me, walking with me as if we are on an afternoon stroll.

"The *hacienda* is beautiful. Is she not?"

This is so much more than a house. It's a fortress camouflaged to look like a palace, and I've never heard of a building, or a home, that was given a pronoun. Cars, trucks, boats, and ships perhaps, but never a house.

Matias walks me down a long, open-aired hallway. Despite the heat, a light breeze cools me. The fine hairs on my arms lift and a shiver slithers down my spine.

Yet, perspiration beads my brow.

Even my body is confused as to what it should feel.

Matias guides me through a set of rooms. The scale of the place overwhelms me. Large groupings of furniture look tiny against the backdrop of arched ceilings twenty feet or more overhead. The whole place is decorated as I would imagine, following local flavors, but it makes me feel tiny.

Insignificant.

Matias marches me toward a set of carved, wooden doors. He steps in front of me, and rather than opening one door, he grabs two thick, wrought-iron door pulls in his meaty hands, opening them at the same time. The scent of cigars, leather, and old books swirls all around me as Matias ushers me inside.

Here, unlike elsewhere in the house, animal skins stretch across the floor. Leather armchairs gather in clusters here and there while walls of books soar three stories tall. Curved staircases curl around the books, ascending all the way to the domed ceiling that looks like it belongs in a church back in Spain.

A massive desk sits at the far wall and the dominating leather chair is occupied by a man its equal. With eyes of Lucifer himself, he glances up at my entrance.

"Miss Isabelle LaCroix …" The man stands. "It is so nice to finally meet you."

Finally?

"I …" Words fail me and I jump when the doors behind me

close me in with the sound of death. I spin around and find Matias is gone.

My entire body tenses, locked somewhere between fight or flight. There's nowhere to go and I'm not trained to defend myself.

I thought Matias was bad enough, but he left me with a monster far worse.

I clear my throat and swallow past the fear closing off my windpipe. "Who are you?" I manage three words before I choke up.

"Now, that is a good question." He gestures to a pair of leather chairs to the left of the massive desk. "Are you thirsty?"

I'm parched. Dying of thirst.

"No."

"You've had a long ride. Come. Make yourself comfortable. Join me."

"Why am I here?" I don't move.

"Miss LaCroix ..." His tone takes on a dangerous edge that sends a chill licking down my spine.

That tingling on the back of my neck returns. I glance at the massive leather chair that's too big for me and swallow the lump in my throat.

"What do you want to talk about? I told Matias I know nothing."

"Please, Miss LaCroix ..." He gestures to the chair again.

"I'm not sitting down. You're a monster and you ..."

"Let's keep this civil." The sharpness of his voice cuts me off.

"Civil?" My voice rises. "Your man kidnapped me, and my father. Forced him to fly me over the border. Then Matias made me drive for days without rest then shoved me into a freezer. How is any of that civil?" The sound coming from my throat is like a screech.

The darkness swirling in his eyes makes my skin prick with chills. He blinks at me with gut-wrenching authority as I foolishly test his patience.

Knowing that throwing a temper tantrum will only make things worse, I huff and stomp over to the chair. Folding my arms across my chest, I drop into the chair and glare.

"Satisfied?"

"You are a very brave woman. If a man spoke to me like that, there would be a bullet between his eyes."

"And why not me?" Hey, it's not like I'm courting death, but I'm genuinely confused. "You obviously have me confused with someone else. Like I said, I know nothing."

He moves to a side table arrayed with crystal glasses and two pitchers. One is full of ice water, the other looks like whiskey.

"If not water, would you prefer whiskey?"

"I don't think drinking anything is a good idea." I'm not backing down. Although, the back of my throat does feel like the Sahara.

"As you wish." He fills two glasses with water, then joins me.

Placing one of the glasses on the table between us, he sinks into his chair like a comfortable friend. The leather creaks as he takes a sip. "It is filtered. No need to worry."

I keep my arms crossed and maintain my silence.

Up close, he's even more intimidating. A distinguished man, he doesn't look like the Nicaraguans I took care of during my ill-fated relief effort with Doctors Without Borders.

A distinct Anglo cast to his features blends beautifully with what I assume are native genes. He's taller too; taller by a foot, at least from the people I took care of. That comes from either good nutrition as a child or genetics.

I'm guessing from the wealth dripping from the walls, it's a bit of both.

As for keeping my silence, my curiosity gets the better of me.

"Who are you?"

NINETEEN

Booker

"It's been three days!" I stomp from one end of the deck behind the duplex I share with Brady to the other end and grip my phone.

He's out with Angie on a *date,* which means they're probably screwing each other's brains out.

"This kind of thing takes time." CJ tries to calm me, but I'm not interested in being *handled.*

"I know. That's what Mitzy said. Sam said it too, and you've said the same thing more times than I care to count. Why can't Bravo head down to Nicaragua to be in place when her team does figure it out?"

"We only assume that's where Matias took her."

"An assumption backed by a lot of solid data."

"Booker …"

"Look, he had her father fly across the border. Mitzy tracked her phone headed due south for Nicaragua."

"It went dead before then."

"Sure, but you gotta drive through Guatemala to get to Nicaragua."

"We don't know that he didn't board a plane. If that's the case, Izzy could

be anywhere in the world. Putting you in Nicaragua could be disastrous if that's the case."

"But it's a seven-hour flight from here. That's seven more hours …"

"Booker, I know how you feel. I was in the exact same place when my wife was abducted. It took forever to find where her kidnapper was holding her, but if I'd gone off half-cocked and failed to lay down the necessary groundwork, I might have found her too late."

"Shit." I knock my forehead with my fist. "I'm sorry. I forgot."

"It's okay, but I bring that up for a good reason. We need actionable intelligence and solid preparation. I can't let the Guardians go into a foreign country drawing attention to Guardian HRS."

"I get it." I hate his words. "Instead of don't-just-stand-there-do-something, we're in don't-do-anything-just-stand-there. It fucking sucks."

"I know, and I know how it feels. Trust me. Izzy is yours, but she's ours as well. This doesn't sit right for anyone. And Forest is already working with his CIA contacts on the ground. We're prepping resources for when you do go in."

"So, you think we *are* going to Nicaragua?"

"I do …" He pauses for a brief moment, *"but not enough to send you there yet."*

"Fuck." It's impossible to keep the irritation from my tone, but thankfully CJ is the best boss on the planet.

He gets it and he's not put off when one of us needs to blow off some steam.

I hate standing on the sidelines. Mitzy's team might be diligently working on finding my girl, but I need to do something.

"I know you said to take time away, but I need time on the range."

"You sure about that?"

"What better way to calm down?"

"I hear you. Sounds good. Take someone with you."

"Why?"

"Because you're a loose cannon right now."

"I'm not *loose* anything. I've got my shit locked down, just need to vent."

"And I know exactly what that means on the range. Take a buddy or stay home." His tone brooks no nonsense.

"Got it."

The moment he's off the phone, another call comes in. It's Gareth, Isabelle's eldest brother, hoping for an update.

"Shit." I've got nothing for him, but I answer the call and resume my pacing.

"Any news?" Gareth's tone is something between frantic and worried.

It's funny how everyone assumes Isabelle and I are an actual couple. From my brothers on Bravo team and leadership to Isabelle's family, everyone acts as if we're joined at the hip.

If they only knew the truth.

The woman I've never held in my arms. Whose lips I've never kissed. Whose body I've never felt wrapped around my own.

I drag my hand down my face and a string of expletives roll through my mind.

"Nothing new. Just got off the phone with CJ. They're still working it."

"God, I hope it works. Our mother is beside herself."

"What about your father? Did he get out of jail?"

"Yes, and thank you for sending support."

"No problem."

Forest sent governmental contacts he has in Mexico to smooth over Isabelle's father's unauthorized border crossing.

Upon landing, he was arrested and his helicopter impounded. With the resources available to Guardian HRS, instead of a conviction and imprisonment in a Mexican jail, Isabelle's father was released and flew home.

I've been balancing calls from her family with my calls to CJ and incessant requests for updates.

"The moment I know …" I stare out across the Pacific and pray for a miracle.

"Thanks." Gareth ends the call.

He knows I'll call, but like me with CJ, he can't help himself from needing an update.

In stark contrast to my mood, the day mocks me.

Another one of those perfect California days, the sky is as blue as blue can be. The ocean stretches out to fill the horizon, still and calm, completely peaceful, like its name.

Cotton ball clouds dot the sky, neither too many, nor too few. The breeze coming off the ocean is warm and inviting, and seabirds circle off in the distance, searching for their next meal.

A perfect fucking day.

"Argh!" My fingers curl into fists as I shout my frustration and turn around to pace once again.

I'm home because after Mitzy kicked me out, CJ did the same. He said I needed to blow off steam and stop making everyone around me jump.

Jump?

Who the fuck cares if people jump around me? They need to do their fucking job so I can do mine. I have half a mind to grab a one-way ticket to Nicaragua and not come back until Isabelle's in my arms, despite what CJ says.

"What's all the yelling?" The back door to Brady's place slides open. He steps out into the sunlight, tipping his head back to enjoy the sun warming his skin.

"I'm so frustrated."

"Mitzy's team is on it." Brady knows my mood. We share a wall between our bachelor pads, and I've cursed and shouted enough over the past few days to raise the dead.

"I know. They're looking into all kinds of shit, but it's the fucking supercomputer that's too fucking slow."

"*Jacen?*" Brady gives me a look. "Hang on. I'll be right back." He returns a few minutes later with a six-pack of beer. "Take a seat."

"Don't wanna sit." A low growl rumbles in the back of my throat. "I'm so fucking tired of sitting and doing nothing."

"I hear you, and as much as you don't want me to say it, I know how it feels."

He's right. The man went after Angie after seeing her face on

TV. Rescued her and Isabelle out of the clutches of the *Coralos* cartel, only to lose Angie at the very end.

It took Mitzy and her team far less time to track Angie down, but it still took time.

I don't remember him coming unglued.

"How did you handle it?" I reluctantly drop into a chair beside Brady. He hands me a bottle.

"I cursed everyone within shouting distance. Tried not to think about it. Failed …"

"So, your advice is, what?"

"I have no advice. It sucks. That's the beginning and end of it." He twists around in his seat. "But the moment we get the green light, Bravo's heading out with a vengeance."

At least we agree on that.

"CJ suggested I head to the range." I take a look at my unopened bottle and set it down. "You wanna come?"

"Now you tell me." He looks at his beer with a grimace. "Waste of a damn good beer."

"I'll buy you another six-pack."

"As you wish. Want me to call the team?"

"Yeah, that might help."

Things may suck right now, and I may be the worst company to be around, but this is when I need my brothers the most.

At least I'll get to blow something up. That should take the edge off my growing frustration.

"We doing sidearms or long range?"

"Sidearms."

I want to punch dozens of holes through the heads of our targets. Each one of them will be practice for putting a bullet between Matias's eyes when I see him.

The motherfucker is going down for taking my girl.

And yes, Isabelle is very much mine. The moment she's in my arms, I'm going to show her exactly what that means, and I'm not taking any lip about it.

Brady texts the team while I put the beer back in his fridge.

TWENTY

Izzy

Before I realize what I'm doing, I take a sip of water from the glass the man set beside me. My first thought is what a fool I am. Anything could be in the water. My second thought is I don't care.

Thirsty and desperate for hydration, my mind isn't thinking about what could be in the water.

Like a drug to knock me out.

"You should drink more. You don't look well." He leans back like a king entertaining a guest. "I promise, it's nothing but water."

I cringe, realizing my mistake. I don't want to give this man anything.

"You'll forgive me if I don't believe you." I set the glass down and fold my arms across my chest.

I've never felt this small and insignificant.

Never this lost.

"I will prove it." He takes my glass and swallows half of it. "Would I drink it if it's poisoned?"

There's no way I'm drinking his backwash. So that doesn't prove anything.

"Maybe." I huff out the word like a petulant little girl.

It's the way he makes me feel and goes with the difference in our ages. He's easily twice as old as me, which makes him even more scary.

"I know Matias and he's not a man who takes care of his charges. No doubt, you haven't eaten or had anything to drink since he took you."

"You mean kidnapped me." It feels important to reiterate I'm here against my will.

This man is too nonchalant about my abduction.

"That is such a vulgar term. You are a guest." The way he says *guest* is twisted and wrong.

"If I'm a guest, then I can leave?" I shift in my seat, testing him. Although, I already know the answer.

"Ah, that wouldn't be wise." He steeples his fingers and holds them beneath his chin. His black eyes glitter with malice.

"Why?"

"Because it's not safe for you out there."

As if *he's* my protector?

"Not safe? You kidnapped me and are telling me it's not safe out there? Seems like it's a whole hell of a lot safer than here."

"Now, now." His tone turns paternalistic and mocking. "Such vulgar language from a young lady is quite unbecoming."

"Excuse me, but you have no right to tell me what is, and isn't, becoming. You *kidnapped* me and are holding me against my will."

"I am protecting you."

"Protecting?" I shake my head, convinced he truly is mad. "Explain how in God's name, you're protecting me."

"Do not take the Lord's name in vain in this household." The way his eyes narrow in warning makes my heart race.

"You kidnap people, hold them prisoner, and you're worried about me taking the Lord's name in vain?"

"Like I said, I am protecting you."

"From who?" Heat fills my cheeks and my voice rises in anger.

"From those who wish you harm."

"I don't have enemies." I enunciate clearly, certain he doesn't understand a word I say. "I'm nobody. If anyone has enemies, it's you."

"Unfortunately, that is all too true." He takes a sip of the whiskey he poured, then gestures to the glass of water. "I must insist. You need to drink."

"I will not …"

"Isabelle LaCroix, you will do as you're told."

"Or, what?"

"Your family will suffer."

My entire world tilts and tumbles into an abyss too vast for words. He knows exactly how to hurt me.

"You wouldn't …" My voice is barely audible, not much more than a whisper.

"You are a guest in my home, and with that you will obey my rules."

"You're a monster."

"Right now, you no doubt think that, but in time, you will come to understand I am your savior."

"You make no sense."

"All will be clear in time. But I must insist. You are dehydrated and overly emotional. Drink." He lifts the glass, handing it to me.

With the threat against my family hanging between us, I take the glass. It's a good thing he drank half of the water because my hand shakes so much I would've spilled that half on my lap. As for the backwash, it's insignificant when it comes to the safety of my family.

With those coal-black eyes watching, I put the rim of the glass to my lips and swallow the rest of the water.

"Now, isn't that better?" He takes the glass, and while I curl in on myself, he rises majestically from his chair to refill it. "Here, have some more."

My hand is less shaky, and I take the glass. Again, he watches over me as I dutifully sip.

Silence descends between us as I finish the water. It's chilled and tastes wonderful. Soon enough, I'll be hydrated enough to generate some of that saliva I want to spit in his eye.

He folds his arms across his broad chest and gives a nod of approval. When I place the empty glass down on the table, he clears his throat.

"Tell me …" There's a pause where I hang on what he says next.

"What?" The urge to tell him I know nothing remains just as strong now as before, but it will do no good.

He thinks I know something, and a man like him gets what he wants.

"Tell me about the men who rescued you."

The moment the word falls from his mouth, my entire body tenses. Not sure what I can, and can't say, my lips press together as my mind whirls.

This is exactly the kind of thing that should be covered in orientation. Maybe it is and I just didn't make it that far, but I'm not telling him shit about the Guardians.

Not that I know much about them.

I'm still such a newbie to the organization.

"I don't know anything."

He rests his hands on the elegantly carved armrests. His left forefinger taps on the wood. Each tap feels like driving a nail in my head.

Dehydration, lack of sleep, and generalized fear sets my head to pounding. The pain makes it hard to think.

Difficult to concentrate.

All I want is to crash in a cozy bed, pull the comforter over my head, and pretend none of this is happening.

"You and I will do much better without threats, don't you think?"

"Anyone would do better without threats." Can't argue with him there.

"Then I suggest you answer my questions."

"But I don't know anything."

"Answer to the best of your ability and I will reward you."

"With what?"

"Freedom."

"You'll let me leave?"

What can I say about the Guardians that won't spill any secrets? I don't want to be *that person*; the one who cracks without a mark on them.

"No, but you will have freedom to move about the estate."

"So, I'll still be a prisoner?"

"You will be my special guest."

Special guest? Why the need for euphemisms?

"I'm not lying to you. I know nothing. I'm no one." This round and round, back and forth frustrates me. I wish it would all just end.

"Yet, someone rescued you within hours of your abduction by the *Coralos* cartel? That doesn't sound like *no one* to me." His tone takes a dangerous edge. "What makes you so special?"

"It wasn't me. It was Angie." I cover my mouth, knowing I fucked up.

"And who is Angie?" Those dark eyes gleam in victory. He pounces on the tiny morsel I let slip.

I can't let him win this easily. Not if I ever want to look Booker in the face again, or Brady. I won't be that girl.

But I already opened the floodgates. If I'm careful about my answers, maybe I can answer enough for him to let me go?

"She's my friend."

"Is she?" He doesn't look convinced.

"Yes, she is."

I don't like the way he questions the simplest thing. If he doubts I'm telling the truth about Angie, how will I get him to believe the lies I intend to tell about the Guardians?

"And did you know her before you entered Nicaragua?"

"Excuse me?"

"Were you friends before you entered my country?"

His country?

"Who are you?"

The way he says *my country* sounds like Nicaragua is something he owns rather than the country he's a citizen of; the difference is slight, but undeniable.

"Please …" His pause sounds gentle, but it's laced with malevolence if I don't respond.

"We didn't know each other until we met to prep for the mission. That's where we met Jerald, who gave me the rabbit's foot." I fumble at my neck, pulling the rabbit's foot over my head. I hold it out. "Take it. I don't want this thing anywhere near me."

The moment he takes the rabbit's foot a profound sense of relief washes through me. The tightness in my chest eases, and I take in the first deep breath since this nightmare began.

"We'll get to this in a moment." He puts the unlucky charm around his neck and tucks it under his shirt.

"But …"

He raises his hand, stopping me. "I'm interested in who rescued you from the *Coralos* cartel and who the men were who killed my cousin."

"Your cousin?"

"Yes." His fist slams against the armrest, making me jump.

My heart pounds like a jackhammer and thunders through my veins. I draw my knees up and fold my arms around them as I press back into the chair, trying to disappear.

"You were there." His tone turns deadly.

"That wasn't me." Again, I cup my hand over my mouth.

What a way to throw Angie under the bus? I'm the worst human being on the planet, caving like a moron.

I bang my head against the back of the chair, hating myself for betraying my friend.

The man's eyes narrow to glittering-black slivers, glaring at me. Assessing my truthfulness.

I hate the only conclusion he can draw.

"The men who rescued you, do you know who they work for?"

I bow my head and press my chin against my knees. Tears prick behind my lids as I close my eyes and try not to cry.

"Did you know them before you came to my country?"

"I did not." It's too late to lie. All I can do is mitigate the damage I've already done.

"Why did they rescue you and not the others?" Curiosity fills his voice.

"It wasn't me he rescued." Realizing I just answered one of his questions, my shoulders slump with regret.

"It was this other woman?" He temples his fingers and rests his chin on the tips of his fingers. "Which is why you weren't there."

"Yes." A single tear leaks from my left eye.

Forgive me, Angie.

"These men—they will come for you." He makes it a statement, without a hint of question lingering in the words.

"I doubt it." I have to hold back something.

"Why?"

"Because I'm nothing to them."

Booker won't stop until he's rescued me. No matter how long it takes, how dangerous it might be, or whether it costs him his life in the process. He will come for me.

I take in a deep breath and do my best to spin a lie.

"There's no way they could've followed me. Your man made sure of that, but even if they could, I mean nothing to them."

"Matias is good for such things."

"Will you demand a ransom?" A glimmer of hope shines in the darkness.

"No. I will not. I have a feeling they will find a way."

"How?"

He finishes the last of his whiskey, then gives me a hard, long stare. "You need rest. A shower, a fresh change of clothes, and a meal." He turns his wrist over. "Dinner won't be served until six, but I will have something brought to your room." His words are dismissal.

My room? Is he mad?

Not that I'll complain about a room. It's much better than a cell in the basement. His civility and polished exterior throw me for a loop. It's almost possible to believe I am a guest and he's my host.

But I'm not.

His men fired on my family. They tried to hurt them. Then Matias kidnapped me and forced me to drive most of the two thousand miles to Nicaragua.

Sleep isn't what I need.

The man abruptly stands, ending our conversation, and holds

out his hand as if I'd let him help me up. I ignore the hand and stand without his assistance.

After the terror of the last three days, I'm ready for more than a nap. Not that I'll sleep. There's no way I can let my defenses down.

Who knows what this lunatic will do to me?

With a gesture toward the door, he follows behind as I attempt to keep my head high, chin up, shoulders back, and ignore the shaking in my knees and the knot of fear coiled in my gut.

When he opens the door, Matias, who leans against the wall, snaps to attention.

"Take our guest to her room. See to it she has what she needs for dinner."

"*Si, senor.*" Matias snaps his heels together and proffers a deferential bow before gripping my upper arm and pulling me down the hall.

TWENTY-ONE

Booker

"Damn, you're on fire." Rafe pulls off his safety glasses as our targets rush toward us.

The paper with the black silhouettes bows back as the cables draw them close.

I opted for small arms precisely so I could imagine putting as many bullets between Matias's eyes as possible. That's the price he'll pay for kidnapping my girl.

"Missed one." One of my shots took out a bite just outside the black silhouette of a human torso.

"Focusing on the positive, I see." Rafe pulls off his hearing protection setting the bulky headset beside his safety glasses.

"Whatever." I put my weapon down, barrel pointed downrange, and yank off my own protective gear.

Instead of sitting on the deck drinking beer and watching the sun dip behind the ocean, the six of us sip soda and water while blasting through target after target.

I've been practicing headshots exclusively, ignoring center of chest shots. It goes against our training, but I don't care.

I'm putting two bullets in Matias's head, then a third in his chest to check off the requisite double-tap box.

In contrast to my performance, Rafe didn't miss a shot. The man has eagle eyes, nerves of steel, and steady hands. He can shoot a nickel from insane distances—repeatedly.

He's our team's lead sniper for damn good reason.

Hayes unclips his target and gives it a good look. "I missed two at the very end. Getting sloppy."

Despite his extensive demolition background, Hayes is second only to Rafe when it comes to hitting what he shoots. He'd rather blow it up but is deadly with practically everything.

I've gone axe throwing with the guys, and Hayes scares the shit out of me with how good he is with anything that has a blade.

His crazy-good aim is a superpower.

"We should put the sidearms away and move to knives. See who wins then." Alec joins in, looking to start a little competition.

"Knives?" Zeb missed three out of the hundred rounds we shot at the range. Our alternate sniper and tech support, he's almost as good as Rafe.

"How about we call it quits and grab a drink?" Brady crumples his target and tosses it in the trash.

I know what he's doing. Brady's trying to keep the guys close, supporting me in the best way possible.

"Only if I get to pick the place," I shout out before Rafe forces us to go to his favorite Chinese buffet. The man would eat nothing but Chinese if he could.

"You don't know what you're missing at Mr. Wu's." Rafe pat's his belly. "Best fucking food on the planet."

"I'm in the mood for steak," Brady chimes in.

"Steak it is." I snicker when Rafe groans.

He's not a meat and potatoes kind of man, unlike the rest of us. It's Chinese or chicken for him.

With dinner settled, we return our weapons to our individual gear lockers in the Bravo bullpen, then head out, splitting up into two cars. We make it half a block when Brady's cellphone rings. He puts it to his ear, then looks at me.

A huge grin fills his face.

"Booker, call the others. We're on."

"No fucking way!" After days of inaction, I question what I hear. "They found her?"

"Yes. They fucking found her. Now, spin this car around. We've got your woman to save."

Eagerness to finally be doing something about Isabelle makes my blood roar. I call Zeb in the other car.

"Yo! What's up?"

"We're turning around." There's no wiping off the victorious grin from my face.

"Why?" Zeb asks.

"Because we're going to Nicaragua." Fire burns in my gut.

"About damn time," Zeb calls out to Alec, who drives the other car, relaying the message.

Executing a tight turn, we head back to Guardian HQ.

Sam and CJ meet us in the Guardian briefing room. Joining them are Mitzy and none other than Forest Summers.

The brooding look on his face makes his solemn expression thunderous. He looks up the moment we walk in, eyes stormy, jaw tight, mouth set with grim determination.

It's enough to pull me up short.

"Brady said you found her." My voice booms through the room. Already, I'm itching to be on a plane, flying out of here to Isabelle's side.

"We did." Mitzy pipes up from the far side of the room. Standing beside Forest, she looks like a tiny fairy—a fairy with pixie dust for hair.

"Take a seat boys." Sam gestures toward the table.

After a brief scuffling of chair legs dragging over the hard floor, we settle around the table.

"Mitzy, go ahead," Sam kicks things off.

CJ turns to Mitzy. Briefly, his gaze locks with Forest. Something passes between them; a grimness, as if they've swallowed rotten meat.

"I'm not going to bore you with all the details," Mitzy pipes up, flashing a graphic on the screen dominating the far wall.

On it are the red lines we looked at before, along with the blue lines I saw earlier.

"As you know, we've been tracing back the men who came after Izzy on her family's ranch. Most of those you captured are low-ranking, street gang members contracted as needed to provide extra muscle. We were able to confirm these men were hired by the *Laguta* cartel rather than their rival, the *Coralos* cartel. Which is interesting."

"Wouldn't they simply be trying to reclaim their lost diamonds?"

"Now that you mention it, those diamonds are quite fascinating." Mitzy's eyes sparkle nearly as much as her hair. "And I'll get to that in a moment."

A mass of blue squiggles fills the screen and makes my head spin.

"We ran into a problem tracking Izzy when her phone died, but we were finally able to pinpoint the signature of her captor's phone."

The blue spaghetti mess disappears and one line remains. She clicks a button and it highlights in bright green.

"This is the phone Matias uses."

Another click of a button and the green line folds in and back on itself, arrowing toward Managua, the capital city of Nicaragua.

"He does not spend the majority of his time in territory controlled by the *Laguta* cartel." Mitzy glances at me. "Which got me wondering."

"Wondering about what?" Brady props his elbow on the table.

"His association to the *Lagutas* is not as deeply intertwined as I initially thought."

"But they're the ones who ordered Isabelle's kidnapping." I tap my fingers on the table. My knees bounce with excess energy; energy trapped with no outlet.

"I'm not so sure about that anymore." Mitzy bites her lower lip and flicks her gaze toward Forest and then immediately turns away.

"What the hell does that mean?" I'm confused and not in the mood for guessing games.

"Only that there is far more going on." Mitzy hedges, something I've never seen the computer genius do from the day I met her.

Mitzy doesn't assume.

She never guesses.

Her currency is in cold, hard facts. If she can't prove something, she won't present it as fact.

"We're going to need a bit more than that." Like me, Brady's irritation grows. "But all we really need to know is where she is and how we're going to get her out of there."

"And that's where things get complicated." Again, Mitzy hedges.

"What's complicated about it? You know where she is. Tell us and we'll build an operation around getting her out."

Mitzy's team accomplishes all manner of modern technological marvels, but when it comes to putting boots on the ground, the Guardians plan the mission.

"Izzy is currently …" Again, she glances at Forest.

He takes a seat, practically falling into it.

The man looks terrible. Knowing him, he's been shoulder to shoulder with Mitzy trying to track Isabelle down and hasn't slept the past three days trying to sort it out.

"She's being held at the private residence of Maximus Angelo." Forest pinches the bridge of his nose. "Seems like I can't escape it." The comment's meant for Mitzy.

"Just another stone. We're taking him down." She places a hand on his shoulder.

"Excuse me, but who is Maximus Angelo?" Whatever private conversation they're having can wait. I'm ready to climb on a plane and extract Isabelle from the lunatic who has her.

"Maximus Angelo …" Mitzy turns back to the screen and flicks a switch on her remote.

The image of a man in his late fifties fills the screen. A mix of Anglo and local features blend seamlessly to give the man a distinguished look.

Bushy brows cap dark-brown eyes, nearly black in appearance. Those eyes stare out of the screen with authority. From the set of his jaw to the lifting of his chin, the man's a predator. The light dusting of silver over his sideburns lends the experience of age to complete his stately appearance.

And why shouldn't it.

The man is Nicaragua's Minister of the Interior.

"What the fucking hell?" I slam my palms down on the table. Anger boils my blood and heats my skin. "The fucking Minister of the Interior kidnapped my girl?"

"Looks that way." Mitzy pauses to let that sink in.

We all stare at each other wondering what the hell.

"How the hell did Isabelle, and Angie …" I include Brady's fiancée. "How did they get wrapped up with him?"

"That's what we need to figure out." Mitzy tugs at a purple spike of hair. "But we can do that after Bravo leaves."

"Right." Brady clears his throat. "You want us to infiltrate the private residence of one of Nicaragua's senior-most governmental figures and retrieve Izzy?"

"That is the objective." Mitzy's snarky comment makes me grind my teeth. "My team's already digging up what information we can. By the time you land, I'll have schematics and security info ready for you."

"By the time we land?" I can't help but scoff at that comment. "Has anyone asked the obvious question of why this guy wants Isabelle?"

"We're looking into that now."

"Seems like we need to do more than that." I can't believe this shit. "Does anything connect him to the *Laguta* cartel?"

"Actually …" Mitzy's voice trails off. She glances at Forest, who waves her on to continue. "The man you shot in Nicaragua, the one who had Angie …"

"Yes?" Brady looks up, eyes pinched at the reminder of what that man almost did to his woman.

"He's a cousin. A second cousin, but a cousin all the same."

"That makes no sense." I bite back a curse.

"That's not the worst of it." Forest's voice is so deep, his words are felt more than heard.

"What's worse than known connections to the *Coralos* cartel?" Brady splits his attention between Forest and Mitzy.

"His brother," Forest clears his throat and continues, "is the leader of the *Laguta* cartel."

"What the fuck?" I don't believe my ears. "He's connected to both?"

"And we're trying to sort through all of that," CJ steps in. "In the meantime, you've got a plane to catch. Grab your gear and load up. Mission planning will occur en route."

Sam stands, letting us know this briefing is over. The rest of Bravo team pushes away from the table.

"Let's roll." I glance around the room, waiting to see if Mitzy has any more information for us. When she says nothing, I look to my team, my brothers in arms.

Bravo team is ready for action. We've got an hour to prep and seven more to fly south, but damn if I'm not going to finally get my girl.

When I do, I'm going to hold Isabelle, kiss her if she'll let me—hell, I'm just going to kiss her and see what happens. She'll either slap me or kiss me back. Either way, I'm not missing out on planting one on her.

Hang on just a little bit longer; I'm coming for you.

TWENTY-TWO

Izzy

Tension mounts as Matias drags me through the opulent estate. Fear knots my shoulders, coils in my spine, and tightens in the small of my back.

Unlike the man in the library—or office, still not sure what that room was—civil is a word lacking in Matias's vocabulary.

There's no pretense about being polite. His fingers dig deep into my arm, tight and unrelenting, as he yanks me down one long hallway and through the next.

The few rooms we pass are more opulent than the one I left, leaving my jaw gaping at the grotesque display of wealth.

Guards dot the halls. They ignore us as we pass, making me wonder how common such a sight is for these men. From their complete lack of reaction, I fear they're used to men like Matias hauling unwilling women through the halls.

What am I going to do?

How am I going to get out of here?

Do I attempt to escape?

Or do I wait for the Guardians to rescue me?

And Booker—the poor guy must be going out of his mind. I've been missing for well over three days.

Three days.

It feels like a lifetime, but also as if no time's passed at all.

I stumble and nearly fall on my face, saved only by Matias's harsh yank on my arm that nearly pulls it out of the socket.

He doesn't slow, leaving me to jog-step behind him.

Panic surges in my veins, and fear licks at my nerves. Each step jangles with electricity, shooting tiny shockwaves through me.

My lips are numb. My fingers tingle. My legs shake and wobble, threatening to send me plummeting to my knees.

If I don't get up, what will Matias do?

Will he drag me along the floor?

I bet he would.

Matias has no regard for human life. I know because I've seen him take a life.

The expression of abject horror on that man's face, moments before Matias put a bullet between his eyes, makes my heart hurt. I shouldn't feel pain for a man who wished me harm, but I understand his horror and the despair he felt when Matias pointed that gun at him.

As for me, and my current predicament, I'm at a complete loss. If I knew where I was, or who that man back there might be, maybe I could get a message out?

"Where are you taking me?" Terrified I'll wind up in a dungeon, allowing Matias to drag me to some dank cell buried deep underground sounds a whole lot like a really bad idea.

Just before an intersection between two corridors, I try to yank free of his grip, but Matias is unstoppable.

"Matias …" A female speaks from down a crossing hall. "Did Maximus give you another plaything?"

Low, and sultry, the voice pulls Matias to a bone-jarring stop.

I nearly run right into him.

The clicking of heels on the stone floor draws my eye.

There are *pretty* women; I classify myself in that category. A little bit of makeup can take me from pretty to beautiful. There are *beautiful* women who radiate near female perfection. They can become stunning with a little work. Then, there's the woman walking toward us.

Midnight-black hair, thick with the slightest wave, cascades over her shoulders to fall down to the small of her back. Mid to late twenties, she's about my age. A formfitting, red dress draws the eye to a slender figure, narrow waist, breasts I envy, and hips that complete the hourglass shape. She's exquisite. Add to that wide, cocoa-colored eyes, specked with gold, arched brows, sculpted cheeks, and full, ruby-red lips; envy sweeps through me before I realize I'm jealous of what she has that I do not.

Exquisite comes to mind.

She's beyond bombshell beautiful.

"I didn't know you were visiting, *Senorita Carmen*." His hungry eyes devour her body.

"I decided I needed time away from the city." Her gaze turns to me, taking me in with a dismissive look. "Who is this?" Icy disdain washes over and through me.

"She is nothing." Matias growls as he yanks me away from the woman.

"A plaything then?" Her tone sharpens, turns not quite derisive, but close enough to snap Matias's spine rigid.

"For your father." That growling in the back of his throat deepens.

"Please …" Her mouth pinches and her long lashes flutter against perfectly sculpted cheekbones. "Another plaything? Why her?" She turns her nose up, but while I continue to stare, she takes another look at me. This time, it's more than casual. "I'm surprised he would bother, considering …" Whatever she is going to say is gone with a flick of her lashes.

For some reason, I hang on those last words.

Considering?

Considering, what?

How much does this woman know about her father?

Clearly, far more than me.

"If you're a good boy, maybe he will reward you and let you

have his toy once he's through with her? But you're never a good boy, are you?"

"How was your visit with Artemus?" Matias looks closely at the woman's hand. "I don't see a ring. Your father will not be pleased."

"I don't care what he thinks. He has no say."

"Is that what you think?" He tips his head back and lets out a caustic peal of laughter.

She folds her arms across her chest and drums her perfectly manicured fingers on her forearm.

"I have better things to do with my time than waste breath on you." Matias's grip on my arm tightens painfully making me cry out.

"*Tsk. Tsk. Tsk.* Be careful, or you'll damage his toy." She lifts her forefinger, shaking it in front of his face.

My insides draw into a tight knot, curling and writhing inside my belly as fear takes root.

A kindness lies in her eyes, completely absent in the callousness of her words.

At first glance, I'd hoped she would be an ally, but that isn't the case. This woman knows what her father does and doesn't seem to care that he ruins lives for a living.

She's also exceptionally comfortable deriding Matias in front of me. She knows how to work a man. Despite her verbal abuse, the sultry tones of her voice cast a spell on Matias.

Completely enraptured, he allows the verbal slights as his body responds to her radiant beauty.

She steps up to me, invading my personal bubble of space as if she owns it instead of me, and cocks her head.

"What game is my father playing with you?" Her attention flits to Matias with a flick of her lashes. She presses a lacquered fingernail under my chin, forcing me to look at her. "I almost feel sorry for you." She practically spits the words at me as if they taste foul.

Not sure what to say, my brows practically touch as they tug together in confusion.

"Goodbye, Matias." She presses her lips to the tip of her fingers and blows a kiss to Matias.

His chest swells even as anger turns his expression stormy and cruel.

With the clicking of her stilettos disappearing behind us, Matias yanks me forward, propelling me toward an uncertain, and dangerous, future.

TWENTY-THREE

Izzy

Numerous cameras lie along our route. Mounted high, they monitor every square inch of this wretched place.

Not a techno-geek like Mitzy, I doubt my mugshot on the surveillance footage here will help her find me.

The last time I was near a camera of any sort was somewhere in Guatemala when we stopped for gas. I managed to convince Matias to let me use the facilities and hoped the gas station cameras were operational.

For all I know, they were as dead as a doorknob, but it was the best I could do.

Not knowing what the Guardians are up to, I resolve to do whatever I can to free myself.

We cross an extravagantly landscaped courtyard laced with the perfume of countless flowers. Water is everywhere, fountains spray into the air, and cascading waterfalls empty into a burbling brook that meanders across the floor until it empties into a Koi pond.

Stone floors spread outward until they flow up, creating marbled walls. Those walls rise proudly, splitting and dividing into magnificent archways that curve overhead. They become elaborately painted domed ceilings shining down on those who walk below.

Monolithic columns support the weight of the ceiling and the tiled roof overhead, giving the entire place the feeling of permanence.

It's a fortress.

While most of the courtyards sport various gardens, some remain frighteningly empty.

Matias pulls me to a set of curving stairs and hauls me up to the second level and then the third. Here, rows of wooden doors march down the long hall. Every one curved at the top, leading into what I assume are private rooms.

He takes me to the very last door on the left and releases me. I rub at my arm where there will be bruises later.

Matias fumbles for a set of keys in his pocket. Once he finds the key he's looking for, he unlocks the door and holds it open.

I expect a cell, something rustic and barely habitable, not the elegantly appointed suite that greets me. A small sitting area is set across from a spacious four-poster bed capped by a canopy stretching over the top, but every window is covered with wrought iron bars.

Off to the side, through another door, is what looks like a private bath.

Standing beside the bed, a woman dressed in a white gauze dress with puffy sleeves and a red sash tied around her waist, suddenly looks up. Her dark hair is pulled up and held out of the way by a handkerchief the same shade of red as the sash.

The moment we enter, she bows her head and kneels. The woman says nothing and Matias gives her a dismissive look.

"Do not speak to Rosalie." He snaps his fingers.

The harsh sound makes me jump. It makes the woman spring to her feet. She rushes to the door, head bowed, hands clasped in front of her. She stops in front of Matias, gives a quick curtsey, then departs in a hurry.

"Why not?" I watch the woman scurry down the long hall. Not once does she lift her chin to look straight ahead.

"You ask too many questions." He grabs my shoulder and bodily shoves me inside.

"I do not."

The scowl on Matias's face is one I know well. He gave me that look all the way from Texas, through Mexico, past Guatemala, Honduras, and into Nicaragua.

"Do not speak to the help. They will not answer and will be punished if they do."

"You can't be serious." I pull back, horrified.

"You are such a naïve little girl. Living the perfect American life."

"Why do you hate me?"

Not that it should, but it bothers me. There's a difference between performing a job his boss ordered—kidnapping me—and this deep-seated, abject hatred.

I mean, he can feel however he wants, but what did I do to spark such loathing?

"I do not *hate* you, *senorita.*" His voice deepens, growing coarse and depraved. "Once Señor Angelo tires of you, you will be mine."

"What?" I falter and take a step back. My heart leaps into a full gallop inside my chest, desperate for escape while my hand presses against my belly.

"Yes, now you see your fate. Enjoy the time you have while he toys with you. It will be brief, and then it will be just you and me."

I stagger back another step, certain I misunderstand his words, but there's no mistaking the desire in his eyes.

The room tilts all around me, spinning wildly as I gasp and struggle to breathe. My legs shake. My knees buckle. I fall to the floor, dizzy and confused. This can't be real. None of it can be real.

Matias glances down. Black eyes, blown out by lust, he takes one step toward me.

When I flinch, his entire body twitches.

He shakes his head, then grips his crotch in a vulgar display.

I choke back a sob when he backs out of the room. As he closes the door, Matias gives final instructions.

"Señor Angelo wants you to shower and dress for dinner. Rosalie will return at half-past five to help you prepare. You have until then to get the rest you will need for tonight."

Why do I think dinner isn't the only thing happening tonight?

My choked sob turns into a complete breakdown as I huddle on the floor and cry until there are no tears left.

Despite what Matias says, I am not naïve. I know what happens when women find themselves victims of despicable men. What I don't understand is how I fit into any of this.

Why am I a prisoner? What value do I hold?

When my eyes make no more tears, and my sobs run out, I push myself off the cold, tiled floor and drag myself into the bathroom.

If I have to endure an evening of the unknown, I'll do it with the benefit of a hot shower and as much rest as I can manage.

The one thing my accommodations lack is a clock. I have my phone. No one cared to confiscate it, but it's been dead as a doornail for a day and a half.

After using the facilities, and brushing my teeth with the toiletries supplied, I take a shower and crank up the steam.

It takes time to wash away the stench of my kidnapping and that terrible ride with Matias.

After scrubbing until my skin is a cherry red, I attack the mess that is my hair. My fingers tremble as I run them through the knots and snarls as more tears spill down my face.

Everything about this overwhelms me. I'm supposed to be strong. Angie was when she was kidnapped that second time. Angelo's cousin tried to rape her. He came close. Fortunately, Brady and Booker got there in the nick of time. Brady put a bullet through the *Coralos'* leader's head, then whisked Angie to safety.

I'd like if that could happen for me, but there's no way Booker can find me now. Not with my phone dead.

If I'd only accepted that tracker.

I hunker down on the floor of the shower, draw my knees in tight to my chest, and cry until exhaustion takes over. Somehow, I manage to fall asleep while in the shower.

Rough shaking pulls me from my dreams.

It's Rosalie.

She turns off the water and holds a fluffy towel for me to dry myself. I'm not supposed to speak to her, but I can't help it. I need the comfort of another human being.

"Thank you." I take the towel and exit the shower.

Rosalie points at the back of her wrist. It's bare, but I get it when she lifts four fingers. Somehow, I managed to sleep until four in the afternoon, although I still feel as if I've been hit by a truck.

I take the towel and rub at my hair. Rosalie shakes her head and takes it from me. She hands me a robe, then gestures for me to sit on a chair facing the vanity.

It's weird not speaking, but that doesn't mean we can't communicate. It doesn't mean she can't answer my questions.

While I sit, she brings out several brushes and combs. Without asking, she dries and styles my hair. Taking all the tangles out of my long, black locks, she manages to smooth out my hair while keeping the loose curls in place.

"I know you're not allowed to speak, but I have questions."

Rosalie shakes her head; real fear rims her eyes. She points up at the corner where a tiny camera sits.

My stomach drops with the realization I stripped and took a shower while under surveillance.

Damn, I suck at this. It never occurred to me to check. Closing my eyes, I give myself grace for missing that and demand that I do better moving forward.

I'm not dumb. I'm a smart and accomplished woman who can figure this out.

But lesson learned.

Assume everywhere I go that I'm being watched, which means finding a way to contact Guardian HQ to tell them where I am is nearly impossible.

Once done with my hair, we move on to makeup. I've never had anyone serve me, and it twists my gut knowing she's essentially a prisoner here like me.

I have to say it like that because I can't bring myself to think the word Matias used.

As for Rosalie, she's a talented genius. I look the best I've ever looked in my life.

Dressed in a slinky ball gown nearly the same corn-flower blue as my eyes, the dress shimmers in the light. One strap over my shoulder, the bust is deceptively modest. I say deceptive because the dress hugs all my curves, drawing the eye to my breasts, my waist, my hips, and my legs. Or, at least, one leg. The nearly hip-high slit pushes decency to the limit, and since the dress is sprayed on, a bra and panties are not provided.

I take one look at the heels she wants me to wear and put out my hand.

"Sorry. No way am I wearing those."

Rosalie insists.

"You don't understand, I sprained my ankle a few weeks ago. It's not fully healed."

I sprained it making my way down a waterfall here in the rainforests of Nicaragua.

I lift the dress and show off my ankles. The left one is still swollen from slipping and sliding down the narrow game trail.

Her brows push together and her lips purse as she tries to force the shoes on me.

"Look, I'll carry them if I must, but no way am I wearing them. I'll turn a healing sprain into a full-on break."

Fear flits in her eyes; there and gone before I realize it. Then an expressionless mask covers her face.

I take the heels from her. "Look, I don't want you to get in trouble. As far as any of them know, you tried."

Rosalie doesn't acknowledge me. Her shoulders slump and her chin dips.

"I really wish you could talk to me." There's so much I want to ask, but my gaze lifts to the camera in the corner.

Everything is monitored.

I take one last look in the mirror, then go to the couch and wait for what happens next.

A knock at the door makes me jump. Not knowing whether I'm to answer or wait for whomever it is to come inside, my hand flies to my stomach as I brace for the unknown.

TWENTY-FOUR

Booker

The flight to Nicaragua takes seven hours. Another hour passes on the ground as we meet up with Forest Summers's CIA contacts in a small village less than two miles from Angelo's private residence.

Sam stands at the front with CJ by his side. Mitzy and her small team hover around a rickety table connecting their gear to banks of lithium batteries.

As for Bravo team, we arrange ourselves in the cramped quarters, leaning against the walls or sitting on the dilapidated furniture.

Joining us are Forest, his sister, Doc Summers, and the two CIA operatives.

"Listen up." Sam clears his throat. "All eyes up here."

He waits for us to pay attention, then crosses his broad arms over his chest.

"Diego Espinoza and Luis Sanchez are our local experts. They're going to brief us on what they know about the major players. After that, once Mitzy's team is ready, we'll go over the operation." Sam yields the floor to a man with dark hair, bronzed skin, and coffee-brown eyes.

"Good evening. I'm Diego Espinoza." He takes a moment to greet each of us with a nod. "I've been on assignment in Nicaragua for a little over a decade. Much of my information comes from contacts I've developed over the years dealing with the *Laguta* cartel and its kidnapping and ransom operations. Luis Sanchez …" He gestures to the other man, "is involved in monitoring the movement of guns, munitions, and the exchange of currency through criminal elements."

Luis lifts a hand in greeting and rocks forward. He takes in a deep breath and takes over.

"The Angelo family is an old family with ties to virtually every industry within Nicaragua, both legal and not. Over the past several decades, they've been increasing their political presence and solidifying their power base."

I check in with my team. We're all familiar with the political climate, especially the CIA's involvement in the '80s and '90s. Our country has its own dark past, specifically, the CIA's role in escalating the U.S. drug crisis and arming of the Contras.

I pay Luis half a mind as he continues.

"Angelo has strong industrial ties and fingers in nearly every criminal organization, including both the *Laguta* and *Coralos* cartels."

"We were told his brother and cousin are the respective leaders." I pull out my Bowie knife and run my finger along its sharp edge.

Briefings are all well and good, but I'm ready for action.

"Correct. At least until his cousin was taken out by your team." Luis rocks back on his heels. "They're struggling to reconsolidate after that loss."

"Why are they rivals if they're in the same family?" Rafe speaks up.

"Maximus created the friction to place pressure on his cousin." Diego takes in a deep breath. "How, we're not certain. Word on the street is Maximus holds sensitive information on his potential rivals, which keeps them subdued."

"And his cousin was a rival?" We don't need a history lesson in Nicaraguan politics. We need to get this show on the road.

My Isabelle's out there, all alone, probably terrified out of her mind, and she has no idea how close we are to getting her out.

"Any rivals bold enough to come at him, speak out against him, or challenge him in the political arena have a nasty habit of disappearing." Diego scratches his chin. "As do those who don't follow orders."

"And you have no idea what kind of blackmail he keeps?" Doc Summers, who's been quiet, speaks up. She and Forest stand together; anxious expressions fill their faces.

"We don't know," Diego answers her question.

"Angelo has done well to secure his position. As Minister of the Interior, his reach extends everywhere." Luis sweeps his gaze around the room.

Does he know who his audience is? This kind of intel is the same page, different day, for our team.

We eat men like this Angelo fucker for lunch. Taking him down will be a piece of cake—if they shut up and let us get on with our fucking job. I stretch out my fingers, realizing I clench my hands. Frustration tugs at me, drawing me toward Isabelle.

The need to get to her makes it difficult to think.

"A man like that will be surrounded by an army." Brady pulls at his jaw. "Makes our job a tough one."

"The security at his private estate, while not insignificant, is nothing you haven't seen before." Sam puts it out there, offering hope.

"His surveillance is second to none." Doubt coats Diego's words. He swallows thickly when both Sam and CJ give him a look. Clearing his throat, he continues. "But I've been assured your tech team can handle that."

No shit we can handle it.

Nothing stops the Guardians.

"We've got it handled and more." Mitzy pops her head out of the dining room. "And Forest brought his new pets along for the ride."

My entire team takes interest.

In our year of downtime, recovering and training, we've been guinea pigs for Forest's newest AI tech. Called R.U.F.U.S., the name is an acronym for Robotic Ultra Functional Utility Specialist, an automated robot powered by artificial intelligence.

Like the others, I welcome this. In the latest iteration, weapons were added to the robots. They enhance our firepower, and since they're virtually invisible to modern detection devices, their stealth allows them to go where we cannot.

I'm happy to bring a robot dog on this mission. Hell, I'll take twenty, although we only brought three.

The automated weaponry is not yet deployable. Too many risks associated with unintentionally injuring civilians. But that's what Mitzy's team is for. They'll operate the weaponry remotely while Rufus I, II, and III do what they do best.

"Considering who this man is, what's the word on lethality?" I want the kill-shot but have a feeling it won't be authorized.

Guardian HRS has gone up against many adversaries—rich and powerful men with unscrupulous morals—but this will be the first time we take out a political figure.

That comes with serious repercussions.

At least not all's lost. Matias will get two bullets between his eyes. That man is going down for abducting my girl.

As my gaze wanders the room, taking everything in, I catch an odd nonverbal exchange between Forest and Doc Summers. The doc places the back of her hand on Forest's arm, then she reaches up to do the same thing to the side of his neck. She asks him something and he shakes his head, saying no.

Giving a light squeeze to his bicep, she leaves him alone. His sigh is nearly imperceptible. I would've missed it, except it caught my eye.

"Angelo is not to be harmed." Doc Summers's soft voice penetrates the rumblings of our team. "Shoot to wound, not to kill. We're not looking to start a war."

It's no secret to anyone in the room, I'm not a fan of that plan. I push off from the wall, hot under the collar and getting angrier by the second. "How are we to mount a rescue mission if we can't shoot combatants?"

Brady gives me a look that tells me to tone it down.

"It's not as if you haven't trained for missions exactly like this in the past." Deep and resonating, Forest's voice vibrates the air. "Your mission is to rescue Izzy. She is your priority, but this is not an assassination. Guardian HRS cannot draw that much attention on itself. We're not taking out a member of their government. Angelo will be dealt with, but not today. Too much is at stake."

Too much?

What the fuck am I missing?

"Yeah, but if we …"

"He's not to be touched." Forest's booming voice silences the room. He looks down at his sister and they trade another odd look. Covering his mouth, Forest coughs. Doc Summers turns to him, looking concerned, but he waves her off and catches his breath.

"Understood." Brady answers for Bravo team, then gives me a what-the-fuck look. He mouths *Stand the fuck down* at me and places his hand over my chest.

I stand down, but only because Isabelle means too much for me to get myself kicked off the mission for insubordination.

Maximus Angelo is the man at the center of everything. If he has Isabelle, there's a reason. Whatever that reason, I'll figure it out. There's more going on beneath the surface, and our CIA contacts are holding back on us.

"As fascinating as all of this is, how does any of this relate to the diamonds?" Brady moves us off the conversation of what to do with the Angelo, back onto the one thing we are one hundred percent sure about.

"That's something we're trying to sort out." Luis Sanchez rubs the back of his neck. "We have an informant within his organization who is reliable. If he was moving something, we'd know." He regards me with caution.

I've seen the look before. The man's hedging.

"Maybe your informant doesn't know?"

The presence of an informant doesn't surprise me, but Luis and Diego's assurance the source is reliable sends up all kinds of red flags. "We believe the diamonds are a ploy to ferret out a traitor in their ranks."

I scratch at my head, confused, but trying to follow.

"So, you're saying Angelo gave his brother millions in diamonds to catch an informant?"

"Yes." Diego's stare doesn't waver. He believes what he says.

"How do you know your informant isn't compromised after the diamonds were lost?" I can't help but push.

"We're certain they are not." Diego holds his ground.

"How can you be certain?" I can't help but press him further.

"Because we would know."

Damn, whoever they have on the inside must be very close to Angelo.

Mitzy would categorize my conclusion as an assumption, but I know it for what it is. Hunches may be hazardous, but there's a place for them. Rather than badger them further about whoever's feeding them intel from the inside, I switch tactics, digging for insight on the warring cartels.

"How does the strife between the two cartels factor in?"

"Angelo is a ruthless individual. Recently, his cousin has been getting more vocal, placing demands on Angelo." Diego steps up.

"Demands?" I look to Mitzy, storehouse of all knowledge, but she returns a shrug.

"Yes," Diego continues. "Nicaragua is one of the poorest countries in the Americas. Poverty is rampant with high inequality between urban and rural populations. They're dependent on agricultural exports, such as cotton and coffee, and have been the victims of several natural disasters in the past decade, which have set back the infrastructure support he's been trying to implement. Nicaragua has the potential to be more, and Angelo wants to be the man to make that so."

"More?"

"His vision is to pull Nicaragua out of poverty, but to do that, he needs money to develop the infrastructure to handle it. Cotton and cocoa only go so far."

"What about drugs?" I arch a brow.

Drugs are exceptionally lucrative.

"Drugs aren't enough." Diego gives a firm shake of his head. "And too much of the profit must stay in the hands of the cartel and gangs who run the drugs and distribute them."

"If he's as ruthless as you say, that wouldn't be a problem." I counter Diego's argument, but it's full of holes. I know it and Diego knows it.

One of the secrets to keeping drugs profitable is making the risk worth it at the lowest ranks. The peddlers and low-level distributors need their cut.

"He needs the money in the hands of the government. Clean money. Sustainable income for the country. That's where the rift came with his cousin."

A rift?

Why is Diego only now getting to this? Big waste of fucking time if you ask me. I peer over Diego's shoulder, trying to see how Mitzy and her gang of techno whiz kids are coming along.

We're really waiting on them. The rest of this is shit, though it impacts our ability to infiltrate Angelo's mansion and get Isabelle out.

"How's that?" Rafe, lover of any and all information, steps in, satisfying his curiosity.

I'm curious too. All of it is connected somehow, just not relevant to my needs at the current moment.

"Nicaragua is rich in natural resources, sitting on what amounts to a modern-day treasure in unexploited mineral resources like deposits of gold and silver. What they don't have is the industry, infrastructure, or capital to exploit it."

"How much are we talking?" I'm curious now.

"Billions to build what they need to pull untold trillions out of the ground." Luis doesn't hold back. "Enough to completely change the geo-political climate of the Americas."

Damn.

"Not to mention iron ore, gypsum, copper, and lead," Diego chimes in. "Those resources are located in the southern part of the country; an area controlled by the *Coralos* cartel, the leader of which the Guardians recently executed."

"I wouldn't say executed," Brady disagrees. "Put down like the dog he was, is what happened." No holding back what he thinks of that man. "Although, it seems we did the man a favor. If his cousin wasn't falling in line, we just took out the opposition."

"And there's still no connection to the diamonds." I kick off the wall, wanting to pace, but there's no room in the tiny house we appropriated as our staging ground.

"According to our source, Angelo's cousin was always a step ahead in negotiations. That led Angelo and his brother to believe they had a rat in the ranks of the *Lagutas*."

"And the best way to ferret out a rat is to set a trap." I see how that might work.

"It's what we speculate, but it's all a moot point now that the *Coralos* cartel is struggling to recover. Before they do, Angelo will have what he needs." Diego chews on his lower lip.

"Seems odd the *Laguta* cartel would give them to a Doctors Without Borders employee." I use the tip of my knife to clean under my fingernails.

"Jerald was nothing more than a courier." Luis clears his throat. "He used your women as unknowing mules. Because of their positions within Doctors Without Borders, they would be the least likely to be searched if something went wrong."

"Like getting kidnapped by the *Coralos* cartel?"

"Exactly. The only reason the cartel didn't find the diamonds was because the information they were fed concerned weapons."

"A deliberate distraction." CJ taps his temple with his forefinger.

"Do you know who the traitor is?"

"Not yet." Diego pulls at his chin. "Although, we're looking to see if any known cartel members are missing."

Missing means killed.

I shift my attention to CJ. "Do we have an action plan? Or are we shooting in the dark here?"

All this information about Maximus Angelo, while interesting, isn't helping me get Isabelle back. We're still sitting on our asses while Lord knows what is happening to her.

"Angelo's estate is uniquely suited to help our efforts." CJ knows exactly what I'm thinking. "Mitzy launched a fleet of drones to map out the property. The house itself is an open-air design. As soon as the sun sets, they'll move in closer and locate Izzy. Bravo team, you'll be in position outside the estate until we have that info."

CJ glances at Mitzy and her team. He presses his lips together and takes in a breath. "In the meantime, along with the Rufuses, you'll patrol the outside of the structure, taking down any surveillance and resistance that you may encounter on your way out."

"Exfil is on foot?" I ask.

If Isabelle's injured, that could prove problematic.

"We do have a plan B."

"And what's that?" My nerves begin to settle. Now that we're on the cusp of actually doing something, I focus on the steps between now and mission success.

"The place is a fortress. Easier to get in than get out," Diego answers my question. "There's a helicopter on standby if required, but we'd like to keep that asset dark for as long as possible. Not that it needs to be said, but our objective is to keep the CIA out of this. We blow that asset if we use it." He glances at Forest, who returns a nod.

"We will make it right if that happens." Forest looks me in the eye. "Exfil will be on foot. Vehicles are parked inside an outer courtyard with heavy gates, spikes, and impact barriers impeding any exit that way. You go in on foot. Come out on foot. Bravo team will be picked up two miles from the estate. It's as close as we dare to go."

"Makes sense." I don't like it, but there's not much I can do about it.

If Isabelle isn't up for the hike—likely more of a run—I'll carry her on my back. I'll do whatever it takes to rescue her.

Over the next hour, we discuss various ways to infiltrate the compound.

As Mitzy's drones gather more data on exterior surveillance and defense, our plans adjust and compensate. The sun sets, bringing on dusk, as we finalize our plans.

"A dozen men patrol outside the walls. The Rufuses …" CJ gives Forest a look. "We seriously need a better name."

"Rufi? Rufusi?" Rafe tries to help, but it makes everyone laugh.

"Well, the damn dogs will tranq the guards. That allows you to get close." CJ rubs his hands together. He's getting edgy, like me.

"The drones are done." Mitzy calls us over to the table.

We gather around her as they piece together a composite of the building.

"How many staff and guards inside?" Brady's back to pulling at his chin. He does that when deep in thought.

Mitzy points to various places inside the compound. "These are staff."

"How do you know?" It's an honest question.

"Guards don't hang out in the kitchen and laundry. They also don't push mops and brooms." She points out the details, making me feel foolish.

"Attempt no contact with the staff." Sam's deep voice commands attention. "But if you come across any, tie them up, gag them, and put them in a place of safety until this is over."

"Copy that." Brady shifts beside me. He gives me a look; one we've shared before. Sometimes, the help is more than just the help.

Bravo team gathers around the table. Brady and I stand across from Sam and CJ. To our left, Rafe and Alec peruse the mock-up Mitzy and her drones generated. Hayes and Zeb crouch down, getting eye level with the display.

Already, they're assessing the best approach, while Brady and I examine how we're going to get Isabelle and the team out.

Mitzy hovers just out of sight, whispering with Forest and Doc Summers. The urgency of their conversation draws my attention from the map of Angelo's estate, but it's the heated argument between them that gives me pause.

Why do Forest and Doc Summers care about keeping Angelo alive?

That's a question for another day because in less than an hour, we're kitted up and on our way.

The night is eerily still, meaning the heat and humidity of the day clings tenaciously to the land. There's no breeze.

No sound.

It's as if time stands still while six warriors prepare for battle.

TWENTY-FIVE

Izzy

The knock shocks my system. I leap to my feet, smooth the dress, and interlace my fingers. Fear closes in on me. My mouth moves, but the words catch on the lump in my throat. While I try to find my voice, the door slowly opens.

My eyes close as a silent prayer runs through me.

Please give me strength. Bless me with courage to face whatever comes next. Comfort me as I face this danger alone.

Expecting Matias, I squeeze my eyes tight, repeating the prayer over and over in my head.

"*Senorita* LaCroix, I hope you had time to rest." The smooth, cultured voice of my captor forces my eyes wide. His arrogance fades for a moment, almost making me feel as if he actually cares.

Not liking the way my mouth gapes, I close it with a snap as the dark stranger pushes the door open. He makes no move to enter, but I take a step back anyhow. Those coal-black eyes regard me; hard, calculating, and monstrous. He takes his time, dragging his gaze from my head to my toes, and doesn't hide his very obvious interest.

"You look as radiant as the morning sun." He scrapes his hand down the angle of his jaw. His five o'clock shadow is thick, nearly a beard, and somehow terrifying. "Stunning comes to mind."

My heart practically leaps out of my chest, taking off like a racehorse with wolves on its heels. I understand that kind of terror. I've lived with fear my entire life, but this is far more terrifying than a fear of heights, or water, or any of the many irrational fears I carry.

This man wants to do very bad things to me.

"Only because of Rosalie." It's all I can think to say.

"Ah, yes. She is a great lady's maid, but you are a beautiful woman, stunning in your own right." He's nearly twice my age and shouldn't be looking at me like he wants to devour me.

My chin tucks down as I avert my gaze. I can't stomach the desire swirling in the dark depths of his eyes. It makes me want to retch. My hand drifts to my belly, attempting to calm the fluttering inside.

Lady's maid?

Did we jump back to another century?

"Why isn't she allowed to speak to me?" Too curious, I can't help but ask. Although why I engage him in any conversation is a mystery to me.

I'm his prisoner. Held against my will. I should make him work for every word uttered from my mouth. Yet here I am —conversing.

"Because those are the rules." His words are more of a dismissal than an answer.

"It's a dumb rule."

He tips his head back and harsh laughter tumbles out of his mouth. It lasts barely a moment.

Before I know it, those soulless eyes are back on me. Assessing. Judging. Weighing my worth. Gauging my strength?

"You definitely don't hold your tongue, do you?" He diminishes me with a flick of his lids.

"Why should I?" My bold comment sounds much stronger than I feel.

It's lunacy to antagonize this man, especially since he controls my fate, but I can't help myself.

"Why indeed." He makes a sweeping gesture with his arm, indicating I exit the relative safety of the room to enter the hallway outside. "Allow me to escort you to dinner."

"Do I have a choice?"

"I like your attitude, Miss LaCroix, but do not test me."

"Or what?"

"That is a question best left unasked." He pivots sharply, giving me space to exit the room. "If you please …"

I do not, but I bite my tongue. Antagonizing this man seems like a poor choice. I should resist him, not blindly comply with his demands.

But I don't resist.

Knowing I tempt fate if I don't do exactly as he asks, I wage a war within myself. Comply with his demands or resist?

I live in a world that no longer makes sense.

It takes every bit of strength within me to force my feet to move. Steeling my breath, I allow my hands to drop to my side and exit the room.

I shouldn't, but it's impossible to silence the thoughts swirling in my head. If I resist, what will he do? Lock me up in that room? Send me to the dungeon?

A house like this, a veritable fortress, surely has a dungeon.

Right?

Bad things happen in dungeons, and I know the limits of my strength. That's something I won't survive.

Until I can figure out a way to escape this place, I choose to remain out of any dungeons, whether they exist or not. Which means giving ground and doing as he says.

The moment I'm out of the room, he shuts the door behind me. Glancing down, he takes a long look at the floor.

No.

Not the floor.

"Where are your shoes?"

"I left the ankle breakers inside."

"Ankle breakers?" One of his brows wings up, curious or amused.

"That's what I call them."

"You can't wander around in bare feet."

"I can't walk in four-inch heels."

"Why not?" He looks at me as if I speak in tongues.

"Because I sprained my ankle a few weeks ago and don't want to turn a sprain into a break."

"You are an interesting woman."

And you're an asshole.

Whatever.

I need to move his focus off of me and try to learn something about him.

"Are you going to tell me who you are? Or am I supposed to guess over dinner?"

"You are a breath of fresh air and an unexpected treat."

"Is that a good thing, or a bad thing?"

"That depends."

"On what?"

"Whether you become a nuisance."

"A nuisance?" My brows tug tight. "Because I won't wear the heels?"

"Because you stand up for yourself."

"And I'm not supposed to?"

"No one goes against what I want."

"No one?"

"No one." He delivers the words with a sense of finality, letting me know not to pursue that line of conversation further. "Not even my high-spirited daughter."

I suck in a breath, realizing how much this man terrifies me. With a flick of his fingers, he can end my life. That's not an exaggeration. Not if a man like Matias works for him. I've seen what Matias is capable of and have no wish to find out what the man standing in front of me can do.

"I'm not lying. I really did sprain my ankle." On cue, my ankle wobbles, nearly giving out.

To my horror, I clutch blindly for support, finding his arm. I steady myself and let go with a hiss.

"So, you have." He speaks as if he made the decision rather

than me. It's slight, but more than that, it's a power move on his part. "In that case, we leave the ankle breakers behind." The ghost of a smile curves the corners of his mouth into a grin.

He offers his right arm, elbow bent, but when I don't accept the very obvious offer, his iron grip encircles my wrist. I flinch and pull away, but his fingers tighten around my wrist, making a show of his power.

He forces my hand under his arm, curling it around until I have no choice but to grasp his forearm. With another penetrating glare, it's a not-so-gentle reminder there is no tolerance for resistance of any sort.

"Maximus." He takes off down the hall.

"Excuse me?"

"My name. It's Maximus, Maximus Angelo. Welcome to my home, Miss LaCroix. With time, you will learn to enjoy your new home and accept your place within it."

"My place?" I pull to a stop and attempt to free my hand, but he places his free hand over mine, trapping it.

"Yes."

"And what place would that be?" I think of my abduction as a short-term thing, but he speaks of something that sounds a whole lot like forever. The entire room spins around me.

"You are not this naïve." He tugs me forward, forcing me to walk beside him. When he places his hand over mine, locking me in place, I swallow down my revulsion.

"Naïve?" That lump in my throat tightens, making it impossible to swallow.

I've entered some sort of ninth circle of hell.

There's little conversation during the long trek to the dining room. I reel from his comment, trying to convince myself it doesn't mean what I think it means. Matias's words return to me. Maximus will hand me over once he's done with me. A chill works its way down my spine, lifting the fine hairs at my nape and on my arms.

"Do you like my gardens?" Maximus doesn't slow his stride, giving me no time to admire anything.

Flickering gas lamps illuminate the halls we walk through, while the courtyards and their gardens sink into darkness with the setting of the sun.

I clear my throat, trying to loosen the hard lump that appears to have taken up residence there, but still can't manage any words. Instead, I give a sharp nod and hurry my step to keep up with his long strides.

We come to an empty sitting room and he guides me inside.

Guide?

It's more like he steers me where he wants. I hate this man. Loathe him on a cellular level. If I could kill him, I would. For me to consider taking a life speaks volumes. That's how much I hate him.

"We will wait here until my daughter comes down. Would you like a drink?"

"Um …" There's simply no way to find my words. With my world in turmoil and my future stretching before me filled with unspeakable horror, I'm completely stumped.

His daughter? I remember the callous woman I met earlier in the hall.

Boy, did she have a lot to say to me about knowing my place.

"Sit." He practically shoves me into a chair. "I will bring you something to help you relax."

I don't want anything that will help me relax. I need to be hyper-vigilant and ready to escape if the opportunity arises. Not to mention, he can slip anything into my drink, taking my free will with it.

"I'm not thirsty."

"This isn't for thirst, but to calm your nerves."

"My nerves wouldn't need calming if I wasn't a prisoner." Knowing I'm not strong enough to free myself, I'll try anything. Even if I'm trying to reason with the devil. "You made a mistake taking me. I really know nothing."

He returns with two tumblers filled with amber liquid. Whiskey, I presume.

"I've accepted that, but you are valuable." He hands me one of the glasses. "There is nothing doctored in your drink. I will not use such things to force you to my bed."

There it is. Irrefutable proof of what he intends. Is it possible to kill another human with a whiskey glass? It's all I have.

"I'm not …"

"Don't misunderstand me, *senorita*, or mistake what I want. Or what will happen. I do not need to drug you to get you in my bed. That is a decision you will make all on your own."

"I will never sleep with you." No way in hell would I ever make such a decision.

He lifts a single finger, silencing me. "Never is a word best used with caution."

"But …"

"Do not underestimate me, nor mistake what I want from you. A person will do things they would not ordinarily do when presented with the proper motivation."

"You're out of your ever-loving mind."

"No. I'm simply accustomed to getting what I want."

"How is that me?" I can't help it; I point my index finger at my chest.

"You are a fortunate consequence of unfortunate events, and I like to take advantage of such things." He leans back, sipping from his glass. His eyes are on me again, roving where they will, without a care for what I want.

"Consequence?" I place the drink on the table next to me. "That doesn't explain why I'm here."

"You are here because, despite what you think, you're a valuable asset."

"Asset?"

"A tool to force my enemies into the open."

"I don't know what you think is happening, but I'm not your enemy. The diamonds were a mistake. I didn't even know I had them. I've told you over and over that I'm a nobody. You can't leverage anything from a nobody."

"That is where you're wrong."

I hate the way he speaks; rarely using contractions of any kind. Makes him sound like a stuck-up pig. Not a pig. The man's a prick.

"I'm not wrong."

"The outfit who rescued you intrigues me, and you are my leverage to force them to reveal who they are, and who they work for."

"Then you're going to be very disappointed. I have nothing to give you, and I'm not worth anything to the man who rescued me."

"One man?" His brows lift.

Shit, it's too easy to forget everything I say will be scrutinized, analyzed, and put to use against Booker and the rest of the Guardians.

"Hate to disappoint you, but like I said before, I was a second thought during the whole rescue. I'm worth nothing. You're barking up the wrong tree."

"In that, you are wrong." He rests his chin on his hand. "You do not understand what makes men tick, or what they will do to protect one of their own. Your friends will come, and when they do, my men will be waiting for them.

"I'm a trap?" A sudden spike of fear rises within me.

"No. You, my dear, are the bait." He chuckles softly, looking pleased with himself. "And while I have you, I *will* make use of your charms."

Charms?

"Why?"

"Because I can." He bolts forward and grabs my chin in his iron grip. His voice hardens and those black eyes of his swirl with malevolent darkness. "I will use their pretty toy and I *will* break you as payment for the inconvenience they have caused me." My pulse spikes and roars past my ears as his grip eases. He releases me, shoving me into the chair while my entire body trembles.

"Why? Why would you do such a thing? Why do you want to hurt me?"

"Because if you're linked to who I think you are, I want him to pay for inconveniencing me."

"I have no idea what you're talking about."

"You don't need to know, and the beauty of this whole thing is I don't have to do anything. They will come for you. All I have to do is bait the trap."

Trap?

My head swims with what he says, making no sense out of any of it.

"Because your courier messed up the delivery of the diamonds?"

"You see only what you want to see." He pulls out the rabbit's foot from beneath his shirt and taps the metal clasp that holds the thing in place. "Diamonds are not the only things I find valuable."

"What's more valuable than diamonds?"

"Information, of course. Diamonds buy things, but information buys loyalty and obedience." He gives me a look, waiting for a response.

"You make me sick to my stomach. As for what you said about me ..." I can't repeat what he implied about having sex with him. "That's never happening."

"Tell me ..." He puts his glass down and leans forward. Reaching out, he touches my knees.

I jerk away, but he captures my knee in that iron grip of his. Fingers dig into my skin, bringing tears. There will be bruising when this is done.

"I will touch and more."

"You're crazy."

"Do you believe you would be so brave refusing me if you knew your mother's life depended on it."

"Leave my mother out of this."

"Like you, she is a tool. I will use you against those who seek to rescue you, and I will use her to compel your obedience." His tone suddenly shifts. "Rest assured, I will not kill your mother, but each time you defy me, she will suffer."

I open my mouth to respond, but he silences me, lifting his forefinger in the air and slowly shaking it back and forth.

"I will begin with her toes, cutting them off one by one. Then her ears. Her fingers follow next."

"You're a monster." I push back in horror, sinking deeper into my chair. "A despicable excuse for a human being."

"Perhaps." He shrugs as if my words mean nothing.

But would they?

To a psychopath?

"I believe you will find your motivation there. If not, I move to your father, your brothers. Anyone you hold dear goes next. Defy me and you will be punished." His lips turn up into a sneer. "Do not force me to hurt your family." He leans back, swirling his drink. Vileness radiates out from his oily gaze, turning my stomach to stone.

"You have what you came for. The diamonds are yours. Why are you doing this to me?"

"Because I can." He squeezes my leg until I cry out in pain, then slowly leans back in his chair. "Because I enjoy it. Now, do you understand the power I wield?"

My lips press together as I take in a long and very shaky breath. Moments ago, if I'd been asked if I would do what this man said, I would've laughed at the idiocy of that comment.

But now?

Now, I understand what true power means, and I know real evil exists in the world.

"Ah, there it is …" He points at me. "Understanding is the first step. Acceptance comes next. After that comes obedience."

"Why? Why would you do something like this?" I can't help it. None of this makes sense.

Booker, if you're out there, please—please help me!

"The pleasure is in the breaking, and you will break very well. Already, you dissemble before me."

"You're evil."

"I am what I am." He turns to the sound of stilettos clicking down the hall. "Ah, that is my daughter. Consider this your first test. Be pleasant and agreeable, meek and mild. Charming and civil. Speak of nothing—*disagreeable.*" The way his lips twist in victory makes my stomach churn and bile rise in my throat.

The thing I hate most is that I will give this man everything he wants. He knows it. I know it. And from the victorious gleam in his eye, he knows I know it.

Maximus rises from his seat as the clicking grows louder. He holds out his hand, waiting for me to take it. My hesitation lasts but a second.

Inside, a war rages within me. There's nothing but defeat waiting for me. I take his hand and let him pull me to his side. While his arm wraps around my waist, the woman I saw earlier sweeps into the room.

If I thought she was beautiful before, that's nothing compared to now. Red silk clings to her natural curves and drapes magnificently down to the floor. Luminous eyes. Luxurious hair. Features destined to drive men mad; she's beyond stunning.

She gives me a look somewhere between a sneer and disgust.

"Papa …" She lifts her hands, waiting for Maximus to release me.

"Carmen, you are as beautiful as ever." He takes her hands in his, pulling her in to kiss both her cheeks. "But you should not be here." His tone takes on a scolding edge. "You were to spend the week with Artemus and his mother planning your wedding."

"Artemus is a dog. I'm not marrying him."

"Carmen …" His tone deepens to a low rumble. "You had better not …"

"Not what, Papa?" She presses first one cheek, then the other, to his face. It's a wooden gesture, done without love. The tension in the room spikes. "Don't you want your only daughter to be happy?"

"Happiness has nothing to do with it."

"I don't favor him." She pushes back, but can she be that oblivious to the bunching in his muscles and the fury darkening his features? "You have a guest." She dismisses her father with a sniff, ending their conversation as if it never began in the first place. "And who is this?" She takes a step back, releasing her father's hands.

She knows who I am—a plaything for her father. The same derisive tone clings to her words as when she watched Matias drag me down the hall.

Nothing about this place makes any sense.

Maximus draws me in close and wraps an arm possessively around my waist.

"May I introduce Miss Isabelle LaCroix. Isabelle, this is my daughter, Carmen Angelo, my pride and joy, if not troublesome, daughter."

"Touché, Papa." Her piercing gaze cuts to me. "We will speak of that later, in private."

"Um, it's nice to meet you." I manage my words carefully, betraying no emotion.

Maximus knows exactly what it takes to control me. I will do anything to keep my family safe.

"And what brings her here?" There's a slight lilt to her voice, a demand disguised as a question. "Another of your toys, I suspect?" Disdain coats her tongue, turning her greeting brittle and cold.

With those words, she dismisses me as something without value.

"Isabelle is one of the doctors Miguel took for ransom. She returned my property."

"I see." Carmen gives me a long once over, then dismisses me with a flick of her lashes. "My father loves beautiful women, Miss LaCroix, but tires of them quickly. Best not grow too attached. He will use you, then abandon you."

"Carmen." Maximus's voice cracks between us like thunder. "Show a little respect for my guest."

"That's what I'm doing, Papa. Showing little respect." With that, she executes a perfect pirouette and heads into the dining room.

"Do not mind Carmen." With that, he guides me into an elegantly appointed dining room set up with crystal, silver, and china. "She's strong-willed and tests my patience at every turn. Regardless, we will enjoy a civil dinner before retiring for the night to indulge in other *activities*." His grip on my arm tightens. "And I expect an exceptional performance following dinner."

My stomach curls in on itself while I force down the bile rising in my throat. Biting my lower lip helps me focus on the pain while trying to figure out how the hell I'm going to survive this night.

The only man I'm interested in spending any evening with is the one man who's yet to take the initiative and kiss me already.

Blowing out a breath, I vow several things.

Whatever comes my way, I'm strong enough to survive it.

My family comes first. No way will this man hurt them.

If I ever see Booker again, the first thing I'm going to do is take the kiss I can't stop thinking about. Then, I'm going to smack him in the face for making me wait.

But first things first.

How am I going to survive this night?

TWENTY-SIX

Booker

HEAT CLINGS TENACIOUSLY TO THE EVENING AIR. IT WEIGHS ME down as we move in toward our target. Unease churns in my gut. Worry over what's happening to Isabelle. Wondering if she's hurt. Suffering? Terrified? Still alive?

Lord, I pray she's alive.

That thought tightens the restrictive band around my chest, making it impossible to breathe.

But I do breathe.

I slow the beating of my heart and force such thoughts from my mind. They distract me, and I need to focus if I'm to get my woman.

All manner of insects are out, biting and stinging those in their path. Fortunately, we're clothed head to toe in black with our faces covered by the integrated helmets created by Guardian HRS.

Which means, instead of bites and stings, I drip sweat head to toe. A minor inconvenience; I've endured worse.

With our integrated displays, we operate in the infrared part of the spectrum, meaning our headsets turn the dark landscape from pitch-black to shades of white and gray. As we move in on Angelo's private residence, Mitzy guides us toward our insertion point.

Her drones remain hard at work. She calls them dragonflies because they're not much larger than a deck of cards. Each one is equipped with high-res cameras and fly on whisper-silent rotors. Covering them, a cutting-edge shielding bends light around them, making them nearly invisible to the naked eye.

Talk about tech gadget cool.

We've got invisibility cloaks for our machines.

A massive wall surrounds and protects the residence, making our entry into the building problematic at best. With no way in, except through the vehicle courtyard, we'll be climbing those walls and dropping into one of the many open-aired courtyards inside.

As for where Isabelle may be—that's yet to be determined. Although, Mitzy's drones are on it.

"A hundred yards out," Brady calls our team to a halt.

We crouch behind dense vegetation, hiding ourselves as much as possible from whatever surveillance monitors outside the walls. Rufus I, II, and III pull up alongside our team.

The doglike robots stand hip high. In addition to their four legs, a fully articulating arm does double duty as a head as well as an arm with a fully functional hand to grab and manipulate objects in its environment.

These things are scary cool.

And damn if my arm doesn't lift all on its own to drape over the back of the robot next to me, just like I did with the real thing back in my team days in the Navy.

Like Mitzy's dragonflies, the same light-bending tech covers the robots. It's disconcerting when I look at them; my gaze slips past the things before catching and trying to resolve their outlines.

"Any word on our target?" I wait for a reply from Mitzy.

"Still scanning. We've ruled out the southern part of the residence. Proceed to the northern aspect for infil."

"Copy that." Brady gathers us together to discuss our approach to the walls.

"*Taking control of the cameras.*" Mitzy updates us on her progress. "*I need five minutes for a suitable loop. Don't move in too close.*"

"Got it." Brady takes off, moving at a steady clip.

"*Taking control of Rufus II and III.*" As Mitzy speaks, the two robots shadowing Rafe, Zeb, Hayes, and Alec, peel off from our group.

While we're inside, they will neutralize any men patrolling outside the walls. Our goal is to get in and get out with no one being the wiser until long after we're gone.

The two robots disappear into the darkness, becoming invisible as they move off. Rufus I stays with us and will remain by our side until we're over the wall.

With the go-ahead given, we move in on the northern wall and wait outside. Mitzy will tell us when to approach. She hijacked the security cameras and will send a repeat of the last five minutes to the security suite inside. The men monitoring those cameras will never see us scaling the wall.

As for scaling the wall, we've got Rufus.

"*Good to go.*" CJ takes over comms. Mitzy's hard at work with her tech. "*You'll be dropping into a courtyard on the other side with plenty of vegetation for cover.*"

"Copy that," Brady acknowledges the communication. "What about Izzy?"

He asks the question burning in my gut. Once we're inside, there's no time to be wandering the halls.

"*Almost there.*" Mitzy's voice sounds strained.

I imagine running three robots, a swarm of drones, and managing her tech team must be taking its toll on her genius mind.

"*Bingo!*" Mitzy's shout makes me jump. "*Target located. Northern wall. One male. Two females. Dining room.*"

"How do you know it's her?" I shouldn't question Mitzy, but I need to know.

"*Height matches.*" She doesn't waste time on details.

"Copy that." If it's good enough for her, it's good enough for me.

"You ready?" Brady clasps my shoulder, giving a solid squeeze.

"Past ready."

Rafe, Zeb, Hayes, and Alec each thump my back in turn.

"Let's get your girl." Rafe knocks the top of my helmet and moves in toward the northern wall.

We approach the last bit of cover provided by the thick vegetation all around us and take a knee.

"I'm in." Once again, Mitzy calls out. *"Give me five to make a loop, then you're good to go."*

About fucking time.

Five minutes shouldn't seem like forever, but I swear, time stands still. With my team around me, I have no worries about how this mission will go. Brady signals us to switch to internal comms.

"Rafe and Zeb, you're over the wall first. Secure our place and take out any opposition as quietly as possible."

"On it, boss." Rafe's grin isn't visible through the black mesh covering our faces but sings in his words.

"Booker and I go next. Hayes and Alec, you guard our rear."

"Hear ya loud and clear." Alec shifts on the ground. Head up. Eyes open. Ears on alert. The man's hearing is a superpower.

"Bravo, you're on," Mitzy calls out. She provides direction via an embedded 3D reconstruction of the building fed to us through the heads-up displays in our helmets. Highlighted in red are the guards inside. Blue figures are noncombatants we're to avoid at all costs.

Rufus moves out, heading for the wall to give us a bit of an assist. Once the robot's in position, Rafe and Zeb sprint the twenty yards to the wall.

The robotic dog rears up on its hind legs and places its two front legs against the wall. That creates a series of steps that Rafe takes at a run. Halfway up, he leaps the remaining distance. Rafe drops down the opposite side while Zeb springs over Rufus and follows him.

The display on our helmets updates to show two new figures lit up in green. Rafe and Zeb move away from the base of the wall and take up defensive positions.

Brady and I wait for the security patrol to create the gap we need to cross the distance unobserved. Once the hole opens, Brady sprints toward the wall with me right on his heels. A series of leaps allows us to scale the wall, using Rufus as our ladder. We jump down into the courtyard below and wait for Alec and Hayes to join us.

A few minutes later, they're on our side of the wall. Rufus moves off under the command of one of Mitzy's operatives to patrol our escape route, ensuring it remains clear. It, and the others, are tiny, yellow lights on our display.

"*We're in,*" Brady reports our progress, although there's no need.

Command knows exactly where we are.

"Sending in best routes." The moment CJ responds, a network of white lines spreads through the expansive retreat.

They've got better eyes than we do, courtesy of the dragonfly drones and the robots outside, but the final decision is Brady's to make. We pause for a second, examining the data fed to us by our technical crew. There is really just the one way in. It's our way out as well, which will be tricky.

Once our presence is known, we'll have to fight our way out, and I want nothing to do with bullets flying anywhere near my girl.

Brady glances at me and the others. He leads us, but we agree as a team. With our decision made, we head out in pairs, leapfrogging our way to the dining room. Rafe and Zeb go first. They exit the courtyard and head down a hall. Once in position, Brady and I go next. We pass Rafe and Zeb, moving deeper into the estate.

Fortunately, with the exception of the cook staff and servers, the rest of the employees are bunked down for the night, leaving the halls clear.

For the most part.

Armed to the teeth, it's not bullets that help us out, but rather silent darts we fire into single guards roving the halls. Silent and fast, the men take two steps before falling to the ground. Each time, we move in, working in complete silence to tie them up and tuck them away to be found later.

Nonlethal.

It goes against my training to leave fighting men alive, but it's much more humane than the alternative. Besides, it's not like we're at war.

We intercept our third guard of the evening and subdue him

before coming within sight of the dining room. There we pause and decide our next step.

So freakin' close.

I don't have a line of sight on Isabelle, but I feel her. She's a part of me, whether she agrees with me or not. The woman can fight it, but I'm going to show her what she means to me. No more pussy-footing around. We've wasted too much time on that shit.

"Hard to say which is her." Brady shifts beside me.

We crouch below a low wall that separates the open hallway from the dining room inside. Lilting female laughter bubbles out of the room. Not our target. Her voice is higher in pitch.

The deep tones belong to the man I want to kill but have been expressly forbidden from shooting. Like his guards, the best we get to do is bury a tranquilizer into his heart.

I wonder if that will kill him.

"Word on the guards?" Brady calls back to Command.

"On set patrols. No one's discovered the ones you took out." CJ gives a bit of good news.

Thank fuck for that.

We all monitor our HUDs, watching the people inside.

"Main course is finishing. Best bet, wait for the servers to clear the plates. They'll retreat to the kitchen, then return with coffee and desserts. That's your window," CJ presents his thoughts, and we mull it over.

Within a few seconds, we give unanimous thumbs up.

"We wait." Brady shifts beside me, getting comfortable but not settling in. We need to be ready to react on a moment's notice.

Behind us, Alec and Zeb guard our rear. Down the hall, Rafe and Hayes will provide cover, sweeping in behind us as we assault the room. Getting out will be problematic. I move close to Brady, voicing my concerns.

"Thoughts on exfil?"

"Challenging." Brady checks his weapon. "We're going to make noise."

"Agree." There's simply no good way to make this silent.

Either the wait staff will return and voice an alarm, or those in the room with Isabelle will do the same. Forced to use nonlethal engagement with the enemy, we're ham-stringed in what we can do.

"If we're going to make noise," I say, "let's start off with a bang.

I pull out a stun grenade and wait for Brady's response. Also known as a flashbang, it's a nonlethal explosive meant to temporarily stun and disorient our enemy. Unfortunately, it'll do the same to Isabelle, but that's okay. I'll get her out.

Voices rise in the dining room. An argument between a man and a woman. Not Isabelle, but someone else. It's the perfect distraction.

Brady gives a nod and counts us down. "*On one… Two… Three…*"

TWENTY-SEVEN

Izzy

IF LOOKS COULD KILL, I'D BE DEAD TEN TIMES OVER WITH THE WAY Carmen glares at me. Beneath her false smile and piercing eyes, the woman wants me dead.

Why?

It's not like I'm here by choice. Maximus says she's strong-willed, but the woman is wicked-smart. There's no way she doesn't know what's really happening here.

Maybe she's in league with her father?

But they argue in front of me. That's weird.

"So, you're one of the doctors who was kidnapped?" Her caustic tone burns right through me.

If I close my eyes and click my heels together three times, will I wake from this living nightmare?

"No." I shake my head.

"But Papa said …" She turns accusatory eyes toward her father.

"I'm a pharmacist. Not a doctor." I wipe my mouth with my napkin and lay it back on my lap. My dinner lies before me, essentially untouched. "Our entire medical team was kidnapped."

"A minor difference." Maximus waves off the error as if it's nothing.

Despite what Maximus says, I don't trust my food isn't drugged. My water and wine glasses remain untouched. Everything about this turns my stomach, and the evening only gets worse with the derogatory stares and not so veiled insults Carmen throws my way.

Either she doesn't know I'm not here by choice or doesn't care.

I imagine a thousand and one ways to give her a message, a desperate plea for help, but abandon each and every one as images of my mother's severed fingers fill my mind.

Maximus's threat is brutal and effective.

Not that Carmen will help. The woman hated me on sight. Why, I have no idea. I've done nothing to her. I wither under her accusatory glare, hunching my shoulders as I desperately try to disappear.

"And how did the two of you meet?" She turns suspicious eyes on me but then suddenly shifts her attention to her father. "Was it before, or after, you had Miguel killed?"

I gasp.

She turns to me. "The man who died was my cousin. Shot in the back of the head. Murdered by my father because he dared to *disagree*." Tossing her napkin on her plate, her attention swings back to her father. In that harsh gaze, victory shines. "Take that lesson to heart. Bad things happen to those who don't do as my father says."

"I had nothing to do with Miguel's murder." Maximus struggles to control his tone. "It was the men who rescued Isabelle who murdered him. They will pay for that."

I look from Carmen to her father and back again, rendered speechless.

"I highly doubt that. You've been after Miguel for years about his territory."

The servers clear our dinner plates, then retreat, leaving us alone.

"My father is not the man you think he is. There's no nobility in what he does. Be very careful jumping into his bed, although it's probably too late for that. Fair warning, it will be the last decision you make. Women in this household are not free to make their own decisions."

"Another word and …" Maximus slams his fist on the table.

"And, what?" She gestures at her dress. "You'll give her away like you did me?" She taps her polished fingernails on the tabletop.

"I did not *give you away*." His voice rises, filling the room.

"You arranged a loveless marriage against my wishes. That's the very definition of giving me away. What did Artemus do to secure my hand in marriage?" Carmen directs her next comment to me. "Tread carefully with my father. You won't be the first woman he's ruined."

"Mind your tone with me, girl. You're dangerously close to crossing a line you don't want to cross."

"I'm not marrying him."

"You will."

"You promised me to a man nearly twice my age, consigning me to a holy union that can't be broken, and for what? What did my hand in marriage cost the great Maximus Angelo? I have a right to know my true worth."

Fury sweeps through Maximus. His face turns beet red and those eyes of his rage with thunderous intent.

My heart slams against my ribcage, trying desperately to escape the confines of this body and run away. I wish it luck. I'd like to get out of this horrible place. I'd love to not be in the same room with Carmen and her father as they argue.

But I'm trapped with no way out.

"You will learn your place, daughter."

"I know my place, Papa. You never let me forget it."

Like me, she's trapped. I may be able to use her after all.

He shouts while she screams back. Their conversation turns heated, switching from English to Spanish as the volume increases.

My Spanish is barely passible, meaning I don't follow what they say. I push back from the table, not wanting to get caught between these two. The moment I stand, Maximus points at me.

"Don't you dare move."

Carmen yells at her father, speaking so fast I barely understand one word in ten, but I pick up a few words: a fiancé, marriage, and wedding she wants no part of.

I want no part of this whole weird conversation and look longingly at the open door leading out of this miserable place.

Movement catches my eye.

Something fist-sized sails through the air. Arcing overhead, it drops to the floor behind Maximus. For a second, I try to figure out what it is, but a blinding flash and a deafening blast force me to the floor.

TWENTY-EIGHT

Izzy

Intense light blinds me. Pain rings in my ears. Metallic smoke and caustic fumes fill the air, choking me after I swallow the smoke. An intense wave of disorientation forces me into a fetal position.

Maximus drops beside me. He cups his ears and curls in on himself. Through the smoke, I can't see Carmen, although she was on the other side of the table from me.

Spots dance in front of my eyes, compromising my vision. It takes a second before I make out dark shapes swarming into the room.

One of them comes at me. My body recognizes Booker on an instinctual level, even if I can't see his face. I cry out and reach frantically as tears rush down my face.

Booker bends down and takes me in his arms. While I cling to his broad shoulders, he places his gloved fingers over Maximus's throat.

The leather thong of the rabbit's foot catches my eye. I blink several times, trying to clear my vision. Spots continue to dance, disorientating me. Booker seems to be fine with whatever he's checking because he pulls back from Maximus.

When he tries to steady me on my feet, I squirm until I'm free and kneel over Maximus's body. Reaching inside his shirt, I wrap my fingers around the rabbit's foot and yank it free.

The damn thing may have caused nothing but trouble, but I want it back. If Maximus wants it, that's enough reason to take it from him. I curl my fingers around the stupid thing as Booker lifts me into the air and carries me out.

My ears ring. My nose crinkles at the acrid smoke clinging in the air. Another wave of dizziness overcomes me and I bury my face against Booker's chest.

He came for me.

Booker shifts me in his arms.

It's hard to see. I blink, but it doesn't help.

When I try to look at Booker, there's nothing to recognize. A helmet with a full shield covers his face. Beneath that, black fabric covers what's left.

His jaw moves, making me think he's trying to say something, but I shake my head and point to my ears. Hopefully, he'll get it. The only sound is that buzzing from the blast.

There are other men in the room.

The rest of Bravo team is here and I want to cheer.

One of them goes to the door leading into the kitchen. He pulls the pin on something that looks like a grenade and tosses it inside. The door closes, and less than a second later, another explosion goes off. I feel it more in my chest than hear it in my ears.

We appear to be done in the dining room because Booker carries me down a long hall. We pass two men crouched in the hallway. They have weapons at the ready. They fall in behind Booker, and we all rush down the hallway.

Pops of gunfire sound somewhere behind us. The ringing in my ears continues, and while I try to say something, I can't hear my own voice.

For the next few minutes, chaos reigns. Men rush us from behind. Booker's teammates take them out. Another group assaults us from the front. Booker shields me with his body as something I can't quite see takes them out as well.

There appears to be a brief discussion between the men, punctuated by vigorous nods. Their deep voices make it to my ears but are still too muffled from the flash grenade. The pounding in my head gets worse as Booker takes me in his arms again and carries me down another hallway. Waves of dizziness surge and subside, a never-ending torment disorientating me.

On the move again, Booker carries me at a good clip as we navigate through the residence. I assume we're headed out, but Booker leads me into the oddly empty courtyard I passed on my way to the room where I showered and cried.

He moves into the courtyard and heads to one of the corners. There, he sets me down and holds me while I find my balance. He speaks, but I shake my head, letting him know I still can't hear. My vision is better, recovering at a fast pace.

I know the men of Bravo team, but the six men decked out in black tactical gear make me suck in a breath. They're impressive. Silent and deadly. Ferocious warriors on a mission to save a life.

My life.

Booker reaches into one of his many pockets and pulls out a tangled mess of one-inch straps. He takes my hands and places them on his shoulders. I almost topple as he bends to one knee. All around us, his teammates take up position, weapons ready, but there is no pursuit.

Booker grasps one of my ankles and gently lifts it. When I do, he places my foot through the mesh. He does the same to my other leg, working efficiently. When he stands, I wobble again. The disorientation fades but is still there.

He works the straps up my legs, then pauses to fumble with the dress. When he yanks up on the silky fabric, he works the straps up and over my thighs. I nearly jump out of my skin when the back of his hand brushes against the bare skin between my legs. He jumps too, perhaps surprised by my lack of panties underneath.

I got groped by Booker, and I didn't get a chance to enjoy it.

There's a bit of a pause while he sorts things out. Meanwhile, a low *thump thump thump* beats at the air.

My brows tug tight as Booker finishes securing what I now

realize is a harness. Up in Booker's arms again, he gently walks to the center of the courtyard, then places me on my feet again.

He reaches between us and clips my harness to his with two locking carabiners. My brain moves at a sluggish speed, trying to figure out what he's doing and why we're not hightailing it out of this place.

A thick rope drops out of the sky.

My head tilts back. My jaw drops. And my heart thunders inside my chest. A helicopter hovers overhead.

One of the men grabs the rope and brings it to Booker. He clips another carabiner around a loop, then takes a step back.

The downdraft of the helicopter kicks up dirt, making a mess of my hair. It forces my eyes closed to protect them from the grit. When I blink, the rest of the men hold various sections of the rope. Like Booker, they're clipped in.

With a flash of thumbs up from them all, the rope yanks me off my feet and lifts me into the air.

A blood-curdling shriek tears free of my throat as the ground disappears beneath my feet. Booker wraps an arm around me, pulling me tight against his chest while I scream in holy terror.

Shots fire from the ground. I barely hear them, but the bright flashes accompanying them are impossible not to see. Booker's team dangles below us and aims back at the ground. Something bright-red streaks toward the last man still on the ground, but I spin on the rope, screaming my head off.

The helicopter flies higher than I've ever been in my life. When I peek, all I see is certain death hurtling below me. I cling to Booker, holding on for dear life as the helicopter speeds us away and out of sight.

I don't think I'll ever stop screaming.

TWENTY-NINE

Booker

The moment I have Isabelle in my arms, that constrictive band around my chest finally eases. I hold her to me, breathing in her unique scent along with her overwhelming fear.

CJ made last-minute changes to our extraction plans while we infiltrated the building, sending the helicopter to extract us directly from the residence rather than completing the two-click run to the original exfil point.

Not sure what he saw, but it won't matter until we debrief. All I care about is that Isabelle is finally in my arms. She's back where she belongs.

Where she's always belonged, even though neither of us has admitted it yet.

As we fly through the air, Isabelle's panic intensifies. Howling at the top of her lungs, she's beyond frantic. She's out of her mind with fear. I yank at the black fabric covering the lower half of my face and try to reason with her.

The flashbang doesn't help, nor do the rotors overhead. The noise they make is deafening all on their own.

A nonlethal device, flashbangs overwhelm and incapacitate without wounding, but that doesn't mean they don't hurt. The concussive wave from the blast can injure lungs and contuse the heart. For most, temporary hearing and vision impairments are the worst of it.

Since she screams at the top of her lungs, there's no reason to worry about lung injury. Her hearing will come back. The temporary deafness will fade over the next few hours. Her vision is likely already back, cleared up from the blinding flash and the intense after images it causes.

She keeps her lids pinched together. Each time she opens them, the first thing she does is look down at the ground. Knowing her fear of heights, I do the only thing I can think of to distract her.

It's the one thing I promised myself I would do when I saw her again.

I kiss her.

Dangling from a rope beneath a helicopter may not be the perfect place for our first kiss, but it'll do. This has been destined from the moment Brady handed Isabelle to me in that clearing in Nicaragua so many weeks ago.

I may not have known it at the time, but when I took her hand, something powerful shook the foundations of my world.

This kiss … It's rough.

Not my best effort, but in my defense, there are extenuating circumstances.

My lips mash against hers, forcing her terrified screams to stop. My hands tighten my hold, unwilling to let go for a second lest I lose her again.

Initially, her entire body goes still. The screams stop. She pushes at my chest, forcing me to reconsider my actions, but a moment later, that push becomes a pull and my senses soar.

Her mouth opens, tentative at first. Her soft lips press against mine. They part, unsure perhaps, but allow me to sweep my tongue inside. The moment the tips of our tongues touch, her mouth opens, and she melds my desire with her own.

Rough and desperate, our teeth chatter against each other as her tiny fists grip my shirt. While I devour her mouth, she works hers against mine. Our tongues battle back and forth, vying for dominance.

But this isn't a battle.

I'm not interested in winning. Instead, I'm here to stake my claim and bind us together into one breath, one beating heart, and one timeless moment that joins us together, from this moment to the next, and onward from there.

Our first kiss is brutal and raw, furious and determined. It's nothing like I thought it would be; it's far better than I ever could've imagined.

As our tongues tangle, we grow more frantic, more determined, more curious about this new sensation we explore together.

Knowing she's securely clipped to my harness, I dare to release one hand. This, I cup behind her neck, fingers gliding through her hair. Her soft exhale heats my blood and tickles the hairs in my nose. I tilt her head, moving her lips where I want them, and kiss her deeper than before.

All around me, sensation beats at me. The helicopter's blades cut through the air, chopping it into a buzzing drone that thumps deep in my chest. The humid air we fly through, parts and flows around us, whipping her hair against my exposed skin.

But those sensations are nothing compared to the explosive feeling of finally holding Isabelle in my arms, locking my lips over hers, and tasting the mingling of flavors that is uniquely her, me, and us.

My chest fills with joy as she embraces the kiss. I could get lost forever in the feeling that comes from kissing Isabelle. I draw her into me one breath at a time until the only thing I feel is her unique essence becoming a part of me.

Why did I never do this before?

What the hell was I thinking?

I don't know and chastise myself for the time we wasted, but this—this is perfection.

I hold my breath, too enraptured by her sweet taste to be bothered with breathing.

This is what I've been missing in my life. I close my eyes,

desperate to fully experience this kiss and sear its memory into my soul.

Holding her, kissing her, it's like finding a piece of me I never knew was missing before now.

She steals my breath, and I slake my thirst, devouring her sweet taste as shivers of sensation rush through me from head to toe. I never want this to end. When it does, I'll only want more.

The question is, what will happen when we're back on the ground?

Will she regret kissing me?

We'll know soon enough.

Our lips pull apart, and I open my eyes. My helmet's HUD returns her image in shades of gray and white. Moving my hand from behind her head, I brush the hair away from her face and rub the pad of my thumb across her cheek.

The thundering of my pulse subsides as she looks up at me. Life will never be the same after this kiss.

I glance down the line, checking on the rest of my team.

Brady would normally clip onto the rope first, as Bravo One, but gave that position to me as he and the others defended us from below. My eyes do a double-take when I look at the last man on the line.

Rafe has a woman clinging to him.

Arms locked around his neck. Legs tight around his hips. He grabs her by the ass, desperately holding onto her. Unlike Isabelle, who wears a harness and is securely clipped to me, nothing protects that woman from a deadly fall except for her grip on Rafe and his on her.

What the ever-loving hell?

THIRTY

Izzy

I've been kissed before, by men who did a relatively good job.

Not a great job.

A good job.

It was almost as if they didn't give kissing me their entire attention.

I often wondered what they were thinking about. Like, one part of their mind engaged in the kiss while another part wondered about something else. Maybe a shopping list? The maintenance schedule of their car? Or perhaps they thought about a project at work, or compared me to kissing another girl altogether? Were they thinking about the backyard barbecue? Getting that raise? It certainly wasn't about getting laid. I've suffered through far too many fishmouth kisses in my time.

The point is, none of those kisses rocked the foundations of my world.

Booker's kiss, however *(dot-dot-dot)*...

He's not thinking about any of those things.

While his lips press against mine, he engages his entire body and his whole soul. In his arms, I feel as if nothing but me exists. As if I am his whole universe.

It's terrifying.

But not as terrifying as dangling beneath a helicopter.

The whole time he kisses me, I forget where I am and what I'm doing.

Where I'm dangling …

With his lips on me, all I can focus on is how amazing it feels.

He kisses me.

I kiss him.

The whole fear of heights thing is a nonissue.

The pad of his thumb brushes across my cheek. All I see is my reflection in the visor of his helmet, but I feel him gazing back at me.

Talk about one hell of a first kiss.

My heart pounds and desire flows. It rushes out from my heart to fill my chest, then moves out from there where it gathers and builds—down there.

Between my inner thighs.

That's never happened before.

As the pad of his thumb traces circles along my jawline, the tiny hairs at my nape stand on end. It's like getting the chills, only hotter.

While I haven't forgotten where I am, my death grip on his shirt eases enough for me to lift one trembling hand to mirror what he does. Rough stubble meets my tentative fingers.

His jaw clenches, then releases, as he leans into my touch. His fingers move, gathering at my nape, then they claw their way through my hair until he gathers a fistful in his hand. In control of my head again, he leans down until his lips are kissably close.

It's as if he asks a question. *Is this okay?*

I cup his cheeks and pull his mouth to my lips.

No words are exchanged. Not that I can hear them. My ears still buzz from that flash grenade.

The moment our lips touch, my heart practically leaps out of my chest. Closing my eyes, I let the world around me fade away and take in a deep breath, flooding my senses with everything that is Booker.

This is perfection.

A giggle escapes me and ruins the kiss.

I remember what my brother said after I mentioned the whole fast-roping to the ground thing. Mom cut him off when he dared suggest doing the same, using one of the three helicopters at the ranch to try it out.

When I tell him what I'm doing now—that I'm clipped to Booker and hang beneath a helicopter as it flies through the air, he's not going to believe me. None of the Dingleberries are going to believe this.

Mom will.

Out of them all, she'll understand.

My laughter breaks the kiss, but Booker is undeterred.

He kisses my cheek and runs the heat of his mouth along my jaw. When he presses his full lips against the soft spot on my neck, below my ear, I just about lose it.

Booker places his lips in front of my ear and whispers, "*You taste like sin.*"

I hear that, and my entire body heats from within as he gently bites my skin.

A love nip, it doesn't hurt.

No.

That's not pain.

It makes me want more.

He grabs my hand and straightens out my fingers, then he places my palm against his chest.

Beneath the dark fabric, below the hard Kevlar bulletproof vest, the thumping of his heart is unmistakable. It may be nothing other than the rotors cutting through the air overhead. It could be my imagination wanting to believe something that's not there. But I know what I feel is real.

Through this whole ordeal, Booker and I have been apart, but there hasn't been a single moment when I didn't feel his presence lending me the strength I needed to survive.

I owe him my life, but I give him my heart willingly.

A smile curves the corners of my lips as I realize I'm exactly where I belong. With that thought in my mind, I open my eyes and stare out over the dense vegetation of the Nicaraguan rainforest passing by hundreds of feet beneath us.

There is no fear. No terror at the dizzying height.

My eyes widen at the beauty of the massive rainforest. From up here, it looks like one massive organism. I lean my head against Booker's chest, thinking about only one thing.

How can I make his heart beat the way he makes mine pound?

With my newfound love of dizzying heights, I brave a look down the rope.

A few feet beneath us, I'm guessing, is Brady. He looks the right build. Beneath him, the rest of Bravo team hangs from the rope.

But what is that flash of red clinging to the last man?

THIRTY-ONE

Booker

SLOWLY, A WENCH DRAWS US UP TOWARD THE OPEN BAY OF THE helicopter. The wench squeals as it brings us in. Navigating up and over the skids is normally not a problem, but then I rarely do that with another person strapped to me. CJ leans down, helping with that transition, while Sam minds the wench. Together, they pull Isabelle and me inside.

I disconnect from the rope once we're clear. Next, I disconnect Isabelle from my harness.

She nibbles at her lower lip and shyly glances at me as I reach between us to unclip the two locking carabiners: one chest high, the other joining our waists. This is officially the closest contact we've ever shared.

With her hearing still affected by the flashbang, I pantomime what I need her to do. I settle her in the middle of the helicopter, fastening the chest harness and lap belt over her tiny frame before cupping her cheek.

The way she leans into my hand means the world to me. It's the ultimate display of affection. Yeah, we kissed, and it totally rocked my world, but that sweet acknowledgment of the shifting dynamic between us says everything.

Unfortunately, I have to let her go and return to CJ and Sam.

Using the comms, I update them on the unexpected passenger, not that they could've missed the woman clinging to Rafe for dear life.

"What the fuck is that?" CJ gives me a look and points down the line.

"No idea." I give a shake of my head and shrug.

"Who is she?" Sam joins in.

"No clue."

I have my suspicions. Maximus Angelo has only one child, a daughter, and I assume that's who clings to Rafe. As to *why* she did such a crazy thing? That's up for debate.

There are three options. One, she's trying to escape, like Isabelle. Two, she's trying to thwart Isabelle's rescue. Three? She's batshit crazy.

A fall from this height is lethal, but it's not like the pilot can land. Beneath us, the rainforest's canopy spreads out in all directions without a clearing in sight.

"I guess we'll find out once we bring her in." My shoulders lift in another shrug. If I'm being perfectly honest with myself, I really don't care who the woman is, or what she's doing clinging to Rafe. All I care about is that my woman is finally safe, and for the very first time, there's not an argument brewing between us.

I cast around the back of the helicopter, looking for what we need to deal with the strange woman and her unusual predicament.

There's plenty of rope.

So, that's good.

This helicopter is a military asset, which means there's not only plenty of rope to go around, but multiple places to tie in. I gather supplies.

Reeling in the line isn't a problem. It's what happens once the line pulls over the landing skids. Maneuvering over that is tricky. If Rafe is going to drop the woman, that's where it's going to happen.

"I'm going out." Using a secondary line, I secure myself to the rope while Isabelle's eyes go wide.

No time to explain. She knows what's happening.

Only I can't rappel out of the helicopter until everyone else is up. Getting tangled with the main rope, as they're pulled on board, will only make things worse. As I ready myself, Brady climbs aboard. He gives me a look, knowing exactly what I plan, and gets ready to assist.

CJ and Sam continue to mind the winch, slowly reeling in the rest of the team.

I step out of the helicopter onto the skids and move toward the nose while Zeb, Alec, and Hayes get reeled in.

"Here." Brady thrusts a modified harness at me, then gets ready on a third line to assist.

Sam and CJ pull up the last of the line until Rafe's head is only a few feet below the skids. With entanglement of the line no longer a concern, I jump off the skid until I hang next to him. Locking off the carabiner, I reach for the shoulder strap of Rafe's harness.

It takes two tries, but I finally grab hold of him. I get one look at the woman and my brows climb up my forehead. She's absolutely stunning. Like Isabelle, her eyes are wide and terrified, but there's a fierce intelligence in her entrancing gaze.

It's too loud to explain what I'm doing, and I don't really need her help. Rafe knows what we're planning. We've practiced numerous iterations of this same thing in training exercises. Brady joins us, taking up position on the other side of Rafe.

Rafe's a tough dude, but his arms have got to be close to giving out. I see the strain in the way he holds himself.

I work quickly, efficiently, like a spider weaving a web, and I don't mind where my hands go, or what they touch. Brady doesn't either.

We pass the canvas strap back and forth between us, tying the woman to Rafe. Hopefully, she'll forgive the accidental boob brush and the intimate sweep of my hands between her legs. I don't mean to touch, but it's unavoidable if we're to save her life.

Save?

Are we really *saving* her if she's the one who jumped Rafe?

It takes a hot minute to secure the webbing. Fortunately, the woman doesn't try to help. Either she's too afraid, or she knows to let me do my thing. Once we're done tying her securely to Rafe, Brady checks our work.

He thumps Rafe on the shoulder and signals overhead.

Slowly, Rafe and the woman ascend. It's not elegant. It's gangly as shit, but CJ, Sam, and the rest of the team get the woman safely on board while Brady and I spot from below. We each have a rope tied to the woman if she falls, but she won't.

We tied her tight.

Once we're all back on board, the rest of us have a little fun with Rafe while CJ and Sam undo our handiwork.

"Got yourself a cling-on, I see." Zeb laughs through the comms.

Rafe shakes his head.

"Rafe's the only man I know who has women throwing themselves at him, no matter where the fuck we are." Alec gets in a dig.

"Ha, good one." He acts like it doesn't matter.

"Yeah, but this is the first time he caught one." I can't help but jump in.

"Caught one? I think she caught him." Hayes chuckles and leans back, watching CJ and Sam try to untangle the mess Brady and I made.

"I've heard of tying a woman to your bed, but Rafe takes it to a whole other level." Zeb's laughter is more of a cackle.

"Fuckers." Rafe punches Zeb in the arm.

"Now that he caught one, who wants to bet on how long he keeps her?" Zeb isn't letting it go. "If she's like any other chick, she'll be gone by morning."

CJ and Sam finally get the woman and Rafe separated. CJ guides her to one of the webbed seats, putting her in the middle, then he buckles her in.

"Y'all are just jealous." Beneath his helmet, no doubt he glares at each of us in turn. "My women come in the morning and I keep them coming through noon." Rafe grabs at his crotch, making a rude gesture.

The woman in red sits rigidly in her seat. For whatever reason, she and Isabelle trade daggers for stares. With a lift of her chin, the woman gives a sniff of disdain at Rafe's crude gesture.

She knows we're talking about her. Thankfully, she can't hear a damn word of it.

The poor thing wraps her arms around herself for solace. Lord only knows what's going on in that head of hers.

Her dark-brown hair is tangled and knotted from the extraction. I'm surprised she doesn't take a moment to fix it. She seems like the kind of a woman who would.

In contrast, Isabelle looks glorious and as beautiful as ever. Her hair is a total mess, but the smile on her face is enough to warm my heart. I go to her, leaving the guys to raze Rafe without me.

I've got more important things to do.

I scoot around everyone and take the empty seat the guys left for me beside Isabelle. The moment I sit down, I grab her hand and take it between both of mine. Pulling her hand to my lips, I gently kiss her skin.

The way she looks at me makes my heart race and my chest swell. Her eyes brim with tenderness and overflow with an emotion I'm almost too scared to name. Leaning down, I press my lips to her ear.

"I always knew you would taste like sin."

I don't know if it's what I say, but she shivers despite the evening heat. A quick glance down reveals tight peaks of her nipples. Which I hope is a sign she's turned on.

Although, the flimsy fabric of her dress hides nothing.

Now, that's a thought to make me hard. I readjust in my seat, trying to be discreet. I don't want her to think I only want one thing. The truth is far scarier.

She pulls back at my comment, eyes wide.

A bit of pink colors her face and spreads down across her breasts. Once again, she points to her ears, but she heard me. That blush doesn't lie.

I place my finger beneath her chin, forcing her to look at me, then I lean in, letting the magnetism between us pull me toward her. It's an irresistible force, one neither of us can deny.

As I lean in, she closes the distance, but our lips don't touch.

Not yet.

Her breaths spill over my lips, making my heart thunder and my senses come alive. The way her fingertips dance across my hand, exploring without purpose, moving without resistance, feels like heaven.

I can't wait to take her hair down and feel it spill all over me. The thought of getting closer sends heat rushing through me. It's a slow burn that will become a raging inferno once we're alone.

The anticipation will consume me, and there's one thing I know for certain. I'm never letting her go. She stirs something deep within me, making my soul shake and my body shiver. Sparks flit across my skin, stoking the embers burning within. I wrap my arm around her, pull her in close, and hold her tight against me.

I understand now what Brady says about Angie.

He told me the moment he held Angie for the first time, he became something more. I feel that truth inside of me, growing bigger and stronger with each passing second.

I've waited my entire life for this moment. Isabelle is my forever. There is no doubt.

Not really sure who leans in first, closing the gap between us, my eyes close as her pillow-soft lips press against mine. Unlike the rawness of our first kiss, this one is sweet, achingly tender, and brings me to making a promise I'll never break.

We may have fought in the beginning, turning the smallest things into raging arguments, but I'm giving this my best possible shot. No more arguing. No more waiting. No more beating around the bush.

The tender kiss ends, and I place her palm flat against my chest. She can't see my eyes, but I make her a promise right there and then. I will love her and protect her. I'll keep her safe. I'll show her patience and respect, encouraging her to dream big and conquer the world. While I'd like to keep her locked up, nice and safe, Isabelle would wither beneath too much protection.

That's one thing I learned after meeting her brothers. They love and adore their little sister, but that love smothers her and diminishes her light.

I want to be the man who helps her shine as bright as she can.

If I do to her what her brothers have done, I'll lose what I love best about her. All of these thoughts run through my mind as I stare into her eyes, knowing she can't read my mind, but that's okay. We have a lifetime to get it right.

Isabelle and I hold hands for the rest of the thirty-minute flight. We don't head back to the staging area, but rather fly directly to the airport, where we're met by a shuttle bus. We all climb on board. Rafe guards the woman in red, staying by her side. Zeb, Hayes, and Alec form a ring around her, preventing her escape.

It's hard to say if she's a prisoner, but until we understand her intent, she remains a dangerous unknown.

The bus taxis around the runway and deposits us at a large jumbo jet. We climb up the stairs and head inside.

Like everything, Guardian HRS doesn't go small with the company jet. The entire inside was scrapped and remade. All seats are first class, two to a side. There's a conference room in the back. Two full-sized lavatories with showers. Those seats recline all the way flat with privacy alcoves for those wanting to sleep.

Sam and CJ take the woman in red from Rafe and escort her to the conference room sectioned off near the tail of the plane. I show Isabelle to her seat and release her hand with reluctance. Pulling off the helmet, I run my fingers through sweat-soaked hair.

"I'll be back in a minute, luv. I've got to store my gear." Resisting the urge to kiss her again, I force myself to leave her and head to the very rear of the plane, where our gear lockers sit.

"Where are the others?" Brady's in front of me. His weapon leans against the wall while he rips off his tactical vest. Like me, he's covered in sweat.

The rest of us follow suit, storing all our gear except for our weapons. Those stay out until the rest of the crew is on board.

"Inbound. Had to stop at the original exfil to pick up the Rufuses. They're five minutes out."

Damn, that's efficient.

"Booker …" Brady clamps his hand on my shoulder. "Go ahead and stow your gear. We've got this." I step to the side as the guys head to the front of the plane.

If there's any trouble, they'll provide support on the ground. I give one sniff of my pits and wrinkle my nose. Not the freshest smelling man in the jungle, I reek.

Knowing I have a few minutes, I grab my Dopp kit, a fresh change of clothes, and head to the restroom in the aft end of the plane. Inside, I kick off my boots and strip all the way down, then I take the modern magic that is a pack of baby wipes and wipe away the stench and grime from my body.

I dress in a fresh pair of black utility trousers and put on a simple black T-shirt.

By the time I'm done, there's commotion at the front of the plane as the tech team loads up and settles in their seats. I glimpse Mitzy all the way from the back, despite her small stature, and exchange a look.

The brightness of her smile brings an answering one to mine. She sticks up her thumb, then rotates it from thumbs up, to neutral, then thumbs down. I know exactly what she's asking, and as my grin grows wider, I give her two beaming thumbs up.

Forest Summers climbs on board. He ducks his head, slanting it to the side, then slides into his seat with a sigh. He looks tired and a bit out of it.

I wait while everyone sorts themselves out. The aisle will clear soon. A peek out the window shows the three robots walking themselves up the ramp to the cargo hold, and I shake my head wondering how their part of the mission went.

Last on board are the men of Bravo team. Brady holds up at the front when he sees me lingering toward the back of the plane. He gestures for me to go ahead, and I quickly slip down the aisle, feeling light-hearted and as goofy as a fool in love.

Isabelle looks up and a soft laugh spills from her luscious lips.

"I was wondering what took so long. Did you shower for me?"

"Not exactly a shower." Although, I did rinse my hair. It hangs in wet strings. And I brushed my teeth.

"For me?"

"Definitely for you." I slide into my seat and take her hand in mine. Once again, I lift the back of her hand to my lips and kiss her knuckles. "Now, about that kiss …"

Her eyes twinkle and that beautiful blush returns.

THIRTY-TWO

Izzy

"So, who is the chick in the red dress?" Booker takes my hand, capturing it for the flight back to California. "And what was she thinking? Is she in danger?"

"That bitch is Maximus Angelo's daughter."

"I take it the two of you didn't hit it off?"

"That woman hated me on sight." I lower my voice to a whisper, not wanting everyone privy to my conversation. "She thought I was Maximus's new lover. I don't think she knows what I truly was."

"And what was that?" Booker's entire demeanor changes in an instant.

"Exactly what are you thinking?"

"Did he …"

"He didn't get a chance. Your heroic rescue came right on time."

I leave out what would've happened later tonight. No need to speak such vileness.

"*Fuuuck.*" Booker releases my hand to pull me tight to his side. "I've been out of my mind with worry from the moment we found out about the damn diamonds. I was always one step behind. Kept losing you."

"You were there when it mattered most." I reach up and cup his face, taking time to really get a good look at him. "My hero."

To my delight, he blushes at that comment. Serves him right.

The man makes me blush with nothing but a look. But there's a reason for that. Booker oozes masculinity. It's in the way he holds himself, the way he moves his body, it's in the filthy thoughts filling his head. He's sex on a stick, and for the first time, he's all mine.

I try to imagine him at eighteen when he was a virile male who danced for money and fulfilled the lusty fantasies of thousands of women during his time as a male dancer in Vegas.

A smile tilts the corner of my mouth, thinking about what he must have been like back then. I imagine a voracious appetite for all things female. With his looks and the way he moves, I bet women fell all over themselves for the tiniest piece of him.

I probably wouldn't have liked him back then. I despise players, men who toy with women's hearts. This version of Booker, a decade older, a real man who rocks confidence like there's no tomorrow—add in the whole protective male thing—and my heart speeds along like a runaway freight train.

There's no stopping what comes next.

Which brings another flush to my cheeks. He knows I wear nothing beneath this dress. I'll give him this; he was a consummate professional fitting that harness to me. The funniest thing is I don't know which of us jumped the most. Me, when he touched my pussy? Or him when he realized I wasn't wearing anything beneath the dress?

I'd love to know what went through his head.

"Are you growling?" I lean back and check if what I'm hearing is really there.

The flash grenade did a number on my hearing, but it's slowly coming back. I would bet a million bucks Booker just growled like an alpha male would when his woman was threatened.

"I have a feeling the Minister of the Interior has a bevy of unwilling women waiting on him." His fingers dig into the armrest. "I wish we'd known."

"Known what?"

"That he had slaves." Booker's fist pounds on the expensive leather of the seat. "We could've saved them."

I remember Rosalie and how beaten down she looked. Horrific guilt rushes through me. I never once thought about her during the whole escape.

"I'm a horrible person." I lean forward and cup my face as shame runs through me.

"No, you're not."

"You don't understand. There was this woman—Rosalie." My voice catches on the lump in my throat.

"Rosalie?"

"She's the only other female I saw." I proceed to tell Booker everything. "But the way she hunched in front of Matias … It didn't even occur to me to find her."

"Don't do that."

"Do what?"

"Beat yourself up over something you had no control over. Our mission was a lightning blitz followed by a rapid extraction. We weren't prepared to search for other captives, but I can promise this …" He takes both my hands in his. "We'll come back."

"Do you think so?" It would help me breathe a little easier. "I can't believe I left her behind."

I'm a horrible human being. I didn't even think about her until now.

"Yes, luv, we will." He speaks with absolute conviction.

"There's something else. Rosalie isn't the only woman I forgot about. Maximus said things to me."

"What things?" Booker's entire body tenses. "What did the fucker say?"

"If I didn't have sex with him, he would send pieces of my mother—"

"Pieces?" Booker's voice rises and I curl in on myself, thinking I've done something wrong.

"Pieces of her toes, her fingers …" I can't finish the rest.

Booker growls low in the back of his throat. For the first time ever, that growly protectiveness doesn't irritate me. It feels different.

Welcomed.

Booker twists in his seat and calls down the aisle. "CJ, Sam …" He waves for the men to join us.

They make their way from the back of the plane to us.

"What's up?" CJ taps me on the shoulder. "Nice to have you home, Izzy."

"Thanks. Glad to be home."

And this is my home. Guardian HRS is my home.

"We need a protective detail on Isabelle's family ASAP." Booker barks out orders. "Angelo threatened her mother if Isabelle didn't …" He clears his throat. "If she didn't—*serve him.*"

Serve?

That's one way to say it.

No reason for Booker to elaborate further. They get it. I wait for questions, but CJ and Sam ask none. The only sign of their concern is a tightening of their jaws and the grinding of their molars.

"Izzy, don't worry about your family. We'll take care of them." CJ rubs at the back of his neck. His eyes pinch and he blows out a breath. "Is there any reason to think more is going on?"

"What do you mean by *more?*" I'm not dense. I know what he's asking. I'm just not ready to face what almost happened.

You can't run from your fears. My father's words come back at me.

Once he saw my phobias multiplying, he tried to nip my anxiety in the bud. It never worked, but in many ways, I wish I'd listened to him. There was wisdom in the message he tried to deliver.

Sucking in a breath, I decide to face this fear head-on.

"I don't know what was going on, except he didn't seem all that interested in the diamonds." I pull out the mangled rabbit's foot and dangle it in the air. "He seemed much more interested in me."

Every word Maximus said runs through my head. I wish I could remember all of it. No doubt there's something important, but I'm at a loss as to what that might be.

"You?" Booker's tone gets rumbly and deep. That growling protectiveness is back.

"More like he was far more interested in *who* rescued me from the jungle than losing the diamonds. He said the man you killed was his cousin, but he didn't seem upset by it. Carmen, however, was furious."

"Carmen?" Sam tugs on his jaw.

"The woman in the red dress." I point toward the back of the plane.

"Any idea why she would do what she did?" Sam's penetrating gaze looks toward the back of the plane.

We're in a modified jumbo jet that's nothing like any of the planes I've ever flown in. Every seat is first-class accommodations. There's a whole room located in the back of the plane.

The Guardians escorted Carmen into that room. One of them stands outside the door, and I think one, or two, are inside with her. I only got a peek inside the bathroom. It's not an airplane lavatory. It's much larger.

"No idea." I shrug. "But she was upset about Miguel."

"Miguel?"

"Her cousin. The leader of the *Coralos* cartel. He seemed to be embroiled in some disagreement with her father. She accused her father of killing him."

"Excuse me?" CJ's brows pinch. "Who accused who?"

Realizing the pronouns could be confusing, I clarify what I said.

"Carmen thought her father killed her cousin, Miguel. He's the leader of the cartel that kidnapped my team. Once she saw you were there to rescue me, she may have decided to …" The right word escapes me. "Um, go with you?" My forehead wrinkles as I try to figure out what I want to say. "The woman is something else and her temper is … Well, it's something. She went off on her father right in front of me."

My words draw a crowd. When I look up, Brady is there. Along with him, Zeb and Hayes gather around. Alec is at the back of the plane, standing guard outside the conference room. I don't see Rafe but remember him coming on board. He must be in the room with Carmen.

"She thought her father killed Miguel Coralos?" Joining the crowd, Mitzy pushes her way in.

"Seemed like it." I can only shrug. "I was really scared, and there was a lot going on."

"Why would she think that? Why argue with her father in front of you?"

"No idea."

"Then she hijacks a ride with the Guardians?" Mitzy taps her lips. "It doesn't track."

"Her father denied killing her cousin and I may have …" I hate this part. They're all so much more in control of themselves, unlike me. I started blabbing the moment I arrived at Maximus's home.

"Maximus was interested in who rescued us. Maybe she believed he wasn't involved and *hitched a ride* to find out for herself." My neck hurts from looking up at everyone.

"That's fuckin' ballsy." CJ grips the headrest of the seat in front of us. "She could've died pulling that stunt."

"You said she argued." Sam joins Mitzy with the chin tapping thing. "About her cousin? The Guardians?" He pauses. "Did they mention us by name?"

"No." At least I kept that bit to myself. "It was all really weird. She went ballistic. Switched the subject to an arranged marriage …"

"Huh?" Mitzy cocks her head to the side.

"Izzy, we need to properly debrief this. There's too much to process." Sam glances down the aisle to where Alec stands guard. "Unfortunately, the conference room is occupied."

"What are you going to do with Carmen?" I clutch Booker's hand, finding his presence reassuring as the Guardians put me to question.

"First, we determine if she's a threat." CJ doesn't hesitate. "Then we ask questions of our own."

THIRTY-THREE

Booker

The flight home raises more questions than answers, but I'll save my questions for later. Right now, I've got a woman to hold.

The seats in the jet are first class, and since we fly at a moment's notice anywhere around the world, they're the fancy ones that lay all the way down.

The last three days have taken their toll on my girl. Adrenaline's run rampant throughout her system; her fight or flight instinct has been on overdrive. Unable to flee, she's been stuck in fight mode with no outlet for all the excess energy.

She's headed for two major crashes.

The first will be emotional.

Now that she's safe, all those emotions she buried to stay alive will rise to the surface and overwhelm her. I wait for that tsunami to try and drown her, but I'll be there to buoy her up.

It'll be hard. There's no privacy on the plane, but I'll shield her the best way I know how.

After that will come the physical crash.

When the last of that adrenaline flowing through her fades, she'll be left with nothing. The drop will hurt, but I'll be right by her side, lending what strength I can. At the very least, I'll watch over her as she sleeps.

Before that, however, are debriefs, both for me and for her. I only hope CJ will allow those to happen together.

"I can't wait to get home." Isabelle slouches in her seat.

Already, fatigue pulls at her. It's evident in the puffiness of her eyes, the yawns that barely stop before the next one begins, and it's in her complexion, which is three shades paler than her normal glow.

My woman looks like she's been run over by a freight train and lived to tell about it. Not that I would ever say that out loud.

I'm not a fucking idiot.

But she looks rough.

"Home?" I'm almost too afraid to ask.

Is that in Leighton, Texas, with her family, or with me in California?

"Yeah. And I want to see Angie. I bet she's freaking the eff-out."

"Everyone was freaking out when you were kidnapped."

"Oh, I don't doubt that." She shifts, turning toward me. "But not you."

"You don't think I was worried?"

"Worried maybe, but not freaking out." She places her hand on my arm. "You came after me."

"Sure as shit, I did."

It's a simple touch, but damn if it doesn't make my heart soar. I love these tender touches much better than the verbal fights we used to engage in.

I place my hand over hers and take a moment to soak in this new normal.

It feels—good.

Better than good.

It feels right as rain.

"You knew exactly what to do." She leans back again with a sigh.

Her faith in me rocks my confidence.

"Not sure if I deserve that." There's nothing but to admit the truth. "I didn't know if I'd find you."

"I wasn't …"

"Wasn't, what?"

"Worried that you wouldn't find me." She looks up through the fringe of her lashes, fluttering them in a way that makes my stomach feel funny. "I knew you would."

"You put a lot of faith in me."

"And look what happened." She reaches up to cup the side of my face. Her eyes shimmer with unshed tears. "You found me, just like I knew you would."

Telling her how much luck was involved in finding her doesn't sound wise. I let her believe what she wants. I know how close we came to losing her forever.

"And I'm sorry." She puffs out her cheeks. "It was all my fault."

"Your fault?" I lean back, surprised by the comment.

"Yeah, if I'd only accepted the tracker instead of getting a bug up my butt about unnecessary surveillance, none of this would've been necessary." She closes the gap between us. "I wouldn't be surprised if they fire me when we get back for how much time and money I've cost Guardian HRS. Do you think I'm going to get sacked?"

"Luv, no one is firing you. There are risks to being a part of this organization. Sometimes, shit happens."

"Well, I learned a valuable lesson."

"What's that?"

"When the company offers to track you for your protection, don't be a snit about it and refuse. I could've saved myself three horrific days."

"You're being too hard on yourself."

"Maybe."

Her hand drops to my forearm and her fingers dance across my skin. Each touch is a tiny electrical spark that speeds my heart and makes me want more.

"I'm just glad we got you back."

"I want to thank you."

"No need for that. I did what needed to be done to get you out of there. We all did."

Another day, I'll let her know how hard everyone worked to find her. Her rescue isn't something I take credit for. If not for the combined might of the Guardians and our technical geniuses, Isabelle would still be lost to us.

For now, though, because I'm a selfish bastard and because I'm enjoying the attention, I'll accept her thanks on behalf of everyone.

It's self-serving, but I don't give a damn.

This is the longest conversation Isabelle and I have shared since she and Angie signed up with Guardian HRS.

"I know that, and thanks for the rescue, but that's not what I was going to say."

"Oh?"

"I wanted to thank you for um …" The way she nibbles on her lower lip shouldn't be legal.

It's hot as fuck and sends my filthy mind to places it shouldn't go.

She looks around, seeing who might be eavesdropping on our conversation.

No one is paying us any mind.

The guys are settling in and getting comfortable for the seven-hour flight home.

Mitzy and her team are doing what they always do. The glow of their monitors casts a blueish hue to their skin.

Sam and CJ are in the back with Rafe and our unusual guest, trying to figure out what that is all about.

Forest Summers and Doc Summers sit at the very front of the plane, heads close, speaking quietly to each other.

"You want to thank me for what exactly?"

I take her hand in mine and press my lips to the inside of her wrist. My hand is huge compared to hers. Not that it's a surprise, but I'm constantly amazed by how tiny she is compared to me. I don't see her as delicate or frail, however, but rather ferocious and fierce.

My woman is one tough cookie.

Everything about her amazes me. I'm in awe of her resilience and strength but know her limits.

She's not indestructible.

With that in mind, I pay careful attention to her state of mind, waiting for that first crash.

"I wanted to thank you for distracting me on the rope." She curls in on herself.

It's an unconscious gesture. I've seen her do it more times than I care to count. She does it to disappear, but she deserves to be front and center. At least, she's the center of my universe these days.

"Stop that." I place my finger under her chin and force her to look up.

"Stop, what?" Her eyes pinch in confusion and she rolls her lower lip between her teeth.

That nibbling on her lip is crack to my dick. Blood rushes down and I forget what I was going to say. She does it again, that nibbling, which forces me to readjust how I'm sitting.

This isn't the time, or the place, for those kinds of thoughts.

"Am I doing something wrong?" She casts about the cabin, then looks down at her dress, smoothing it with her fingers. "Am I giving the guys a peep show?" She carefully draws the silky fabric over her leg, minimizing the near thigh-high slit in the gown.

"No, luv. You're perfectly covered." I place my hand over her fidgeting fingers.

I took her dress into account when I picked our seats, placing her in the window seat with that slit facing away from prying eyes.

Not that anyone on this jet would violate Isabelle's privacy. If they saw something they shouldn't have, like Brady who took the position below me on the rope, it'll go with them to their grave.

"Then what are you talking about?" Her unease manifests in more lip nibbling.

"That." I touch her lower lip and gently get her to stop.

"Why?"

"Because it *distracts* me."

"It does?" She does it again, then flutters her lashes.

I can't believe it, but she's teasing me. Or flirting.

"Yeah, it most definitely does."

"How?"

"It's a major turn-on, and this isn't the place I want to be sporting a boner for all to see."

"Boner?" She shoves me playfully in the arm. "I haven't heard that word in years. These days, we call it an *e-rec-tion*." She makes a point to enunciate each syllable.

"Shh." I make a point of covering her mouth.

"Why?"

"Do you want everyone to hear?"

"I don't mind." She glances around the cabin again. "It's not like they don't know."

"Know, what?"

"*Puh-lease* …" Her dramatic eye roll is Oscar-worthy. "After that kiss, they all know we're going to be boning once we get back."

"Boning?" A chuckle escapes me. "And you complained about me using the word *boner*."

Damn, she gets straight to the point, which means I don't have to do the whole song and dance thing to convince her to get in my bed.

She's there already—in a metaphorical sense.

"I wasn't complaining." She blows a puff of air to move the hair out of her eyes. "It was an observation." She gives me a sly look. "What else does it do?"

Her pink tongue slips out of her mouth to moisten her lips. She draws out the motion, making sure I watch every second of it, then she rolls her lower lip in and nibbles on it.

"You know what it does." There's no way to suppress the low groan in the back of my throat. Once again, I shift in my seat.

"No, I don't. Why don't you show me?"

Damn, but she's a little minx. Which means we're going to have tons of fun. I grasp her wrist and place her hand over my groin, where my dick stands ready and at attention.

"That's what it does to me."

"Really?" Her left brow arches and a mischievous grin curves her lips. Her fingers curl around the bulge in my pants, making my breath catch.

"Yes."

"Good to know the equipment works." The tip of her tongue peeks out from between her lips again. "But there's only one way to know for sure."

"Is that so?"

"It is." She pulls her hand off my cock.

"And how's that?"

"Take it for a test run?"

"A test run?"

"Yeah, you know ..."

"Oh, I know." My grin is a mile wide. "But I want to hear you say it."

"I can't." Suddenly shy, her boldness falters.

"Here, let me help you out." I take her hand again to show her exactly how much harder I've gotten in the past few seconds. "You're interested in taking my equipment on a test drive because you want to know how good it's going to feel when I finally fuck you. You've been wondering that since the day we met."

"Booker!" That blush is back, brighter than ever. She places her hands to her cheeks. "I wish that didn't happen. I hate that I blush so easily."

"I think it's adorable."

"I'm not trying to be adorable."

"What are you trying to be?"

"Sexy. You know ... Dirty talk."

Her voice lowers to a whisper at the end. The way she's flustered by her blush brings lightness to my soul and laughter to my lips.

"Luv, you have no idea how fucking sexy you are, and I can't wait to be alone with you. As for the dirty talk, leave that to me. That's my department."

If possible, her cheeks turn a deeper shade of pink.

"I really wish I wasn't a blusher."

"It's fucking adorable, luv, and sexy as fuck. I bet you'll turn bright crimson when I eat that pussy you're barely hiding beneath that dress."

"Oh my god." She muffles her shriek and squirms in her seat. "Stop."

"Stop, what?" The look I give her is positively sinful. "You've got to know that barest brush of my hand over your pussy would never be enough."

"Booker." She tries to get me to hush.

My voice is low, perfectly controlled, and audible only to her. No one's paying us any mind, and I'm having tons of fun making her blush.

"Your cheeks are rosy now. I wonder how red they'll be when you're riding me."

"Booker." Again, she glances around the cabin.

"Although, I won't be looking at your face." I place my fingers on the tip of her shoulder and slowly walk them down her bare arm. As I do, my knuckles brush against the swell of her breast. I lean in and whisper in her ear. "I'll be watching your luscious tits bounce as you come all over my cock. Of course, I'll definitely be looking at your face when you wrap those sinful lips of yours around my cock, but I won't be watching you blush."

"Okay. Okay. You've made your point."

She pulls away, but not before her entire body shivers in reaction to my touch. Her nipples react and there's no way to hide their tight little nubs beneath the flimsy fabric of her dress.

"That I'm looking forward to fucking you? Making you come on my face? Or that I can't wait to slip my cock in your perfect little mouth and feel those luscious lips wrap all around me. After our kiss, I know exactly how talented that tongue of yours is."

"O-M-G. You're killing me." She lifts her hands in mock surrender. "You win the dirty talk award. Okay?"

"Fine by me." I shrug as if it doesn't matter. But it does. It matters a lot. "But seriously, which one do you want to do first?"

"You're incorrigible."

"Luv, I've been waiting to fuck you since the day I took you out of the jungle. I just need to know how you want to begin. Or is that something you'd rather I decide? I tend to be a bit dominating in bed, so if you like a man who takes charge … What are your thoughts about rope?" I can't help but wink.

This is so much fun.

Her cheeks darken another shade of red and the blush extends down her neck and across her chest. I enjoy the view as I watch her blush spread.

"I'm dead." She crosses her arms over her chest and sinks in her chair. "Absolutely dead. You know this isn't fair." She peeks up at me, fluttering her lashes.

She's fucking incredible.

"How's that?"

"Because you know exactly what I'm thinking when I blush."

"I do, and that's why it's sexy."

"Because you make me blush?"

"Because you blush when you're thinking about having sex with me. That's fucking hot."

"Oh lord, just kill me now."

"I have no plans to do that, but do you know what the French call a woman's orgasm."

"I'm afraid to ask." She places the back of her hand over her forehead.

"La petite mort."

"And that means?"

"A brief loss of consciousness following particularly powerful orgasms. I see many *petite morts* in your future, my dear."

"You do?"

I love the way she peeks up at me, not afraid to show vulnerability. It's an incredibly intimate admission.

"If you say yes, but you have to say. Now tell me, when we get home, and all the debriefings are over, will your answer be a yes, or a no?"

I'm all about obtaining consent. In today's sexual climate, it's a no-brainer. Consent is essential, but I hate the whole dancing around the issue.

"Do I have to wait until then?"

"For the inspection of whether my equipment works as advertised?" I lean close to whisper in her ear. "You say the word and I'll take you right now. I've waited long enough to make you scream, but we have a bit of an audience." I exaggerate looking around the cabin.

Isabelle looks at me, tries to say something, then dissolves in a fit of giggles. Those giggles turn into true laughter, and that laughter brings a lightness to my chest. Her lids do that fluttering thing again, teasing me, and it's as if I've died and gone to heaven.

"What's so funny?" Brady stops by, checking in.

My woman gives him one look and her laughter dissolves into full-on belly laughs. She tries to speak, but her laughter doesn't allow it.

Brady arches a brow. I give him a look he understands all too well.

Laughter always comes before the fall.

We've seen it far too often.

I truly believe it's the mind's way of dealing with tragedy, a way to soften the hard, ragged edges left behind.

And right on cue, Isabelle's laughter turns to sobs.

I take her in my arms and hold her through the cascade of emotions breaking through her carefully shored-up defenses. In my arms, Isabelle lets loose a torrent of fear and rage, despair and helplessness, and she allows me to hold her through it all.

I spend the rest of the flight with her in my arms, and why shouldn't I?

It's exactly where I belong.

THIRTY-FOUR

Izzy

By the time the plane lands, I feel as if I've run a marathon of emotions. What began as simple laughter at Booker's outlandish, but oh-so-sexy dirty talk, turned into something I can't describe.

A catharsis?

It's as if those giggles unleashed the dam I put around my emotions. They all came pouring out at once. Fear for my safety, for my family. Worry over Rosalie, who I left behind without a thought, and the horror she endured and continues to endure. Anger at the way my family was threatened and chased down as we literally ran for our lives. The way the Dingleberries defended me without a single word about how it was my fault their lives were in danger. My father's stalwart support and the terrible position he was put in when he had to watch me go.

Rage.

That's a powerful one.

Booker held me through that unsightly bit.

I may have said things about what I planned on doing to Maximus and his balls. Embarrassment followed after that. Worry about how the others on the plane saw me after that particularly expressive emotional display.

Through it all, Booker never once let go.

I really hate to say it, but I fell in love with him on that plane. I think there's always been a little piece of me that knew he was the one, but I was too prideful to accept it.

To blind to see it.

"I must look a mess." I swipe at my puffy eyes and feel crusted salt from far too many tears that dried as they fell down my face.

"You look like a beautiful mess." Booker gazes down at me, his expression serene and full of an emotion I'm not ready to accept. "But you're *my* beautiful mess, and all I see is how incredible you are." He kisses my forehead and checks on me.

I mean, I know I'm in love with him, but I'm not ready to see that emotion reflected in his eyes.

But it's there.

Dear lord, it's there.

And I find that terrifying.

The next few hours after we land are all a blur. Booker isn't wrong about the debriefs. To be honest, it feels a little like an interrogation as Sam and CJ try to wring as much information from me as possible.

Forest Summers and his sister, Skye, sit in on my debriefs. They don't sit at the table but rather in a pair of chairs set off to the side. The entire time I talk about my abduction, they trade stares filled of pain and smoldering rage.

My throat hurts from speaking. I take another sip from my water glass and blow out a sigh.

"How much longer?" I look at Sam and CJ, then glance toward the door Booker and the others disappeared behind.

How long has it been?

A glance at the clock over the back wall says an hour at most, but it feels as if days have passed.

"I think we're done." Sam and CJ look toward Forest and Skye, waiting for something.

Once again, the two founders of Guardian HRS exchange an indecipherable series of expressions.

Forest looks about how I feel, a bit haggard. No doubt he's had little sleep since this whole escapade began. I'm coming to understand the man likes to have a hand in most things.

Although, he lets Sam run the show with his two captains, CJ and Mitzy.

But it's not Forest who speaks.

Skye rubs her hands on her pants and stands. "I'm sorry this is dragging on. I know all you want is to go home, take a warm bath, fall into bed, and put all of this behind you. I promise, we're almost done."

"It's no problem. Whatever I can do to help wrap this up, or make sense of it all, I'm yours."

"That's incredibly kind." She twists to look at her brother. Her lips press firmly together when she spins back around. "You mentioned something I wanted to explore."

"What?"

"Something Maximus said."

"Okay?" I'm a little confused, but I'll do what I can to help.

"Who did Maximus think you were linked to?"

"Huh?"

"You mentioned he said … *If you're linked to who I think you are …* Did he mention who that might be?"

"No." I remember Maximus's words verbatim.

Because if you're linked to who I think you are, I want him to suffer and pay for what he's done.

"He said whoever it was would pay. Did he mention what it was they did?" Her voice may be soft, but it carries easily throughout the room. There's a quiet strength to Skye Summers. One day, I hope to have that same strength within me.

"No. I assumed he meant the diamonds. He kept inferring there was more to the diamonds than the diamonds themselves."

"Do you have any idea what that might be?" CJ props his elbows on the conference table and leans forward.

"He said diamonds weren't the only things that were valuable. They bought *things*, but information bought *loyalty*. Or … maybe it was obedience?" I scrunch up my nose trying to remember. "It may have been both?" I don't like the uncertainty in my voice.

"It was most definitely both." Forest's deep rumble brings a chill to my spine. "Now, do you believe me?" That comment isn't for the rest of us, but rather for his sister.

"Yes." Her shoulders slump and a little bit of the light in her eyes goes out. "It never ends, does it?"

Without a word to the rest of us, she pivots and heads for the door. Forest is right behind her, moving his towering frame faster than should be possible.

He wraps an arm around her shoulder, which leaves me with a whole slew of questions. However, that isn't happening. CJ places his palms on the table and stands.

"I guess that's it. Izzy, thank you for being as patient as you've been. I know you're eager to get out of here, and there's someone eager to take you home." CJ exchanges a look with Sam. "I think another one's been bit."

"I think you're right." Sam clears his throat and stands. "I do appreciate your patience. Booker is waiting for you outside. I assume you're okay with him seeing you home?"

"I am." What an odd question?

"And, Izzy," Sam cocks his head to the side, "we contacted your family the moment Bravo team liberated you. I know we haven't given you a chance to speak with them. If you want, please feel free to stay here for a bit. Mitzy set things up so you can video chat with them. If you would rather wait, you can do that too."

"Wow. Thank you."

I'm a bit torn, to be honest. The moment Sam mentioned Booker was waiting for me, all I could think of was running into his arms, but my family deserves to see my face.

"Sam?"

"Yes?"

"Can you tell Booker I'll be a moment?"

"Absolutely." Sam signals to CJ, who goes to the media wall to set up the call.

Sam doesn't lie about it being all set to go. CJ clicks one button and the wall screen comes to life. With that, Sam and CJ leave me alone.

My family answers on the first ring, and I lose my bet with myself as to whose face would fill the screen first. I expect Gareth, my overly protective brother, but it's my father's face I see first.

"Dad …" My eyes mist with tears. "I'm so sorry." My shoulders slump with the weight of everything I put my family through.

"Sorry?" His face brightens with a smile. "I'm just glad you're okay." He hesitates. "You are okay, aren't you? When Booker called …"

"Booker called you?"

"Yes. He called with minute-by-minute updates from the moment you were taken." Gareth pushes my dad to the side. "Told us when they finally found you, how they were going to get you out, and sent several texts after he found you."

"He did?" For some reason those are the words that bring back my tears. Knowing Booker cared enough about me to keep my family in the loop to that degree means everything to me.

"You got a solid man there, Izzy." My dad takes over. "He gave his word he'd find you and did just that. I couldn't want a better man for my daughter. When you have the time, I'd really like to fly out there and get to know him better."

"Dad, we're barely together and you already have us at the altar."

"No barely about it."

"Mom, will you talk some sense into Dad?"

"Honey, I would, except I agree with your father. Booker will need to mind his language when y'all visit, but other than that tiny flaw, you found your perfect match."

"Oh my god, we haven't even had sex yet." My fingers curl into fists and I stomp my foot.

Damn, it's easy to regress with my family. When will they see me as the adult I am instead of the baby of the family?

"Luv—TMI." My mother shakes her head and gives a flick of her lashes. "But for the record, some people still wait for marriage before having sex."

I cannot believe I'm talking about my nonexistent sex life with my parents.

"Don't know what people you're talking about, Mom, but it ain't any of your kids." Colton's bright face fills the screen. "How ya doing, little sis?"

"Not so little anymore."

"Ain't that the truth." He glances off-screen. "For what it's worth, I agree with the 'rents. Booker is a good man. Unlike Mom, however, if you haven't jumped his bones, what the hell are you waiting for?"

"Colton!" My mother's response brings a smile to my face. The familiar snapping of a kitchen towel sounds, along with an *oomph!* from Colton.

I cover my mouth as a fit of laughter overcomes me. Not to take the Lord's name in vain, but I have the best goddamn family in the world.

Sorry, God!

I glance up and say a short prayer of repentance while the twins take the screen.

"You look like crap." Jude gives me the once over.

"Thanks, Jude. In my defense, I've been too busy to put on my makeup."

"Sounds to me like she needs to get off the *Gam-dod* phone and do something about that." Parker throws a little wave at me. "If you need help, I bet Booker won't say no."

"You are all incorrigible bastards." My mother's voice cuts in. "I swear I didn't raise a bunch of hellions."

"What?" Parker defends himself. "Not like I cursed."

"You *Gam-dod* did," Mom replies. "And no more encouraging Izzy to do anything with any man she's not ready to do stuff with. It'll come on its own time."

"Oh, Mother," Gareth says, "I think that time is now." He snags the phone from whoever was holding it and pans around the kitchen where my entire family is gathered. "Say goodbye to Izzy." He jumps back when Mom tries to grab the camera. Jude and Parker help, holding Mom back by the arms. "Have a good time, little sis, and don't forget to use protection. Mom may say she wants grandbabies, but I don't think she's ready for them to be popping out of you just yet."

"Gross." I shake my head. "You're all so gross … But I love you."

"And we love you." The Dingleberries wave as one. Dad takes Mom in his arms, and I swear that shimmering in his eyes are the beginnings of tears.

"I'll call you all later. I promise." I blow them a kiss and cut the connection.

That call will definitely go on record as the shortest family group call as well as the most uncomfortable.

But Parker might be on to something.

A shower sounds like exactly what I need.

With my spirits lifted, I don't think I realized how much I needed to hear from my family. Knowing how Booker went out of his way to keep them in the loop only makes me fall in love with him even more.

He's a Guardian and a fierce protector, but he's a softy at heart.

I'll be adding that to the list of things I love about Booker Holloway. Speaking about the man of my dreams, he's right where Sam said I would find him.

THIRTY-FIVE

Booker

The moment Isabelle exits the main HQ building, it's as if the sun shines down on me. My breath eases and my heart kicks into high gear. I hold my arms out and watch with joy as she runs right into my embrace.

Talk about movie-worthy.

The moment she jumps into my arms, I lift her off her feet and spin us in a circle as our lips lock and our mouths fuse in a beautifully chaotic frisson of need.

Knowing there are plenty of eyes on us, I keep things as PG-13 as I can. I stop spinning and lower her to her feet.

"Now, that's one way to say hello." I grip her arms. "You feeling okay? Did they work you over too hard?"

"No." She slaps me playfully on the chest. "But they sure know how to ask the same question from ten different angles. I'm beat."

"I bet." I stoop down until we're eye to eye. "I have only one question."

"Hit me."

"Where exactly am I taking you? Your place or mine?"

"That depends."

"On what?"

"How big is your bed?" Her eyes twinkle with mischief and a whole lot of sexy. Right on cue, here comes the pink coloring her cheeks.

"Big enough for two." I take her hand and thread our fingers together, interlocking our hands.

"And your shower?" She peeks up at me through her lashes, gorgeous and adorably shy.

"My shower?" It's not the direction I expect, but I'm more than flexible.

A bit of shower sex is never a bad thing. It's actually one of my favorite ways to fuck. Not that I need a shower. A sturdy wall will do. I love holding a woman in my arms and having complete control. Nothing like her legs wrapped around my hips while I raise her up and down, thrusting with my hips like a pile driver.

Hot and sweaty is good.

Dirty is better.

Absolutely fucking filthy is the best kind of sex on the planet but may be a bit too much for Isabelle at the start.

"Oh yes. I need a thorough washing." She's cute when she tries to talk dirty.

"Washing?" My brow arches. "Are you looking for assistance?" I'm more than willing to engage in that activity.

Running a bar of soap over every crack and crevice? Hell yes, sign me up. Take one of her legs and drape it over my shoulder while I devour her pussy?

Fuck yes.

"I do." She does that thing with her lip, nibbling it, and I groan with frustration. "And a massage." She lifts on tiptoe to give me a quick peck on the lips.

"A massage?" My brow arches, enjoying this. It's a great window into the sexual side of Isabelle LaCroix.

"Definitely." Her head bobs vigorously.

"Would that be a back massage? Or are we talking a whole body, deep-tissue massage with a happy ending?"

"Ew! Only men get happy endings."

"Is that what you think?"

"Yeah. I have four older brothers, and they've told me a thing or two."

I dip down and whisper in her ear. "It's not just the men who get happy endings. I'm more than happy to be your masseuse and finish you off with a bang." I nip at her earlobe.

"Oh my God. Stop that."

"Stop? Not on your life." I tug her toward my truck, eager to get away from prying eyes and someplace much more private where we can explore all her fantasies.

"Well, a whole-body massage sounds fun."

"Demanding, aren't we?"

"A little."

"Well, you can demand all you want until the clothes come off, but remember what I warned you about."

"What did you warn me about what?" Her voice grows quiet, unsure but still interested.

"I'm the boss when it comes to sex. Unless you're against the man taking charge?"

I hope not. I can adjust and adapt to meet her needs, but I know what gets me going. That push and pull of power is a total game changer when it comes to sex.

The way her pupils dilate tells me everything I need to know.

I give a light smack to her ass. It's the tiniest test.

Her little squeal, and lack of irritation or indignation, make my dick take notice. I'm hard as a rock by the time we get to my truck.

When I pull into my drive, I'm fucking aching.

I turn off the ignition and get ready to exit the vehicle, but Isabelle doesn't move.

"What's wrong?" I place my hand on her thigh, looking for a reaction, good or bad. If she's not ready, I'll wait. There's no need to push, and I'd never force anything when I've got all the time in the world.

"It's really happening." She nibbles at her lower lip.

This time, I see it for what it is.

Isabelle's unsure.

"It?" I try to draw her out, looking to see where her head is at.

"You know." She's too fucking cute the way she squirms in the seat.

"You're blushing again."

"Am I?" Her hands fly to her cheeks. "I hate that."

"Because you know that I know you're thinking about having sex with me?"

"Yes … Ugh, I hate that." She squirms again. "Fair warning, but I'm not …"

"Not what?"

Not interested?

It can't be that, not with all the vibes she's throwing.

"I'm not as open about sex as you are. I'm not as …" She makes a vague gesture and takes in a deep breath. Peeking up at me, she struggles. "I'm not as comfortable talking about sex as you are."

I grab a lock of her hair and twine it around my finger. "You don't have to be anything you're not comfortable being, and you don't have to do anything you're not comfortable doing. If you need time, we can grill dinner on the deck, watch the sun slip below the horizon, and marvel as the sky turns to flame overhead. We can wish on shooting stars and do nothing more than that. We don't need to rush anything."

"I know, and thank you for that. It's one of the many things I'm coming to realize I love about you. I'm just nervous, I guess. Technically, the last time I saw you we were …"

"Arguing?" I nod. "I know. And now everything's different. We're different." I take her hands in mine. "I've always wanted you. Since the moment your hand touched mine in that clearing, I've wanted you. At first, it was purely physical. I'll admit that. You were a conquest I wanted but couldn't have. It made me irritable."

"And you were an incorrigible prick who argued with me nonstop."

"Yeah." I rub at the back of my neck. "Guilty as charged. But things are different, right?"

"Yeah."

"And this feels …" I leave room for her to finish that statement.

"It feels all kinds of right. I'm not saying I have cold feet. Or that I don't want to be here. Or that I don't want to spend the night and indulge in whatever crazy monkey sex you have planned."

"Crazy monkey sex?" I can't help but laugh. "I assure you, there will be no monkeys involved."

"You know what I mean." She shoves me playfully.

"I do. Or I hope I do." I lift her hand to my mouth. "How about we open a bottle of wine, take a seat outside, and watch the sun go down? Whatever happens after that, happens. We search for shooting stars or make some of our own in bed. We've got the rest of our lives to figure out the rest."

"We do?"

"Yes, Isabelle. We do."

"Why do you call me Isabelle?"

It's too early to be professing my love, but I know in my heart she's the other half of my soul. We'll get to the gooey love stuff later. "Because everyone else calls you Izzy. But you, Isabelle, are mine."

"What if this …" She gestures between us. "What if it's just a temporary high from the whole abduction and rescue thing? What if it's not real?"

"Are you asking if we'll ever argue again?"

"Maybe."

"I hope so."

"Why?"

"Because makeup sex is going to be fucking phenomenal."

Damn, but I love the way she blushes. My dick is rock-hard now.

"I bet it will be. Any kind of sex with you will be phenomenal." Her tone turns wistful. She leans over and kisses me on the cheek. "How about you show me your home?"

"Sounds like a fucking good plan." Despite the aching in my dick, I'm not pushing sex.

At least, not right away.

Isabelle's in a strange headspace right now, one I haven't quite figured out. If I have to guess, she's still processing what happened. I mean, *of course* she's processing. She went through hell, and that kind of a thing leaves a mark.

Matias took not only her freedom but threatened her family. He reached out and touched her life. Things will never be quite the same, at least not as long as he still draws breath.

I regret not putting a bullet through his head.

As for Isabelle, I'd be a total dick to think she's going to sort through everything in less than a day.

To be honest, a tiny part of me hopes she will, because I can be a selfish ass sometimes, but also because I want that pain to magically go away.

Unfortunately, I'm well acquainted with the residual trauma that simmers in the background in those we rescue. It can take months, maybe years, for Isabelle to fully process what happened.

I'm not an insensitive prick. When we have sex, it will be *we* who are having it, and not just *me* getting off. I'm not going to use Isabelle for self-gratification.

Not when I feel the way I do about her as a person.

"Well, let me show you around." I point to the left. "Brady and I bought this duplex together. He's got the unit on the left, and we're on the right." I pause to see if she catches the pronoun. The *we* kind of slipped out. If I have it my way, she'll be moving in with me the moment she's ready.

I jump out of the truck and race to get to her door before she can get out on her own. I'm eager to show her I can be a gentleman when I want to be.

She takes my hand, steps out, then leans into me.

"You smell amazing." She takes in a deep breath. "Did you take a shower while I was being interrogated? You smell minty clean instead of powder fresh."

"Hey, don't *diss* the power of a baby wipe. It's powerful stuff, but guilty as charged. I'm more than willing to offer my services to help you clean up, if that's what you want."

"If that's what I want?" She grabs my neck and forces me down to her level. A gentle press of her lips brings joy to my heart. "I think I want that very much, but I'd be lying if I'm not a bit nervous. Do you mind if we open that bottle of wine first?"

"Luv, I don't mind in the slightest." I take her hand and lead her inside my half of the duplex.

Modest on the inside with a million-dollar view on the outside, my place is a small, two-bedroom unit that is pretty much devoid of any personal touches. When I moved in, I hired an interior designer, telling her my favorite colors were gray, black, and white. She got carte blanche, and I got a modern design out of the whole thing.

With slate floors and an open-concept floor plan, it's ridiculously easy to clean, and easy to leave at a moment's notice when duty calls.

"It's not much, why don't you look around while I grab the wine. I'll meet you out back?"

"Where's the bathroom?"

"First door on the left. The master is last on the left, and the …" I pause, considering what to say, "the other is on the right, obviously."

"Obviously." She leaves me to freshen up while I grab a bottle of Pinot and two wine glasses.

It's a beautiful day outside. Standard California weather, it's balmy warm, no jacket required, a smattering of high, wispy clouds overhead, and a relatively calm ocean extending to the horizon.

I uncork and pour the wine, sit back in my favorite Adirondack chair, and wait for Isabelle. She wanders outside a few minutes later.

On my feet, I hand over her glass of wine. "I hope you like Pinot Noir. I forgot to ask what you like, but know it's not beer."

"Definitely not beer." She takes a sip, then suddenly pauses. "I'm sorry. We should toast, shouldn't we?"

"What would you like to toast to?"

"How about new beginnings?"

"Sounds absolutely perfect. To new beginnings—with you."

"And you." Her smile is as bright as the noonday sun, and that blush reminds me of dawn peeking over the hills to the east. "You are absolutely stunning." I wrap an arm around her waist and lead her to the railing. "What do you think of the view?"

"It's gorgeous. How did you …" She gestures at the single massive deck.

"When Brady and I bought the place, we thought we'd gut the interior and share it, but after thinking about our various—um, lifestyles—we decided to keep the interiors as two separate units. Here, have a seat. Let's watch the sun go down."

I hold her wine while she gets comfortable.

"You did? Why?" She reaches for her glass and takes a sip.

"Because …" I purse my lips, debating how much to tell Isabelle, but fuck it. I want her to know everything about me. "Because the women I used to bring over tended to make a lot of noise."

"From screaming."

"Yes." I rub the back of my neck.

"Orgasms?"

"Not just orgasms." There's a bit of hesitation in my voice.

Which is strange. I've never balked at letting a woman know about my kink.

Not that I'm all in.

I'm not a lifestyle guy, but I like to spice things up from time to time, and hey, a bit of fantasy and pretending never hurt anyone.

"What does that mean?" Her brows lift, curious but guarded.

"Did you look in the guest bedroom?"

"No. I didn't want to pry." She takes a sip of liquid courage—it's one of my best Pinots—then turns back to me. "You don't have a *Red Room* hidden back there. Do you?" Her words are a tease because she doesn't expect them to be the truth.

I return a stony look, giving her an answer she may not be ready for, or may not want to hear.

She almost spits out her wine and covers her mouth.

"Oh my god!" Her eyes grow wide. "Don't tell me you have a Red Room."

"Okay, I won't tell you I have a Red Room, but red isn't really my color. It's more a mix of dark gray and black."

"Holy fuck." She shoves her wine glass at me. "Hold this."

Before I know what's happening, Isabelle races back inside. I leap to my feet, spilling red wine all over my shirt.

"Fuuuck!"

I run inside, right on her heels, juggling two wine glasses, spilling wine all over the floors, but I'm not quite fast enough. Isabelle is already down the hall.

She opens the door to the spare bedroom as I slide to a stop a few feet away, holding my breath. Her jaw drops, and her eyes grow as big as saucers. She looks at me, then looks back inside.

I know exactly what she'll find. I'm paid well as a Guardian, and I like nice things. Everything in there is custom-made, and the leathers are second to none.

"Holy shit, batman." Isabelle doesn't run.

I gulp as she crosses the threshold and hold my breath.

"Tell me what's going on inside that head of yours." My voice deepens. Can't help it. It's the way I'm wired, especially when a woman enters that room. It's like a switch flips in my brain.

"What's going on in my head?" She looks up at me. "I don't think I'm ready for that."

Not ready? Or not willing?

Isabelle moves deeper into the room, running her hands across the various apparatuses inside.

Watching her explore is torture. Not knowing her thoughts is driving me insane.

"I can always move things out." I offer an olive branch.

When it comes down to it, this room isn't an integral part of my makeup that I can't leave it all behind. It's more of a way to spice things up and have a little fun while having sex, but I don't need it in my life to be happy.

She makes a complete circuit of the room, saying nothing. Her fingers run across the various implements hanging on the wall. She looks up at me several times, but her expression is indecipherable, and her thoughts beyond me.

She makes it back to the door, takes her glass out of my hand, and sips the rich wine. Without a word, she wanders down the hall and heads back outside.

I follow behind, not sure what to think. When I make it outside, she's back in her seat, staring out over the horizon.

I grab what's left of the bottle and top off her wine before sitting down beside her.

Side by side, we sit in silence as the sun dips below the horizon and the sky turns to sheets of fire overhead.

Whatever thoughts are swirling in her head remain hers alone as the first stars peek through the blanket of night.

The weirdest thing about the whole Red Room thing is I don't feel uncomfortable about it, especially when she reaches across and takes my hand in hers. We sit there in easy silence until the wine is done and millions of stars twinkle overhead.

Next time, instead of the Adirondack chairs, I'm sitting us on the outdoor couch, where we can snuggle, or fondle, probably both. I'll take her hand for now. All the rest can wait.

Half an hour later, Isabelle crashes. I've been waiting for it, knew it was coming. I hoped to forestall it with some epic sex, but her body is finally shutting down after her ordeal.

I wait until she's fully asleep, then gather her in my arms and carry her to bed. She barely stirs as I undress her. I do my best not to stare, but while I may be a gentleman, I've never claimed to be a saint.

Hard and aching once again, I leave her in my bed while I head to the shower to relieve the aching in my balls. With visions of all the things I want to try with Isabelle, my release comes quickly, but it's not enough.

I need more.

I need her.

THIRTY-SIX

Izzy

Bright sunlight shines in my eyes. I lift my arms overhead and point my toes in a whole-body stretch as a yawn works its way free.

Then I freeze.

Where am I?

I fight momentary disorientation, but it all comes back to me.

All of it.

My lids pinch together with memories of last night. A peek beneath the covers reveals my bra and panties are intact.

"Guess we didn't have sex." I mumble my disappointment out loud, but it's for the best. To not remember our first time together would be an egregious sin.

Stretching my hand out to the side reveals I did not sleep in the bed alone. There's the distinct impression of Booker's body beside me. I curl on my side, grab his pillow, and breathe in the scent of him.

There's no clock and I have no idea where my phone might be. Damn, if I'm going to laze around in bed all day. I sit up and swing my legs around. Blinking through sleep-blurry eyes, I peer at a chair tucked into the corner. Propped on top of it is one of my bags and there's a note placed on top of it.

Curious, I wander over. The note's from Angie.

Dear Izzy,

I hope you're having a fabulous time with Booker. I am going to want all the gory details later. For now, Booker asked me to pack you a little care package. I delivered it early this morning and heard you were still fast asleep. I guess your Guardian kept you up all night. Such a lucky girl.

Anyhoo, I'll see you when I see you. Don't do anything I wouldn't do, unless it's cool as shit, then do it. Do it all and tell me about it later.

Xoxoxo

Your Bestie,

Angie.

I clutch the letter to my chest and beat back a flood of tears. I've never had a bestie before and cherish the friendship Angie and I forged amid that crazy escape through the jungles of Nicaragua.

With all the debriefs yesterday, I have yet to see my best friend and can't wait to catch up. But first …

First, I need to brush my teeth, wash my face … I smell my pits and wrinkle my nose. No. First things first, a shower, wash my hair, then all the rest.

Knowing somehow that Booker is giving me space, I don't rush through the morning. I take a long, hot shower. I need a moment alone with my thoughts.

I soap and rinse no less than three times and run shampoo through my hair three times before applying conditioner. Anything I can do to rid myself of the stench of Maximus Angelo will be done.

In addition to very practical, and comfortable clothing, Angie tucked in a few fun, personal pieces of lingerie. I put those on beneath a pair of loose-fitting jeans and a pretty pink blouse.

Nothing fancy on top, but oh so sexy underneath. What will Booker think about the red lace?

Shame it's not dark gray.

Not a normal color for lingerie, I make a vow to find some.

We have a date in the guest bedroom. Not today. Maybe not for some time to come. I'm not quite that confident to dip my toes in those waters, but it's always fascinated me. That he's into it makes me want to explore it with him.

The dark-gray lingerie will wait. Today, it's all about sexy and sinful scarlet lace.

With my hair combed through and tied up to air dry, I look in the mirror and decide there's no need for any of the makeup Angie added to my bag.

Slowly, I open the door leading into the hall, then give a soft laugh.

Why am I sneaking? He knows I'm here.

I push open the door and take in a deep breath. Today, Booker and I will have sex—and it's going to be amazing.

With that thought in my head, I wander down the hall leading to the open-concept living area and pull up short.

Standing with his back to me, Booker swings his hips to music piped in through the headset he wears. I cover my mouth, trying to silence my surprise, because holy hotness on steroids, the man can shake that ass.

And what a mighty fine ass it is. Tight. Toned. Well-defined. His black boxer briefs sway to what must be a slow, sultry beat.

Shirtless—what a treat—he's muscle packed on muscle. It's basically a job requirement for a Guardian, but knowing something and seeing something, renders me speechless.

Speechless because I'm practically drooling at the mouth. I shouldn't stare, but if he's going to put on a show, I'm going to watch.

I lean against the wall, cup my elbow in the opposite hand and lean my cheek on my palm.

Holy hellfire, I can't wait to run my fingers all over that body.

A wicked idea pops into my head. I may not be the stealthiest person on the planet, but I figure I've got half a chance of sneaking up on him.

I imagine moving in behind him and wrapping my arms around his waist. Maybe, I'll let my hands travel up to explore the definition of his pecs? Or … I might let them trip over the ridges and grooves of a well-defined six-pack. Hell, a guy like him is packing an eight-pack.

Lifting on tiptoe, I slowly make my way over to the kitchen. I pause several times, thinking he hears me, but he inevitably goes back to swaying those hips. As for what he's cooking, it's hard to tell. Delicious and complex aromas percolate into the air. There's a hint of garlic, the one spice to rule them all, plus other, lighter scents.

Is that lilac?

Is that even used in cooking?

So far, so good. The kitchen island is several feet away from the cooktop, plenty of space for me to slip in behind him. I move in, hands ready to grab his hips, when Booker suddenly spins around and grabs me.

"Oh no you don't!" He plants a fat kiss on my lips, then grabs my hips, moving me in synch with the rhythm of his body.

"How did you hear me?" I loop my hands around his neck and giggle as he grinds against me.

"Huh?"

"How did you hear me?" I raise my voice and tap the headset.

He flashes me a wicked grin and winks with those devilish eyes of his. "Didn't have to hear you." Booker yanks off the headset. He buries his nose in my neck and flutters kisses all along my neck. "I smelled you the moment you entered the room."

"Ew … You smelled me?" Somehow, that's not a positive image. "I took a shower."

"I know. Heard the water running for a really long time."

"Why didn't you join me?"

"Because I'm whipping you up something special."

"You are." I try to peek around him to see what's on the stove. "What is it?"

"Ah, that is a cook's secret. You're not the only one who can cook."

"I don't know about that. You've never cooked before."

"Why should I when you're so good at it, but I do have some secrets." He grips me by the waist and lifts me off my feet.

I squeal in surprise as he carries me the few feet to the kitchen island.

"How do you like my kitchen?" There goes another of his devastating winks.

"Um, it's cool?"

"What about the island?" He gestures to the long expanse of the center island. "I had it built special." He wedges himself between my legs.

"It's cold?" Even through the thin fabric of my pants, the cool surface makes itself known.

"Is it?" He leans back. "Hmm, I thought I turned on the heat."

"You have a heated kitchen island? Is that like a California thing?"

"It's a specialty thing." He gives me a look like I'm missing something obvious.

I take a moment from admiring his half-naked body to examine the countertop, but I see nothing unusual. It's a flat piece of granite. Large. Exceptionally large. All up and down are what look to be those pop-up power ports. I only know about those because my mother wants those installed when they redo the kitchen.

With my arms draped around his neck, I let my fingers twirl in his hair. He keeps it a little longer in the back, but it's otherwise what some would call an out of regulation haircut. You can put a man in the military, but you can't take the military out of the man when all is said and done.

"Are you going to tell me?" I'm still confused.

"Look down, luv." He wiggles in, forcing my legs wider. One glance and it all becomes clear.

"Oh my god!" I cover my mouth and can't help but laugh. "Please tell me you didn't design it for that."

"Luv, you bet your britches that's exactly what I did. And speaking of britches, why did you bother putting on pants? You could've at least worn a skirt. Then I would have easy access. This way …" He shakes his head. "This is an obstacle that must be overcome."

"You're crazy."

"Not crazy, luv, just horny as shit. Sleeping next to you all night, without touching you, qualifies me for sainthood."

"About last night …"

"Oh no." He presses a finger to my lips. "We're not doing the whole, *about last night thing*."

"But …"

"You were mentally, physically, and emotionally exhausted, and as much as I would've loved to jump your bones, you needed rest. I was happy to give you a safe place to sleep."

"And today?"

"Today depends on you."

"How so?"

"In there lies the path to as many orgasms as you can stomach, if that's what you want." He gestures to a ceramic jar with a lid on it. "If not, I was thinking about a walk on the beach. We can do either, or both, or none at all. I am, as they say, at your service."

The way his voice vibrates when he says that makes my toes curl and other parts of me throb with anticipation. Considering his kitchen island was specifically designed so that his parts meet up with my parts, I know exactly what I want.

"Before this goes any further, luv, take a look at that." He uses his chin to point to a small ceramic jar sitting on top of the counter.

Curious, I lean over, lift the lid, and look inside at a treasure trove of condoms.

"Well, what do we have here?" I sift through, admiring what I find. "Cherry flavor?"

"That's for you."

"Me?"

"When you decide to wrap those luscious lips around me. I'm always thinking of the ladies." He pulls the jar over and pulls out a ribbed condom. "This is for you as well."

"And this one?" I turn an odd foil package in my hand.

"Ah, that one glows in the dark."

"You're kidding me?"

"Not in the slightest." He returns a stone-cold expression. It lasts for a good while before his face breaks out in a grin.

"Glow in the dark?"

"It goes with the lighting in the room that's not red."

"Ah, your personal dungeon."

"I prefer to call it a pleasure palace."

"Looks more like a dungeon, or den of sin."

"All I ask is that you reserve judgment until you experience it yourself." He dips down to get eye to eye. "Does it freak you out?"

"Not really." I hold up a hand. "But maybe we take that one slow and focus on the other bit first?"

"The other bit?" He arches a brow.

"You know."

"Are you asking me to have sex with you?"

"I think it's implied."

"I don't want to assume." He rocks his hips forward. He's hard and fully erect. The tip of his penis bumps up against my pussy. If it weren't for our clothes being in the way, we'd be fucking by now.

"You're nothing like I thought."

"Really? Should I ask?"

"I thought you were a player, focused on only one thing, but you've shown incredible thoughtfulness. It's unexpected."

"I'll take that as a compliment. Although, I'm not sure if I should be offended. I do come with a past, as I'm sure you do. We can talk about all of it if you want, find the skeletons and such, but one of the things I've learned along the way, especially when it comes to the room, which is not red, is communication always comes first, followed by consent. You may be disappointed when you find out how much of a player I was not."

"I didn't mean to offend."

"Luv, I'm not offended in the slightest. However, the fact you're still wearing pants while my dick is drilling a hole through my briefs is pretty offensive. Pick a condom, babe, and get ready for the time of your life."

"I've never met a man like you."

"No doubt about that." He reaches into the jar and hands me three condoms. One is cherry flavored. Studs cover the next. The last one is ribbed. "Pick one."

"Studs?"

"I hear only good things." His wicked grin is back, along with a gleam in his eye.

"Studs it is." I pull the studded condom out of his hand and rip the top of the foil. "Is that enough consent for you?"

Booker grabs my neck and pulls me in for a hot and ferocious kiss. It reminds me of our very first kiss dangling beneath a helicopter as it lifted me to a staggering height.

We're both a frantic mess of clashing teeth, dueling tongues, and hands that go everywhere, groping as they explore.

He shoves his hand under my shirt and cups my breast while I free his engorged cock from his briefs. A hiss escapes him as I wrap my hand around the thick shaft. He nips at my neck, kissing and sucking as I lightly stroke him from root to tip.

He takes his time warming me up, driving me crazy as he hits all the erogenous zones in my neck, behind my ear, and even tugs provocatively on my ear lobe.

I go from curious to hot and bothered in zero seconds flat. Tearing at my shirt, I can't yank it off fast enough.

Booker works at my pants, freeing the button and lowering the zipper. He works them down my hips. I lift up as he pulls them over my ass and frees my legs.

He stands in front of me, breathing hard, admiring the red lace lingerie barely clinging to my body.

"You are fucking hot." He takes his time, nibbling my neck, kissing my lips, and trailing down to the other side.

His hands cup my breasts, squeezing and stimulating until my breaths turn short and ragged. Nearly panting, I whimper as his palm glides over my belly and his fingers dip beneath the lace of my panties.

He makes me gasp when his fingers explore my folds, pressing lightly at first, then exploring further. I sigh as his teeth graze across my shoulder. When he swirls a finger around my pussy, I'm way past panting. Guttural sounds escape my throat as he sinks first one finger and then another inside.

My entire body jerks as he stimulates my pleasure centers and makes my body come alive. His fingers curl and rub against my inner walls sending jolts of electricity coursing through my body.

"Oh my god, Booker …" My words are mostly intelligible. "Please, I need you to fuck me."

"We'll get there, luv. For now, enjoy the ride." He pumps his fingers in and out, sending shockwave after shockwave pulsing through my body. It's a sizzling current of liquid heat, surging in and out, frying my nerve endings as they build and build and build.

I cling to Booker through the whole thing and dig my fingers into his skin, clutching as he works me into a frenzy. The words coming out of my mouth make no sense. They're barely human.

Booker reduces me to nothing but need and want and pleasure, almost too painful to bear. I cry out as he presses against my chest, forcing me to lie down on the granite countertop.

I think he's going to stop when he pulls his fingers out, but then his mouth takes over.

Heat is everywhere.

The heat of his mouth. The heat of his tongue. The heat of his breath washes over me as my body liquefies beneath the intensity of sensation.

I laugh.

I cry.

Tears fall from my eyes as my entire existence narrows down to raw, sexual desire as he probes deeper and licks faster. He adds his thumb to the mix, circling around my clit, stroking rhythmically until I can't take any more.

My entire body is on fire, consumed by the passion flowing

through me. I dig my fingers into his hair, pressing his face against my pussy as my entire body trembles.

Booker continues to stimulate me. Heat coils within me, building and tightening like a spring, until it suddenly peaks and releases all in a rush. I'm carried over the edge. All that pleasure releases in a blinding flash of liquid pleasure.

A scream erupts from my lungs as a firestorm of sensation engulfs every cell, obliterates every thought, and takes me to a place of intense bliss as sensation powers through me wave after incredible wave.

His lips press tenderly against my inner thigh, and his fingers caress my skin. It's the most erotic and sensual experience of my life. He effectively turns me into a quivering mess.

Booker rises over me as I pant and attempt to gather all the pieces of my soul he sent into oblivion.

La petit mort?

I know why the French call it the little death.

"Fuck, but you taste like sin." Booker reaches beside me where I dropped the foil packet, leaving it discarded beside me. "I'm going to fuck you, Isabelle. I'm going to fuck you until you come apart and your voice is hoarse from screaming my name."

I place the back of my hand over my eyes as flickering aftershocks of the orgasm continue to spark within me. Then the bulbous tip of Booker's cock presses against my entrance.

"It's going to be a tight fit. If it hurts, tell me to stop."

"I'm never going to tell you to stop." I drop my hand long enough to gaze into his eyes. Blown black by lust and masculine need, he grips my hips and pushes inside.

Sensation sparks again, more intense than before. My walls pinch and burn, protesting the invasion, but there's no way I'm stopping this.

"You doing okay?" His fingers dig into my ass and his body trembles. He's having difficulty going slow.

"Yes." I nod, vigorously and grab his wrists, letting my fingers dig in. "Don't stop."

"Not if the world itself were ending." Booker's nostrils flare. No man deserves to smell as good as he does.

My back arches as he pushes further inside me, thrusting my tits up in invitation. Booker obliges, and the heat of his mouth covers my breast. I shiver against the sensation.

He stands tall and stares down where our bodies are joined together.

"You might want to hold on for this." He helps me to sit up, then sweeps the mess of my hair off my face. "You are fucking incredible." With that, he wraps his hand in my hair and pulls me in for a devastating kiss.

And then, Booker's hips move …

Holy hell, I've been transported to another plane of existence where every breath is liquid pleasure.

Booker fucks me on the kitchen island until I come on his cock. He pulls out, swaps out the condom, then takes me from behind, driving into me like a man on a mission.

We move from the kitchen to the couch, to the floor, and then to the wall.

His powerful arms hold me fast as he impales me on his cock and takes me again. All day long, we fuck. Like rabbits, we go at it nonstop.

Whatever was on the stove burns and is completely unsalvageable, not that we care. Food means nothing as he carries me to his bed and takes me again.

In the shower, he grabs the back of my neck and forces me to my knees. I would go willingly, but it's so much hotter when he makes me obey.

I wrap my lips around his cock and swallow him whole as he fucks my face, almost collapsing when his legs nearly give out. We sit on the floor of the shower, talking, holding hands, kissing softly, longingly, then more ferocious as our need overcomes us once again.

By the time we crawl into bed, the sun's already down, and the stars shine overhead. Booker pulls me close and cradles me in his arms.

"I'm never letting you go." He seals the promise with a kiss, and we both fade into dreams of what tomorrow will bring.

THIRTY-SEVEN

Booker

After two days of blocking calls and ignoring messages, I finally succumb to the loud knocking at the door.

"What the fuck?" I glare at Brady and give him a look that can kill. "Do you know what time it is?"

"Looks to me it's about fuck o'clock." He tries to barge in, but I block him with my arm.

"No one's coming in. You got something I need to know. I'm here. Spit it out."

"What I have to say is that you and your woman need to climb out of this fuckfest you've got going on and get your asses to HQ."

"Why?" I exaggerate with an emphatic sigh. "There ain't nothing I need to do at HQ."

"You might not, but Iz sure as shit does."

"And what would that be?"

"Nobody knows. Rafe's cling-on isn't speaking to anyone and says she'll only talk to your woman. So, get your dick out of your girl, put on some clothes, and get your sorry ass to HQ with Izzy in tow." Brady doesn't have to shout to get his point across, and he's not talking to me like his best bud.

That's Bravo One issuing a direct order.

"Copy that." I take in a deep breath. "We'll be there within the hour."

"I'd love to tell you to hurry the fuck up and make it ten, but I know you're going back inside to fuck her brains out before you leave."

"Be careful what you say about my woman."

"Ain't saying nothing that isn't true, and I'm not saying it to anyone but you." He thumps his chest. "Respect, but get your fucking ass in gear and answer your damn phone."

With that, Brady executes a precise about-face and storms off to his side of our conjoined domiciles.

"Who was that?" Isabelle peeks out from the hallway, clutching a sheet to her naked body.

"Brady."

"What did he want?"

"He said we've got to stop screwing around and get back to work."

"Oh." Her eyes grow wide. "Did something happen?"

"Don't know." I stalk toward her, hungry for what I can't seem to get enough of. "Don't care."

I rip the sheet from her body and body slam her against the wall. We've yet to cross the threshold into the one room of the house where we haven't fucked, but I've learned enough to know what gets Isabelle's juices flowing the fastest.

My girl loves a rough fuck, and I'm more than happy to nail her against the wall. I fuck her in the shower and put her on all fours, taking her from behind. It's rough as shit, and damn, does she know how to scream. It's like a mainline of crack going straight to my dick.

Somehow, we manage to make it out of the house and arrive at Guardian HQ two hours later. Brady waits for us in the main lobby and greets me with pinched eyes and a you'll-pay-for-this-later promise. I say nothing as I escort Isabelle inside and come to a halt right in front of him.

"We have arrived."

"A full fucking hour late."

"But Brady said …" Isabelle looks between me and Brady, then rolls her eyes. "Oh lord, Brady, I swear I didn't know."

"No doubt that's the truth. You would never dare to keep the brass waiting, unlike Booker here, who's flirting with death."

"Them?" Isabelle stands a little taller. "By them, who are we talking about?"

"Your boss, for one, and my boss and my boss's boss and fucking Forest Summers. They're all waiting for you in the conference room."

"Holy shit." Isabelle gives a little squeak beside me. Then she turns and shoves me. "Did you know?"

"Brady may have mentioned a meeting."

"I told your boyfriend to get his ass here over an hour ago."

"Sorry." She tugs at my hand, but I don't budge.

I can't. Brady and I have to do the macho-stare-and-glare-while-measuring-our-dick-sizes thing before either of us can move.

"Oh, for the love of all that's holy, will the two of you stop." Isabelle marches off in a huff, but she stops a few feet away. "Hello? I have no idea where I'm headed. One of you needs to put your dick-measuring pencil away and tell me where everyone is waiting."

Brady does this slow blink thing. It takes a moment before Isabelle's words sink in. He huffs a laugh and shakes his head. The two of us turn as one and he slings an arm over my shoulder. Thumping my chest, he shakes his head.

"Dude, I'm happy for you. I really am, but don't …"

"Can't make any promises, but message received."

We're the best of buds, but he's still, technically, my superior. We stride over to where Isabelle waits for us. Once we're close, Brady drops his arm from my shoulder, allowing me to reach out and capture Isabelle's hand.

"This way." With a sweep of his arm, he gestures toward the executive conference room.

Isabelle moves in close. Her hand twitches with nervousness as Brady holds the door. I walk in holding hands with Isabelle, wanting everyone to know we're officially a couple. As for who's inside, that comes as no surprise.

Forest Summers and the doc are seated on one side of the long conference table. Sam and CJ sit opposite them. They push back from their chairs and stand to greet Isabelle.

"How are you holding up?" Sam reaches for Isabelle, and to my surprise, she allows him to wrap his arms around her.

The contact's brief, but it takes everything within me not to snarl like an animal. When Sam releases her, CJ also gives her a quick hug. Unlike Sam, CJ kisses the side of her cheek. I swallow that snarl as well.

The kiss means nothing. Like Isabelle, CJ's from Texas, and that's just a normal greeting for them. They're not as standoffish as the rest of us.

Forest and Doc Summers do not stand but rather wait patiently for Isabelle to take her seat at the head of the table. Brady and I are not offered seats, but neither are we excused from the room. We take up position holding up the wall and wait for whatever this is to begin.

"Why do I feel as if I've done something wrong?" Isabelle swivels in her seat, revealing her nervousness.

The urge to go to her rises within me, but a curt glance from Brady keeps me right where I am.

"We've had a bit of a development." Sam presses a button on a panel in front of him.

"Hey, boss, what's up?" Mitzy's perky voice rises from a hidden speaker.

"Izzy's here."

"About time." Her chipper voice makes me irritable, but then I've been running on little to no sleep. "I'll be there in a jiffy."

Sam leans back. "You said something during your debrief that's had us all wondering."

"What was that?"

"It was the comment Angelo made to you about the diamonds."

"Yes?" Isabelle realizes she's fidgeting and tries to sit still. It lasts about a nanosecond before she gives up. "But I don't know what it meant."

"Do you remember what he said?"

"Sure, it was something about diamonds buy things, but something-something buys loyalty."

"Yes, I've been trying to wrap my head around that and fit it in with what happened to Angie."

"What do you mean?" Isabelle leans forward. "Are you talking about our abduction?"

"More about how Jerald fits into the picture. We've been discussing it on and off and something has always felt a bit off about it."

"I suppose. Honestly, that's a bit out of my scope."

"Maybe, but I think it all fits."

"If you say so." Isabelle doesn't look convinced, but then neither do I.

"What the fuck's been happening around here?" I keep my voice nearly sub-vocal, for Brady's ears only.

"If you'd been on time, I would've briefed you." He rocks back on his heels and refuses to say anything else.

"Asshole."

"Everyone has one." His response is clipped and sharp.

The door to the conference room bangs open and Mitzy barges in carrying something bulky in her arms. One of her assistants follows behind pushing a cart.

"Hey, Izzy, have they briefed you?" Mitzy's chipper voice is bright as bright can be.

"Um, I'm not sure if what they've said counts as a briefing. I'm not sure why I'm here."

"You didn't tell her?" Mitzy turns accusing glares at CJ and Sam. "Typical." Her attention sweeps across the table to Forest. "You know I blame you. It's your job to get your people to do the talking thing. Y'all can't keep expecting me to connect the dots."

Skye covers her mouth, hiding her laughter, while Forest flinches as if stung.

"I'm not …" he begins, but Mitzy cuts him off.

"Oh, I know. I'll deal with it." She turns toward Isabelle and props her fists on her hips. "You are here because the princess in the dungeon says she will only speak to you."

"Excuse me?"

"The woman in the red dress? Carmen Angelo? Daughter to Nicaragua's Minister of the Interior? The man who …"

"We know who the fucker is." I cut Mitzy off before she goes any further.

In contrast to the many shades of beautiful blushes I've come to adore, Isabelle turns white as a ghost. She's not ready to face those memories, and Mitzy should know better.

"Why would she want to speak to me?" Isabelle's voice shakes nearly as much as her body.

"Don't know. She specifically said you are the only one she will speak to and only if there is no recording and no witnesses."

"What?" Isabelle sits straight as an arrow. "That makes no sense. She literally hates me."

"Well, I suppose she miscalculated when she hitched a ride with the Guardians." CJ presses his palms to the table. "The thing is, we're running out of time. The Minister thinks his daughter was kidnapped. It won't take long for him to figure out *who* rescued you, and we can't afford for him to connect the dots. Which means, we need to know what she has to say. Right now, the only person she will talk to is you."

"But I don't know anything about interrogating a prisoner."

"Carmen is not our prisoner." CJ leans back.

"But you said …"

"I said we tried to question her, but we are not keeping her under lock and key. She's able to get up and leave anytime she wants."

"Then, why hasn't she?"

"That's what we want you to find out," Skye answers for the room.

"Look, I'd love to help, but I don't think I'm the right person for this job."

"Maybe not, but you're the *only* person for this job." Sam twists in his seat. "Mitzy, show her what you found."

"One sec." She whispers something to her assistant.

He connects a few cables and the wall screen opposite Isabelle reveals a picture of a mangled rabbit's foot and nearly ten million in diamonds.

"Jerald, as far as we know, was a courier for the *Laguta* cartel," Mitzy begins. "The very dead, Miguel *Coralos*, thought Jerald was using your Doctors Without Borders mission to smuggle weapons, which lead to your capture, but no weapons were discovered. No explosives. No munitions. Nada. But he came after Angie demanding she give him back the rabbit's foot, which was filled with ten million in diamonds. We thought that was the end of it. Jerald was working for the *Laguta* cartel, and he was smuggling diamonds, not weapons. It appears our Minister of the Interior friend was shifting large amounts of cash to the *Laguta* cartel, which is run by his brother. His cousin, poor dead Miguel, was in some kind of disagreement with Angelo."

"If you say so." Isabelle shrugs.

"Actually, you said so," Mitzy fires back.

"I did?"

"Yes, but we investigated and did some digging. Regardless, we thought it stopped at the diamonds. But your comment about buying loyalty and obedience struck a nerve." Mitzy glances at Forest. "A very raw nerve."

"I'm sorry. I don't understand." Isabelle looks to me, but I don't know anything more than what's been said here. I return a shrug and hate that I'm not by her side.

"We'll get to that later. The point is, Miguel thought weapons were being smuggled. He was wrong. Angelo's brother, leader of the *Laguta* cartel, used the diamonds to flush out a traitor. Turns out it's probably some combination of it all."

"Why would he do that?" I jump in, curious enough to open my mouth.

"We *assume*," Mitzy uses air quotes, "and you know how I hate to assume, but we figured it has something to do with mining the mineral deposits found in *Coralos* controlled territory."

"Okay." I shrug. It's not enough, and I agree with Mitzy about assuming too much.

"The thing is, we were all wrong." Mitzy spins around and glances at the blank screen at the end of the room.

"Huh?"

"The diamonds were a distraction for what was really being moved."

"And what would that be?"

"Show them." Mitzy points to her technician.

The view on the screen zooms in, not on the diamonds, but rather the raggedy rabbit's foot. Specifically, it zooms in on the metal brad that attaches the rabbit's foot to its chain.

"Keep going." Mitzy gestures to her technician to continue.

The view zooms in until metal scoring marks are visible on the brad.

"Keep going." Mitzy points her finger and rolls it, gesturing for the tech to zoom in further.

The view intensifies, gets fuzzy, then jumps again in magnification.

"What you're seeing is the brad as viewed by a scanning electron microscope. Are you familiar with those?"

"Not really."

"A scanning electron microscope is more powerful than a light microscope, the ones you probably used in your high school biology lab. Your typical microscope can magnify things up to two thousand times. A scanning electron microscope can magnify up to a million times. A transmission electron microscope can zoom in fifty million times, but we didn't need that for this."

We all return blank stares, or maybe it's just me.

Mitzy puffs out a breath. "Let me put it in terms that make sense. Imagine a single grain of sand. Just one grain. A tiny crystal. If a light microscope magnifies it two thousand times, it's suddenly about the size of an average adult footstep." She puts her hands out in front of her about a foot apart.

"Now, if you magnify that same grain of sand a million times, which is the average power of a relatively low-powered Scanning Electron Microscope, or SEM, that grain of sand is suddenly the size of the Eiffel Tower. Pretty damn huge. Not to get too technical, but there's a more powerful electron microscope, a TEM, or Transmission Electron Microscope. It's the one that can magnify up to fifty million times. That makes that single grain appear to be the size of two Mount Everest's stacked on top of each other. We started with the SEM. I want you to imagine for a moment how much information you could write on the Eiffel Tower if you had a spray can and could write all over it." Mitzy signals the technician.

"Izzy, when you said Angelo mentioned information, I went looking. First, we looked at the diamonds, both from your rabbit's foot and then from Angie's, but there was bupkis to find. Then I had an idea when I saw the brad. Normally, it's made of a flimsy metal; think tin. These were made from copper and you can use different techniques to engrave that metal. So, I threw it in a SEM for shits and giggles, and this is what I found."

The resolution suddenly jumps a thousandfold, or rather a millionfold. My head hurts imagining the scale Mitzy refers to, but sure as shit, there's writing on the metal.

"Fuckin' A."

"Exactly." Mitzy gives a little bow. "What we have here is another one of our favorite things; a cipher without a key, and that's where you come in." She points to Isabelle. "You're going to have a nice, long chat with Maximus Angelo's daughter."

"Me?" Isabelle points to her chest. "I know nothing about interrogations, and like I've said a million times, Carmen hates my guts."

"And yet, she will speak only to you." Sam presses his fingertip on the table, emphasizing his point.

Isabelle gulps and slowly gives in with a nod.

When they take her, I push off the wall to join her, but Brady places his hand on my shoulder.

"Sorry, dude, but she has to do this alone."

"Alone, my ass." Nothing's keeping me from Isabelle's side.

"Stand down, Bravo Two." Brady clears his throat, telling me not to push.

"Fuck." I push off the wall and clench my fists. "You're cool with this?"

"All I know is what I've been told. Carmen will speak to Izzy, and Izzy alone. We'll only get in the way." He runs his fingers through his hair. "I don't like it one bit, but it is what it is."

And he's right about that.

Isabelle disappears for two hours. When she returns, it's with an apologetic shrug and to tell us she's been put under a gag order.

I don't like it, but when we need to know, Bravo team will be briefed on our next steps. I hope whatever they discussed helps Mitzy's team figure out what the information scribed into the metal collars of the two rabbit's feet is important enough to kill for.

Until then, I've got my girl and two weeks off from my duties at Guardian HRS. Isabelle and I are headed back to Leighton, Texas, where I have a very important question to ask her father.

THIRTY-EIGHT

Booker

"You're not nervous, are you?" Isabelle takes my hand in hers as we exit the plane and head down to baggage claim.

"Not at all." I unthread my fingers from hers, but only to loop an arm around her neck to pull her in for a sloppy kiss.

"Ew … Gross." She wipes at her mouth and gives me the stink eye. "You slobbered on me."

"I'd rather pin you to that wall and fuck you until you scream, but I think the other passengers would take offense to that."

"Agreed … But slobber?" She wipes at her cheek again.

"It was one wet kiss. Deal with it."

Isabelle rises on tiptoe and licks my face.

"Fair's fair."

I shake my head and we continue on.

"So, which of your brothers will be picking us up?"

"If I had to guess, Gareth and Colton." The bounce in her step reveals her eagerness to see her family again. Her excitement is infectious, and I share her eagerness. Although, mine is for a different reason.

"I like them. Your family is pretty cool."

"Thanks, but please remember, Mom doesn't like swearing."

"I will do my *gosh darn* best to keep a clean mouth, but I can't promise."

"Well, that'll have to do." She loops her hands around my neck and pulls me down for one of her simmering, sweet kisses that never fails to get me going.

"Not fair." I reach down to make a quick adjustment, then wrap my hand around the back of her neck, trading a sweet kiss for hot and steamy. One that's guaranteed to turn her face a pretty, scarlet red.

"Holy shit." She's breathless and panting, mirroring my state of arousal. Unfortunately, there's nowhere private where we can slake our hunger for each other.

"Yeah—can I just say I can't wait until tonight?"

"Tonight?"

"Yes, luv. I'm going to finish that kiss and make you scream."

"You can't tonight."

"Why?"

"Because we're staying at my parent's house."

"So?"

"We won't be in the same room, and there's no way I'm having …" She peeks at the steady flow of people passing us by without a care in the world. Lowering her voice she whispers the rest, "Sex."

"You're kidding, right?" I've heard of old-fashioned, but her parents can't be that old-fashioned. "Do your parents know where you've been sleeping?"

"They don't ask, and I don't tell. So, no. They do not, and we're not having sex under their roof."

"What if we're married?" I toss the comment out there to see how she responds.

"Surely you can go a few days without sex?"

"A few days?" I gasp in mock horror. "Surely, you jest?"

"You'll live."

"If you call walking around with a boner and blue balls living …" I love the light teasing back and forth.

I love every damn thing about Isabelle, and I plan to make our current living arrangements permanent. I'm a man on a mission.

We make our way through baggage claim, grab our luggage, and head outside to meet her brothers.

As expected, Gareth and Colton are there to pick us up.

"Nice to see you again, Booker." Gareth gives me a solid shake.

"Likewise." I load our bags into the back of the truck while Gareth and Colton greet their sister. Once Colton is done hugging Isabelle, we do the manly shake and greet.

"How was the flight?" Colton asks.

"We didn't crash." Isabelle's excitement at seeing her brothers is a palpable thing. "So, win-win all around."

I can't help but laugh.

One of Isabelle's many fears, she seemed to manage the flight without a hitch. Honestly, I forgot all about that being one of her phobias, but I suppose it's because I managed to keep her mind off her fear of flying with a bit of groping and magic fingers. Not officially a member of the mile-high club, she's one step closer.

"We're meeting up at the ranch, if that's okay," Gareth says. "Construction at the new drill site is almost finished, and Dad didn't want to wait to see you."

"Sounds fun." I hold the door for Isabelle and lightly slap her ass as she climbs into the truck. "I'd love to take a tour of the ranch under better circumstances than last time."

"Well, I think we can handle that." Gareth glances at me through the rearview mirror. "It'll be far less exciting than the last time you were here."

"I'm totally good with that."

Isabelle and I sit in the back, while Colton and Gareth sit up front. On good behavior, we leave the middle seat between us vacant. If Isabelle sat beside me, there's no way I'd be able to keep my hands off her hot body.

I crave that constant connection.

"Are you nervous?" I lower my voice and get Isabelle's attention. "Last time you were here …" I let my voice trail off.

During the rare times we're not fucking, Isabelle and I have had a chance to share bits and pieces of her past. I've learned quite a bit about my girl, like where her fear of water comes from, her fear of heights, and her fear of flying.

They were all precipitated by a traumatizing event. Considering the last time she was on her family's ranch, Matias kidnapped her at gunpoint, I hope she doesn't transfer some of that fear to the ranch.

"No. Not nervous." She fidgets in her seat. "Excited."

"That's good." I reach across to hold her hand.

"How are Sam and Charlie doing?" Isabelle's voice is tight, strained with worry.

"Very good, considering." Colton spins around in the passenger seat. "Fred and Bruce had minor concussions. They were released the same day. Charlie and Sam were in longer. They were lucky."

I remember the wounds sustained by Charlie and Sam and breathe out a sigh of relief. If something happened to either of the men, Isabelle would never be able to forgive herself.

"After we see Mom and Dad, I'd like to visit them in the hospital." Isabelle's concern over the men who work for her family warms my heart.

"You'll see them sooner than that." Gareth switches lanes, moving us onto the freeway. "They're meeting us at the ranch."

"They are? Shouldn't they be at home, resting?"

"You think they'd miss out on seeing you?" Gareth gives his sister a look. "I'm not supposed to say this, but you've got a bit of a surprise party planned for your homecoming."

"Ugh, I hate surprise parties. Couldn't you talk them out of it?"

"We tried." Colton leans forward to turn on the radio. "But you know how Mom is when she gets an idea in her head."

"But she knows I hate them."

Colton spins around again. "Just go with the flow, sis. This party isn't for you."

"Ugh …" Isabelle leans back and closes her eyes. "I hate surprise parties." Her grumpy tone brings a smile to my face.

There's more to the surprise party than she knows, and more than her brothers realize as well, even if they're unknowing accomplices.

I've been in secret conversations with her mother, planning this party, and getting everything set up. After today, I'm hoping Isabelle's thoughts about surprise parties change.

The drive from Laredo to Leighton is a little over an hour. It takes almost as long to get to the ranch. By the time we pull up to the main gates, I'm ready to stretch my legs. However, the LaCroix ranch lives up to the Texas motto where *everything* is bigger.

About half an hour later, we pull up to a grouping of temporary buildings surrounding the newest drill site.

"Wow, it's almost ready." Isabelle is the first to jump out of the truck. It takes less than a second for her to look at the construction and determine it's nearly ready. There are so many layers to my girl.

A group of people exit the largest of the three buildings and begin walking toward the truck. I recognize them all from the last time I was here, trying and failing to keep Isabelle from getting kidnapped.

Her father walks behind the main group of people with three men. I recognize Fred Asher, Bruce Ackles, and Tom McBride. Both Fred and Bruce were knocked out cold last time I was here.

While Isabelle runs to her twin brothers, I angle off to the men.

"Mr. LaCroix, it's nice to finally meet you." I hold out my hand and wait for him to take it. Unlike the rest of Isabelle's family, this is the first time I'm meeting her father.

"Nice to meet you." His grip is firm but not overbearing. He grabs hold of my arm while we shake. "You know Fred, Sam, and Tom?"

"I do." We quickly shake and exchange greetings. "I thought Charlie Tompkins and Sam Hodges were going to be here?"

"They're here." Isabelle's father hooks a thumb over his shoulder. "But they're staying in the air conditioning. It's too hot out here for them. The docs weren't happy releasing either of them early, but no way were they going to miss this."

"I take it Mrs. LaCroix spoke to you?"

"She did, although I'm not supposed to tell you. I have to pretend I'm surprised, but I want to tell you I'm impressed."

"Impressed?"

"That you're asking for my blessing."

"She wasn't supposed to tell. I wanted to do this thing right."

"You've already done it right, but let's do it, son. Go ahead and ask."

Totally not how I saw this going, I clear my throat and swallow down the nervousness fluttering around inside of me.

I envisioned a private conversation with Isabelle's dad, not one with witnesses. Since it looks like Isabelle is nearly done hugging her mom and brothers, I take a swallow and just do it.

"I know it hasn't been that long that I've known your daughter, but I know one thing for sure. She's the other half of me, and if you'll allow it, I'd like to ask for her hand in marriage."

"And you think she's going to say yes?" Her father isn't letting me off the hook easy.

Wasn't expecting a question, but I grin from ear to ear.

"I don't *think* she's going to say yes, Mr. LaCroix, I *know* she will."

"Ha! I love your confidence, son." He sticks out his hand. "Welcome to the family. If my daughter will have you, I'm pleased to give you my blessing."

"Daddy!" Isabelle shouts and comes running.

Her father releases my hand, then holds his arms out wide to give his daughter a hug.

"Are you okay? Did you get arrested? Did they hurt you? Impound the helicopter?" She's one long string of questions. "I've been so worried about you."

Her father answers none of her questions as he holds his daughter in his arms and fights off the mist in his eyes.

I take a step back and move over to Isabelle's mother. "Mrs. LaCroix, it's nice to see you again."

"Likewise." She grips my arms and kisses my cheek. "Are you ready?"

"Is it all set?"

"You know it is."

"And did everyone make it?"

"Flew in this morning and are waiting inside." She leans in close. "You know she hates surprises."

"She's going to love this one." I turn to my girl, adoring how she's surrounded by so many people who love her.

I made the right choice asking her family to be here today.

Her mother gets everyone corralled and headed toward the main building. Inside, the newer members of Isabelle's extended family wait to bear witness to what I hope is the beginning of a new life with Isabelle by my side.

I drift back from everyone, letting them go inside ahead of me and Isabelle.

She takes my hand in hers. "I'm so glad Skye let me come back."

"Technically, you never got to take your leave."

"True, but I *technically* haven't banked any time off yet. I have to say Guardian HRS is a really cool place to work, and I'm so happy they didn't can my ass over the whole abduction thing."

"You're going to love working for them."

She tries to tug out of my grip, but I hold her back.

"Let the others go in. I want to hang back for a second."

"Why?"

"To admire you of course."

"You say the corniest things." Her cheeks turn pink.

"It's true." I pull her into my arms, hugging her tight. "I never want to forget this moment."

"Why?" She cranes her neck, looking up at me.

"Because."

"Because, why?"

"Ever inquisitive, aren't you?"

"It's just, you're acting a bit weird."

"No, I'm not." The thing is I'm scared shitless, and that's saying something for a man like me. What if I've gone to all this trouble and she says no?

Honestly, I haven't thought of that possibility. In the days leading up to this, all I've thought about is the joy on her face and the *yes* on her lips that will irrevocably join us for life.

I kiss the top of her head and swoop down for a truly swoon-worthy kiss. When I let her go, her cheeks are the proper shade of red.

"Um …" She fans herself. "We should go inside. They're probably wondering what we're doing."

"Probably."

Only, I know Isabelle's mother is getting everyone in position.

The moment we walk through that door, her family won't be the only ones inside. All of Bravo team flew down for this. Angie came with Brady, and even Skye Summers flew down to be here. Sam, CJ, Mitzy, and Forest weren't able to come.

They're busy trying to figure out how to break the cipher on the information engraved on the pair of rabbit's feet Angie and Isabelle brought out of the Nicaraguan jungle. In solid Mitzy fashion, however, they will be present virtually.

I reach inside my front pocket and pull out the engagement ring. Angie and Brady helped me shop for the perfect ring, and Mitzy added a bit of Guardian HRS tech that will help me sleep well at night.

"After you." With a gallant gesture, I usher her over the threshold and wait two beats before joining her inside.

"What the …" Isabelle presses her hands to her cheeks at the massive "Welcome Home" sign strung up in the middle of the room.

She's cute, trying to pretend she's surprised. Sitting in two chairs a bit off to the side, Charlie Tompkins and Sam Hodges take a load off. They're still recovering from their respective gunshots to the chest.

Isabelle spins around in a circle. My girl is such a bad actor, but when she turns all the way around and sees me on one knee, her pretend surprise turns real.

"Booker? What are you doing?"

"Isabelle LaCroix …" My eyes suddenly mist up, and I cough to keep them from turning to tears. With a goofy grin on my face, I make a show of pulling out the ring and lifting the lid of the velvet box. Sitting inside is a one-carat diamond ring. "Will you do me the honor of becoming my wife?"

"Oh. My. God!" Her blush turns bright pink, and happy tears fall down her cheeks. "Yes! Yes!" She wriggles her fingers, thrusting out her hand. "A million times, yes!"

Jumping up and down, it's difficult placing the ring, but I somehow manage it. Up on my feet, I pull my girl to me and kiss her in front of her family and ours.

On cue, Isabelle's mom pulls on a lever.

A loud pop sounds as confetti bursts into the air. A hundred white and silver balloons drop on all of those gathered, and the Welcome Home sign flutters to the floor.

Stretched out behind it is another banner with just three words.

SHE SAID YES!

Stepping out from behind the banner, my buddies from Bravo team stand witness.

"Angie!" Isabelle screeches and runs to her dear friend. The two women jump up and down, then Isabelle shows Angie the ring.

Angie looks at me and winks. Without her, I wouldn't have known what to get for my girl. Brady breaks away from the girls. He comes to me and sticks out his hand.

"Congratulations."

"Thanks." I can't keep my eyes off my girl.

Rafe, Zeb, Hayes, and Alec bring beer. I stand with my brothers, fellow Guardians united by the same vision. We're Guardians, hostage rescue specialists. We used to hunt dangerous men. Now, we do whatever it takes to retrieve the fallen, the broken, those who've been taken.

And we never fail.

I look at my wife-to-be, to her family surrounding her, and to my brothers standing by my side. What I do matters.

It's the best goddamn feeling on earth.

"To the first man down." Rafe lifts his beer and cuts his gaze to Brady. "When should we expect you to fall?"

"Ha!" Brady takes a swig. "In good time." He looks over to Angie, eyes full of love. "When she's ready, but this is Booker's day."

And he's absolutely right.

Today is the best day of my life.

BRAVO TEAM; A WHOLE NEW SERIES OF PROTECTOR ROMANCES showcasing the Guardian Hostage Rescue Specialists. Rescuing Carmen is the next book in the exhilarating new BRAVO TEAM series.

Read Rafe and Carmen's story, grab your copy of Rescuing Carmen HERE.

These former Navy SEALs, DELTA Operatives, and Special Ops soldiers turned ***Guardians & Protectors*** are guaranteed to capture your heart and leave you breathless.

Have you met the men of ALPHA team? Their series is complete; seven sexy, swoon-worthy book and all the gritty suspense you love.

If you haven't check them out: Guardian HRS Alpha Team series.

Turn the page for a sneak peek at the explosive combination of Rafe and Carmen. Grab your copy HERE.

The End

ELLZ BELLZ

ELLIE'S FACEBOOK READER GROUP

If you are interested in joining the ELLZ BELLZ, Ellie's Facebook reader group, we'd love to have you.

Join Ellie's ELLZ BELLZ.
The ELLZ BELLZ Facebook Reader Group

Sign up for Ellie's Newsletter.
Elliemasters.com/newslettersignup

Also by Ellie Masters

The LIGHTER SIDE

Ellie Masters is the lighter side of the Jet & Ellie Masters writing duo! You will find Contemporary Romance, Military Romance, Romantic Suspense, Billionaire Romance, and Rock Star Romance in Ellie's Works.

YOU CAN FIND ELLIE'S BOOKS HERE: ELLIEMASTERS.COM/BOOKS

Military Romance

Guardian Hostage Rescue Specialists

Rescuing Melissa

*(*Get a FREE copy of Rescuing Melissa when you join Ellie's Newsletter*)*

Alpha Team

Rescuing Zoe

Rescuing Moira

Rescuing Eve

Rescuing Lily

Rescuing Jinx

Rescuing Maria

Bravo Team

Rescuing Angie

Rescuing Isabelle

Rescuing Carmen

Military Romance

Guardian Personal Protection Specialists

Sybil's Protector

Lyra's Protector

The One I Want Series

(Small Town, Military Heroes)

By Jet & Ellie Masters

EACH BOOK IN THIS SERIES CAN BE READ AS A STANDALONE AND IS ABOUT A DIFFERENT COUPLE WITH AN HEA.

Saving Ariel

Saving Brie

Saving Cate

Saving Dani

Saving Jen

Saving Abby

Rockstar Romance

The Angel Fire Rock Romance Series

EACH BOOK IN THIS SERIES CAN BE READ AS A STANDALONE AND IS ABOUT A DIFFERENT COUPLE WITH AN HEA. IT IS RECOMMENDED THEY ARE READ IN ORDER.

Ashes to New (prequel)

Heart's Insanity (book 1)

Heart's Desire (book 2)

Heart's Collide (book 3)

Hearts Divided (book 4)

Hearts Entwined (book5)

Forest's FALL (book 6)

Hearts The Last Beat (book7)

Contemporary Romance

Firestorm

(Kristy Bromberg's Everyday Heroes World)

Billionaire Romance

Billionaire Boys Club

Hawke

Richard

Brody

Contemporary Romance

Cocky Captain

(Vi Keeland & Penelope Ward's Cocky Hero World)

Romantic Suspense

EACH BOOK IS A STANDALONE NOVEL.

The Starling

~AND~

Science Fiction

Ellie Masters writing as L.A. Warren

Vendel Rising: a Science Fiction Serialized Novel

About the Author

Ellie Masters is a USA Today Bestselling author and Amazon Top 15 Author who writes Angsty, Steamy, Heart-Stopping, Pulse-Pounding, Can't-Stop-Reading Romantic Suspense. In addition, she's a wife, military mom, doctor, and retired Colonel. She writes romantic suspense filled with all your sexy, swoon-worthy alpha men. Her writing will tug at your heartstrings and leave your heart racing.

Born in the South, raised under the Hawaiian sun, Ellie has traveled the globe while in service to her country. The love of her life, her amazing husband, is her number one fan and biggest supporter. And yes! He's read every word she's written.

She has lived all over the United States—east, west, north, south and central—but grew up under the Hawaiian sun. She's also been privileged to have lived overseas, experiencing other cultures and making lifelong friends. Now, Ellie is proud to call herself a Southern transplant, learning to say y'all and "bless her heart" with the best of them. She lives with her beloved husband, two children who refuse to flee the nest, and four fur-babies; three cats who rule the household, and a dog who wants nothing other than for the cats to be his best friends. The cats have a different opinion regarding this matter.

Ellie's favorite way to spend an evening is curled up on a couch, laptop in place, watching a fire, drinking a good wine, and bringing forth all the characters from her mind to the page and hopefully into the hearts of her readers.

FOR MORE INFORMATION

elliemasters.com

facebook.com/elliemastersromance
twitter.com/Ellie__Masters
instagram.com/ellie_masters
bookbub.com/authors/ellie-masters
goodreads.com/Ellie_Masters

Connect with Ellie Masters

Website:
elliemasters.com
Amazon Author Page:
elliemasters.com/amazon
Facebook:
elliemasters.com/Facebook
Goodreads:
elliemasters.com/Goodreads
Instagram:
elliemasters.com/Instagram

Final Thoughts

I hope you enjoyed this book as much as I enjoyed writing it. If you enjoyed reading this story, please consider leaving a review on Amazon and Goodreads, and please let other people know. A sentence is all it takes. Friend recommendations are the strongest catalyst for readers' purchase decisions! And I'd love to be able to continue bringing the characters and stories from My-Mind-to-the-Page.

Second, call or e-mail a friend and tell them about this book. If you really want them to read it, gift it to them. If you prefer digital friends, please use the "Recommend" feature of Goodreads to spread the word.

Or visit my blog https://elliemasters.com, where you can find out more about my writing process and personal life.

Come visit The EDGE: Dark Discussions where we'll have a chance to talk about my works, their creation, and maybe what the future has in store for my writing.

Facebook Reader Group: Ellz Bellz

Thank you so much for your support!

Love,

Ellie

Dedication

This book is dedicated to you, my reader. Thank you for spending a few hours of your time with me. I wouldn't be able to write without you to cheer me on. Your wonderful words, your support, and your willingness to join me on this journey is a gift beyond measure.

Whether this is the first book of mine you've read, or if you've been with me since the very beginning, thank you for believing in me as I bring these characters 'from my mind to the page and into your hearts.'

Love,
Ellie